Secrets of the Sonnets

Shakespeare's Code

For Sandy

*And for my students
& friends who asked me
so many pesky questions*

*And in memory of
Sam Schoenbaum*

By Peter Jensen

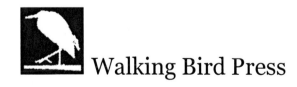

Walking Bird Press

 Walking Bird Press

340 North Grand Street
Eugene, Oregon 97402
chickadeeacres@yahoo.com

About the cover: A digital, collage "painting" by Michael Backus
with images manipulated after the following: Shakespeare
(the Chandros portrait by Richard Burbage, c. 1594-99);
Henry Wriothesley (miniature by Hilyard, 1594);
Christopher Marlowe (painter unknown, 1585); and "An
Unknown Lady in Black" (by Gheeraerts, 1592)—owned by
descendants of Lord Hunsdon.
The background is taken from a famous woodcut from a
book by Camile Flammarion (1842-1925).

The four **name code** lines quoted are from *Shakespeare's
Sonnets:* **Will** #136.14, **Kit** #84.9, **Henry** #81.5, and
Aemelia #151.5.

Jensen, Peter J. (1942—)
Secrets of the Sonnets: Shakespeare's Code
Includes bibliographical references and index.

ISBN 978-1-4303-0923-9

1. Shakespeare, William, 1564—1616—*Shakespeare's
Sonnets*—Substitution code—1609 Quarto—
2. The Poet William Shakespeare—The Youth Henry
Wriothesley—The Dark Lady Aemelia Bessano Lanyer—
The Rival Poet Christopher Marlowe—Deciphering—
Time and Timeline—Names and Identities.

Published by Walking Bird Press in paperback in 2007

Ghost Story

When Borges met Shakespeare in the library
Of the dead, he felt Will's face with his finger-tips
And said, "William, please don't tell me who
The dark lady was or who the youth. I don't

Want to know your secrets. I wish to wonder
About your mysteries forever." Shakespeare
Took both of Borges' hands in his and said,
"Welcome. You're the first person to say, 'Don't tell.'

But we dead don't have any secrets! They're all
Here: the lady, my wife, the youth, my rival.
They're all quite famous and will tell you all.
No one comes to me when they can hear

My originals perform. But tell me, Man,
About yourself." So, Borges began.

—*Peter Jensen*
12 October 2003

"My intentions are, as you well know, more readily
arguable and, in many cases, more conscious, more
mathematical, more cerebral if you will than those
of most of my colleagues, whose more directly-aesthetic
and unconsciously-sensitive impulses can sometimes
be more easily felt than put into words."

—M. C. Escher
from a letter to B. Merema
10 May 1952

"Use your eyes!"

—Leonardo Da Vinci

"In general we look for a new law by the following process.
First you guess. Don't laugh, this is the most important step.
Then you compute the consequences. Compare the consequences to experience. If it disagrees with experience, the
guess is wrong. In that simple statement is the key to
science. It doesn't matter how beautiful your guess is or
how smart you are or what your name is. If it disagrees with
experience, it's wrong. That's all there is to it."

—Richard Feynman

Jeff Larkin, my doctor, said to his son Chris, "So if
Peter's right, how big is this?"

Chris, a Ph. D. candidate in English Renaissance
Literature, answered, "It's big. It's VERY BIG!"

One of my son's best friends, Alex Taylor, who is
studying to be a lawyer, advised me to, "Copy
all the sonnets by hand. I did it, and I understood so much more! Petrarch did it, too,
when he wanted to master Greek and Roman
classical works."

4

Table of Contents

Tables & Figures

Secrets of the Sonnets:
Shakespeare's Code

By Peter Jensen

"Dear son of memory, great heir of fame,
What need'st thou such weak witness of thy name?"

      *   *   *

"Then thou, our fancy of itself bereaving,
Dost make us marble with too much conceiving [.]"

From John Milton's Sonnet,
"On Shakespeare," 1632
(Sonnet written by Milton at age 24
for publication with the Second Folio
of Shakespeare's plays. This was
Milton's first publication.)

Introduction: a Preview

This Stratfordian study reveals how I discovered code words and letters that name key persons of *Shakespeare's Sonnets* as well as key code numbers that may give us a timeline.

The word that enables the naming code is **"name."** This word is used **17** times in **14** sonnets. **14** is an obvious sonnet code number.

In those sonnets can be found **doublets** —**2** is another key code number—used as name words or embedded letters for Will Shakespeare, Henry Wriothesley, Kit Marlowe, and Aemilia Lanyer.

In other sonnets, the doubled (and multiplied) code words may reveal new, autobiographical details, other identities, and evidence of Shakespeare's sense of humor and the depth of his language play that uses all the tricks of Renaissance England's love for classical rhetoric.

In addition, Sonnet **52** is found by the same doubled word and letter code to be a key **Summer Solstice** sonnet. If we count back from 21 June to Sonnet 1, we arrive at May 1st (our new calendar or N. C.) or April 24th of the Old Julian Calendar (or O. C.). If we count ahead to Sonnet 126, we arrive at September 3rd or August 27th O. C.

If Sonnets **40** and **133** are contemporaries, both revealing when Will first admits that the youth and the dark lady are having an affair, we can give them both the date of June 9th (N. C.). This lines up Sun & Moon.

Then, Sonnet 127, the first dark lady and lunar sonnet, becomes our June 3rd (along with its solar twin Sonnet 34), starting one possible **28** day (14 X 2) lunar cycle within the **126** day (28 X 4.5) summer solar cycle of the youth's sequence.

If any year is referred to, it might be **1592**, but Shakespeare probably wrote and revised the *Sonnets* over the **20-year** period **(1589—1609)** that spans the main years of his wonderful career as a dramatist.

A more complex view of this great sonnet sequence—and its ties to the plays and Shakespeare's other poems than any of us has to date—is called for.

If, like me, you are a reader of all 154 sonnets and the attached "A Lover's Complaint," both published in 1609 as Shakespeare wished, then you and I may have wondered about many of the same topics. Please remember that I offer you all these insights in the spirit of scientific speculation with evidence and full of love for reading and puzzling over repeated patterns in William Shakespeare's texts.

—Peter Jensen
Eugene, Oregon
February 2007

Chapter 1   Long Interest and Discovery of Code

For the last forty-five years, I have loved William Shakespeare's high-school humor, his love of silly people, his willingness to joke in a graveyard, and his high-spirited playing with words. But despite all the giggles and guffaws, I never expected to be able to use my plastic, 10-box-top decoder ring to probe the darkest secrets of his sonnets. But I think I have done it!

Shake the scenery! Roll a thundering cannonball down a wooden trough! While reading the Arden Edition in April 2002, I discovered the names of the author, the youth, the dark lady, the rival poet, and others systematically **encoded** in *Shakespeare's Sonnets*. I know this is a very controversial and wonderful claim.

A Shakespeare scholar I really admire—Stanley Wells—published with Paul Edmondson their book-length essay on the *Sonnets* from Oxford University Press in 2004. I had looked forward to reading their ideas and hoped to see new ground broken on puns and other rhetorical figures. But Wells had already made his views on name puns quite clear in an earlier 2004 book, *Looking for Sex in Shakespeare:* "And I have said, the only name that emerges is Shakespeare's own, Will, relentlessly and bawdily punned upon in some of the later sonnets" (53).

Despite this learned man's warning, I want to take a chance and reveal what I think is a far more extensive, punning name code, which I have been working to uncover since 2002. Since then, I have also discovered overall organizational patterns and timelines that lend support to those who believe, as I do, that the 1609 version of *Shakespeare's Sonnets* is based on the author's approved (if imperfect) text and order, which he worked on over Time, the fourth dimension, that major entity often addressed in the sonnets.

My analysis makes me ask these basic questions: what if Shakespeare started writing in 1589 and revised right up to 1609? Would the 1609 text look as it does now? My answer is: yes, I think so. In articles on the *Sonnets*, Michael Dobson suggests there may have been two major periods of revision: 1603—4, when Shakespeare wrote "A Lover's Complaint," as a young maid's lament to contrast with the very male sonnets, and just before publication in 1608—9 (Wells & Dobson 262, 438). Both of those periods were plague years when theaters were closed, and Will had time to write.

I have been reading all 154 of the sonnets since I was nineteen and have been teaching them to undergraduates since I was twenty-three. Like many college English instructors, I have regularly taught 15 to 20 of Shakespeare's greatest sonnets in a class called "Introduction to Poetry." (We number it English 106.) But I have always been suspicious of the things people—from my students to famous scholars—say when they pull only popular sonnets from the sequence and isolate them from all the rest. By Winter of 2007, I have read nine major, annotated editions of the *Sonnets*. All of these editions have taught me how to think or not to think about this great work.

I have also been amused to read comments from scholars (quoted by my students or read by me) that make claims like: "This sonnet is not worthy of Shakespeare." Or: "This sonnet must be from his juvenilia." This failure to understand that the full, 154-sonnet sequence was given a design by the sonneteer is quite misleading. I think we always need to struggle to comprehend as many meanings as we can inside the full sequence.

I am now a community college English Instructor and a published poet, and I turned sixty-four in the summer of 2006 as I worked on this latest draft. I find myself an elder with something to say. But my interest in these sonnets is not sudden; inspiration for this investigation had much earlier roots. I've had help from my family. When I was a little boy in Brooklyn, New York, my Scot-Irish Grandmother Sadie McClean Ebbers read the sonnets to me. I yawned and thought she was reading the *King James Bible*, but she laughed and told me, "No, these poems are about much more earthly love."

More recently, in the late 1990s, when my son Daniel Applegate was in high school, he and his cousin Colin bought the computer game *Riven*. They started the game together and took notes as they explored deep into its "little r" (reality), its virtual world. Their plan was to play it continuously until they won. Life and school were put on hold. While one played and took notes, the other slept. They briefed each other at "shift changes." It took them five continuous days and nights to learn the culture, crack open the secrets, solve the mysteries, and win the game.

I understand their game-playing completely. One of my main, "little r" games has been *Shakespeare's Sonnets*. In addition to those nine, book-length, annotated editions (listed at back), I have read many biographies of Shakespeare. I have slowly come to the conclusion that, in the *Sonnets*, we have the real autobiographical text of *Shakespeare in Love*. The movie was fantastic and fictionalized. Big question: are the sonnets?

It's easy to make too much of little clues, but it also may be worse to ignore them. What if Shakespeare hid the name of the dark lady in the sonnets as Sidney "hid" the name of Penelope Devereux Rich (sister of Lord Essex and namesake for the Earl of Southampton's oldest daughter) in Sonnet #37 of his sonnets to Stella, with seven puns on her last name "Rich?" And what about puns? I've been told and read too often that the pun is "the lowest form of humor." But here is Sir Philip Sidney caught punning and seeming to be pleased with his own wit. Have you ever wondered how the Elizabethans viewed puns?

In his *Introduction* to Shakespeare's other *Poems* besides the Sonnets, John Roe comments on the increased punning rate by Elizabethan poets:

> For the Elizabethans rhetoric constituted one of the great discoveries of antiquity. ... Yet the Elizabethans' self-conscious display of wit in creating verbal effects exceeds anything in classical literature and is probably greater than in contemporary Europe. Petrarch certainly knew how to pun, as his wordplay on the name Laura makes clear, but Elizabethan poetic punning seems to be of unprecedented intensity. (4)

Roe thinks there is an historic linguistic reason for this:

> ... the English language was expanding at a considerable rate ... In such circumstances, it is not surprising that the trope of oxymoron, or antithesis, inherited from Petrarchan poetry, should register changes in how it was used and a marked increase in frequency. Punning similarly indicates division or unsettled meaning. (4)

Punning can also mix emotions in one word and give that word both an everyday and a second comic or tragic ironic intent. Punning can introduce a whole "range of meanings to be comprehended at once (which no other deployment of language can do)" (5). Punning can contain contraries. "The pun accordingly signals the ideal capacity of language to bring different and discordant meanings together while yet underlying the differences that exist in reality" (5). And punning can be used to create worlds of meaning that are far apart. Punning can deliver both an ordinary word and a code word in one. If you get it, punning can be the key to a secret inner world creating a "plain text" and a "cipher text."

Shakespeare's fondness for punning goes well alongside one of his favorite ways of writing plays full of "double writing." If you try to read *Hamlet* two ways, you can imagine the play full of many unsettling meanings for the court and also full of other meanings at the public Globe.

New slang words often operate as codes for younger generations or in-groups or whole communities, and slang often derives from a witty pun. As Republicans were attending Ike's Inaugural Ball in 1952, African American citizens were singing and talking about how they wanted to "ball" all night. I grew up in Brooklyn, New York. We learned the puns of Harlem as soon as they were recorded and played on the radio. Shakespeare had a very good ear and did the same kind of coining of puns. He was one of the good, bad boys from Stratford, and many Londoners loved to laugh with him.

Punning on names appears in other Renaissance arts as well. There is a famous painting in the National Gallery in London by the Venetian painter Lorenzo Lotto (c. 1480—post 1556). It is entitled "Portrait of a Lady Inspired by Lucretia" (c. 1532). It depicts a young woman in a "showy" black and red dress.

The unknown Venetian lady sternly gazing out at the viewer was probably named Lucretia, for she points to a drawing of Lucretia, an ancient Roman heroine who stabbed herself rather than endure the dishonour of having been raped, and thus made unfaithful to her husband. (Langmuir Plate 13)

Langmuir writes that, "Lotto often made punning allusions to his sitters' identities." In addition to the "ink drawing" painted in oils, there is a piece of paper on a table quoting a passage from Livy about Lucretia as well as a cut wallflower, which "may be a reference to the mythological rape of Persephone" (Plate 13). Of course, in 1594, Shakespeare also published a long poem about this Roman heroine, "The Rape of Lucrece," dedicated to the Third Earl of Southampton. Her rape and the revenge of her husband's family led to the downfall of the Roman Kings and the establishment of the Roman Republic.

Lotto's unknown lady painted during the reign of Henry VIII, the punning on her name Lucretia, a poem by Shakespeare on the same Roman subject—all this forms a heady mix of cloudy speculation and wonder. Who owned and displayed that painting in the early 1590s? But all we need right now is to establish a keen, long-standing Renaissance interest in name puns and code. Next, we need to focus on Shakespeare's need for secrecy and ambiguity and his conflicting desire to make the persons of the sonnets "immortal."

Just for fun and to expand my views of Renaissance studies, I read a complete pictorial biography of another genius, *Leonardo da Vinci* by Pietro C. Marani. I was pleasantly surprised to find many of the same themes and biographical notes I am exploring in this study of Shakespeare:

1. **Name puns** (Ginevra and juniper in Italian, *ginepro,* as well as Lorenzo and laurel in Italian, *lauro*);

2. **Identities** of sitters and patrons and platonic lovers revealed (Ginevra de' Benci, Bernardo Bembo, and Lorenzo de' Medici);

3. A gift of two **sonnets** from Lorenzo de' Medici to Ginevra;

4. **Symbolic emblems and slogans** full of family and historic meaning (mainly plants and Latin mottos);

5. **Use of geometry and numbers** to signify meaning;

6. Leonardo's middleclass **father** Ser Piero, who was a notary; and

7. The **education** of a young painter, who did not finish grammar school, but was sent to the professional workshop of a great master, Andrea del Verrocchio, alongside other great students like Sandro Botticelli (38—48).

I often tell my students when we begin studying Shakespeare that we are studying a man like Da Vinci or Mozart. Leonardo lived about one hundred years before Shakespeare, and his career in painting (and so much more) reveals some powerful Italian biographical and cultural themes that replay and echo in the career of William Shakespeare and his chosen fields of writing aristocratic style lyric poetry to publish in his lifetime and dramatic texts for his company and the English commercial theater.

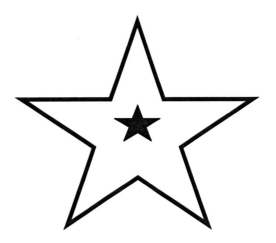

Chapter 2   Shakespeare's Time and His Need for Code

Shakespeare lived in a time when civil rights were limited. Yet it was also an intellectual boom time when the energy of writers was very high. Lots of opinionated broadsides, anonymous posters, and doggerel verses were published, hung up, read, and taken very seriously by the Elizabethan secret police. Lots of subversive sounding stuff was produced. Lots of nameless and faceless informers informed and misinformed the authorities. Tons of awfully pious tracts preached to true believers and the unfaithful. Elizabethans enjoyed their access to the new mass technology of the printing press, as we enjoy the Internet today, but back then, the presses were regulated, so each authorized work (not anonymous tracts or broadsides) had to be pre-read, censored, and registered.

Robert Greene was a very jealous hack writer, who launched attacks on the two most successful playwrights of his time: Marlowe and Shakespeare. His pamphlets are used as evidence of both these men's successes. But not even Greene dared to name names. He used a punning code and instead attacked "Merlin" and "Shake-scene." Not only did this get him off the legal hook; it was part of the satirical game. Some say that the 1592 attack on Shakespeare was not even authored by Greene. Perhaps it was launched by playwright Thomas Nashe (1567—c. 1601) hiding behind the name of the dying Robert Greene. Much of the literary evidence of that time should not just be taken at face value. Shakespeare himself used these methods and warned us to watch out as he played along the borderlines between author, audience, and censor quite bravely. Attacks were launched by allegory and code, and readers and playgoers enjoyed the gossipy guessing games.

This was also a dangerous time for writers. Marlowe was brought in for questioning when a poorly written broadside (not by him) attacked the Dutch immigrant community and merely mentioned his plays and ideas. Marlowe's ex-roommate, playwright Thomas Kyd, was interrogated about Marlowe's religious beliefs by state prosecutor Sir Francis Bacon. During this questioning by Bacon, Kyd was tortured on the rack. Kyd told them what they wanted to hear about an atheist tract that he confessed "belonged" to Marlowe, but Kyd's health was ruined, and he never wrote again. Then, despite his service to the crown as a spy against Catholics in France and Flanders, Marlowe was caught up in a domestic power struggle and murdered.

Near the end of Elizabeth's reign, after the failed Essex rebellion, Shakespeare's company was investigated for staging *Richard II* about a weak King who was deposed, and the company was cleared of possible treason because the company was paid. And Ben Jonson was jailed when he made fun of the new King James I's money-making scheme of selling knighthoods. Jonson called these newly minted Sirs, "forty pound knights," and that got him put in prison, where he was investigated behind bars by Robert Poley, one of three spies present at Marlowe's murder. When Ben was released, his mother gave him a joyous coming-out party at the Mermaid Tavern. But it's obvious; writers had to be wary.

Sir Phillip Sidney's puns on a married woman's name, "Rich," in his sonnets never got him into trouble. Although he was a lord, his sonnets were published after his death in battle. This publication was part of a hero-making campaign by his family and his father-in-law, Sir Francis Walsingham, who wanted to distract people from Walsingham's invasive investigations among conspiratorial, foolish English Catholics. Walsingham's agents pushed conspirators around Mary Queen of Scots so hard that they wrote letters (in a code that Walsingham's code breaker had broken) condemning themselves. So, in a great show of patriotism, after Mary was executed, Walsingham honored Sidney as a Protestant hero with a state funeral, and Sir Phillip's sonnets were a great hit a few years later in 1591.

Shakespeare read Sidney and took note. He had just started his own sonnet sequence to a young lord. He would have liked his sonnets to be a big hit as well, but, I believe, his life intervened. The young lord became much more than a patron. Will's sonnets are not about unrequited or neoplatonic love like the sonnets of Sidney, Wyatt, Surrey, and Petrarch. Will's sonnets are about passionate friendship and love between himself and the youth and then between Will and a lady. There are also rival poets for the youth's affections, especially one who is more dangerous and talented but who suddenly disappears and is referred to in the past tense. And the lady becomes a rival, too, and has an affair with the young lord. Unlike Will's entitled mentors in the song and sonnet sequence, middleclass Will gets sex, is betrayed, loses his faith in love, wonders at love's continuing burn, suffers, tries to understand his suffering, gets some kind of clap, matures, revises himself, and is enmeshed in the lives of his profitable theater company and his lively family.

Will is also a cautious publisher. He is very successful at play writing, acting, and being a partner in a great company. He has a lot to lose. So he reads some of his sonnets to his friends—perhaps he circulated or gave away some copies—but he put off publishing for both personal and political reasons until it was almost too late. I believe he followed the practice of Sidney and many others and used a punning code to name major and minor characters in his sonnets. When he wrote most of these sonnets during the last decade and a half of Elizabeth I' s reign, some of what he was doing and writing about could have been risky. He wanted to immortalize at least the youth. I believe he encoded identities and put off publishing until the sixth year of the new King's reign, until a year before he retired (or perhaps was forced to retire by hardening political lines) from fulltime playwriting.

Always great at seeing from many perspectives, Shakespeare does warn all of us about making too much of code letters with one very funny incident in *Twelfth Night* (c. 1601). In Act 2 Scene 5, love sick Malvolio tries to turn the letters M. O. A. I. —that appear in a love letter forged by Maria—into his own name "MALVOLIO." In line 120, he begins,

"'M.' Malvolio—'M'—why, that begins my name." He goes on, making too much of the false code, which Maria left as bait for him: "'M.' But then there is no consonancy in the sequel. That suffers under probation. 'A' should follow, but 'O' does" (123—25). "… and yet to crush this a little, it would bow to me, for every one of these letters are in my name" (132—33). Later, I will make much more of **Malvolio minus love:**

$$\textbf{MALVOLIO} - \textbf{MOAI} = \textbf{LLOV.}$$

Now, I don't want to be remembered as another snookered Malvolio (his name another pun, "bad will" or sick volition in English), but once I found some code that made sense, I had fun following the clues that Shakespeare left. Is he diddling with me as he had Maria diddle Malvolio? Would Will do that to one of his most

amused and honest readers? O well, I guess that aging community college teachers and poets can rush in where PhD's fear to tread. I'm a fool for Will; I admit it.

$$\textbf{MALVOLIO} - \textbf{LLOV} = \textbf{MOAI.}$$

But I'm not a Bardolatrist. What I love about him has nothing to do with idealizing the poet. I am much more interested in trying to hear the man. I just love his jokes, his verbal intelligence, and his odd, inventive ways of shaping a river of words as it flows through him. I want to string my "discovery" of code out as far as it

takes me and see where it goes. As the licensed fool Feste tells Malvolio, "… thus the whirligig of time brings in his revenges" (5.1.371-2). I am committed to taking the time and trudging all the way to William Shakespeare's North Pole with or without dogs!

16

Chapter 3　Shakespeare: Great User of Sources

Those of us who teach both the Survey of English Literature and Shakespeare realize that it's so important not to teach William Shakespeare in a vacuum. He, above all others, was the greatest, most exciting user of sources. Some people can't imagine what a great reader and rewriter this theater man from Stratford was. They wind up believing that only someone with direct, royal experience and/or more of a formal education could write as Shakespeare writes. They cannot see how hard he worked to use all his sources. He finds, reads, and borrows from famous, great, popular, as well as rarely read originals. He is such a great workman, such an exemplary tradesman, and such a meticulous craftsman! That is his genius. And when investigating the roots of *Shakespeare's Sonnets*, it is almost impossible to overemphasize Shakespeare's debts to and improvements of the sonnets of Wyatt and Surrey (from Will's copy of Tottel's *Songs and Sonnets*, 1557) and also especially, the sonnets of Sir Phillip Sidney. Sidney's sonnet sequence, *Astrophil and Stella,* was published in 1591, a year or so after Shakespeare had started his own, and Sidney's sonnets sold almost as well as London hot cakes.

Will Shakespeare is not the first sonneteer to pun on his own name Will. **Phillip** Sidney does it on the first name in his title "Astro**phil**," which means "star lover." Sidney also puns on Stella's (star's) real name, Penelope Devereux **Rich,** in a total of four sonnets: #24, #35, #37, and #48. In Sonnet 24, Sidney puns on Stella's married name four times starting out line 1 with a slam of her husband, Sir Robert Rich: **"Rich** fools there be ..." (Sidney 50). And in Sonnet #35, line 10, Sidney says that he, her love "slave," "Doth even grow **rich, naming** my Stella's **name**" (54). I want to say that I hear echoes of that Sidney line in Shakespeare's Sonnets 95.8 and 151.8, and an imitation of that naming method as well.

In fact, the relationship between *Shakespeare's Sonnets* and Sidney's originals is so rich that we can view Sidney's book as a prompt book from which Shakespeare writes sonnets that dialogue with Sidney's. Many of the tricks of the trade that Will Shakespeare, Gent. used may have been used first by Sir Phil including a **naming code.** So if there is a naming code in Will's sonnets, could we crack it by unpacking each pun? Is Will's code based on what Sam Johnson (always wonderfully misleading, like a Tory Falstaff of moralistic taste) put down as Will's greatest weaknesses, falling for the "quibble" and the pun?

Although Dr. Johnson and his good friend, actor David Garrick, were responsible for so much important work on Shakespeare in the 18th century, I do not want to follow their leads. According to Anthony Davies,

Garrick's version [of *Romeo and Juliet*] was closer to the original, though he increased Juliet's age to 18 and eliminated much of what he dismissed as 'jingle and quibble,' cutting puns, simplifying diction, and rewriting rhyme as blank verse (shortening even Romeo and Juliet's sonnet on meeting at the feast).
(Wells and Dobson 401)

This is a good example of **bias** against many of Shakespeare's favorite tricks and one of his most common kinds of jokes. This bias against puns is still a common problem in many of the annotated, unfunny, or even **anti-funny editions** of the *Sonnets*.

But if you are writing about Shakespeare's works, you should not impose stuffy, anti-Shakesperean values on his wit. We have to remember what Chris Baldick described as "Shakespeare's notorious devotion to punning" (Wells and Dobson 359). If we really want to understand Shakespeare's art, Will Shakespeare is right; Sam Johnson and others are wrong.

This devotion to puns is part of Shakespeare's artistry. It may be the missing key that we need to solve some very old mysteries hidden in the puns of his sonnets. Could it be that bias against punning is why the code has not **popped out** at people? Yes, I think so. But puns are really a crucial part of Elizabethan sonnet writing, and Will puns much more than most others.

After the posthumous success of Sidney's sonnets, many other Elizabethan poets wrote and published sonnets, too. Shakespeare's times were crowded with scribbling poets and rhyming lovers. There may have been as many as twenty-two sonnet sequences published in the 1590s in England. Shakespeare's sequence was not one of those published back then, yet it is now the only one regularly studied outside of Sidney and Spencer classes. Here is a chronological list of 17 historically interesting sequences with their dates. I have added **nine**—one by Christopher Marlowe's friend Thomas Watson and one each by Giordano Bruno—his sonnets in Italian were dedicated to Sidney and published in London (Bossy 57), Robert Sidney, Constable, Percy, Drayton, Barnfield, Linche, and Wroth—in square brackets [   ]—that were not listed in the Oxquarry on-line source:

Table 1. Elizabethan & Jacobean Sonneteers

[1. Watson #1: *Hekatompathia* (written)	1582]
[2. Bruno: *De gli eroici furori* (*Of Heroic Passions*)	1585]
3. Sidney: *Astrophil and Stella*	1591
[4. His brother Robert Sidney: recently discovered sequence	n. d.]
5. Daniel: *Delia*	1592
[1. Watson: *Ekatompathia* (#1 from above—published)	1592]
[6. Constable: *Diana*	1592]
7. Lodge: *Sonnets to Phillis*	1593
8. Watson #2: *The Tears of Fancie or Love Distained*	1593
9. Barnes: *Parthenophil and Parthenophe*	1593
10. Fletcher: *Licia, or Poems of Love*	1593
[11. Percy: Coelia	1594]
[12. Drayton: *Sonnets to Idea*	1594—1619]
13. Spencer: *Amoretti*	1595
[14. Barnfield: *Cynthia. With Certaine Sonnets*	1595]
15. Griffin: *More Chaste than Kind: Fidessa*	1596
[16. Linche: *Diella*	1596]
[17. Wroth, Lady Mary, née Sidney: *Pamphilia to Amphilanthus*	1621]

Source of data not in [ ]: Oxquarry Books

We can see how Shakespeare's sonnets, perhaps written and worked on **from 1589 to 1609**, fit in. Some poets rushed into print; Will did not. Like Drayton, he revised. He also put off publishing. For this we can be thankful, and we should also be very careful about dating Shakespeare's sonnets and his revisions. Perhaps others should have revised and punned more and used puns or codes for names. Consider the last two lines of Sonnet #1 from Thomas Lodge's *Sonnets to Phillis* (1593):

"Show to the world, though poor and scant my skill is,
How sweet thoughts be, that are but thoughts on Phillis."
(Oxquarry Books)

Well, hit me over the head and call me a sonneteer! So there were many other educated and half-educated Elizabethan men writing sonnets to named or unnamed lovers in the 1590s and three very interesting examples before (Watson & Bruno) and after (Wroth) that key decade.

The Sidney family had much to do with this literary sonnet fashion. Like fossils all found in the same lakebed proving kinship, the titles and lover's names and their methods show the sonneteers' appreciation and their desire to ride on the hem of Sidney's cape. Many of these sequences are linked by word play. Sir Philip Sidney punned on his name in his title (*Astrophil*) and on his lover's real name (Rich) in his sonnets. Lodge wrote sonnets to a lover with the female form of Sidney's name: *Phillis*. Daniel took the "n" from his own name and came up with his title and name for his lover *Delia*. Shakespeare may be glancing at this taking away of an "n" whcn in Sonnet #15, line 14, he contrasts himself to Time, "As he [Time] takes from you, I **engraft you new**." (In all lines from the *Sonnets,* I quote the Duncan-Jones edition, and my **emphasis** is added here as well as in all examples.)

In this pun, married to an orchard image of grafting a new variety on an old trunk, Will grafts an "n" on "you" to make the **you**th "new." Later, Drayton took the "l" out of Daniel's *Delia* and came up with his more Neoplatonic and intellectual title: *Idea.* Barnes named his male character after Sidney: *Parthenophil.* Shakespeare may have also punned on Sidney's name in Sonnet #85, one of the rival poet sonnets, and the one that commentators say has the most echoes of Sidney's sonnets. Line 85.4 reads, "And precious phrase by all the muses **filed**." In this line, Shakespeare seems to be saying that "all the muses" of all the rival sonneteers, many of whom are writing lines for his young patron, have their phrases "filed" or polished or Philed by a "golden quill" named Philip Sidney. Later, it may be Sidney's nephew William Herbert (W. H.) who pays for the publishing of *Shakespeare's Sonnets.* And finally, in 1621, Lady Mary Wroth, née Sidney, may be the only woman of note besides Aemelia Lanyer (there are two fourteeners in her book in 1611) to publish sonnets. All this playing of the sonnet sequence game leads to great and to not so great works. Ever since the Romantics gave new breath to the sonnet form that may have drowned after Milton, poets have been scribbling thousands of good and bad sonnets.

Shakespeare makes fun of bad sonnet writers in *Much Ado About Nothing* (c. 1598). In Act 5 Scene 2, Benedick offers to write Margaret a sonnet, "In so high a style ... that no man living shall come over it" (lines 6—7), if she will bring her lady Beatrice to him. She jokes about a man "coming over" her and goes for Beatrice anyway. But once he's alone, even witty Benedick (good dick) admits he's having great trouble writing a love poem for Beatrice (the name of Dante's girl muse). And the trouble comes because rhymes in English are not so easy (as rhymes can be in Italian):

> Marry, I cannot show it in rhyme; I have tried: I can find out no rhyme to 'lady' but 'baby,' an innocent rhyme; for 'scorn,' 'horn,' a hard rhyme; for 'school,' 'fool,' a babbling rhyme; very ominous endings: no, I was not born under a rhyming planet, nor can I woo in festival terms.
>
> (Lines 35—41)

Many Elizabethan poems are full of forced rhymes, lip-tripping lines for lovers, and odd, awkward phrasing. The difficulty of saying sensible, iambic pentameter lines that must always rhyme could and did drive poets to blank verse or prose. Many modern writers have simply given up and call it all "free verse." But song lyric writers are still struggling with rhyme, and some can do no better than Benedick or hope to do as well as another love-sick fellow, Romeo, and his love Juliet, who speak a very fine dialogue Sonnet about pilgrims and saints of love when they first meet at a ball at her house when both are in disguise. This is how the sonnet craze shows up in Shakespeare's plays. There are at least three sonnets embedded in *Romeo and Juliet* [I've found four and a half] and at least seven in *Love's Labour's Lost* (Wells and Dobson 438).

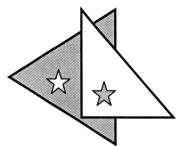

Later, in *Romeo and Juliet*, Mercutio wants to be sure that Romeo is okay after he went over the wall into the Capulet's orchard to woo Juliet:

> Speak but one rhyme, and I am satisfied;
> Cry but 'Ay me!' pronounce but 'love' and 'dove.'
>
> (*R&J* II.1.9–10)

A rhyme, any rhyme will do (as any radio or CD player or singing cell phone or IPod will demonstrate these days) when one is acting or rapping like a fool for love.

Chapter 4   Rhetorical Figures and Real Secret Code

In his *Teaching Shakespeare*, Rex Gibson notes that young Will, "like most other Elizabethan grammar school boys, would have memorized a very large number of [over 100] figures of rhetoric" (74). I wish I could find a list of those figures, which young Shakespeare had to memorize. Of the ones Gibson covers, the following four are most relevant to the code of the Sonnets: *1. "Ploce—* repeating words in a line or clause"; *2. "Antanaclasis—* punning on a repeated word to obtain different meanings" (74); [I want to add *3. Anagram—*words that contain the letters of each other, only scrambled as in the famous, anonymous (or some say written by "holy" George Herbert) example of "Mary" and "army:"

"How well her name an **army** doth
      present,
In whom the Lord of hosts did pitch
      his tent."]

and *4. "Deixis* (usually pronounced dake-sis) [which] is Greek for 'pointing'" ... "elements of speech" or "pronouns" that point out (84). Shakespeare may have learned tricks of his trade early, but he also laughs up his sleeve when he thinks about school, as he did in *The Merry Wives of Windsor* (c. 1597) by showing a little boy named Will using macaronic "pig" Latin to impress his mother in front of his Welsh Latin teacher.

I always assumed, incorrectly, that university students in the late 1500s learned more than Shakespeare did about rhetoric and writing. But apparently, this was not so. Just because I teach all levels of writing classes in the first two years at a community college, I assumed that Shakespeare missed some basics and more advanced training. But Schoenbaum sums up

"... the education that an Elizabethan grammar school provided. It offered about as much formal belletristic instruction as was available in those days for an incipient man of letters. The universities had little to add, for their task was to train up men for the professions: medicine, law, above all, divinity" (58 f).

Schoenbaum goes on to quote T. W. Wilson, "Shakespeare ... had as good a formal literary training as had any of his contemporaries" (59). No wonder Marlowe had Faustus rail against "all" that Wittenburg had to offer! Maybe Marlowe learned nothing about play writing at Cambridge. My own son Daniel went to a very good high school, South Eugene, and found the first year at the local University of Oregon a lot less advanced.

Perhaps Shakespeare discovered early for himself a connection between figures of rhetoric and secretive, encoded writing. A pun could mean one thing to the uninitiated and at least two things to those in the know. Most of us go through the grades and high school making up puns and secret language that we hope our parents and teachers don't get. In middle school, my son and his friends used to ask each other if their "stocks and bonds were going up or down?" (They were actually talking about girls and their love lives.) As for the use of serious code in England, even in the late 1300s, the use of cryptography was fairly common, and it was not only used in statecraft. Simon Singh tells us that "alchemists and scientists [used] … it to keep their discoveries secret" (27). Geoffrey Chaucer was one of Shakespeare's constant sources, and Singh surprised me by revealing that

"… Chaucer was also an astronomer and a cryptographer, and he is responsible for one of the most famous examples of early European encryption. In his Treatise on the Astrolab he provided some additional notes entitled "The Equatorie of the Planetis," which included several encrypted paragraphs. Chaucer's encryption replaced plaintext letters with symbols…" (27).

So, the example of a great writer of the Middle Ages, who was also a diplomat and a scientist, encoding his astronomical findings is closer to regular practice than I thought. I've always been amused by thinking about Leonardo da Vinci writing his notebooks backwards by using a mirror. I've read that originally, in the Middle Ages, looking in a mirror was a sin called "speculation." How many people had mirrors back then? How much could da Vinci count on mirror writing as an encoding device?

But what about the real secret codes used by spies in Shakespeare's times? In his book, *The Elizabethan Secret Services*, Alan Haynes tells us that

Elizabethan ciphers had two principle forms: **transposition**, where characters were shuffled but retained their actual meaning; and **substitution**, which omitted the change of sequence while replacing characters with other letters or symbols—often **numbers** served this purpose. (23) [my emphasis]

We will see that Shakespeare's code **substitutes** sound-alike, punning words (but very few true homophones) and look-alike, spelled words (but not perfect homographically) for the names of his principal people. Jonathan Crewe notes, "The sonnets … prove … Shakespeare's marked attention to both voiced and inaudible letters" (41). We will see that he also uses code **numbers** and scatters **doubles** or buries **letter code** or **transposes letter** order through key lines after his main clue word tells us to look around for encoded data. If he uses code he must tell us when and how to look for it. That is, any encoded message must have both a key and a code.

Haynes writes of many other methods of encryption used by Elizabethan spies: blank parts of pages were written on with invisible ink made of milk and lemon juice (22); tiny messages were written by experts in microscopic writing (15) as on many paper currencies today; code grilles had holes that fit code letters in known texts (22); and an old book English agents bought on the continent contained hundreds of alphabets in Latin where letters could be ciphers, and keys were provided (22). One such cipher-key and letter code list belonging to the spy Robert Poley—one of three spies present when Christopher Marlowe was murdered—has been published. (See Nicholl, Plate 18.) Most commonly, there was direct **substitution** of a **number** or a **code name** for principal players such as "32" (23) or "Pallas" (157)—perhaps too obviously a pun on "palace"—for Queen Elizabeth. It should be noted that use of number codes was common. Rowland White wrote a letter to his patron Sir Robert Sidney in which Essex is 1,000 and Cecil is 200 (Trevelyan 268). This direct substitution method is more Shakespeare's style (although maybe we'd better check the blank places in the 1609 text for milk and lemon juice).

The breaking of a nomenclature, consisting of the combination of a cipher alphabet and code words, led in 1587—during his "lost years" when Shakespeare was 23 years old and probably quite fascinated—to the conviction and execution of the most famous plotter in Queen Elizabeth's prisons, Mary Queen of Scots. This was the biggest, public case of Shakespeare's young life.

Singh writes,

> When Phelippes [Walsingham's code breaker]

deciphered Babington's message to Mary, which clearly proposed the assassination of Elizabeth, he immediately forwarded the damning text to his master.... Walsingham [who] ... bided his time in the hope that Mary would reply and authorize the plot, thereby incriminating herself. (40)

Not only did Mary endorse the plot in a letter that was detoured and deciphered, but Phellipes was able to forge a postscript in code that made it seem as if Mary were asking for the names of "six gentlemen" who were in on the plot. Singh goes on to explain,

> The cipher of Mary Queen of Scots clearly demonstrates that a weak encryption can be worse than no encryption at all. ... their faith in their cipher made them particularly vulnerable to accepting Phelippes's forgery. (41)

Not only was Mary beheaded, but Walsingham organized a spectacular state funeral for his son-in-law, Sir Phillip Sidney, a Protestant war hero who was killed in 1586, to distract people from seeing a Catholic martyr in Mary. The Earl of Essex had brought home Sidney's sword from Flanders; he also married Sidney's widow, Frances Walsingham. Then, four years later, when Will was 27, Sidney's sonnets were published in 1591. These linked events may have started Shakespeare's interests in Sidney and in code, especially since

Sidney had his own punning code for key names.

Even in this book-length essay, I don't pretend to have found all of Shakespeare's code; I only want to question Shakespeare, not torture him! In his time, agents were sometimes tortured on the rack for their "alphabets." Haynes writes about the usual cast of suspects: Walsingham, Burghley, and Essex as spy masters and all sorts of funky operatives, including the deadly projector Poley and the over-educated Marlowe, the son of a cobbler from Canterbury trying to live well as a college student by spying and treating his friends at school to butter and beer. Years later, Ben Jonson promises a friend, whom he invites with a poem to supper, that they can drink wine and speak freely because there will be no government spies at their table. He puns on the names of two famous spies: "And we will have no **Pooly** or Parrot by" (Abrams 1398). Poley, who survived the death of Elizabeth as Lord Cecil's man, had investigated Ben in prison and perhaps even tempted him to treason. Ben was smarter than Poley. As any deep reader knows, Ben's older friend, William Shakespeare, leads all the rest of the writers in saying what he wants while leaving most would-be censors, Masters of the Revels, self-appointed Puritans, agents, spies, and current "authorship" idiots all puzzled and choking in his literary dust asking: "Which of all the possible meanings does he really mean?"

In the world of diplomatic and military actions and the field of history, codes are famous and vital, and they must be clearly understood. But in the world of literary interpretation, a claim of finding code is looked down upon. I blame all those who tried or are trying to grind some anti-Stratfordian, authorial axe for giving all other eye straining conspiracy theories a bad name. I quote Leonard Woodcock, former President of the AFL-CIO here, "I am against all conspiracies that I am not a part of." I want you to follow the cipher I found.

But there is great resistance to **all** deciphering of the *Sonnets:*

> To read Shakespeare's sequence in the hopes of decoding an implied story, keen though some of these poems seem to encourage this strategy, is inevitably to do violence to the lyric compression and self-enclosure of the individual sonnets which compose it, and to the rich variety of tone and technique they achieve despite or rather through the formal limitations of their strict fourteen line structure.
> (Wells and Dobson 440)

But these are traditional, not logical reasons why a code is not to be looked for or why a code might not be present. All of these formal considerations are moving and fun to follow, too, but none of them rule out the use of a cipher. But this anti-code bias runs strong in literary studies, as do all devices and forms of truth deemed to come from "outside the field."

We have only to look at how stubbornly standard English Literature texts held onto the Queen's Coroner's Inquest version of Marlowe's death, which accepted as gospel the version told by three, self-serving spies, who were with Marlowe when he was murdered. Even almost ten years after the publication of Charles Nicholl's 1994 best seller, *The Reckoning*, anthologies still mouth the dubious cover story that Marlowe's murderers told the Queen's coroner, and they even add the further lie that Kit's murder happened in a public tavern. The film *Shakespeare in Love* goes on to immortalize this suspect disinformation on the silver screen. Yet Shakespeare is more rigorous than his imitators. In *As You Like It*, the fool Touchstone proves that Shakespeare had read the coroner's— "a great reckoning in a little room" (*AYLI* 3.4.10)—report and had serious doubts about its truth. That's what I love about Shakespeare: he really does his homework!

But once a dogma is born in literary studies, it takes reasonable doubt far too long to arrive. But I must say that my own doubts about Marlowe's death were raised in 1967 when I took Professor Schoenbaum's course on Marlowe at Northwestern University, and he said in a lecture, "There is something wrong with the usual story of Marlowe's death. It wasn't in a tavern, and the three other men with him were all spies." I had to wait twenty-five years for Nicholl's brilliant book to give my doubts more reasons. But some Marlovians simply take off from there. There are also improbable explanations about escape and covert

names—posted as if proven—on the Marlowe Society Home Page, and there's a whole host of loony theories afoot about Marlowe and Shakespeare based on claims of codes, secret names like *"Monsieur Le Doux,"* Thomas Walsingham's deceptions, and other dead "authors" of Shakespeare's plays.

So my idea that Shakespeare might have used code in the sonnets is in with some very bad or silly company. John Hollander, a poet and an introducer of the *Sonnets,* speaks for many when he writes,

> Serious readers of poetry today, whether professional scholars or not, would certainly stop short of the kind of near-paranoid cryptanalysis that used to be pursued by those who felt that they had been given the key to Shakespeare's "heart" rather than his art.
> (Orgel *Introduction* xxx)

Hollander goes on, as many Moderns and Post-Moderns do, to take Robert Browning's side of the "art" versus "heart" debate against Wordsworth. Now, I really admire Hollander as a analyzer of formal poetry, but I teach the phony dilemma of false extremes in logic class, so every time I get told I can have only one of two choices, I feel as if I'm being set up to stop thinking. I feel like the Presidents of India and Egypt during the Cold War being told I must choose between the West and the East. I feel as if I'm in the presence of some kind of ideological bully, so I will see if I can invent (at the very least) a "Third World." When I think of

Shakespeare's complex approach to the heart/art split, I know I need views that let me explore both of them and a mixture and more than either or.

Why do we have to choose between Browning and Wordsworth? And what is the difference between "near-paranoid cryptanalysis" and valid cryptanalysis? Is all code breaking off limits? I need some principles to guide me; and I can't lean on either Browning or Wordsworth to be my guiding Virgil here. We are far beyond the heart-felt Romantics and the more skeptical but too dismissive and Puritanical Victorians. Neither the Romantics nor the Victorians were famous for dirty jokes, but Shakespeare is!

I am fortunate to have met at the Oregon Shakespeare Festival in Ashland, Oregon in May 2003, one of the best-known American commentators on the *Sonnets,* Stephen Booth. I was delighted with his talk about finding "patterns" in two of the sonnets enclosed in *Romeo and Juliet.* I had not yet read his famous commentary, so I rushed out to buy and read it. I am glad that I came to his book after most of this study was written. I find in his four hundred pages of notes some very persuasive arguments against my point of view. I had to reevaluate everything I have thought about these sonnets as I read his long book during the Summer of 2003. As I said, I really am inspired by his finding of **rhetorical patterns** in Shakespeare's lines. But, while Stephen Booth is very open to detailed sexual and musical interpretations, he seems to have an allergic reaction to all "substantive" or biographical interpretations. He even worries that his deep readings will mislead others like me: "Although I have taken pains to keep suggestions and echoes and wordplays in perspective by labeling them as such, I still fear that I will seem to be a crazy advocate of crazy interpretations" (Booth 371). So I want him and others to know that his was the next to last of eight editions of the *Sonnets* that I have read. Any "crazy interpretations" here came first, and I must claim them as my own.

Interpreting the *Sonnets,* as you can hear in the tone of these warnings, is a very touchy subject for leading academics. Since I am not one of those, I have had to be my own guide and think my own thoughts. To help me in this work, I made up a list of principles that may help me avoid the faults of what I see as the two extremes:
all autobiography versus all fiction.

Table 2. Ten principles of my investigation

1. I will not declare any sonnets "spurious," "inferior," "not by Shakespeare," or "juvenilia" as a **dodge** of trying to explain why they are placed where they are in his 1609 sequence.

2. I will not prefer any **critic** to Shakespeare. I will avoid the common mistake of preferring Dr. Samuel Johnson's Tory tastes to William Shakespeare's sexy sense of humor and tasty use of words.
3. I will try not to prefer any **"tradition"** to the text.
4. I will not declare that the sonnets are one **extreme** or another.
5. I will not declare that a "double meaning" cannot have **both or more** meanings. I do not want to shut down speculation.
6. I will not pretend that mere **words** like "great," "occasional," or "inferior" get an investigator off the hook of explaining all the sonnets if he or she can. I can't help but leave plenty of room for new investigators.
7. I will not declare that "we can **never know**" means the same thing as "I cannot explain this right now."
8. No matter how delicious and tempting, I will try not to substitute **name calling** of opponents for reasoning about the sonnets. O, all right, I will do a little insulting and name calling—it's so much fun and Falstaffian & Shakespearean: "Thou whoreson, son of a bitch!"
9. I will try to write this discovery narrative of my investigation as an **adventure** for all kinds of readers who simply love Shakespeare.
10. I will write in **plain English** and define all technical terms.

I admire and have read many people who do not follow all ten of these principles, but I get very impatient with scholars or others who tell me where to stop thinking, no matter how they say it. These 154 sonnets have made me very curious. Since I don't know if I have the "right" answers, I am willing to consider lots of possibilities and questions. I am willing to follow leads that go nowhere. And I am willing to show my mistakes and my blind spots. I have read about other published code theories, but I have not read all the books. One claim is that Giordano Bruno—that monk of science and a peace activist between Catholics and Protestants or perhaps even a spy for Walsingham—brought a code from Italy (perhaps from Galileo) to England and that Shakespeare uses it in the *Sonnets*. Another person tries to prove that Shakespeare's family was secretly Jewish and that Shakespeare used Judaic, Cabalistic code in his *Sonnets*. A third code lover wants us to believe that Shakespeare was the founder of the Masons, and that we cannot get what he's driving at unless we see all the Sonnets and plays as Masonic texts. A fourth writer would have you believe that Shakespeare was a believing English Catholic, who always used common words with Roman Catholic meaning. You can find all these code breakers on-line simply by searching under "Shakespeare + code."

All or some of this other code work may or may not be true. I don't see why Shakespeare would not play with other codes if he knew them. But those writers are so sure of themselves, and I am not. My find of a humbler, more humorous and obscene, autobiographical code with a Stratfordian bent seems more useful, funny, obvious, and immediate to me. The fact that it has not been found until I found it troubles me and makes my claims seem very dubious. But unlike Malvolio, I have a sense of humor about myself and my professional standing. At the end of all this word play, I don't mind being seen as a fool, perhaps not as wise as Feste. But I want to share all of what I think I have found and add to the discussion.

Let me restart my direct narrative of discovery by asking: without the code maker's originals or code sheet, what proof does a code breaker have? A real code must be complex and serve the needs of the code maker. Any real code must work on many levels. Real people and places must be named. Times and dates must be precisely given. Complex text messages must be both hidden yet easy enough to translate once the key, cipher, alphabet, or methods of encryption are known. Shakespeare had some real reasons to hide names and dates; but he also had some literary reasons to reveal names and dates and make his code fun to find and comprehensive. Like many encryptions used by states and businesses, Shakespeare's code must work on many, interactive levels. The code I believe I've found uses a key word, doubled sound puns, spelling look-alikes, doubled letters, and interlocking numbers. Most importantly, it should help many readers see into the sonnets as if through the windows of Sonnet # 24 into Shakespeare's workshop.

I wonder if this fine Sonnet 24, where Shakespeare says, "Mine eye hath played the painter…" (line 1)

"And perspective it is the best painter's art;" (line 4) reveals that Shakespeare read a translation of Piero de la Francesca's Latin work *De Prospectiva pingendi* (On perspective in painting) "written in the mid-1470s to 1480s" and discussed at length by Giorgio Vasari in the 1500s (Livio 126). Lines 6 and 7 of Sonnet 24 (as edited by Katherine Duncan-Jones) offer us this view in:

"To find where your true image
        pictured lies,
Which in my bosom's shop is
        hanging still [.]"

Shakespeare touchingly portrays himself as a craftsman like his father, only, Will's workshop is, like that of W. B. Yeats, in his heart. I have wondered why Sonnet 24, such an obvious time number sonnet, does not make more use of 24 hours a day. Perhaps it does contrast the sunlight coming into the windows of Will's workshop—where a painted "image" of the youth can be seen—to the darkness and more powerful truths in the youth's heart, which cannot be "known," except perhaps in lines of poetry.

But what else can we see in that workshop on his table? Are there also sheets of code words and notes about substitutions? Did he dream up a systematic code, insert it in the sonnets, and then burn his notes? In the next run of eight chapters (5—12), I want to prove that Shakespeare worked out a code that named his key "characters" and set key dates.

Chapter 5   The Code: Name Puns, Doublets, Letters, & Numbers

I will state my simplified conclusions about Shakespeare's code first and then trace (sonnet by sonnet) how I discovered it. The obvious "magic key word" that turns on Shakespeare's naming code is **"name."** There are only **14** sonnets with **17** lines that contain the word **"name."** The first number is the code number **14 (also a code number for Shakespeare himself)**, the most important number of all in 152 out of 154 of these 14 line sonnets. The second number **17 (also a code number for the youth)** is less obvious, but it refers us back to the first **seventeen** sonnets that we think Shakespeare got paid to write for the youth's seventeenth birthday, perhaps one celebrated in October 1590. When we see the key word **"name,"** we should look around for **doubled words** (or doubled **letters** or scattered **anagrams**) that could be clues. In his flawed book, *Elegy by W. S.*, Don Foster makes a still valid point by reminding us of Shakespeare's frequent use of **doublets**: "W. S. does not share the predilection of John Donne and many others for three items in a series. He thinks rather, like Shakespeare, in paired nouns, paired phrases, paired clauses" (125).

For example, when I read Sonnet 121, I wondered if the **two** uses of the word **"vile"** in line 1 were puns on his name, Will: "'Tis better to be **vile** than **vile** esteemed [.]" In May 2003, I attended a workshop on *Romeo and Juliet* at the Oregon Shakespeare Festival in Ashland. Professor Stephen Booth's presentation was about "patterns" he found in two of the sonnets embedded in that play—the Prologue and the first flirtatious exchange of the young lovers. Booth used bold **"distressed typography"** on words or parts of words to point out the **patterns** he had found. That is what I have been doing—but I have been making **code patterns** bold— since April 2001. I am thankful to Booth to have a **name** for this way of marking high lights in text.

So I have lit up the two uses of "**vile**" in sonnet 121, line 1. But should I think that there is a punning code operating when line 8 states, "Which in their **wills** count bad what I think good?" There appears the **plural** word, **"wills."** The very next line, line 9— "No, **I am** that **I am**, and they that level"—contains the words, **"I am that I am,"** which quotes what God said to Moses when Moses asked God his **name.** God was unwilling to give a name to himself, but these words are coming from Will's mouth, and they also make, with the line before— two **Will-I-am-s**—who sound here a little to me like Popeye, not Jehovah or *Adoni!* Should this odd, comical example inform us how to look for names?

Did Shakespeare write sonnets before his great sequence of 1—154? He must have to get so good at them. He may have written some to interest Henry Wriothesley's mother, Mary Browne Wriothesley, the Countess (or Baroness) of Southampton, to pay him for a birthday set of 17. Peter Levi found one anonymous sonnet to, "John Florio, Southampton's Italian and French tutor, installed by Burghley as a spy in his [Southampton's] household" (96). This may be Sonnet # minus 1. Perhaps Florio read it to Henry's mother to get her to ask Shakespeare for a short, pro-marriage sequence. After all, when Henry was only 16, his mother had agreed with Burghley that his granddaughter Elizabeth de Vere would make an excellent match. I think that it's important to remember that the intimate, family voice in Sonnets 1—17 shows Will's skill and daring when he speaks to the fatherless Henry as an older brother might. But the intimacy of the voice may also come from the fact that these are occasional birthday poems, perhaps ordered, paid for, and designed to be read aloud by a very frank mother to her son in private or at a small party.

When I first read this sonnet to Florio, I noticed its puns on flowers and Florio's name. Levi thinks, "almost no other poet in 1591 could have written the sonnet" (96). In fact, the first line echoes the first line of Sonnet #1: "From fairest creatures we desire **increase**." The date 1591, given to it by Levi, does not mark when it was written, but from when it was first published by Florio. So it could have been written in 1589 or 1590. Here is what I'd like to call Shakespeare's Sonnet Minus 1:

Phaeton to his friend *Florio*

Sweet friend, whose **name** agrees with thy **increase**,
How fit a rival art thou of the spring!
For when each branch hath left his **flourishing**,
And green-locked summer's shady pleasures cease,
She makes the winter's storms repose in peace,
And spends her franchise on each living thing:
The daisies sprout, the little birds do sing,
Herbs, gums, and plants do vaunt of their release.

So when that all our **English** wits lay dead
(Except the laurel that is evergreen),
Thou with thy fruits our **barrenness** o'erspread
And set thy **flowery** pleasance to be seen.

Such fruits, such **flowers** of mortality,
Were ne'er before brought out of **Italy.**

(qtd. in Levi 96—7)

Of course, the **five-fold** pun on flowers, flora, Flora, Florio, and Florence works in Latin, English, and Italian, and it shows up in *La Primavera*, a great painting by Botticelli, and it is not original to this sonnet or Shakespeare. Note the Italian abba/abba, envelope rhyme scheme the poet uses here in the octet for an Italian friend. Then, his rhymes go "English" in the sestet: cdcdee. This does sound like young Shakespeare, eager to compliment a tutor and gain access to a powerful house that would benefit him more than he could realize prior to 1590. Florio was so impressed, he saved this sonnet and published as a preface to one of his own works in 1591.

I also wonder how far back Shakespeare's family connections go with Southampton's family. Henry's father was "lord of the manor in Snitterfield where John Shakespeare was born" (Levi 10). I think the word **"barrenness"** (above) is a pun on the title **Baroness** of the powerful lady and widow, Henry's mother, also known as Mary, the Countess of Southampton. When Shakespeare dedicated *The Rape of Lucrece* to Henry, he used **both** of Henry's titles after his name: "TO THE RIGHT HONOURABLE, HENRY Wriothesley, Earle of Southampton,

and **Baron** of Titchfield."

Of course, this sonnet to Florio, if Shakespeare's, is pre-code, but it shows some of Shakespeare's early passion for precise nature images, for **name word play,** and for the people and the art of Italy. Of course, other Elizabethan sonneteers shared all these passions. This poet's pen name "Phaeton" shows him using an alias or code name, and it may document his fear of borrowing the sun's (Henry's) horses and driving them so badly that he falls from heaven. Once we enter the book of his numbered sonnets, we know it is William Shakespeare writing, and we find all sorts of the same kinds of clues and puns verified and agreed to by many scholars as well as many other possible puns that make my ears ring.

One note about proving puns: some are obvious and can be agreed upon. Some have quite a consensus built up around them. Others are a little or a lot less obvious. Some may seem very far-fetched. But how can a subtle pun be proven? If I hear or see a pun, how can I use logic to persuade a skeptic? Sometimes, only a pattern of use and repetition can be used as further evidence. That is why the **method of the code** is so crucial to understand if it is correct.

Chapter 6   The Author's Name: Will

I began looking with amused suspicion at all doublets as if I was a detective, and they were all twin, Gemini perpetrators of the low-life pun. I never cease to be amused by Shakespeare's use of doubled twins in *Comedy of Errors* and his later gender games with twins in *Twelfth Night*. Of course, the father of twins might make quite a few jokes about his hard-to-tell-apart, twin children. (I must be a simple fellow, one of Shakespeare's groundlings. For me, double identities, meanings, and puns are a code set up for laughter.) I discovered that in encoded lines of the *Sonnets*, there are both homophonic and homographic puns, both sound and sight gags. This was fun. Here's how I progressed.

First, start at the most obvious example, the two lines that form the final couplet of Sonnet 136:

"Make but my **name** thy love, and
         love that still;
And then thou lov'st me, for my
         name is **Will**."

In this most straightforward sonnet, hardly in code, the word **"name"** is used **twice** in the couplet, and the word **"will"** is used **seven** times as a pun on his name, as a word variously meaning: "will power," desire, lust, a future helping verb, and as a contemporary joke word meaning both male and female genitals. That's my Will!

We still make jokes about "willies" and "Slick Willie." When in London in Summer 2001, my wife and I went to see the Reduced

Shakespeare Company, still running to full houses after six years then, and I bought a T shirt with a picture of Shakespeare on it with a motto under him saying: "I love my Willie." After too much pointy-headed studying of Will's texts and especially all the blooming, bloody notes, my students and I love to watch the zany Reduced Shakespeare Company act out America's revenge for (or is it a response to?) Monty Python & the Flying Circus! I think Will would enjoy the reduction, too, but he might want his cut.

Mario Livio reminds us that even Johann Sebastian Bach (1685–1750), "… encrypted his signature in some of his compositions via musical codes. In the old German musical notation, B stood for B-flat and H stood for B-natural, so Bach could spell out his name in musical notes: B-flat, A, C, B-natural" (183). Livio then quotes Altschuler, who compares, "Bach's obsession with encrypting his signature [to] Alfred Hitchcock making a cameo appearance in each of his movies" (184).

All these wonderful artists can't resist tagging their works like graffiti artists and saying: "I was here, and I made this." Leonardo da Vinci left his thumbprint in his oil paintings: "Leo made this." "Shakespeare wrote this." "Kilroy was here!"

So maybe Shakespeare's obvious name pun couplet in Sonnet # 136 is a key we can use to unlock a code. Maybe it can be translated:

"**Name** is the key word, and I've used it twice just this once where I name myself. Seven uses of Will times two uses of name interlock with Sonnet #135." In Sonnet 135, just before this one, he puns with **13 wills** and **one wilt** for a total of **14.** It's all sexy and goofy. But the word "name" does not appear. Perhaps he used this sonnet to light up the code number **14**, as in "13 wills and one wilt equal the number of my name. Now, go look for 14 sonnets that use the word **'name.'**" I began to wonder what other sonnets name **Will** (lots) or also use the word "**name**" (only 14).

Is this punning on names one of his regular habits of thinking? It is fascinating that Shakespeare punned on his name elsewhere, not only in his writings. In her rough book, *Ungentle Shakespeare*, Duncan-Jones points out that the design Will wanted for his coat of arms is a piece of "'canting,' or punning heraldry" (92). "Laid on a 'bend sable', or black band, is a golden tilting spear" (93). She reminds us that the Wriothesley (Southampton's) coat of arms has four silver falcons on it, and while they are, "shown in profile, the silver falcon on the Shakespeare crest has 'his wings displayed.' The intention is to suggest the moment called 'shaking', which in falconry was the bird's action immediately before taking flight. Rather than shaking the spear that it holds, bolt upright, in its right claw, the bird is itself enacting the 'shake' part of the bearer's name" (95—96).

It is as if Will's family coat of arms is speaking a visual pun: "Shake Spear!" Even though this was a proud and serious image to Will, going back to spear shaking warriors in the past who may have fought for William the Conquerer, he couldn't help playing with words and images, and I will never see it again without smiling. In fact, his own name contains a bawdy joke, and so do the names of some of his best-loved comic and other characters. Who can forget the line-up of shake spear, fall (or false) staff, hot spur, and touch stone?

This is a writer who loves to play name games. In Sonnet 71, the third sonnet to use "**name**" in the series, I found this plea in line 12: "Do not so much as my poor **name** rehearse," and, instead of "will," I found the two punning words "**vile**" and "**vilest**" in line 4, "From this **vile** world, with **vilest** worms to dwell" [.] (Very "poor" Will indeed.) I wondered if the word **name** turned on the code, and then some key name word (that sounds or looks like a key name) was used **twice**. I had counted all uses of the word "**name**" in all 154 Sonnets and had found **seventeen** lines using "**name**" in **fourteen** sonnets (with one of those lines containing an additional "**naming**" in gerund form). The number **fourteen** is the most obvious magic number in a sonnet cycle. The number **seventeen** is also important in this sequence because it was the commission to write the first seventeen sonnets that got Shakespeare started in a short sequence for a total of 17 x 14. Next, I listed all the lines in which the word "name" appeared and did deep reading around them to find doubled words.

For example, in Sonnet 72, line 11, I found: "My **name** be buried where my body is," but the "buried" doubled words were in two similar-looking pairs: **willingly/ well** and **worthy/ worth**. "Will" is **buried** in "**will**ingly," and since I believe that the young man was most likely Henry **Wriothesley**, the Third Earl of Southampton, I wondered if **worthy/ worth** were sort of a sight gag, a homographic, spelling pun on Henry's last name. If so, there is some old family name history buried in this pun. (Heraldic punning was common. See puns and geometry buried in **Tudor Rose** below. **)

Duncan-Jones reports that [Henry's] "great-uncle Sir Thomas Wriothesley had been Garter King of Arms for nearly thirty years. ... It was he who, after some experiment, evolved the elaborate spelling of the family name, once plain '**Writh**', as 'Wriothesley', pronounced 'Risely',

which was to be adopted both by his own descendants and those of his brother" (Ungentle ... 84).

So Shakespeare's sound pun on **worth** is very close to the root form of Henry's family name **Writh**, and the spelling of **worthy** is buried in **Wrioth**esley.

In the next instance, Sonnet 76, line 7, I found: "That every word **almost** doth **tell** my **name**," and there are three double-**ll**, rhyme and off-rhyme words with will: "**still**" (twice), "**all**" (twice), "**tell**," "**telling**," and finally, "**told**." I began to wonder if he were teasing us. I worried about my madness or his **method**. Well, he did write "almost." This subtle word-play made me want to tease him back and call him "William Tell."

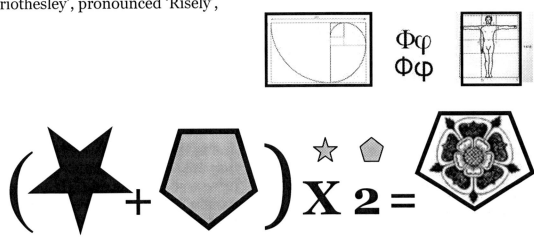

** <u>Tudor heraldic Golden Ratio Φ</u>

(Greek letter *phi*) X **2** (puns): **Tu**[2]**dor**[door] **Rose**
Doubled red & white symbolic flower (rose within rose)
2 geometric 5's (penta-): York white in Lancaster red
pentacles **(pent)** inside pentagons

Chapter 7   The Youth's Name: Henry

In his narrative about "Mr. W. H.," Oscar Wilde reminded me that the great painter, "Michael Angelo plays with ... [the] name" of "the young Tommaso Cavalieri" in his sonnets (1175). The whole inherited Italian and English sonnet tradition seems to require some kind of name play. Perhaps the first of *Shakespeare's Sonnets* to code name the youth was Sonnet 36, line 12: "Unless thou take that **honour** from thy **name**:" and the word **"honour"** is used a second time nearby in line 11, "Nor thou with public kindness **honour** me," as an **honorific** for "Henry" as in the dedication to *The Rape of Lucrece:* "HONOURABLE, HENRY." Maybe Shakespeare is doing simple arithmetic: take (subtract) the British spelling of **"honour"** from Henry. What do you get? The answer is in the leftover vowels:

> HeNRy
> — HoNouR
> ey[e] **(I) O, O, U** (you)!

Is that **I. O. U,** with doubled **O** for owe? Is this sonnet a promissory note with a doubled "owe?" I have to say maybe, maybe not. As in all detective work, it's easy to read in too much. A good detective gets the correct focal length and keeps things in focus.

Sonnet 36 is only one of **two** sonnets containing the word **"name"** before the middle of the youth's sequence. In fact, these two sonnets may contain early number clues planted by Will to point out his **double** word code. The first line of

this Sonnet 36 admits: "Let me confess that we **two** must be **twain**." This is circular reasoning, perhaps a confession of number code, a repeated magic number: two said twice. If "two" is "twain," then we are each one: 2 divided by two is 1. Most of the math in the *Sonnets* is schoolboy math—adding, subtracting, multiplying, and dividing—and Shakespeare uses his math to encode, to fool around with math that sounds like logic, and to reinvigorate clichés that use numbers to make jokes or proverbial sayings.

In the next instance, Sonnet 39, line 6, he is still playing with simple numbers: "And our dear love lose **name** of **single one**," and the possible code name words include a **single** use each of **"worth"** (Wroithesley) in line 1, "O how thy **worth** with manners may I sing," and **"hence"** (which could introduce the youth's first name, Henry) in line 14**.** The number logic of this sonnet is a play on two and one: they are two who are one. Will is pretending in line 14 to be one with Henry while they are apart: "By praising **him here** who doth **hence** [Henry] remain." After these two sonnets, 36 & 39 (that may play on both the youth's names), the word **"name"** doesn't show up again until a cluster that begins with Sonnet 71, but there it refers to Will.

Everyone wonders if the plays written at the same time as the *Sonnets* also contain important identity clues. An article about the use of language in *Love's Labour's Lost,* adds one piece of pro-Southampton data. D. Carroll Allen finds, "The **code** for the "College de Montaigu" is also **code** for "Montague House"—a solution that suggests the Southampton component in the play's make-up, and probably John Florio. Montague House was Southampton's mother's family residence in Southwark ... If the play was designed for a private performance ... it would probably have been one at Montague House" (10).

The Globe wasn't built yet in Southwark, but it's fun to think of Shakespeare's company in the streets going to Montague House to dress up as four lords, who were in the audience, and play them setting up a Platonic Academy ruined by the appearance of four pretty women. Every time the youths try to study philosophy, along comes Venus and her sexy train. And, of course, the name Montague suggests a strong connection to one family in the feud in *Romeo and Juliet.*

The next sonnet along my trail of breadcrumbs to have **name** in a line and point toward the youth is #80, line 2: "Knowing a better **spirit** doth use your **name**," and we know this is about the rival poet using the young man's **"name,"** a very scary event for Will before his patron helped him become a full partner in the Globe Theater in 1599. The suspicious-looking name words found are: **"worth," "wilfully"** [sic], **"will," "whilst," "wracked," "worthless,"** and **"worst."** (Notice that there are seven words in this string as there were seven uses of

"rich" in Sidney's most punning sonnet. When we get to the use of numbers as code, we will see that number 7 is one of the key numbers linking the sonnet form and time.) When I found these seven words, I began to try to read the code as an embedded message by filling in my words where needed. We again have **"will"** and **"worth"** in one poem, with **Will "willfully"** worried **"whilst" "wracked"** about losing **"worth"** to the rival poet. Will would then be **"worthless,"** and that would be the very **"worst."**

This is **not** just a paraphrase of the poem; it is the overt statement in plaintext of what a covert string of code words (or cipher) might imply. As in real intelligence work, it is very important to get the covert message right. In this sonnet's line 7, Will compares himself to a "saucy bark," the kind of small, shallow draft English warship that defeated the Spanish Armada in the Channel. Will's rival, on the other hand, is compared to a larger "tall" ship riding on the youth's "soundless deep." Perhaps this is a very well known ship, the main playwright for the Admiral's Men, the poet who launched a thousand verses and curses, Christopher Marlowe.

Here we must use our naval intelligence. Perhaps we could name the "saucy bark" *Puck* or *Venus* and the rival's man of war *Faustus* or even *Neptune.* Shakespeare is clearly worried about losing this battle at sea: "Then if he thrive, and I be cast away,/ The **worst** was this: my love was my decay" (lines 13 and 14). But as Shakespeare already knows, the small English ships barked like the dogs of war around the Spanish men of war in 1588 and drove them on the Flemish coast to be scattered by English fire ships, which forced the rest to sail north and around into the stormy Atlantic off Scotland and Ireland. So Shakespeare's small ship barks like a terrier, and by Sonnet 86 the danger from the main rival is over. The rival is referred to then in the past tense.

Sonnet 81, line 5 may again pun on the young man's first name, Henry:

"Your **name** from **hence** immortal
    life shall have,"

and the word **"hence"** is **doubled** before that in this sonnet in line 3, "From **hence** your memory death cannot take" [.] I speculated that the simplest code is to write a key word just **twice**, so the reader knows that it wasn't a one-time, random event. And if there are hundreds of examples (See Appendix A, pages 164—169.), all that evidence adds up. Suddenly, if we read line 5 again, we might read, "Your **name** [Henry] from [the word] **hence** immortal life shall have." Shakespeare wanted to and promised to immortalize the youth. I think he did it in this code.

But then, in Sonnet 89, line 10, Will seems to be worried that he has over- exposed Henry's name, in his two dedicatory letters to "Venus and Adonis" (1593) and "The Rape of Lucrece" (1594) and perhaps even here in code, so he writes: "Thy sweet beloved **name no more** shall dwell," and this sonnet may have **no name word** for the youth (unless the single word **"Haply"** is

"perhaps" one for Henry—as a tripled **"happy"** may be in Sonnet 92), but this Sonnet 89 does contain the author's **"will"** four times, **"tell"** once, **"I'll"** twice, and **"ill"** once. **Will** may be feeling a little **"ill"** about telling his love because he has told too much and exposed Henry's name and patronage and their love to what we call "publicity."

Sonnet 89 is still reflecting in the aftermath of the rival poet sequence and its dangers. In line three, Will says, "Speak of my lameness, and I straight will **halt**" [.] He is not lame like Socrates or Oedipus. He can "halt" limping. He says so with this pun on stop (halt!) and lame, so I see him smiling here. He can't help joking a little even about being abandoned by Henry. The first quatrain limps along like this in one reading with the stresses in bold:

"Say that thou **didst** for-**sake me**
    for some **fault,**
And **I** will **com**-ment up**on that** of-
    fense;
Speak of my **lame**-ness, **and** I
    straight will **halt,**
A-**gainst** thy **rea**-sons ma-king **no**
    de-**fense."**

This lameness must refer to an implied pun about Will's lame "feet" in poetry; perhaps his iambic footwork sounds a little hobbled by all this naming code with its interlocking numbers. The proof here is in the scansion. Line one begins with a stress on "Say" that knocks the meter a little off balance, and we fall toward "didst" over two unstressed sounds. Then we hit two back-to-back stresses that slow the line down, but then we must tumble over two small words toward "fault." This is like a rougher line from a Wyatt sonnet. Line two has ten syllables and an odd misstep between "upon" and "that," and that makes us put stresses down next to each other with a missing syllable before the strangely stressed pronoun "that." We have here almost a caesura as we look around for the missing syllable. Line three starts again with a stress followed by two unstressed words, and there's an odd softer stress placed on the small word "and" as if putting down this foot hurt. Only the fourth line is regular, so he shows he can stop this limping along as soon as Henry says, Halt!" This fourth line is like a more popular, smooth Surrey sonnet line. And it might be a joke that says, "See, I can count to five." Perhaps if he stops punning, his lines will flow beautifully again. But can he stop?

There's wit and planned artistry here even when he pretends to write badly. (See essay p. 214.) This is a funny man, who, like Alexander Pope, rewards deep readers with all kinds of rhetorical jokes. If Shakespeare's lines sound like miscues out of Mozart's "Musical Joke," we must see if it's Will doing a silly dance skillfully. He does this so well in the "Pyramus and Thisby" skit in *A Midsummer Night's Dream*. The worse job acting it out my students do, the funnier it gets. It's a "rude" skit that cannot self-destruct! But there the meters and repeating sounds help the actors rant and rave. Here in Sonnet 89, we just have trouble walking along, so we become "lame" readers.

Next, Sonnet 95 has two lines with the word **"name"** inside. "Doth spot the beauty of thy budding **name**:" (line 3) and in line 8, as a gerund "naming" and then the noun repeated: "**Naming** thy **name**, blesses an **ill** report." Even hearing Henry's name in a bad report of ill gossip is a blessing to Will. The problem is that Henry has "sins" but makes the "shame" so "sweet." Here, **"rose"** in line 2, "Which like a canker in the fragrant **rose**" is a sound-alike to Henry's last name (pronounced **Risley**) and an emblem of Henry's family (as well as the Tudors'). **"Rose"** is used as Henry's "budding" last name word. Perhaps the three h-words—**"heed," "heart,"** and **"hardest"** in lines 13 and 14—point toward (thy name) Henry. "Take **heed**, dear **heart**, of this large privilege;/ The **hardest** knife ill used doth lose his edge." The gossip about and the sins of the youth's "sport" are clearly sexual. **"Rose"** was used for Wriothesley before in the famous Sonnet 18 to Henry, "Shall I compare thee to a summer's day" where the first syllables of **both** their last names are either stated or implied in line 3: "Rough winds do **shake** the darling [**rose implied**] buds of May."

Sonnet 108 is tricky. Its name line 8 recalls, "Even as when **first** I **hallowed thy** fair **name**." But there are none of the name code words here. Perhaps this paraphrase of the Lord's prayer (in Will's religion of "divine" love) is looking all the way back to Sonnet 1, **"first"** written for Henry's seventeenth birthday in 1590, where we find the possible **single** name words **"herald"** and **"rose"** for **Henry**

(Harold) Wriothesley (Riz).
Sonnet 1 probably recalls Henry's
"coming out" as a herald at the St.
George's Day, Order of the Garter
ceremony on the 23rd of April 1590.
The first seventeen sonnets were
probably written at the request of
Henry's widowed mother Mary
(nicknamed **"April"** twice in the
Sonnets), who may have been one of
Will's first patrons.

The pun on Henry's name in
Sonnet 1, **"herald rose,"** is closer
than it looks. Rowse points out that
Henry's

> ... grandfather, Sir John
> **Writh**, was the third Garter
> King-of-Arms and held the
> office at the time when the
> College of **Heralds** was
> incorporated in 1483. As such
> he was frequently employed
> on diplomatic missions by
> Edward IV and Henry VII. He
> ... was not merely a **herald**
> but a man of diplomacy [who]
> died in 1504 ... His elder son,
> Thomas, [Henry's uncle] ...
> had much the same kind of
> career, court ceremonies,
> diplomatic missions,
> **Heralds' Office** work,
> though to these he added
> scholarship and was a noted
> collector of **heraldic**
> antiquities. (1-2)

The name pun on **herald** and
Harold is close, especially since
Henry was often called "Harry" as a
boy. It was this uncle Thomas who
changed the simple name Writh to
an older form—Wriothesley—from a
family member who lived back in the
reign of King John (3).

If my favorite time scheme is
correct, which I will explore and try
to prove in the second half of this
study, then Sonnet #1 could be seen
as a flash back to April 24, 1590,
when Henry was only 16. On the day
before (April 23rd), Henry might have
been the "herald" in a royal coming
out celebration of the annual Order
of the Garter on St. George's Day
presided over by Queen Elizabeth I.
(Henry's great-uncle had been Garter
King of Arms for thirty years.) That
day was also on or near
Shakespeare's 26th birthday and may
have been close to when he started to
write the first seventeen sonnets at
the request of Henry's mother. (In
one possible timeline I suggest later,
Sonnet #1 starts on April 24th of the
Old, Julian Calendar, near or on
Will's birthday, and the youth's
sequence runs 126 days until August
27th.)

As a reminder of St. George's
Day (April 23rd), the Order of the
Garter, and his own birthday,
Shakespeare may have given Henry's
mother the code name **"April"** in
Sonnet #3, who "Calls back the lovely
April of her prime;" (line 10) and a
second time in Sonnet #21, "With
April's firstborn flow'rs, and all
things rare" (line 7). Then we have
only to remember back to Chaucer's
Prologue for *The Canterbury Tales*,
when **April** rains end the drought of
March, to wonder if Henry's mother
ended a long drought in
Shakespeare's income and brought
about the flowers of May for Henry's
October 1590 birthday. Certainly,
Sonnet 18, no longer paid for by
Countess Mary, celebrates "the buds
of May" and the blossoming of a real
personal friendship between the poet

and the youth. But right away, the realist Shakespeare hits us with Sonnet #19, the first great Time sonnet. "Devouring time" poses a dangerous, criminal threat to the youth. Time is the great enemy, which the sonnets set out to conquer through the "immortality" of verse. I believe that through the use of numbers and time words, Shakespeare linked his name code to an internal timeline and number code in the sonnets. To prove this will take quite a bit of investigation and elementary math. Shakespeare's sense of Time in these sonnets is almost as complex as Einstein's in his theory of relativity.

But Shakespeare starts with the seventeen-sonnet birthday sequence, where each sonnet equals one year in the life of the youth. In this first, seventeen part beginning of his sequence, Shakespeare (like Ovid's Tiresias, an ally to Henry's mother) warns Henry to marry and avoid the fate of (Ovid's) Narcissus, as explained in Sonnet 3, line 14: "Die **single**, and thine **image** dies with thee." A code of scattered **doubled letters** (not words) links two key sonnets (1 & 62) in a Narcissus/Tiresias pair. Shakespeare is quite sexually explicit from the start. In Sonnet 1, he speaks like an older brother to the fatherless youth and quite bluntly tells him to procreate, not masturbate. In lines 11 and 12, we find the name of **Onan** in doubled **letters** (not doubled words):

"Within thine **ow**n bud buriest thy content,   **on/on**
And, tender churl, mak'st waste in niggarding."   **An/a/a/nn**

Narcissus and Onan have a lot in common as lovers of self.

Then, in Sonnet 62, which in my favorite timeline (See Table 9, page 115.) comes right after 28 sonnets to the youth linked to dark lady sonnets, when the affair with the lady is over, and the youth is separated from Will, Onan's name— interrupted at least twice by a pun on Will's wife's name **Anne** at the beginnings of two middle lines— appears again in lines 1—4:

"Sin **of** self-l**o**ve **p**ossesseth **a**ll mine eye,   **o/o/o/a/n**
And **a**ll my soul, **an**d **a**ll my every part;   **Anne/a/an/a/a**
And **fo**r this si**n** there is **no** remedy,   **Anne/o/n/no**
It is **so** gr**o**u**n**ded i**n**w**a**rd my **h**e**a**rt."   **o/o/n/n/a/h/a**

Well, it's a little more jumbled and obsessive and comic than in Sonnet 1, and perhaps he exclaims here, "O Anne, Anna, Anna!" and "Anne. O, N-No!" and "Aha!" To underline this obsession, he uses "self" or a form of "self" seven times and forms of "my" or "mine" nine times, a perhaps sexual use of those two climacteric numbers. In his emotional loneliness, Will portrays himself as narcissistic and masturbatory as the youth, and he tells us this in code. Perhaps he even comically portrays himself getting caught by his wife. I don't know for sure, but I find it possible.

I found a long, Freudian analysis of Shakespeare's "Poetics of Narcissism" by Jane Hedley. Like many of the unfunny articles I've read, this one had me laughing very quickly. What it is about "lit crit" that is so damned serious (besides tenure)? Some University Wits have always had trouble enjoying and really "getting" Will. While he talks or jokes around, his commentators drag him down in "discourse." But they can have good ideas, and Jane Hedley reminded me of the rest of Ovid's narrative about Narcissus. Hedley leaves out Tiresias, but she includes Echo, who fell in love with Narcissus as the poor boy gazed at his own reflection. Echo, of course, couldn't speak first, but she had to repeat whatever Narcissus said, thus reinforcing his illusion that his image in the pool is another person. Hedley portrays Shakespeare's stance in his sonnets "in terms of Freud's account of 'the inclination toward a narcissistic object choice' in homosexual men" (Hedley 1).

I am not so sure. I think Shakespeare is a greater general psychologist than Freud (as opposed to being a doctor who tries to heal mental illness) and a much more potent and comic thinker than a simple narcissist. I remind us all that comic vision is tied to the human intellect, and Keats was right when he praised Shakespeare's deep, double consciousness. But Hedley, quite correctly, reminds me to pay attention to all the mirror images in the sonnets, and she has some good material on what she wants to point out as rhetorical devices that best express or expose narcissism and obsession. But when it comes to wordplay, I'm not sure I see Will as in any way "unconscious" of all the implications of all his words.

Of course, the use of the rhetorical device of the *chiasmus* presents an **abba** mirror image in the word order inside his lines, as in line 14 from Sonnet 154: "**Love's** fire heats **water, water** cools not **love**." This is a miniature image built into the word order of love looking into its reflection in water that ends the whole sequence. But the device that most reminds both Hedley and me most of Echo is punning, technically called "syllepsis." Hedley quotes, "The sixteenth-century rhetorician George Puttenham [who] called syllepsis "the figure of double supply" [where] … a single word is doubly contextualized … and thereby has more than one of its possible meanings brought into play" (10).

So I think that Shakespeare is making very sophisticated use of the Narcissus story to describe his love for the youth. It's as if he wrote a dialogue in punning code between himself and Echo:

Poet:	"Hence!"
Echo:	"Henry!"
Poet:	"Rose!"
Echo:	"Risley!"

But Shakespeare is not stuck under some shallow Freudian diagnosis, where the doctor knows all, and the patient is ignorant. I think his self-consciousness (as he developed in the language use of the sonnets) is incredibly complex, intellectual, and ironic. Perhaps Shakespeare is making funny faces behind the much too serious doctor's or commentators' backs.

As if to trick simplistic thinkers, Sonnet #62 shows Shakespeare at his most narcissistic. But, although he says he "paints" his "age" with the youth's "beauty" in line 14, in line 5, he ridicules himself: "Methinks no face so gracious is as mine," but then, he looks in his mirror, and, in line 10, he sees himself as older Tiresias: "Beated and chopped with tanned antiquity," so Shakespeare returns from narcissistic self-deception to his stance of realistic irony. In fact, he uses the same kind of rough wording to describe himself here that he later flings at the dark lady in Sonnet # 130, "Black wires grow on her head." And Tiresias is, famously, one of the world's most experienced lovers, one who is cursed with bisexual, visionary powers that neither the goddess Hera (Roman Juno), the Queen of the gods, nor Oedipus the King of Thebes can handle.

But the insult of calling young Henry "Narcissus" may or may not be original with Shakespeare. Peter Levi found that in 1591, Lord Burghley's secretary John Claphorn wrote Southampton "an insulting Latin poem" called "Narcissus" (96). Levi wonders if Sonnets 1—17 (or perhaps those parts revised after 1591) are "a counter blast" to Claphorn's poem (96). Maybe Claphorn's Latin insult takes off from the first 17 sonnets instead. The date 1591 fits with my thinking that Sonnet # 19 may be a blast against the Burghley/de Vere plan to force young Henry to marry Elizabeth de Vere and force the future Earl into their court faction.

Certainly, Will's insults of the youth are more personal as well as sympathetic. Will takes the stance of an older, married-with-children brother speaking with tough love and warning his younger brother. Perhaps some of his more intimate sonnets were even written with the idea of a persona, that of Henry's mother Mary—one of Shakespeare's first patrons—reading them to her son. Will gives her a voice and well put poetic arguments for her to read on her son's 17th birthday. Claphorn, on the other hand, may be representing Burghley's plan to force young Henry to marry Burghley's granddaughter, Elizabeth de Vere. As we will see, this plot may give Sonnet #19 a whole new meaning, which can only be spelled out with knowledge of the code.

In the next code Sonnet 111, line 5 goes: **"Thence** comes it that my **name** receives a brand [.]" Shakespeare's name receives a brand from the public nature of his theater work. Perhaps Lord Henry has criticized funny Will for his "low-life" manners. Will bluntly reminds Henry that the goddess Fortune didn't give him wealth or a title. Will apologizes for his work a little, too, explaining that he has to keep the groundlings laughing. I must be part groundling myself. I have always read for, listened for, and enjoyed his jokes. Here in this sonnet, we have a great comedic writer privately excusing himself to his lordship, patron, and (not always approving) friend. Here are the burdens of loving someone from the upper class; a comic genius cannot express the true range of his wit for fear of hurting or offending the youth's feelings, at least not without apologizing in private.

Since **hence** may also be a Henry word, it's interesting that **"thence"** (or "from hence") is used twice as is the word **"will"** with one use of **"willing."** Of course, he may want to remind Henry that there are **two** major events (and maybe some minor ones) where Henry's deeds **"brand"** Shakespeare's **"name."** The first is very personal, and that is caused by Cupid's **"brand."** Henry was not so honorable that he turned down the dark lady's invitation to play at love. And the second comes later and is political. Although Shakespeare supports the Essex faction against the older men around Elizabeth, he was never part of the Essex rebellion in 1600-01 as Henry was. Will was never **branded** a traitor, but his company was suspected and investigated and cleared. The fact that they were **paid** just before the rebellion to perform *Richard II*, where the overthrow of a weak king is shown, got them off the hook. By the use of code, Sonnet 111 may be the last to **name** Henry in **"thence."**

I have had some trouble finding any code or way of explaining deeply Sonnet # 126, the twelve-line envoi at the end of the sonnets to the youth. At first, I wondered if they were just the leftover couplets to six unfinished sonnets. Eight of them are end stopped and could be self-contained. The middle four lines are linked in a couplet quatrain. Do all twelve lines say in bunches of four and two "the end" five times over? The two missing lines in the traditional couplet position struck me in two ways: the first was a reference to the silence after death, as in *Hamlet*. The second is a

happier note: in 1609, this relationship was on-going and had not ended. Or is it a sigh by the author meaning, "This will have to do. I can't go on?" No one seems to know if the two sets of parentheses were written there by Shakespeare or by an "editor" at the printer's. But I don't want to let anyone else into *Shakespeare's Sonnets* in the position of "author" if I can find a good reason to say I think Shakespeare did it. I want to point out that lines 5 and 11 both contain parentheses in the 1609 Quarto: "(sovereign mistress over wrack)" and "(though delayed)," and they may set up an echo effect in the parentheses around the two non-existent final lines, the emptiness of death that can be delayed no longer. This argues for Shakespeare as the person who wrote the empty pair of **(**   **)**'s there with his quill.

I think it's also significant that "... in the 16th century Erasmus gave the attractive name 'lunulae' to round brackets [what the English call American **parentheses**], in reference to their moon-like profile" (Truss 161). They look like the first and last phase of the Moon (with twenty-eight days in between). Thus, the double sets of "lunulae" form both an end to the youth's sonnets (like a double bar in music) and a silent, double transition to the 28 dark lady sonnets. Perhaps the moon month is doubled because she is driving both the youth and the poet loony. Anyway, we have seen almost all important code elements doubled, and the missing twin lines at the end of this envoy sonnet are no exception. Since they denote both the end of time in the sonnets and the end of the first 126 sonnets before the sonnets to the lady, they must work both ways two times.

Fortunately, I found an article by Neil Graves, who takes us as far as we may want to go on Sonnet #126. The main reason I like this piece is that, of all the commentators, Graves is one of very few with a sense of humor and a deeper understanding of puns as sound code. He actually tackles all three of the "odd" sonnets (# 99, # 126, and # 145), and I am grateful for his help. In Sonnet 99, Neil thinks "violet" can be said in three syllables as a pun on "violate." Thus, the extra line comes first and "violates" the form to "bother the reader" (203). Another point of the poem is that all the "flowers" of the court have "violated" Henry Wriothesley by robbing his best qualities.

John Kerrigan has found Shakespeare's source for Sonnet 99 in Constable's *Diana* published in 1592 and 1594 (300). Perhaps # 99 is also "odd" because it may announce the failure of the Essex rebellion with picked, funereal flowers, which have all stolen qualities from the youth as (from Shakespeare's point of view) the Earl of Essex also "robbed" Henry's loyalty. Line 13 (an unlucky number) may announce the death of Essex, "A vengeful canker ate him up to **death** [,]" but it is not part of the usual couplet in this fifteen-line sonnet. And in line 11, "And to his **rob**b'ry had ann**exed** thy **breath**;" Shakespeare may give us sound and letter hints of **Robert**, the **Ex**-Earl of Ess**ex**'s name. And to annex Henry's breath is to force him

through military and family loyalty to **conspire** (or breath together) in the Essex rebellion. I know it's standard to called this failed rebellion "foolish" or "ill-advised," but, once again, from the point of view of one who dotes on Henry and in the mind of Essex, it really looked as if their enemies at court were trying to crush them just before they rebelled. Perhaps Essex and Southampton were as boxed-in as Hamlet and Horatio were in the final duel scene by the two poison users Claudius and Laertes. Perhaps the whole play *Hamlet* was written like "The Mousetrap" to test the Queen and Lord Cecil, to plead for Henry's life, and to remind the court that a new king was coming from the north like Fortinbas.

As for the other, robbing flowers of the court that Shakespeare mentions, what can I do but guess? The **violet** may even be the aging Queen Elizabeth. She's earlier (older) than all the rest, and soon after the play *Hamlet*, which is filled with some very anxious content about the aftermath of the Essex rebellion, Shakespeare will write *Twelfth Night* with a plucky heroine, **Viola**, for the Queen's Christmas court celebrations. The **lily** may be Lyly's patron de Vere, whose white hand is behind the boys' theater mentioned in *Hamlet*. **Marjoram** may be Henry's very Catholic Grandmother Lady Marjorie still tolerated by Elizabeth but a dangerous relative for Henry. And the shameful **red roses** are the Lancastrians while the despairing **white roses** are the Yorkist lords. Some of them judge Essex and Henry; some of them do not intervene. Of course, one of the more interesting players in the trial is a man said to have been in Essex's faction—Francis Bacon—but once again he turns state prosecutor against his former "friends." Is he the **"canker"** (or what we would call a "mole") of quatrain three? After that possible third quatrain mention of the death of Essex himself—and notice that the **third quatrain** is where Shakespeare refers to Hamnet's death in Sonnet 33, Marlowe's death in Sonnet 74, and now Essex's execution here— the couplet returns to other flowers—all the other lords of the court—which have stolen their sweet scents or colors from Henry. Suddenly, this fifteen-line sonnet, which some dismiss as mechanical or a piece of trifling flattery, may reveal another political allegory of a threat against Henry similar to Sonnet 19, which is placed 60 sonnets before this one.

Neil Grave's work on Sonnet #126 goes quite far into sound puns, a possible acrostic, and typography jokes. He gives us the pun on "audit" in line 11. We should *hear* from the original spelling of "audite" the word "oddity," which acknowledges this envoi's odd form. Neil wants to bring in Shakespeare's wife Anne Hathaway as Nature and wants us ("humorously") to see a heavy-set woman and also an hourglass shape of Time (206) in the two pairs of parentheses as lines 13 and 14:

(   )
(   )

whose audit all of us must answer when Nature says, "It's Time!" The last two lines of all (11 and 12) before the empty lines are:

"Her audit, though delayed,
    answered must be,
And her **quietus** is to render thee."

(Note that Duncan-Jones has unfortunately edited the parentheses in lines 5 and 11 into commas. This ruins Shakespeare's soundless (   ) typography pun.)

I also hear "her quietus" in line 12 as one final joke, "her coitus," our final mating with our "sovereign mistress," Nature. And if you read these double parentheses as an envoi's transition to the dark lady sonnets, then we already know that both the poet and the youth will end up being **rendered** by her **audit** and her **coitus**.

I also remember that double bars show up at the end of every piece of music. Was Shakespeare trying for a print equivalent of the double bars here? Could this pair of parentheses be the precursor to shaped poetry, such as "The Altar" or the angel wings in "Easter" by "Holy George" Herbert? If these parentheses lines stand for an hourglass, it's clear that the sand has run out. The end of time in this whole sequence comes not after Sonnet #154; it comes after #126 when time is over for Will and Henry in 1609.

But although their Time is over, the love and inspiration remain. Will decided to publish the *Sonnets* to save it all. Back in sonnet 38, Will named Henry the "**10th Muse.**" This has an historic, almost an immortal, ring; it is what Plato called Sappho (Livadas 188).

46

Chapter 8   The Dark Lady and Her Name

Φ *phi*

Once we turn ahead to the dark lady sonnets, Shakespeare takes us (back in time) to his anti-idealistic lover's views that started in Sonnet 34 with doubts about Henry. His lady is the opposite of Wyatt's Anne Boleyn and Sidney's Stella, Lady Penelope Rich. Will's lady is both available and has a will of her own. She is not a member of the dangerous upper class; she is dangerous because she makes love with the upper class and has the same needs as Will. He will describe her, but will he name her? In almost everybody's favorite dark lady sonnet, #130, Will pretends in the first line to mock her by saying what she's not. Her "eyes are nothing like the sun;" but many have pointed out, he is mocking his model Sidney who, in his Sonnet #7 compares Stella's eyes to the blinding sun. Will may also be mocking an even earlier model by Thomas Watson, a great madrigal writer, early sonneteer (1582), and close friend of Christopher Marlowe. Both Daniel's *Delia* Sonnet 31.7 and Linche's *Diella* Sonnet 31.2 may also be mocked

models (Kerrigan 359). Shakespeare objects to the extreme comparisons, not to the qualities of his dark lady.

Sonnet 130 sets up another satirical contrast with lines of yet another sonneteer, Edmund Spencer. "In the early 1590s the widowed Spencer wooed and won Elizabeth Boyle, who became his wife in 1594" (Abrams 863). In 1595, Spencer published his 89 sonnets *Amoretti* ("little loves" or "little cupids"), which details their courtship. With his sonnet sequence, Spencer published one of the great wedding poems in English, *Epithalamion*. In both, he describes his lady in idealized terms. In Sonnet 37, he "covets" yet fears her golden hair "under a net of gold" (865). When he describes her as a bride in the ninth stanza of *Epithalamion*, he goes over the top: "Her long loose yellow locks lyke golden wyre,/ Sprinckled with perle" (872), and I wonder if we can hear Will laugh at "wyre" and write in his Sonnet #130, line 4: "If hairs be wires, black wires grow on her head;" once again, it's the exaggerating lover using funny language that sets him off, not the faults of his lady.

With Spencer's works, we may have another chicken and egg problem. Could Shakespeare have written or revised Sonnet #130 in 1595? We don't know what his sonnets looked like as a work in progress. Did he try to write them in chronological sequence, or did he decide at some point on an over arching design and write sonnets to fill in spaces? I think the textual evidence points to both methods. A sonnet sequence, with one poem per page, can easily be reshuffled, revised, and renumbered. When Will read Spencer's Sonnet #64 in 1595, he may not have laughed at first because it speaks of kissing, but he may have laughed when Spencer swears that Elizabeth's lips "smell lyke unto Gillyflowers" (866), and all her parts smell like different flowers. "Her ruddy cheeks lyke unto Roses red;" swears Spencer. And overall, "her sweet odour did them all excel" (866). This was too much for Will. He may respond in Sonnet #130, lines 6—8,

"But no such roses see I in her
        cheeks;
And in some perfumes is there more
        delight
Than in the breath that from my
        mistress reeks."

Spencer's fond clichés could have engendered the funniest lines in Will's #130. And if some of the dark lady sonnets were written after Will studied Spencer's two works in 1595, could Will have also borrowed

something deeper from Spencer's *Epithalamion?*

This innovative wedding poem is embedded with the **numbers** of a **time code.** As Abrams and other editors point out, it has 365 longer lines of pentameter (or longer) for the days of the year. It has 24 stanzas for the 24 hours in a day. His wedding day is set on the Summer Solstice, so this wedding song covers 16 hours of daylight and 8 hours of night, the same ratio of light to dark on that day in Ireland (864). This is the poem's deep, temporal structure. Did Will borrow the idea of a time code from Spencer? Later, I will say yes to this claim and try to prove that Will's Sonnet #52, at a key point in the sonnets to the youth, is by placement and code a Summer Solstice sonnet, and its matching Moon Sonnet #145, is written in praise of Will's wife Anne with short lines (tetrameter) for the shortest night of the year.

Spencer does not have to use code to name his beloved. In his Sonnet #74, he names his three Elizabeth's: his mother, his Queen, and his lover (867). But Will has personal reasons to hide his names. He is still married to Anne. Their daughter Susanna gets married in 1607 and gives birth to their granddaughter Elizabeth in 1608, and Shakespeare's own mother Mary is still alive. Interestingly, Mary dies in 1608, a year before he publishes his sonnets. Perhaps he wanted to hide the existence and the identity of the dark lady from his mother and Anne. But, of course, Anne finds out his infidelities; in Sonnet #145, she pities him and does not "hate" him.

In line 13, she throws "hate away," a pun on her maiden name Hathaway. But, before that, there are more uses for code than fooling the censors or deceiving an enemy. There are some dear family members to deceive and protect as well.

Bear with me here. There are only three sonnets in the dark lady sequence that use the word **"name."** We move to Sonnet 127, the first of the "dark lady" songs. But its line 7 seems to warn us in double negative no's: "Sweet beauty hath **no name, no** holy bower," and the key repeated word here is **"black"** three times, which left me (along with many others) in the dark. In Shakespeare's time as in ours, a double negative grammatically and mathematically also implied a positive. Feste jokes, "... your four negatives make your two affirmatives" (*12th Night* V.1.20-21). But is Shakespeare's double denial in Sonnet 127 a clue that he will name the lady later? Line 2 also uses **"name"** in the negative: "Or if it were, it bore **not** beauty's **name**;" Shakespeare may be toying with us here and setting up a later answer.

But does he give us any word clues that point to a specific woman? I wondered if Will had seen the painting "Unknown Woman in **Black"** at his patron's (Hunsdon's) house after 1592—which might be Aemilia Lanyer—painted in 1592, just before she is dismissed by Hunsdon as his pregnant mistress (Woods *Lanyer* 18). Line 4 of Sonnet 127 does bemoan, "... beauty slandered with a **bastard** shame [.]" Is this a reference to her being pregnant with Henry Carey's baby and "slandered" by him? Who is the real "bastard," the powerful father or the innocent baby? Line 6 contains an image of **"black"** beauty, "Fairing the foul with **art's** false borrowed face [.]" Is this "art" reference to the painting? Did the painter clean her up and "fair" her "foul" for an aristocrat's art gallery? Is this a more typical reference to a lady's make-up as "false" painting or a portrait that makes her look more aristocratic or both? Line 9 sets up a nice contrast to her eyes compared with the sun, "Raven **black"** is the color of "my mistress' eyes." Does her shameful situation explain why, in line 10, she has eyes so black "they mourners seem [?]" Will seems very sympathetic here and falling under the spell of those dark eyes. If she is his Raven, then he is her Crow.

Sonnet 136 gets hotter by ending on a couplet of name lines 13 and 14, but they are not about **her** name:

"Make but my **name** thy love, and love that still;
And then thou lov'st me, for my **name** is Will."

Well, that's clear! And this is one of that pair of Sonnets (135 & 136) where there are precisely numbered **"wills"** splattered all over the place, an orgy of **"wills"** (13 **"wills"** and a **"wilt"** in #135 and 7 **"wills"** in #136). By the way, I don't think her **"will"** refers to her husband's name. Line 2 clearly refers to Shakespeare and his willie: "Swear to thy blind soul that I was thy Will [.]" Her **"will"** is also where **"Will"** wants to put his **"will,"** and he wants to be her **"one" "sweet" "Will."** He uses key numbers like **14** and 14 divided by **2** or **7.** In these two sonnets, his code numbers (14 and 2) interlock with his most obvious code words for his name to give us a master key and clarify his method. The directions he gives may be: look for **14** sonnets where there are **doubled** words for **name** clues and good luck after that.

Much has been made of Will's anger toward and despair about the dark lady and the youth and their **double-crossing** love triangle, but there are quite a few funny, forehead-slapping poems for her, too. Some sonnets that others see as insulting, I see as very funny. But Duncan-Jones, in her attempt to prove Shakespeare "ungentle," shows how far some commentators are willing to go. She writes, "The so-called 'dark lady' sonnets constitute a poetic equivalent of the beating up of whores that was such a popular holiday pastime for young men of high status" (215). Wow! I was shocked by her conclusion. I feel this a wider gulf than that between most male and female readers of Shakespeare. I find this an extreme charge and very misleading. I often borrow from Duncan-Jones and her very good specific findings, but, even though I borrow from her, this quote from her new book proves to me that—whatever is true about the idealization of Will that is worth debunking—she is less gentle than Shakespeare. I don't trust her here at all.

This quote is trying to bolster her case that Shakespeare in the sonnets is only a misogynist, and it makes me distrust this seemingly trust-worthy scholar and source. I

knew she was very willing to go far out of her way to stack her revisionist deck for William Herbert as the youth. But here, she takes advantage of Will's real, hot hatred for the dark lady after his new love for her is so disappointed. This turn takes place so quickly from the two optimistic sonnets (127 and 128) to the darker sonnets about lust and "false compare" and her tyranny and "black deeds" (129 through 132). This sad run of four sonnets ends with the fifth, Sonnet #133, lines 3 and 4) "Is't not enough to torture me alone,/But slave to slavery my sweet'st friend must be?" where Will admits the lady has betrayed him with the youth.

Sure, he hates the dark lady for betraying him, but he had also felt intense excitement and hope that she would be a true and literate female lover, a rarity in his time for a man of his class: an educated, musical woman. After hate, he goes through a wide range of passions about her. He curses her. He praises her love making skills. He feels destructive lust for her. He tries to figure out one of his favorite themes: love versus lust, which he explores in great detail in "Venus and Adonis" and "The Rape of Lucrece" and many of his plays. He teases the dark lady and makes fun of himself. He humiliates himself with a smile and with tears. He uses broken logic to reason himself out of love for her. He cries out in despair. He cracks jokes about how other poets make silly descriptions of their lady loves. (He says he loves Henry, too, yet there are no truly funny poems for Henry. He can't afford to despise or make fun of Henry.) What is really interesting about the dark lady sonnets is the complex conflict between what he sees and what he feels about her and the enormously wide range of emotions he expresses. Any study of Shakespeare that hits just one of his notes is as shallow as propaganda and yesterday's lies.

What makes William Shakespeare stand out from all his rivals and all that speculation about "other authors" of his plays is that he is a wonderful comic. Ben Jonson was right when he wrote in 1623 about his "beloved" William:

Shakespeare is a Renaissance Sophocles and Aristophanes rolled into one! He would have had a ball with his contemporary Spanish counterpart, Cervantes, who died the same year in 1616. England and Spain, Protestant and Catholic could've made a lasting peace with those two laughing at the helm. So why don't we elect funny men? I jest. But I do regret that most current scholarship still says that *Cardenio: Or the Second Maiden's Tragedy* is a "lost" play that may have been by Shakespeare and might have

been based on Will's reading of *Don Quixote*. There is a text for *Cardenio*—it has merely been "lost" in a box labeled, "minor plays by John Fletcher." This gets us very close to Will. Fletcher was his replacement and late co-author of at least two plays for The King's Men.

Now we come to the end of the dark lady sequence and a possible pay off. The last of the 14 sonnets and 17 lines to contain the word "name" is 151, line 9: "But **rising** at thy **name** doth **point** out **thee** [.]" Now this is really tantalizing! Henry's name has been

thrown in the ring as the youth ever since folks noticed that both "Venus and Adonis" and "The Rape of Lucrece" were dedicated to him. But there never was any paper trail to a name for the dark lady until now. Is her name **embedded** in Sonnet 151? I think so. I am going to side with historians and biographers, not my sonnet isolating, horse-blinder wearing, text-happy, New Criticism, fellow English teachers, on this. With A. L. Rowse and Peter Levi and Michael Wood, I like Aemilia Bessano Lanyer (1569—1645) best for the dark lady.

Chapter 9   Aemilia Bassano Lanyer
as the Dark Lady

Here are some of the possible matches between Aemilia Lanyer's life and the dark lady of the *Sonnets:*

• She was probably a musician and could play the virginal as the dark lady did in Sonnet 128. In her book on Lanyer, Woods interprets lines from Lanyer's poem about the country-house Cooke-ham as showing that Aemelia "served as music tutor for Anne Clifford" (daughter of Margaret Clifford, countess of Cumberland).

• She probably had "wiry," black hair (Sonnet 130) from her possibly Jewish, definitely Italian father, Baptist Bessano, who came from Venice to London to be a court musician under Henry VIII.

• Her breath may have "reeked" (Sonnet 130) along with Will's after she cooked Italian garlic dishes for him. Remember Bottom's advice: "And, most dear actors, eat no onions or garlic...."

• She was a famous mistress to Henry Carey, Queen Elizabeth's cousin, who cast her off—the cad— and married her off on October 18, 1592 to another musician, Alfonso Lanyer (her second cousin), after Carey got her pregnant (Woods *The Poems...* xviii).

• Carey was also known as Lord Hunsdon, the Lord Chamberlain, the Queen's personal supervisor of both the theatrical and the musical scenes, and he became patron of Shakespeare's company starting in 1594 (Gibson *Sonnets* 147; Woods *Lanyer* 93).

• Her (possible) cousin, Robert Johnson (c. 1583 —1633), related to her mother Margaret Johnson, wrote music for Shakespeare's (and Ben Jonson's) songs and was "musician for Shakespeare's company" (McBride n. p.).

• Aemilia was considered a "brave," loose, and independent woman by a horny astrologer Simon Forman (Woods *The Poems...* xx). Forman winds up calling Aemilia a "whore" because she didn't sleep with him— Men! But Forman gave Rowse his first (perhaps mistaken) clues, and Woods uses Forman as a straw man in her battle against Rowse's claiming Aemilia was "promiscuous" (Woods *Lanyer* 25). Later, I want to say how I think both Rowse and Woods may be right about Aemilia Lanyer at two very different stages in her life.

• Aemilia may or may not have been writing poetry in 1592, which she later published in 1611 containing her feminist views. She failed to get the kind of female patronage from her book that she really needed. But back in 1592, she may have been looking for both a male writing mentor and a male poetic patron, which may make her the second, main rival poet to seek financial help from Henry and challenge Will as well as want to learn writing from him. Maybe it is the angry and ambitious, 23 year old Aemilia, dark haired and olive skinned, who Tom Stoppard should have written into *Shakespeare in Love*.

• When she and her husband Alfonso were having hard times in 1604, none other than Henry Wriothesley (our hero) suggested that Cecil and the new King James I give her husband a hay and straw weighing position in London.

• Oscar Wilde brings up two women's names that make glancing references to the dark lady. Cranley wrote a poem, published after Shakespeare's death, for a woman named "Amanda," who sounds like the dark lady (1188). And Wilde thinks Shakespeare's love for the dark lady had ended before 1594 because Henry Willobie writes asking love advice about a reluctant woman named "Avisa" from his "friend W. S.," who was "newly recovered from the same infection" (1190). So I wondered if the Amanda/Avisa/Aemelia three syllable, A-a names were any kind of historic echo among Shakespeare's contemporaries, who heard more current London gossip than we ever can.

• In 1592, Aemilia was 23, Will was 28, and Henry was 19.

• After the birth of her first baby, Henry (Hunsdon's child) in early 1593, Aemilia had trouble carrying babies to term. Woods quotes Forman, who writes, "She hath mani fals conceptions" (23). She had another miscarriage in 1597. Forman writes that before this

miscarriage, she had "moch pain in the bottom of the belly, womb, stomack and hed / & redy to vomit" (23). Finally, her baby daughter dies at nine months old in 1599. In a group of ten sonnets in which he discusses his own venereal disease, Shakespeare says he believes he caught some kind of venereal disease from the dark lady.

In a January 2007 interview with Chris Larkin, son of my doctor Jeff and a Ph.D. candidate planning to write his thesis on Alchemy, Chris mentioned **Chlamydia** as the most likely disease. A visit to the *Wikipedia* web page on "Chlmydia" reveals a possible symptom list for both Will and Aemelia: **him**—fever, burning urine, and eye infection; **her**—burning urine, womb pain, spontaneous abortion, and pneumonia for any new born.

In addition to all this, there is a very good Chapter 8 (entitled "Was Emilia Bassano the Dark Lady of Shakespeare's Sonnets?") by Roger Prior in a book called *The Bassanos: Venetian Musicians and Instrument Makers in England, 1531—1665*. Although Prior is a Literature researcher and writer, this book is essentially on musical history and musicology. So I have found it quite useful to go outside "the field" of Literature to gain new and "forbidden" insights. This pastoral vision of the "field" of Literature as the sole property of Ph.D.'s in English is a quaint notion that begs the question of who owns the pasture.

The truth is, Shakespeare owns this pasture. Some times it is imperative to leave the "Literary" pasture behind and join the wild men in the woods. I have found that historians, poets, musicologists, art historians, mathematicians, chemists, journalists, and many others are sometimes much more willing to be daring than some "great" professors of Literature. Perhaps some of their "greatness" stems from their unwillingness to stray from the "party line," the great consensus of slow-to-change opinions that has hardened into "Shakespeare Studies."

But within the protective cover of a musical family's history, Prior feels freer to explore if Aemelia were the dark lady. He thinks that Aemelia was forced to have sex with Hunsdon even after she was married off to Alphonse Lanier (118). Thus, Shakespeare could see her as a raped wife like Lucrece. Prior also questions whether the dark lady is playing a "virginal" in Sonnet 128. He believes the word "jacks" points to a different instrument that the Bessanos made as well as virginals: the clavichord (119). This instrument required its player to dampen the sound with the palm of her hand, thus coming in contact with the strings and the jacks. The Bessanos made and sold those jacks. Prior believes this explains why Will envies those wooden jacks and sees them more blessed than his "living lips" (Sonnet 128).

Prior finds a three-way tie for the phrase "base touches" in Sonnet 141. But these touches are "base" in four ways: 1. They are base because both Aemelia and her infant son Henry were illegitimate; 2. They are

base because they are (both wanted and unwanted) sexual touches; and 3. They are base notes on the strings of a lute or a keyboard (124), and I want to add 4. They are **base** because her name is **Bassano**.

Prior finds, as I do, name code in Sonnet 127 in the phrase **"each hand."** He spells it out: each = **H** (spoken with a dropped h) + hand = **Hund**, so these 2 words are a name code reference for the unwelcome, continued "base touches" of Lord Henry Hunsdon (130).

Prior is right to point out that Sonnet 127—on the surface, a clichéd protest against the false picture cosmetics can create—actually conceals a meaning below blonde versus black beauty. A very powerful nobleman is continuing to make Aemelia miserable. She is not just superficially protesting against social "racism" and bigotry against dark women. She is mourning her continued sexual slavery under the man who would not help her enough after he got her pregnant (131). Thus, the superficial social contrast between dark and light women and fashions covers over a much more dangerous personal situation that Aemelia is in and that she tells Shakespeare about. Once again, thanks to Prior this time, the code reveals new depth and power behind Shakespeare's surfaces.

But (I hear you say) this is all circumstantial evidence. So I tore Sonnet 151 apart looking for her name, and I found it! Get ready for one of Will's funniest, bawdy jokes. Remember the rhetorical figure *Deixis*, which means "pointing" in

Greek? In this Sonnet's **name** line, Will brags about getting an erection after naming her, and what does he **"point"** out her **"name"** with? His penis! Line 9 again says: "But **rising** at thy **name** doth **point** out thee [.]"

This Sonnet has 7 p-words, so if we didn't get it the first time, he ends the couplet with a repeat,

"I call/ Her 'love' for whose dear love I **rise** and **fall**."

I wondered what line 9 was pointing at. Well, if it is pointing up like Will's proud member, then it is **pointing** at the second quatrain right above it, which reads like this (with my emphasis and analysis added) in lines 5—12:

"For, thou betr-**A**-ying m**E**, I do betr-**A-Y**   **AE/AY**
M-y nobler part to **M**-y gross body's tr-**EA**-son;   **MM/EE (sound)**
My soul doth te-**LL** my bod-**Y** th-**A**-t h-**E** m-**A**-y   **LL/YA/EA**
Triumph in love; flesh stays no further reason,

But rising at thy **name** doth **point** out thee   **Name** pointing line
As his trium**phant prize**, **proud** of this **pride:**   **6 p-sounds**
He is content thy **poor** drudge to be,
To **stand** in thy **affairs**, **fall** by thy side."   **stand/fall**

So I didn't find doubled code words punning on her name; I found doubled letters instead:

AEAYMMEELLYAEA!

(a lover's elongated call) a **double** anagram with **two** spellings of her name embedded in three lines like the letters for **Onan** used earlier. It's interesting to note that Shakespeare may be contrasting a wonderful **double** orgasm with the lady here to the earlier empty results of masturbation. Here, Will is not alone or lonely; he is creating "the beast with two backs" with the dark lady. Many have commented on the sexual nature of this sonnet, but they should not stop there as if there were nothing deeper than sex and climax.

As always with Shakespeare, explaining the hidden "dirty joke" may not be going far enough.

The doubled word **"betrAy"** in line 5 starts off the code with the fact that the lady is also sleeping with Henry. A sexual triangle generates a moral triangle. Since she **betrays** Will, he must **betray** his own reason to make love to her. Of course, the doubled word **"betray"** may also point out other doubled betrayals: Will betrays Anne; the lady betrays her husband. The "body's treason" comes at a cost, but his soul gives his body permission. Does this trouble his "conscience?" The Latin proverb says, "An erect penis has no conscience." But yes, his betrayals do trouble his conscience. Nothing in

Shakespeare's thought is simple or one-sided for long.

But once given the reason that he "may triumph in love," Will's flesh does grow erect with pride and points her out. And Aemilia is on top in this love-making, double orgasmic sonnet, a position in which Will still **points** to her with **"pride"** here as he identifies her. First, he calls out her **name**; then, he reaches climax with six, pulsing **p-words or sounds: point, —phant, prize, proud, pride, and poor**. Finally, he is "contented" to go from triumphant **pride** to **poor** drudge and fall by her side. (Elsewhere, he laments when she is really on top and in control of their love affair.) But here, in the next to last personal sonnet, that double spelled out name may be the only laughing, sexy proof of the dark lady's identity we'll ever get from Will. But of course, her married name is close to **Lunar**. Should we call the 28 sonnet cycle of the dark lady—Will's own, very mysterious **Mona Lisa**—the **Lanyer** cycle?

Sonnet #152 is the final personal sonnet for Will's Queen of Summer, the "inconstant Moon." While Sonnet #151 is all about sex, pride in her, and the dark lady's name, the next sonnet is all about lies and vows broken and oaths taken and cursed. In this sonnet, Will places the blame on himself. True, he begins with blame for the lady and her willingness to break "thy bed-vow." But the sonnet's turn comes early in line 5 this time. In lines 5 and 6, he accuses her of breaking her vows to her husband and to Will. "But why of two oaths' breach do I

accuse thee, / When I break twenty?" He has sworn and forsworn ten times what she has, and all his "vows are oaths but to misuse thee" (line 7).

Those who would brand Shakespeare a "misogynist" should reread with a sharper eye and wonder instead at his intelligent complexity. In this sonnet, his final speech to the lady, his final judgment goes against himself. Honestly, he swore falsely to sleep with her. All his swearings by her "kindness," "love," "truth," and "constancy," had a dishonest, foul, sexual motive. In lines 13 and 14, he delivers his final judgment of himself:

"For I have sworn thee fair: more perjured eye,/
To swear against the truth so foul a **lie**."

His very last personal word to her is a pun that tells the truth about his loving lies. He swore twenty lies to lie with her. Turn the pages beyond the double envoi Sonnets 153 and 154, and, in "A Lover's Complaint," the maid says that she would fall for the youth's lies all over again. Here, Shakespeare seems to say he would lie again to the dark lady. He spends almost twenty years revising his sonnets to her. She may have been the love of his life, his only chance for a literate, female soul mate. No one should discount the importance of this half-Italian, possibly Jewish, half-English woman poet and lover to him. Almost half of his plays have Italian settings or connections. Some of his most wonderful female characters may be based on her, too. All of this is worth a much more rigorous, long study.

The lunar cycle ends with double envois in Sonnets 153 and 154. Not only does he end the dark lady sequence with love that burns him, Shakespeare also has a case of venereal disease or **Chlamydia** that he cannot cure in the hot waters of the Roman baths of Bath or the "mercury-infused sweating tub" (Duncan-Jones *Ungentle...* 219). In fact, images of disease show up in ten sonnets and give us some medical evidence to speculate about the identity of the dark lady. Here's a possibly chronological list of those ten, disease-related sonnets:

Table 3. Ten sonnets that may track venereal disease.

1. #137:   "this false plague"
2. # 140:   "As testy sick men" ... "No news but health from their physicians know."
3. #141:   "my plague" ... "she that makes me sin awards me pain."
4. #144:   "her foul pride" ... "Till my bad angel fire my good one out."
5. #145:   "But when she saw my woeful state"
6. #147:   "My love is as a fever" ... "nurseth the disease" ... "preserve the ill" ... "Past cure I am"
7. #60:   "the pebbled shore" ... "And nothing stands but for his scythe to mow."
8. #153:   "seething bath" ... "Against strange maladies a sovereign cure" ... "love's brand new fired" "I sick withal the help of bath desired" ... "a sad distempered guest" ... "But found no cure"
9. #61:   "My slumbers" ... "broken" ... "From me far off, with others all too near."
10. #154:   "fire" ... "bath" ... "remedy" ... "For men diseased" ... "Came there for the cure" ... "Love's fire heats water, water cools not love."

From this chronology, we can glean some possible conclusions about Shakespeare's love and his disease. He believes he caught both love sickness and venereal disease from the dark lady, who perhaps caught it from her husband. (Today, of course, people have to do such path of infection charts when faced with tracking the much more deadly, sexually transmitted disease, AIDS.)

In Sonnet #144, Will is in doubt whether the dark lady and the youth are still making love because he says that if the young man gets VD, it will constitute proof they are. This is true even though he was so sure they had double-crossed him back in the time-paired Sonnets #40 and #133. We could assume that he is not sleeping with the youth in Sonnet #144, if ever. Who knows? Perhaps we can think that Anne in Sonnet #145 saw signs of Will's disease, realized it meant he'd been unfaithful, but took pity on him.

He has a fever from the disease. Perhaps it went dormant

during his later life and flared up again when his fever came back during his fatal illness in 1616. Many feel that he went to the springs at Bath to try hot water as a cure. Today, you can ride a canal boat down the River Avon to Bath. But the waters did not cure either his VD or his lust. Many see this as the sad end of the sonnets in #154, but I think we need to go from there to Sonnet #62, which appears to be a lonely, honest, funny, masturbatory poem, and then read from #63—the mid-point of the solar sonnets—through to Sonnet #126, which finishes off the real time of these *Sonnets* with a twelve-line envoi ending in two silent lines both encased in the little crescents of parentheses, perhaps signs for (two times) a lunar month.

I do not know if this medical analysis and symptoms of Chlamydia will ever give us scientific proof that Aemilia Lanyer, with her difficulties in carrying babies to term, was the dark lady, but I wish we could find more information and a picture of her. I asked in the library at the Shakespeare Birthplace Trust in Stratford in the summer of 2001 with no luck. According to Forman, she had a mole "in the pit" of her throat in 1597 (Woods *The Poems...* xxi).

Susanne Woods has come up with an intriguing, plausible painting, "Unknown Woman in Black," who may be Aemilia Lanyer, but this woman has red hair (dyed like older Queen Elizabeth's?) as well as dark eyes. She wears a high collar, so we can't see if there is a mole. In 1592, she was painted by the same painter, Marcus Gheeraerts, who had painted Hunsdon in 1591. Perhaps he

wanted a memento of the mother of his bastard to remember her by. Woods reproduces both paintings from collections of the Lord Chamberlain's descendents (*Lanyer* 17, 18).

Like a zany Shakespeare detective (think of me here as Peter Seller's Inspector Clouseau), I want to make an identification mountain out of Aemelia's **mole**. In Hamlet's early, oversimplified theory about the tragic flaw, before he knows that Claudius is a murderer and thinks of him only as a heavy drinker, he uses the image of "some vicious **mole** of nature ... the stamp of one defect" (*Hamlet* I.4.23 ff). At the end of *12th Night*, when Viola and Sebastian are reunited, they can hardly believe it, so they trade family identification secrets such as the fact that their father had a **mole** "on his brow." There is a third important **mole** in *Cymbeline*. When Iachimo wants to falsely prove that he and Imogen have made love, he describes to her jealous husband Posthumus, "On her left breast/ A **mole** cinque-spotted, like the crimson drops/ I'the bottom of a cowslip" (*Cymbeline* II.2.37-39). This "stain" hooks Posthumus, who is as easily deceived as Othello.

I don't know why Shakespeare didn't use the **mole** as an identifying mark in the *Sonnets*. Perhaps it was too visible in the pit of Aemelia's throat, and Will is no Iachimo. The lady may be flawed, but a gentleman doesn't go out of his way to identify his lover to her husband or the curious mob. Use a secret code perhaps—see how long it has taken to find out—but a mole? Monsieur, do you take William Shakespeare for a *paparazzi?*

Susanne Woods really objects to A. L. Rowse's interest in Aemelia Lanyer as the dark lady, but it seems to me they may both be right. They may be talking about the same woman 19 years apart: a sexy, angry, cast-off, pregnant, 23 year-old mistress in the spring of 1592 and a radical Protestant, 42 year-old feminist poet hoping for female patronage in 1611. I know my friends and I changed a lot from ages 23 to 42. Certainly, our theories of both the dark lady and Aemilia should allow both women (or are they the same?) to mature and change.

Two years after Will's *Sonnets* were published, Aemilia Lanyer published her own book of religious and personal poetry (which includes 2 sonnets or fourteeners). So we have a clear self-portrait of her feminist, independent, and poetic intelligence, a lady lover who once may have been worthy of both Will and Henry (neither of whom is just any "downstream" man), and a woman who may have changed quite a bit between 1592 and 1611. (Think of John Donne's changes from young rake to older sermonizer and writer of Holy Sonnets that pun on his name Donne and on his wife's name Ann More, as well.)

By 1611, Lanyer had grown into the first English woman to publish her own book of poetry, some good proof that she was a great, love-worthy woman. Unlike William Shakespeare, she is a sincere believer at age 42, and she gives voice to her beliefs without much

irony (except that directed at sexist men) and without using much of the more famous "double voice" techniques of Shakespeare.

I have not found any reference to a relationship with William Shakespeare in her work. Woods believes her poems show that she was influenced by her reading of Will's "Venus and Adonis" and "The Rape of Lucrece"—both dedicated in public writing to Henry—and may have met Shakespeare (98). These two long, published poems are quite powerful and were popular and may have interested Lanyer in meeting both Will and Henry. I can't help thinking about the importance of this possible meeting for both Will and Aemelia. Neither of them seems like the kind of person not to recognize the high value of the other. Whatever happened, I think this possible love affair is worth a speculative book and movie of its own. Too little is known about the women who influenced Shakespeare to let go of this possibility easily.

In one of Lanyer's sonnets, addressed to King James I's and Queen Anne's 15-year-old daughter, Princess Elizabeth, Aemilia writes,

"Though your faire eyes farre better
        Bookes have seen;
Yet being the first fruits of a woman's
        wit,
Vouchesafe you favour in accepting
        it."

(Woods *The Poems...* 11)

There are many "better Bookes" she could mean, including *Shakespeare's Sonnets.*

Unfortunately, none of the ladies or royals she appealed to for funding—including Prince Henry (Stuart) on whom so many disappointed hopes were pinned—helped her enough for her to publish more poems. The first English woman poet to publish her own book may have stopped writing in 1612, the year of Prince Henry's death and about the same time as Shakespeare retired.

Perhaps both writers were disappointed when in 1611 King James appointed a right wing Archbishop of Canterbury, George Abbott, who began a crackdown on Catholics, Puritans, and all those in favor of religious tolerance using the 1611 King James Bible. Of course, the earlier Gunpowder Plot and the assassination by a "deranged friar" of the tolerant King Henry IV of France in 1610 may have caused the English King's crackdown. Was this the end of royal tolerance for Shakespeare's complex views? Some scholars, including Clare Asquith, believe that Shakespeare was asked to write simplistic, pro-Stuart, religious propaganda, and, when he refused, he was forced to retire (263 & 271). It was in this period of religious repression that *The King James Bible* was published and that both Ben Jonson and Henry Wriothesley converted from Catholicism to the Church of England.

What of Shakespeare's feelings for the dark lady after the *Sonnets*? We know of his passionate interest in Italy and in Rome. Could Cleopatra be a farewell portrait of Aemelia Lanyer with Will imagining himself as a fading Mark Anthony? Back in Sonnet #40, in lines 1—4

addressed to the youth, Shakespeare had punned (twice) on Aemelia's "darkness:"

"Take all my loves, my love; yea, take
	them all;
What hast thou then **more** than
	thou hadst before?
No love, my love, that thou mayst
	true love call;
All mine was thine, before thou hadst
	this **more**:"

"This **more**" is a pun on **Moor**. But, before those wanting the lady to be an African-English woman (like madam Lucy Morgan) get too excited, I want to warn you that there's **more** going on here as well. I have a Cockney friend who grew up in Britain, who married an Italian woman from Brooklyn. When his mother first met his bride, all were shocked when the mother called her a "darkie!" Both husband and wife were shocked at his Mum's racist word, but could this be a Cockney leftover from Elizabethan days when it was really common to call almost any Mediterranean woman "dark?"

There is a second, more personal pun in this word "**more**." One of Leonardo da Vinci's patrons was Luduvico il Moro. In one painting of the walls in a room in Milan, there are the large trunks of decorative trees whose "branches rise to intertwine on the ceiling in a sort of fictive pergola" (Marani 245).

This decoration has been interpreted as a representation of the classical literary *topos* of the Vale of Tempe—the wilderness where Apollo dwelt. The trees may be mulberries, a pun in Italian on Ludovico's nickname,

Moro, since the Italian word for **mulberry** is *gelsomoro*.

(251)

Oddly enough, on the coat of arms of Aemelia's Bessano family from Venice, there is a **mulberry tree**, *morus* in Latin. It is emblematic of their family tree. Does the presence of that tree as their family icon mean that the Bessano family was engaged, along with Ludovico, in planting mulberry trees around Milan or Venice in order to start a domestic silk-producing industry in Northern Italy to compete with more expensive silk from China? Do the Jewish loan-maker Shylock and his daughter Jessica, the name of one protagonist Bassanio, the name of the merchant Antonio (Aemelia's Italian uncle in England, whose grandson Alfonso Lanyer she married), and the character of the cross-dressing Portia as a lawyer in a Venetian court in *The Merchant of Venice,* owe anything to Aemelia's Italian roots, family, and stories she told Will?

What does the legendary mulberry tree Shakespeare planted in his garden behind the New Place say about the dark lady, his old flame? What year did he plant that tree? After his death, people came from all over to get a cutting from that tree. How many descendants of that tree now grow in England? The new, cranky owner of New Place was so "bothered" by "relic" seekers, he cut down the tree and tore New Place down. Ah, the innocent, peaceful days before tourism became a part of the economy! Did that tree in his family yard make Will Shakespeare smile at his private joke? In the dark lady Sonnet #135, the one that uses 13 wills and one wilt for a total of 14, he again puns on "**more**" two times in lines 3 and 12:

"**More** than enough am I, that vex thee still,"

*   *   *

"One will of mine, to make thy large Will **more:**"

What **more** could we ask for? The pun is threefold or more. This is a common Renaissance name pun. And it's Shakespeare's funny naming code! Once you accept the code, you see it pop up everywhere. For those who don't see it, I repeat the punch line to a joke about a complaining believer stuck on a roof in a flood. He had prayed to God for deliverance, but he drowned when God did not lift him up. God responds: "What do you mean I didn't try to save you? I sent a floating tree, a rowboat, and a helicopter!"

In the winter of 2006, I wondered where to go to get more of the latest information on any proven ties between William Shakespeare and Aemelia Lanyer's large family. I know this is an exciting new area for research. I hope my discovery and/or merely my claim of cracking a name code here will help stimulate more work. After reading of a relevant 1995 book in an academic chat room, in June 2006 I sent for and read Lasoki and Prior's book, *The Bessanos*, which answered much of my need for more about the Bessano family.

These two writers—Lasoki a musicologist and Prior a literary author—gave me a new boost and took me from the Bessano family straight to Aemelia and from the *Sonnets* to the plays and back again. I have added their specific insights where they seemed to be needed in my text. To any one wanting more reasoning about Aemelia as Shakespeare's dark lady, I refer you to Prior's Chapter 8. In it, he looks at name puns as evidence in both the *Sonnets* and the plays. I will return to this subject in Chapter 24, pages 147—163.

Note: The spelling of the Bessano name is as varied as most names were then: Elizabeth Woods uses "Bassano" while Aemelia's father Baptist spelled it "Bassany" in his will. In some of the plays, Shakespeare spells it "Bessanius," and "Bessanio."

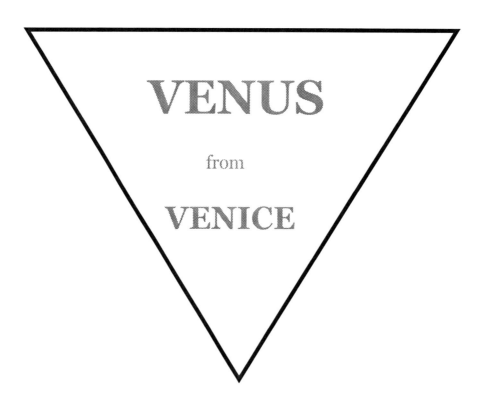

Chapter 10 Seventeen Code Lines Containing "Name" in Fourteen Sonnets

When my wife Sandy Jensen heard me say that there are **17** lines with **"name"** in them in **14** of Shakespeare's sonnets, she asked, "Do they make a sonnet embedded in the sonnets?" Could this be the 155th Sonnet? Could it act as the **crown** sonnet in a crown of sonnets, a kind of condensed code sonnet using all the **"name"** lines? I arranged and rearranged those 17 lines. (I also wondered if two odd sonnets contain a part of his number code. Sonnet #99 does have an extra 15th, introductory line just as Sonnet # 126 is "missing" its couplet and is only 12 lines long. Could the numbers 15 and 12 help our understanding? I cannot take them further.) Unfortunately, the seventeen lines didn't make much sense in the order in which they were printed from Sonnet 36 to 151, and the end rhymes don't promise much at all.

But I put them in the lines in which they appeared, each in their own sonnets. Let's do the math. Here is what I found: **no lines** 1, 4, or 9 (1 + 4 +9 = 14) have the word "name." However, lines 2, 5, 7, and 12 (2 + 5 + 7 + 12 = 26, & 26 — 12 = 14) do have "name" in **two** lines each. And line 8 has "name" **three** times (17 — 3 = 14). I think all these interlocking numbers and **results of 14** may be part of the code; and the numbers of the code become a new formal challenge that generates new parts of the puzzle. Placed exactly in those seventeen lines, there are 6.5 Wills, 7.5 Henrys, and 3 Aemilias for a total

of 17. Seventeen is not as important a number as fourteen, but it does remind us how this sequence was started: with an order for seventeen birthday sonnets to celebrate Henry's seventeenth birthday, one for each year. I was very interested to lay out this Table 4. It made me wonder if Shakespeare kept a table like this in his notes.

In typical groundling fashion, I must grumble about not being able to muck about in Will's foul papers. I often wind up feeling like a twenty-first century Caliban struck dumb by the magician's powers. My desire to know more about his books and my admiration for this Prospero called Will are my only excuses for all my speculations. I grew tired of the old, much repeated saws about the *Sonnets*. I felt that they represented a false consensus and an artificial stopping place. Even these wise Stratfordian lines sounded to me like the odd claims of "final knowledge" in science and the "end of Physics," and I doubted that we really know Shakespeare in all his Renaissance complexity.

I longed to make a breakthrough into new territory. Perhaps that comes from living more than half my life in the American West close to the wonderful Oregon Shakespeare Festival theaters in Ashland. So I tried to imagine I could see into Shakespeare's workshop to his work table and his notes as he worked on the *Sonnets*. In this next table—**17 lines that contain "name"**—we have data that must make or break my thesis about Shakespeare code:

Table 4. 17 Lines that Contain "Name"

#/# line Line	Sonnet#—Name
First, there are 8 lines for an octet:	
1.2 Knowing a better spirit doth use **your name**,	80—Henry
2.2 Or if it were, it bore **not** beauty's **name**;	127—Aemilia
3.3 Doth spot the beauty of **thy** budding **name**:	95—Henry
4.5 **Your name** from **hence** immortal life shall have,	81—Henry
5.5 **Thence** comes it that **my name** receives a brand,	111—Will
6.6 And **our** dear love lose **name** of single one,	39—Will & Henry
7.7 That every word **almost** doth tell **my name**,	76—Will
8.7 Sweet beauty hath **no name**, no holy bower,	127—Aemilia
Then, there are three 8th lines before the turn in the middle:	
9.8 **Naming thy name**, blesses an ill report.	95—Henry
10.8 Even as when first I hallowed **thy** fair **name**:	108—Henry
11.8 But rising at **thy name** doth **point** out thee	151—Aemilia
Finally, there are 6 lines for a sestet:	
12.10 **Thy** sweet beloved **name no more** shall dwell,	89—Henry
13.11 **My name** be buried where my body is,	72—Will
14.12 Unless thou take that **honour** from **thy name**	36—Henry
15.12 Do not so much as **my** poor **name** rehearse,	71—Will
16.13 Make but **my name** thy love, and love that still;	136—Will
17.14 And then thou lov'st me, for **my name** is Will.	136—Will

---

Well, the only lines that read well are the last two. That's too bad, but this was worth trying, and I'll leave this in as a kind of **index** to the **17 name** code lines. Here's where *Shakespeare's Sonnets* become even more like a deep computer game, and I never know how ingenious Will is trying to be. There are all kinds of formal poems, like the sonnet or the sestina or the villanelle, that contain and obey important number rules that dictate what parts of poems must do. But what about the numbers used in this sonnet sequence? There don't seem to be universal number rules for whole sonnet sequences, so Shakespeare was free to create a numbered structure. For example, two times seventeen equals thirty-four, and Sonnet 34 is an important sonnet—coming at the end of the second set of 17. Sonnet 34 is about despair when the youth (celebrated in the first 17 sonnets) has betrayed Will. Listen to the famous opening question of Sonnet 18, line 1, **seventeen** sonnets earlier: "Shall I compare thee to a summer's day?' and contrast it to the response and question in Sonnet 34, also line 1:

"Why didst thou promise such a beauteous day" [?]

The covenant between youth and poet is broken early by the youth.

And if we are looking at the numbers of the two ending sonnets of the whole sequence, the double envoi Sonnets 153 and 154, why is it that **17 X 9 = 153**, and **14 X 11 = 154?** Do these two results have a lot to do with each other and Shakespeare's clever design and his use of personal code numbers?

Is **11** a code number for his son Hamnet? Is **14** a code number for Will? Is **17** a code number for Henry? Is **28** a code number for the dark lady? Do these numbers prove that all 154 sonnets are by Will and are all rightly placed in his precise sequence? Yes, I think so.

Then there are other key numbers, like the socially important, climacteric numbers **7** and **9**.

Unlike some of the personally meaningful numbers, some of these numbers are important to the numerological society Shakespeare lived in. Numerology—isn't that a strange part of astrology? Yes, but when specific numbers have social significance, they take on a "magic," secret feeling. A few years ago, at a large convention, 20th century physicists voted that there are eleven dimensions in the universe as we know it, not ten or twelve. Perhaps you think I have gotten too tangled up in too much "secret code!" Or perhaps you see more clues than I do? Feel free to do more math. I think Shakespeare did.

Chapter 11   Backyard and Horse Riding Code: Scenes from Life

One of the funniest sonnets in the dark lady sequence sounds as if it were written or dreamed up in a backyard in Stratford amidst farm birds and babies. Sonnet 143 starts out with a mock epic, "Lo," also a pun on "low," and portrays the lady as a housewife (**"huswife,"** an H-W word), who sets down her crying baby (named Will), so she can run after a runaway chicken. Nowhere is this barnyard fowl named in the sonnet, so there's this key word (hen) that is left out of the sonnet on purpose. Perhaps, here we see Aemilia, as a housewife, running after a **Hen** named Henry. And Will humorously portrays himself in lines 13 and 14 as a big baby in need of "mothering" and kisses: "So **will** I pray that thou mayst have thy **Will**,/ If thou turn back and my loud crying still." Of course, this is a grown man's game. He really wants her to come back, so he can have his **will** with her. "Stop chasing that **Hen [.],** and come back to **Will**, Baby!" He portrays himself as a silly man willing to say almost anything to get a kiss from her.

When this sonnet 143 is left out of the anthologies, teachers can't teach it. Then students get a very wrong picture of Shakespeare's range. They tend to believe that he is "above" them. This is akin to leaving all the comic scenes out of the tragedies or claiming that the tragedies are more "Shakespearean" than the comedies. What if we cut the gravedigger scene from *Hamlet?* Of course, then we leave out

Shakespeare's unique sense of humor, the humane side of his intellect, and we deprive ourselves of his gift of laughter about all kinds of subjects. Why would we want to do that to our students and ourselves? Will has called the dark lady's deeds foul; here he is showing her chasing a fowl. What a fowl deed! The old pun with fowl and "fool" from Chaucer is a good joke. Here Will shows himself and the lady in a humble farmyard, and Will is trying to compete with a runaway chicken! Showing himself as a big crybaby also allows him to make fun of the lady and the youth. She becomes a cook like Anne running after a chicken, and the young lord is reduced to a flapping chicken trying to stay out of the pot. This is comic relief on the scale of the Marx Brothers. Run, Henry, run!

I believe that understanding the name code makes the autobiographical case for the *Sonnets* much stronger, reveals Shakespeare's true character as a funny, ingenious poet, and also makes one's reading a heck of a lot more fun! We might imagine Will the comic in Stratford watching Anne or his daughter Susannah chasing after a hen and laughing at the mess he's in. We might even see the baby as little Elizabeth Hall, his granddaughter, born in 1607. This Sonnet 143 shares the middleclass and the Stratford flavor of his Falstaff comedy, *The Merry Wives of Windsor.* After reading works by Don Foster and being inspired by his methods, if not all his conclusions, I saw that no clue is too small, and sleuthing through famous texts is still and always worth doing. In fact, it's one of the main reasons for being a literature instructor or student.

The two horse riding sonnets, 50 and 51, seem to be about going away from Henry on horseback to Stratford. Sonnet #143 (above)—set in a yard—is the next companion piece to Sonnet #50, and coming back toward Henry and London on that same slow horse is portrayed in Sonnet # 51. Will rides back to Sonnet #144 and his "two loves of comfort and despair [.]" I wondered if Will were playing with the second half of his name with the word **"spur,"** which appears in both Sonnets 50 and 51. I remembered that famous Sonnet 18 uses the word **"shake,"** and then, by using an on-line, word search concordance for the *Sonnets*, I found out that another use of **"shake"** is in another famous sonnet, Sonnet #73. There is yet another use of "shake" in Sonnet #28 & "shaken" in #116. So, overall in the sonnets, those words appear in the following order: **shake (18)/shake (28)/spur (50)/spur (51)/shake (73)/shaken (116)**, which is an expanded, chiasmus-like
[A] ABBA [A]
pattern that both Sidney and Shakespeare use quite often. So Shakespeare did not leave his last name out of the *Sonnets* and pun only on his first name Will as some experts say.

Unlike the winged Pegasus of the classical poets or the white horse of Petrarch, Will is stuck on a slow horse both going to Stratford and returning to London. Lords may have fast chargers or war horses, but Will has only a slow nag, who does not speed up when he is spurred. The pitiful horse only groans, and his groans reminds Will that he is leaving his "joy" behind in London. But, of course, the dark lady sonnets show what he is leaving behind is more complicated. In Sonnet 133.1 he had cursed, "Beshrew that heart that makes my heart to groan" as he admitted that the lady had also enslaved the youth. And before that, in Sonnet 131.10, he had cried out, "A thousand groans but thinking on thy face:" and that is an echo of the line Marlowe wrote in *Faustus* about Helen: "Was this the face that launched a thousand ships?" So Shakespeare and his old horse are both groaning. Perhaps Shakespeare is laughing at himself as if he sees himself being ridden by this lady. That's not as funny as the chicken and the baby, but it implies that she may spur him on, but he can only groan.

These "shake" "spur" puns on his last name go along with the amusing old tale that Shakespeare was the translator of the 46th Psalm in the *King James Bible*. Perhaps, as these tale tellers say, Will chose #46 because it was twice his birthday, the 23rd. Those who believe this ask us to find in the translation his name split into two. The 46th word from the beginning is **"shake."** The 46th word from the end is **"spear."**

Whatever the truth of this story, it is true that this kind of name game is not trivial or dumb to famous English writers. From Sidney to Donne, authors see this punning on names as a cute bit of wit, another sign of intelligence, and a dare or challenge to the readers to find them out. So why should we ever accept Dr. Johnson's or any one else's bias against the pun when William Shakespeare appears to love this game? In fact, he rolls in it like a happy dog having fun! It seems to

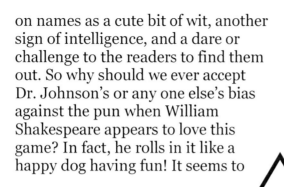

me to be anti-Shakespearian not to tease our noodles with puns. After all, even Leonardo da Vinci called himself "Lion ardor" and joked about Petrarch loving "laurel" so much because it tasted so good with lamb.

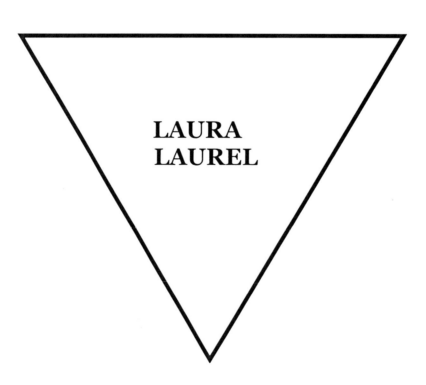

**LEONARDO
LEON ARDO
LION ARDOR**

**LAURA
LAUREL**

Chapter 12   The Rival Poet's Name: Kit & the Need to Investigate How Time Is Bent by the Fate of Marlowe

What about that fourth mysterious name, the name of the rival poet? Is his name also embedded in the sonnets? Using the **double code**, I believe we can find him. First, let's look at indirect evidence. There were other "rivals" dedicating works to Henry Wriosthsley back then: Barnaby Barnes dedicated his sonnet sequence *Parthenophil and Parthenope* to Henry in 1593, the same year as "Venus and Adonis," and Nashe dedicated his *The Unfortunate Traveller* to Henry in 1594, the same year as "The Rape of Lucrece" (Schmidgall 56). This may account for Shakespeare's feelings that he made Henry's name too public by advertising his patron in his two dedications. So, there were rivals, maybe as many as nine.

But in the early 1590s, there was only one true rival in the theater who could give Will a scare by approaching Henry as a lover or a patron or both, and it was that shoe cobbler's son from Canterbury, educated at Cambridge, Christopher Marlowe, the spy who was murdered after an all day meeting at a "safe house" in Deptford on May 30, 1593 (Nicholl 329). Remember, we are looking for one true, threatening rival in the early 1590s to William Shakespeare **in Will's mind**, not ours, not just someone like Chapman, who later put a weakened finish on Marlowe's strong, unfinished narrative poem, "Hero

and Leander." Both Marlowe's and Chapman's versions of that poem were not published until 1598 (Duncan-Jones 282). But if Marlowe first read "Hero and Leander" with Henry and Will present or gave a copy to Henry, who showed it to Will, that could feel like a threat to Shakespeare in 1592 or 1593.

Many of *Shakespeare's Sonnets* are crawling with both obvious and hidden references to Marlowe and with echoes of his lines. There is even a translation of Marlowe's Latin **motto** (from Ovid) that was included on the painting of him dated 1585 (when both Marlowe and Shakespeare were 21) that now hangs in his eating hall at college:

"QVOD ME NVTRIT ME DESTRVIT."

In one of Shakespeare's most famous Sonnets, number 73, the 12th line translates that motto and reads:

"Consumed with that which it was nourished by."

Before the Rival Poet sequence, there is an odd temporal anomaly, as if a premonition of Marlowe's murder came to Will before Marlowe became a rival. But this must be the result of twenty years of revision. We can speculate that quatrain three of Sonnet #74 was written even after Sonnet #86, when Marlowe is referred to in the past tense. Sonnet 74 begins with Will's fear of being arrested (by death). Many agree that line 12 might be a reminder of Marlowe's murder: "The **coward conquest** of a wretch's knife," but what did Shakespeare know of this murder? We know he read the Queen's coroner's **inquest** because his clown Touchstone quotes its key word **"reckoning"** with a Marlovian twist in *As You Like It*:

"When a man's verses cannot be understood, nor a man's good wit be seconded with the forward child, understanding, it strikes a man more dead than a great **reckoning** in a **little room**." (*AYLI* 3.4.6-10)

If this **"coward conquest"** is a reference to that murder, then hasn't Shakespeare figured out something like what Charles Nicholl figured out in his book, *The Reckoning*, that Marlowe was held fast by two spies and stabbed accurately above the right eye by a third "**coward**?" The "**little room**" is both a reference to the private room where the murder took place in Deptford and a sly, off quote from Marlowe's *The Jew of Malta,* about "great riches in a little room."

Was Shakespeare at first afraid he'd be killed as Marlowe was? What was their relationship besides rivals in the theater and rivals for Henry's love? Who from that time could shed light into the dark corners of these questions? For me, that someone could be Edward Alleyn. One of surviving, original copies of the 1609 Sonnet edition belonged to Alleyn, Marlowe's great leading actor: "he bought a printed copy for sixpence in June of 1609" (Levi 109).

(I assume someone has read any notes Alleyn may have made in the margins of his copy of the *Sonnets*. Or did he write in his copy? Has anyone published a facsimile containing his notes? Inspired by William Blake, I want to be the proverbial fly on Edward Alleyn's shoulder as he first sat down to read *Shakespeare's Sonnets.*)

Like this intrusion of a future event about Marlowe back in Sonnet 74, Shakespeare had used this same position in quatrain 3 of Sonnet 33 to introduce his grief about the death of his son Hamnet (which took place 4 years later in 1596) into Sonnet 33, perhaps written in 1592, which is about Henry's betrayal of Will's love with the dark lady. Hamnet died at age 11, and he is represented (replaced) by that number in the sequence. Here, in quatrain 3 of Sonnet 33, Hamnet is remembered, and 3 X 11 = 33.

Both Hamnet's death and Marlowe's were shocking to Shakespeare. I believe both deaths gave some of the raw emotional power to the play *Hamlet,* along with the death of John Shakespeare, the failed Essex rebellion, and the jailing of Henry for three years in the Tower. In Sonnets #33 and #74, Shakespeare writes as if chronology did not matter. He thinks a little like T. S. Eliot finding time future embedded in time past. Future tragedies can bleed down into sonnets written before they happened.

Today, we enjoy such events when they happen in science fiction novels. But what shall we make of Shakespeare's implied, odd theory of time? Are these made to look like premonitions? Or is Shakespeare playing with loops in time? Why does he allow his later self to insert later events in earlier sonnets? This leads us to the biggest question of all: what else can be said about how time is structured in the sequence? The whole sequence ends with Sonnet 154, but that is not the end of its time. In these sonnets, time moves in complex loops and lines. I think it would make great chronological sense to read Sonnets 1—33 first, then read Sonnets 34—61 and 127—154 alternately as matched pairs, and finally read Sonnets 62—126. I think that after Sonnet 154, Sonnet 62 is the next sonnet in linear time that then runs straight again and finishes at Sonnet 126 with its missing couplet trailing off like Hamlet's death speech, "The rest is silence."

Shakespeare's sense of time in the *Sonnets* was first warped by the double cross of the youth and the dark lady in 1592. That event cements Sonnets 40 and 133 together in one 24-hour block: day and night. Since I believe that Marlowe's murder in 1593 was the second event to warp Shakespeare's sense of time, let's get a first look at the overall structure of Time in the *Sonnets* and get a clear idea of how the youth/dark lady twin sonnets relate to the nine rival poet sonnets.

(See Figure 1, next page. This is my diagram of the linear time sequence based on our calendar—the Gregorian—not the Old Calendar—the Julian—of Shakespeare's time. There will be more discussion about conversion to Shakespeare's Old Calendar later. After this diagram, I will continue with details about how Marlowe's name is encoded in the *Sonnets*.)

Figure 1. The Shape of Time

The Youth: the Sun

MAY

OUR CALENDAR
May 1: Sonnet 1
May 5: Sonnet 5
May 9: Sonnet 9
May 12: Sonnet 12
May 15: Sonnet 15
May 17: Sonnet 17
May 18: Sonnet 18
May 20: Sonnet 20
May 25: Sonnet 25
May 29: Sonnet 29
June 1: Sonnet 32
June 2: Sonnet 33
June 3: Sonnet 34
June 4: Sonnet 35
June 6: Sonnet 37
>June 9: Sonnet 40-
June 10: Sonnet 41
June 11: Sonnet 42
June 12: Sonnet 43
June 17: Sonnet 48
>June 21: Sonnet 52-
June 27: Sonnet 58
June 30: Sonnet 61
July 1: Sonnet 62
July 2: Sonnet 63
July 6: Sonnet 67
July 10: Sonnet 71
July 13: Sonnet 74
July 17: Sonnet 78
July 23: Sonnet 84
July 25: Sonnet 86
July 28: Sonnet 89
July 31: Sonnet 92
Aug 1: Sonnet 93
Aug 7: Sonnet 99
Aug 10: Sonnet 102
Aug 15: Sonnet 107
Aug 20: Sonnet 112
Aug 24: Sonnet 116
Aug 27: Sonnet 119
Aug 31: Sonnet 123
Sept 1: Sonnet 124
Sept 3: Sonnet 126

Side
By
Side
In
JUNE ☽
Moon
(28
Days) ☾

JULY

AUGUST

SEPTEMBER

Dark **Lady: the Moon**
127—154 (28)

June 3: Sonnet 127
June 4: Sonnet 128
June 6: Sonnet 130
June 9: Sonnet 133—40/133←
June 10: Sonnet 134
June 11: Sonnet 135
June 12: Sonnet 136
June 17: Sonnet 141
June 21: Sonnet 145—52/145←
June 27: Sonnet 151
June 30: Sonnet 154

Rival Poet(s)
78—86 (9)

Note: triangle with lady in **June**
triangle with rival in **July**

Solar time flows 1—126 with side
bar for **June nights** with lady.

72

We got lost and then found our way in time for a good cause by wondering why a reference to Marlowe's murder might show up early in Sonnet #74. Now let's come back to the second triangle inserted in the sequence. Sonnets 78—86 are rightly called the "Rival Poet" Sonnets, and in them Shakespeare worries about his own lack of invention and the "proud" power of his main rival's lines. He begins Sonnet 86 with lines that describe his rival as a pirate ship and his patron Henry as a treasure ship:

"**Was it** the **proud full sail** of his
     great verse,
Bound for the **prize** of all-too-
     precious you,"

and, in the first line, I can hear again Marlowe's most famous line from *Doctor Faustus*, the one that Tom Stoppard, in his script for *Shakespeare in Love*, used as the line about Helen of Troy that amazed other actors, who used it in auditions, and annoyed Shakespeare:

"**Was this** the **face** that launched a
     thousand ships?"

Listen for the echo and note the use of the past tense, which suggests that Sonnet 86 was written after Marlowe's 1593 murder, to end the Rival Poet section:

"**Was it** the **proud full sail** of his
     great verse [?]"

I was happy to read that Oscar Wilde, who had a much better ear than mine, also heard this as an echo of Marlowe (1169) as did Rowse, who points out yet another

Shakespeare/Marlowe echo between Marlowe's *Tamberlaine:*

"And all his **captains** bound in
     captive chains."

and Sonnet 66:

"And **captive** good attending
     captain ill:"

and Rowse asserts that no one of Shakespeare's contemporaries influenced "Shakespeare's mind" more than Marlowe (76). These constant echoes—like Ariel's spirits on the magic island—may be the sounds that are driving the Marlovians of the Marlowe Society Homepage so crazy. Shakespeare often feels deep sympathies with this great "spirit," immortalizes him in the sonnets, and continues to be inspired by him for the rest of his writing life.

Sonnet 86 ends the nine sonnets (is this because there were traditionally nine Muses, and were there, in addition, nine rivals?) of the Rival Poet section, which seems to progress from saying that there are **some** rivals to there is only **one** who matters and finally to say that **one** is no longer a threat. Sonnet 86 ends with the lines, which speak in the past tense about Henry's **face** showing up in Marlowe's "Hero and Leander." Marlowe has Neptune see Leander as a possible male lover, like Jupiter's Ganymede. And Shakespeare admits:

"But when your **countenance**
     filled up his line,
Then **lacked** I matter, that
     enfeebled mine."

Shakespeare is freaking out at seeing Henry's feminine **face** (the face of a **count** but like a boy actor's face playing Helen) in Marlowe's homoerotic lines about Leander being made love to by Neptune as the poor boy tries to swim to the woman of his dreams, Hero. Perhaps, at least this once, Kit Marlowe was trying to catch up to Will Shakespeare's very successful "Venus and Adonis" (dedicated to Henry) by writing a more powerfully explicit, erotic poem. "Hero and Leander" was written in 1593, just before three spies (Robert Poley, Ingram Frizer, and Nicholas Skeres) murdered Marlowe and ended his rivalry with Will. I wonder what exact codes Marlowe used while working as a vulnerable Renaissance James Bond. And did Kit, Will, and Henry ever talk about these codes or poetry or play writing at Henry's Titchfield estate in Hampshire or any where else? Once again, my wish to turn into a fly on a tapestry has got me wondering. I hope no one swats me when I am acting like a fly.

But this is all indirect evidence, good material for historic fiction or the movies. Is there any direct **code on Marlowe**? Yes, there is. I believe his street name "Kit" (equivalent to "Will") is embedded (twice) in Sonnet 84 and alternates with a possible negative code word for Henry's last name, **"worse."** Sonnet 84, Line 1 begins with a question in the present tense:
   "Who is it that says most?" The answer is found twice in the sestet in lines 9—14:

"Let him but [**K** sound] **copy** what in you is wr-**IT**,	**K—IT**
Not making **worse** what nature made so clear,	**WORSE**
And such a [**K** sound] **counterpart** shall frame his w-**IT**,	**K—IT**
Making his style **admired** everywhere.	**admired**
You to your beauteous blessings add a curse,	
Being fond on **praise**, which makes your **praises worse**."	**WORSE**

KIT COPIES & IS MY COUNTERPART & IS ADMIRED, & YOU SING HIS PRAISES, TOO: WORSE & WORSE.

Here the code reveals Will's greatest fear: **"Kit"** and Henry intermingled in a **"praise"** giving and **"praises"** accepting love affair: **"worse"** and **"worse!"** Will and Kit and Henry form the second poetical/sexual triangle of the *Sonnets*. And Sonnet 84 is in the present tense; Marlowe was still alive, and he and his **Admiral's** Men at the Rose Theater were more **"admired"** than Shakespeare.

74

We hear another echo of Marlowe when Will describes his fever for and from the dark lady in Sonnet 147, line 1: "My love is as a fever, longing still," and the fever is from both lust and some kind of venereal disease. Shakespeare writes a second, negative version of Marlowe's Latin motto in line 3:

"**Feeding** on that which doth **preserve the ill** [.]"

This line and Marlowe's motto may be a remake of lines from Ovid's *Metamorphosis*, 15.234-6, which Katherine Duncan-Jones translates,

Eaten up by that which **ate** it up" (256).

So Shakespeare's main rival Marlowe is destroyed by that which nourished him, in line with his chosen motto from Ovid. It is Time that brings us into being, nourishes us, and seems to loop back at us with opened jaws and take us away. Time is the great devourer of all things, like a serpent that devours its own tail and will even destroy itself. That is not only Christian and classical pagan belief about Time; it may also be the view of 21st century physics.

Chapter 13   Two Interlocking Triangles

If both sexual/poetic triangles of Will/Aemilia/Henry and of Will/Henry/Kit were happening in the same year—say **1592**—or 1592 and 1593—the **autobiographical** reasons for all Will's stormy and dramatic emotions don't seem very "fictional" after all. I know some very good Shakespeare scholars (like Helen Vendler) have great distaste for the "biographical fallacy." But I believe that these sonnets are both an autobiographical mine and mine field. Will was a jesting, flesh and blood Stratford boy; a great, groaning London theater man; and a laughing anti-Puritan. He is not afraid to write about his "darkest" secrets. He hated hypocrisy; many of his own confessions and his defenses against the accusations of others in these sonnets prove that. He also makes good fun of pedantic "discourse." Many university wits then and still today were and are nonplussed by his plain speaking, his double-edged puns, and his coarse jokes. But not even the liberated academics who revel in his sexual jokes go far enough. His puns may not only be sexual; they may be personal as well. This man stuck in two triangles can make very complex comments about his love and life.

In addition to the triangles of the sonnets, two interlocking triangles suggest sacred geometry that most Renaissance artists believed in. These triangles are embedded in many Renaissance paintings. The upward pointing triangle is male; the downward pointing triangle is female. The union of these two triangles is such a powerful symbol—the six-pointed star—that it became the seal of King Solomon, which became the Star of David, which became the star of the state of Israel. And this symbol is not only a Jewish symbol. I don't know how far back its use goes, but I do know that in the 1100s, a French mathematician built the six-pointed star into a formula for a new form for poetry: the sestina. This form, like the sonnet, was part of the dawn of the Italian and French Renaissance in poetry. In the Oregon woods, we have a delightful, white wild flower that hangs like a line of bells off a lily like stem. When you look at the small flower from the open end, you see two interlocking white triangles. Pioneers gave this flower the folk name "Solomon's Seal." There is even a look-alike flower that is called the "False Solomon's Seal" because it doesn't make the structure of two interlocking triangles. I am certain that Shakespeare loved this six-pointed symbol of union, too, and built it into his sonnet sequence.

But in the feverish world of Will's late twenties—when he experiences both triangles in 1592 (aged 28) and 1593 (aged 29)—Henry is like fair Helen, and Aemilia is like Medea, the dark, beautiful "witch" of the Orient. Will is strung out between them like **Faustus** between Angel and Devil (as in Sonnet 144, line 1: "Two loves I have of comfort and despair"), and Kit is also wooing Henry/**Helen** for a kiss. Marlowe, that very talented scholar/poet, may be seeking patronage beyond Thomas Walsingham and trying to quit dangerous spy work. Those who doubt that Henry was a "fair," attractive "master mistress of my passion" (Sonnet 20, line 2) and someone who could break Will's heart should look again at the paintings of Henry done in his lifetime (including the new portrait that was for so long classified as a woman but is now found to be Henry as an older boy). Remember that Henry and his wife Elizabeth Vernon had a daughter named Penelope. Penelope married Baron Spencer. Thus, Lady Diana Spencer (Princess Di, a tragic beauty and very hot celebrity in her time) was descended from "fair" Henry, and so are her two sons Wills and Harry both heirs to the British throne (Wells 402). So Henry Wriothesley was a beautiful boy/man, who broke Will's heart.

But are all these men in *Shakespeare's Sonnets* bi-sexual involved in both straight and gay triangles? Typically, the Sonnets are cryptic and swing both ways. Remember, homosexuality was a capital offense in Elizabeth's England. Sonnet 20, often quoted by us heterosexuals, was written when Henry was younger and seems to prove that Will is interested only in Henry's heart. But the more you read it, the more you realize that Sonnet 20's words can be bent either way. And that was earlier. In Sonnet 31, Will says in line 14, **"And thou** (all they) **hast all the all of me."** "All" does not mean some. I once read that Henry had a homosexual partnership with another lord, who shared his tent when they were with Essex's army in Ireland, but that may be nasty army gossip. Homosexuality was a capital crime in Shakespeare's

lifetime, so don't expect any unambiguous confessions from Will. The only man charged under that law was Edward de Vere, the Earl of Oxford, and he was charged with the rape of a boy. But he seems to have survived that charge; who would believe a boy against such a powerful Earl? Or was there a fine involved?

In 1889, Wilde wrote "A Portrait of Mr. W. H." where, in a delightfully "wild" framed narrative, he pleads for a Neo-Platonic, loving friendship (not gay love) between actor/writer Shakespeare and boy actor Willie Hughes, his fictional contribution to a solution to the W. H. mystery. I do know that Oscar Wilde used *Shakespeare's Sonnets* as part of his defense when Wilde was on trial in 1895 for being a great, bisexual playwright having a homosexual love affair with a young lord (Duncan-Jones *Introduction* 32). Wilde knew lots more about this stuff than I do, but *Shakespeare's Sonnets* couldn't help him, and he was found "guilty." England sent her greatest comic playwright since *The Tempest* to jail to break his health with two years of hard labor. And those who had been delighted by *The Importance of Being Earnest* couldn't save him. I know Will would have been just as horrified at Wilde's imprisonment as he was at Marlowe's murder.

In Sonnet 131, where Will finds Aemilia to be angry and **"tyrannous,"** like Medea once she was wronged, Will again echo's Marlowe's famous line about Helen with a dark difference in line 10: "A **thousand** groans but thinking on thy **face"** [.] These groans come early in their affair. I think her sudden anger may have sprung from Will's revealing his knowledge of her affair with Henry and Will's asking her to be true only to him. Will has become like Jason moaning over Medea while possibly losing Henry, the Golden Fleece. Will also wonders if he is also like Menelaus, who will lose Helen to Paris, Prince of Troy. Shakespeare's 28-year-old grief is triangular and real. Both 19-year-old

Henry and 23-year-old Aemelia share the blame for Will's distrust of them and his loss of love. For once, just imagine being in Will's place! But what was raw in 1592 may turn artful by 1609. Revisions that Shakespeare added by age 45 in 1609 may lend eloquence and mature grief and even ironic humor to his 28-year-old self.

Triangles—both signs of gender and relationship—may create strong dramatic tensions, but they also cause suffering. Will suffers two painful, triangular relationships with Henry: the first with a woman writer Will wished to enjoy as his own soul mate, the second with a great writing rival, who wants to steal away his friend and patron. Will the dramatist and poet used these triangles to amplify the literary power of his sonnets. But Will the lover groaned like a man bent over love's rack.

Chapter 14   Will's Wife Anne in Code

But where is Will's wife Anne Hathaway in all this? She is punned on in Sonnet 145's last two lines 13 & 14:

"'I hate' from **'HATE' AWAY** she threw, **HATHAWAY**
AND saved my life, saying 'not you.'"
ANNE

I don't think this "odd," tetrameter sonnet was written earlier, before Shakespeare mastered pentameter as some imply. I believe he learned to count and scan lines in Stratford grammar school. I also believe Anne found out in Stratford (from his case of VD: "when she saw my woeful state") or was told by Will about all this, and she forgave him. I wonder: what is the real reason this sonnet is in a more song-like tetrameter? If my favorite timeline is correct, Sonnet 145 represents the night of June 14th O. C. (or June 21st of our calendar), the **shortest night of the year,** so it is written in the **shortest lines** of the sequence. Here we may be seeing both time structure and line length inspired by Spencer's "Epithalamion." It's always odd to really think about what the critics of this sonnet mean when they call it "juvenilia." Do they mean at some point in his young writing life Shakespeare could not count to five and so wrote four beat lines? This is a very silly idea. Even when commentators have other evidence, they still repeat this old saw.

For example, Kerrigan repeats it (376) and, at the same time he quotes a **tetrameter sonnet**

embedded in *As You Like It* III.2.121-50 (perhaps written in 1600). Kerrigan compares this sonnet in content to Sonnet 53; Shakespeare presents it as written by Orlando to praise Rosalind. It begins,

"Therefore Heaven Nature charged
That one body should be filled
With all graces wide-enlarged."
                    (Qtd in Kerrigan 237)

There were no "sonnet police." Sonnets did not have to be written in pentameter, or the poet was busted. There are other examples of non-pentameter sonnets from that era. Sidney wrote hexameter sonnets as well. Sonnet 145 could have been written earlier during Will and Anne's courtship. Will's "woeful state" back then could have been his boyish erection, for which she had "mercy." But even if it were written in that time (the early 1580s) and saved, why did Shakespeare insert it here in his 1609 sequence?

Does it form a Stratford pair with Sonnet #146, with its puns on body and soul? Is his soul in Stratford, where he is building up protection for his body and his family? Certain key words could be puns about his financial dealings in his home town: "painting," "walls," "costly," "cost," "short a lease," "fading mansion." Could these be references to the cost of buying and fixing up Clopton's New Place and buying leases on farmlands? In line 7, he wonders if his family or "worms" shall be "inheritors of this excess." Just like Will to worry about his family in the middle of a remodeling project. He is a caring man.

Yet just before this sonnet worrying about the dialogue between his soul and his body, the threat of Anne's hate goes to hell "like a fiend." I find other telling puns in Sonnet 145, line 8, **"And taught** it thus **anew** to greet:" in which he states that he cannot hide his secrets from his wife, for "Anne taught" and "Anne knew." This time, his "woeful state" could be his venereal disease, evidence of his infidelity, for which she also has "mercy." As Neil Graves wrote about Sonnet 145, "Here the Stratford-focused playfulness inside the poem shows the author's gamy spirit at work" (204). Yes, and it shows a second instance of forgiveness from Anne. The spirit of forgiveness that takes over his later Romance plays and culminates in the farewells and pardons of *The Tempest,* may have been taught to Will by his wife.

Perhaps the songlike, non-sonnet tetrameter is also a clue to the source for Will's puns on **And** and **Anne**. Will had a copy of Tottel's *Miscellany*, 1557, which he mentions in *The Merry Wives of Windsor.* This old anthology included pre-Elizabethan sonnets and songs by one of his main poetic mentors, Sir Thomas Wyatt, and there's one sonnet in that book that expresses, with a pun, Wyatt's love for the untouchable **Anne** Boleyn, Queen Elizabeth I's mother, who belongs to Caesar, Henry VIII:

"Whoso list to hunt, I know where is **AN** hind."   **ANNE** (dear)

In another poem in loose tetrameter lines, written while Wyatt was in the Tower in 1536, Wyatt describes witnessing the beheading of Anne Boleyn from his cell:

"These bloody days have broken my **heart,**
... The Bell Tower showed me such sight
That in my head sticks day **and** night."
(Abrams 534)

What a terrible thing for Wyatt, a prisoner, to have seen: he is the **hart** who saw the death of his queen and lady **Anne.**

William Shakespeare never rejects his Anne. He returns to her and their daughter Susanna for comfort. He is rewarded by Anne's forgiveness, which he records in Sonnet 145 and in many of the Romances. He is also rewarded with at least one very solid son-in-law, Dr. John Hall in June 1607, and a grand-daughter Elizabeth in February 1608. But he is still worried about the fate of his younger daughter Judith. He records some beautiful wishes for her happiness in the Romances, especially in speeches of Prospero for Miranda. But, just before his death, she marries poorly, and he changes his will. Will, the father, cannot win for his younger daughter what Will, the playwright, created for her on stage. Will's final dreams come true for both his older daughter Susanna and his wife Anne but not for Judith.

80

Chapter 15   Anne and Henry and Will

Will's dreams come true, I think, about Anne and Henry. Perhaps after Will's affair with Aemilia ended (maybe in 1592 or 1593—maybe even later in 1595), Will continued with Anne as one of the (somewhat) estranged loves of his life, and I believe that Will and Henry were also life-long, loving friends. The sonnet that seems to record the death of Queen Elizabeth I and the crowning of the new King James I—Sonnet #107—is followed by sonnets of reunion, new, refined love, and time that may run right up to 1609.

According to the on-line Oxford University Press Shakespeare encyclopedia, in 1605, about a year after he was released from the Tower by the new King, Henry put on a production of *Love's Labour Lost* in his London Montague House for his royal guest, Queen Anne. In it, she saw satirical scenes and references to what Shakespeare called "The School of Night," that shadowy group formed around Lord Ralegh, Marlowe, Chapman, Hariot, and others, who may have or may not have met, said, and planned awful things in the early 1590s against both church and state.

In Shakespeare's play, perhaps also full of encoded references to named people or a similar circle around Henry Wriothesley, the new queen would have seen a harmless group of four male wannabe Stoic philosophers undermined by the appearance of four beautiful women. Maybe Henry was trying to indirectly tell King James that Ralegh was not a danger to him. If so, it didn't help Ralegh because the Spanish made his arrest a condition of peace with England, and King James gave in. After Ralegh's main royal supporter, Prince Henry, died in 1612, King James gave into the Spanish and had Ralegh executed.

There is also reason to believe that Henry Wriothesley, who was on the London Board of the Jamestown settlement, showed Will a copy (one of three circulating before it was published later) of William Straichey's 1610 letter about the wreck of the flagship on Bermuda that became one of Will's sources for *The Tempest*. (William Herbert was also on that Board and could also have been a sharer.)

Perhaps in 1617, before the memorial year of 1623 (7 years after Will's death, when the two actors, Heminges and Condell, were reconstructing the First Folio, and Ben Jonson was writing his loving introduction poem to these plays by the "Sweet Swan of Avon"), Henry may have helped the family to pay for the limestone bust of Shakespeare that now sits above Will's grave in Stratford (Wilson 399). The sculpture workshop in Southwark was the same one where Henry had much earlier (when he was 21 in 1594) ordered his own father's grave sculpture (399). (See new material on Shakespeare images and busts—bottom of next page).

Then, after Will's bust was in place—with its warning not to move his bones (perhaps written by Shakespeare's medical, Puritan son-in-law in 1617)—the First Folio was published, Anne died in 1623, and Henry died during a war in Flanders with his son Thomas in 1624, still carrying a flame for Shakespeare in his heart. Why wouldn't Shakespeare still be loved eight years after his death? The *Sonnets* promised this kind of love after death to Henry, and, I believe, they delivered it by naming the youth:

"Your **name** from **hence immortal life**
shall have."

(Sonnet 81.5)

Time has turned the *Sonnets* into fractals of sound and meaning that can be traced back to the poet, and his code may give us many more direct connections with Will than we had before.

Fractal Phi

In addition, in 2006, a new book called *The True Face of William Shakespeare*, uses new science and technology by German federal police forensics experts, medical pathologists, and computer imaging experts, to validate six images of Shakespeare and give us this probable timeline:

1. The Chandros Portrait (c. 1594—99) painted by Richard Burbage perhaps for Globe opening;
2. The Flower Portrait (1609) perhaps from a companion life mask and live sitting to celebrate the year of the publication of the *Sonnets*;
3. The Davenant Bust (1613);
4. The Darmstadt Shakespeare death mask (1616);
5. The Stratford Bust (after the death mask—c. 1616—1617); and
6. The Drocshout Engraving for the First Folio (1623) after The Flower Portrait from 1609.

(Hammerschmidt-Hummel 47—95)

Chapter 16 Minor Characters: Greene, De Vere, & W.H.

I know there are all sorts of rival theories and even a comic play, *The Beard of Avon* by Amy Freed, about who wrote these sonnets and the plays, and who made love to whom and how. I don't expect to surprise anyone with the names I found in the Sonnets—**Will, Henry, Aemilia, and Kit**—but I reckon my "proofs" and my finding of "code" will make some people upset, incredulous, dizzy, faint, and even air sick. One retired high school English teacher overheard me telling an Anthropologist friend of mine at an Oregon conference about my discovery of code, and this older man exclaimed, "The hell you have!" I have found no indifferent responses. Fortunately, most responses I have heard have been, "Tell me more!" Both positive and negative responses like these have pushed my work along in the years from 2002 until 2007.

I am glad that one of my favorite biographers of Shakespeare—Peter Levi in his *The Life and Times of William Shakespeare*—agrees with all these three, central names (as does Rowse). Levi is a former Professor of Poetry at Oxford University, and he is a scholar I like to debate, agree with, and disagree with when I am muttering in my study at my computer. He also gives me, an American, some clear English notes, which I lack, for this work. I hope all sides will take what I've found seriously enough to do their homework and read all the *Sonnets*, especially the so-called minor ones. I happen to like some of them more for their difficult, brainy wit and wacky humor than some of the "lollipop" sonnets that "everyone" loves. Read them all! I admit it; that's my secret agenda. I think the greatest disservice to Shakespeare comes from those scholars who dismiss some sonnets as "inferior" or "juvenilia" or even argue that they "could not have been written by the 'divine' Shakespeare." Notice that some commentators do this without explaining the part these sonnets play in the sequence. Isn't it silly Bardolatry to dismiss poems written by Shakespeare as "not worthy" of him and then ignore them?

The so-called "minor sonnets" contain joys and jokes and details all their own. Many agree that Sonnet 112 contains a reference to an insult that pamphleteer Robert Greene paid to Shakespeare in 1592. Greene had mocked Will's name, calling him "Shake-scene" (Gibson *Sonnets* 204). Jealous Greene wrote an attack on Marlowe, too, calling him "Merlin." The "bridges" for this pun are two other spellings of Marlowe: "Marlin or Merling" (Nicholl 203). In Sonnet 112, Will asks why he should care about Greene's old insult as long as Henry is his friend and patron. Line 4:

"So you **o'er-green** my bad, my good allow?"

Henry covers Will's faults with a **green** cover crop. But the code shows us one further joke embedded in lines 1—4 of this sonnet. In 1592, Greene (or perhaps Thomas Nashe using Greene's name for safety after Greene had just died) had famously called Will "an upstart crow," but Will likes the image and plays in his code with it:

"Your love and pity doth th'impression fill	
Which vulgar s-**C-A**ndal stamped upon my b-**ROW**	**CA/ROW**
For **W**hat **C-AR**e I who **C-A**lls me well or ill	**W/CAR/CA**
So you **O'ER-GREEN** my bad, my good all-**OW**.	**R/GREEN/OW**

I believe we have caught Will triumphantly **crowing** twice (**CAW CAW!**) over **R. Greene: Crow Caw, Crrrow CaCaw!**

I want to crow (like Mary Martin singing Peter Pan) about finding this code, but I also want to say that if I could put a question mark of speculation after every one of my assertions and include a laugh or two after each discovery, then, I believe my words would be closer to the spirit I'm trying to achieve in this study and closer to Will's spirit as well. I am just an Oregon Fish Crow picking up tasty scraps and laughing on the Pacific shore.

An Aside on Authorship Versus Stratfordian Code

Now, I will throw a couple of bones to rival identities, but I don't think Tory Oxfordians or the fans of William Herbert (W. H.) will like what I've found. Here I go onto somewhat dangerous turf. There's a very vocal, fanatic minority of Tory buffs, Conservative revisionists, crazed de Vere fans, and war-like Oxfordians, who carp at Stratfordians but do not themselves really accept the burden of proof once shifted to Oxford or the difficulties over any 400-year-old evidence. When I ask local Oxfordians I have met pointed questions, they blink and act like my students when they haven't done their homework or like Owls in daylight being mobbed by Blackbirds. But I will give only a little time and space to debate non-Stratfordians. There is too much wonderful William Shakespeare material to revel in and play with! I must leave the full impact of my discovery of Stratfordian code on questions of authorship to others.

Recently, one self-appointed, Oxfordian guard dog found my 18 November 2004 draft of this essay on my web page and emailed me. In an insulting way, he referred me to the almost worthless Oxford Society Home Page. But I had already done that homework two years before when I read that fake scholarship and had had a good laugh. The Bacon Society and Marlowe Society Home Pages are worth a little more because they actually contain original works about and by **great writers**. I still invite my students, who express interest, to visit and evaluate all three "Society" web pages equally. Although Films for Humanities made a DVD *The Shakespeare Enigma* and although in Summer 2005 the Ashland Shakespeare Festival hosted an "authorship" debate and although this has become an overwrought, popular topic in our current culture "wars," I think it's a silly issue. We all could stand to learn a lot more about Shakespeare; Queen Elizabeth I; Sir Francis Bacon; Edward de Vere, Earl of Oxford; and Christopher Marlowe, but people who can't tell these people apart are not very good or trustworty readers.

In a style calculated to insult or amuse, I sum up my "authorship" findings this way:

1. **QE I:** too busy, wrong class and politics, & dead too soon.

2. **Oxford:** not a great writer, a corrupt character, wrong class, & dead too soon.

3. **Marlowe:** a great, unfunny, rival playwright, & dead too soon.

4. **Bacon:** a great essayist, totally humorless, wrong class & politics, a cold fish, but at least he lived long enough. There's a problem with Bacon —he lived too long. He died in 1626, 3 years after publication of the First Folio, with not a word about his "authorship."

I don't think that quick sketch will end all the authorship noise, do you? I don't attend trendy conferences on this bogus topic, but some of my students want to research this "authorship" topic, so I have read a lot of this shit. Now here is this: **all** evidence I offer is based on what I think William Shakespeare of Stratford may have said **in or out of code** about these people and more.

Most authorship fanatics have not read Ben Jonson's poem for the First Folio, so they cannot see around that big rock in the stream, the great author William whom Ben called the "Sweet Swan of Avon." In a recent PBS *Frontline* show, whose thesis wanted to prove how Marlowe "survived" his "staged" murder and went into exile in Italy and "sent scripts" to Shakespeare to put his name on, one Marlovian said that Jonson was paid by William Herbert to write a "falsified introductory poem" to the plays in 1623. I fell out of my chair laughing at this personage, who insulted two of the greatest friends and writers of an age—Jonson and Shakespeare—in one sentence! But at least Marlovians have a suspect who can write great works. Oxfordians don't.

Here Oxfordians will see what I found as "evidence" in the text of the Sonnets, and what I think of the Earl of Oxford (de Vere). Reading all the *Sonnets* carefully and letting Will's words sink in should be required of everyone who wishes to speculate about Will's life. Of course, the author of Sonnet 25 tells us he is not a nobleman; lines 1 through 4 are very clear:

"Let those who are in favour with their stars
Of public honour and proud **titles** boast,
Whilst I, whom **fortune** of such triumph **bars,**
Unlooked for joy in that I honour most[.]"

Oxfordians cannot apply Sonnet #25 to their "Shakespeare" because their candidate for author is an Earl. There are so many Oxfordian web sites and books that my undergraduate students sometimes think some proof for the Earl must exist, but the issue of Shakespeare's class is clear. He came from the same class as his two brilliant rivals and more learned friends in the theater, Marlowe and Jonson. And to judge from the plays put on and loved by the public to this day, Marlowe's and Jonson's greater book learning is not as important in the theater as Will's sweet, wordy humor.

Oscar Wilde, in his "Portrait of Mr. W. H." also makes mistaken use of Sonnet 25 for the opposite reason. Wilde wants to prove that Mr. W. H. was not an Earl, so he confuses "I" in the sonnet with the youth (1154). That way, he can rule out both Southampton and Pembroke and advance his fictitious "real" name, "Willie Hughes," for the actual brilliant boy actor Dicky Robinson, which he says may have been Willie's "stage name" (1179). But the "I" in Sonnet # 25 is clearly the poet. At least Wilde from Dublin is under no early 20th century, Reverand Looney delusions about the poet not being William Shakespeare from Stratford.

Cast of Characters for Allegorical Code

Early in Henry's young life, the Earl of Oxford did play an important, negative role. I think that Will's code of double naming does **name de Vere** in the famous early Sonnet 19, lines 1 & 2:

"Devouring time, blunt thou the **lion's paws**,
And make the earth **devour** her own sweet brood;"

This may be a reference to the Earl of Oxford and his father-in-law, Lord Burghley, who were trying to force Henry to marry **de Vere's** daughter, Lady Elizabeth Vere. But Henry rejected her, started an affair in 1594 and later, in 1598, secretly married Elizabeth Vernon, lady-in-waiting to that other Elizabeth, the Queen. Sonnet 19 contains **code** name words for Henry, perhaps **"heinous"** and more likely **"worst"** and **"wrong."** According to Shakespeare, **"Devour**ing Time" (de Vere) is threatening to commit a **"heinous** crime" (**"he-i-n**-ous c-**ri**me"—Henri) against Henry and force him to marry the **"wrong"** Elizabeth. Will thinks the **"worst"** of fathers who try to force young people to marry someone they don't love.

In a brief study of Sonnet 19, Robert Jungman expanded my understanding of a key term in a key line, number 11: "Him in thy course **untainted** do allow [.]" Shakespeare is pleading with Time to let the youth remain "untouched" as in a jousting run and "unharmed " as in hunting. Jungman points out that the word "untainted" also came from the **field of law,** where it could mean "unarrested" or "unimpeached" (19). So Will may also be pleading with Burghley and de Vere not to arrest or impeach young Henry for some kind of "breach of promise" as they perceived it. Perhaps they felt that since Henry was a minor and his mother seemed to consent for him, they had the law on their side.

86

However, these two lords didn't need to go to court; they had the power of the law and perhaps the Queen's approval.

It may seem odd that they could order an Earl-to-be to marry. But remember, even Sidney's Stella (in real life Penelope Devereaux) was forced to marry Sir Robert Rich, and Henry was fined the huge sum of 5,000 pounds by Lord Burghley for refusing to marry Elizabeth Vere. Peter Levi points out that later, not only were Henry and pregnant Elizabeth Vernon jailed by the Queen for marrying without her permission, but that Elizabeth Vernon was the first cousin of the Earl of Essex, and Henry and Elizabeth Southampton named their first daughter Penelope after her cousin, Robert Devereaux's sister and Sidney's love, Penelope who he named Stella (97).

I do not share Peter Levi's very British admiration for the aging Queen Elizabeth I, nor, I believe, does Shakespeare. An old queen who jails a pregnant Lady in Waiting and her husband can't be all good. It's true, they failed to get the queen's permission to marry. Perhaps they knew she would not give it. Perhaps that is why Sir Walter Ralegh also failed to ask her permission to marry and was also jailed. I guess we should face it; the Queen, who never married her lovers, was obsessed by the marriage plans of others.

Perhaps, for Lord Essex, who had been under house arrest since his unapproved return from Ireland in 1599, this jailing of his first cousin and one of his most faithful officers in 1598 was one of the seeds of the ill-fated and poorly-conceived Essex rebellion. We must remember that the Queen was also micromanaging how Essex conducted the Irish war. Later, Essex was placed under house arrest, and it may have seemed to him that launching a rebellion was the only way to survive the power plays of his enemies.

We know Essex and the Queen were incensed against each other by his appointing Henry General of the Horse (even after Henry led a heroic charge to save the British army) and by his making peace in Ireland and failing to ask her permission to do both. The anger in the Queen's chamber scene in *Hamlet* (often played as a bedroom scene back in the Freudian 20th century) owes much to a similar scene of Essex wearing his sword and barging into the Queen's rooms. Henry probably told Shakespeare all about that. You see, Shakespeare did not need to be a lord in order to get a lord's eye view. Later, it was reported that the furious Queen took down an old rusty sword and stabbed the arras in that room repeatedly.

But back in kinder times, perhaps summer party-goers at Henry's mother's wedding to the older Thomas Heneage (May 2, 1594) saw Hermia's dictatorial father Egeus ("Obey me and marry Demetrius or die!") in *A Midsummer Night's Dream* as Will poking fun at the Earl of Oxford. Levi reminds us that Henry's mother Mary was in favor of a match between her son and Elizabeth de Vere, but Shakespeare must have known more about Henry's heart. Egeus/Oxford cannot force a wrong marriage. The Fairy

King Oberon will order Puck to see to it that both Hermia and Helena get their right, loving husbands.

Will later pokes fun and Hamlet's deadly sword at Oxford's father-in-law, Burghley, by portraying him as another father, Polonius, who is using and risking his daughter Ophelia as innocent spy bait against Hamlet. Once again, the speculative fly in me would have liked to have buzzed around and seen Queen Elizabeth I's face and the face of Lord Cecil, Burghley's powerful son, when Hamlet drew his sword on the old spy behind the arras and stabbed him to death while calling him, "A rat!" Some people have seen the Earl of Essex in the character of Hamlet. I have written a paper to spell out my idea that the character of Hamlet was also partly based on the murdered Christopher Marlowe. That would have made *Hamlet* a true "ghost story" (about two ghosts, Essex and Marlowe) for the court. And the whole play would then become a "mousetrap" for the Queen and Cecil testing their guilt and perhaps pleading for the life of imprisoned Henry Wriothesley.

But Sonnet #19 may be about the attempt to forge a wedding between Henry's future money and Elizabeth de Vere. He gets his money in 1594, the year he starts a secret affair with Lord Essex's first cousin, Elizabeth Vernon. Burghley and de Vere's scheme for more power and money is quite a serious threat to Will's young lord's happiness.

I think that there may be a complete allegorical code set up in Sonnet #19 of substitute words for names of important characters in the early 1590s:

Table 5: Code List for Sonnet #19

1. Devouring Time	Edward de Vere
2. The Lion	Lord Burghley
3. Sweet brood	Elizabeth de Vere
4. The Tiger	Francis Walsingham
5. The Phoenix	Queen Elizabeth I

Reconsidered this way, Sonnet #19 almost reads like a name code list for an encoded letter from the spy Robert Poley with substitute names for the powerful players. We know that Walsingham used the tiger as an emblem on his stationary, and we know that Elizabeth was referred to as "the Phoenix of the World."

Sonnet 19 is a key Time sonnet. It links up to Sonnets 52 and 60 and others. After Shakespeare finished his first seventeen, commissioned sonnets for the youth's birthday, he makes a fresh start on his own with the gorgeous Sonnet #18. But once he quickly knows the young man's heart, he realizes that the force of his first seventeen sonnets—persuading the young lord to marry and have children—is also being manipulated to make Henry marry someone he does not love. With Time, the Lion, the sweet and wrong lady, the Tiger, and the Phoenix (as well as Henry's own mother Mary) all pushing Henry toward the wrong match, Shakespeare realizes the youth needs his help. Sonnet #19 records Will's realization, and he is quite brave and blunt: he pleads with Time, "O carve not with thy hours my love's fair brow," (line 9), and "hours" is quite a common pun for "whores." This is quite a slap at de Vere, who is treating his daughter like a whore to be sold, but money was also quite a commonplace motive for arranged marriages. Henry has to buy his way out of de Vere's trap with money provided by his mother's fortunate second marriage to the very rich Thomas Heneage. Then, sonnets to follow declare Shakespeare's love and support as he watches the youth mature and find his own power.

Besides perhaps writing or paying for some comic masques for the court in the 1580s, whose scripts did not survive for us to judge, de Vere did play at least one key role in Elizabethan drama. He was John Lily's patron. Lily's *Euphues and His England* (1580) was dedicated to de Vere. And under his patron's influence, Lily set up and wrote plays for a company of boy actors (Magill 99). Of course, de Vere was himself

devoured by time in 1604. That is, he died a year after Queen Elizabeth I, which usually takes a person out of the running for "author" of all the great plays put on by the King's Men for the court of James I or sonnets written after 1604 for sonnet readers of the Jacobean Age and beyond, much less a romance—*The Tempest*—based on a 1610 ship wreck report. In addition to this dated evidence, two very thorough women scholars, Leah S. Marcus in 1988 and Clare Asquith in 2005, have explored many of the hundreds (perhaps actually thousands) of post-1604 **topical references** in *King Lear, Macbeth, Othello, Measure for Measure, Coriolanus, Cymbeline,* and *The Winter's Tale.*

The "chest full of Oxford's scripts" left to a country bumpkin named "Shakespeare" is just a silly figment. It is probably based on the much later tale from 1742 of two chests full of Shakespeare's "loose papers and manuscripts," which were supposedly carted off from the New Place by Will's granddaughter Elizabeth long after Will's death (Schoenbaum 249 f). The trouble is, no one has found these invaluable chests. They may have just as well contained pillowcases embroidered by Anne and Susanna. One cannot just make up evidence when there is none and base a whole authorship theory on such a busted bubble.

The Problem of W.H. and Code

I am friendlier to those who want the youth to be **William Herbert** (son of Mary Sidney, nephew to Sir Phillip Sidney, and cousin to "Holy" George Herbert), but according to the timeline and the evidence I envision, he's too darned young. He was born in 1580, which makes him only 12 in 1592. He just doesn't fit in with Will at 28 or Aemilia at 23. And if Marlowe, who was murdered in 1593, is the main rival poet of Sonnets 78—86, then I don't think that 12- or 13-year-old William Herbert can be the youth, who was courted by Marlowe or made love to by Will, both aged 29.

In fact, some authors go to great lengths to avoid naming Marlowe, the most obvious suspect, as the rival poet just because they want William Herbert to be the youth, and "Kit Morley," as he signed himself in his only surviving signature, really screws up the William Herbert timeline. It's not that he wouldn't be interested in a boy, I guess. I don't know really; many of the reports on the vices of Marlowe come from his political enemies and right wing preachers and very ignorant, suspect sources. It's also hard to believe that this young boy and his mother would have been that interested in Marlowe.

If you want to say that Sonnets 1-17 were written for William Herbert's 17th birthday, then, like Katherine Duncan-Jones, you have to start the timepiece of the sonnets running very late in 1597. And then, like the White Rabbit in Wonderland, you have to run very hard all the time to catch up with your own fluffy tail while singing, "I'm late. I'm late for a very important date!" Oscar Wilde takes care of ruling out William Herbert in his own way. He remembers that

Meres listed *Shakespeare's Sonnets* as known and being circulated in 1598. Herbert was seventeen in 1597 and didn't come to London until 1598. Anyway, Wilde wants to start Shakespeare's relationship with the youth in 1594. Whatever the year, Wilde concludes, "Shakespeare ... could not have known Lord Pembroke until after the Sonnets had been written" (1154).

Duncan-Jones admits that some of the Sonnets 1—17 were written for Henry Wriothesley's 17th birthday in 1590, but she goes on to suggest that 1—17 may have been rewritten and recycled for William Herbert's 17th birthday in 1597 (*Ungentle* 216). But that still begs the question of whether sonnets 18—126 were written for Henry Wriothesley. William Herbert may or may not be the publisher Tom Thorpe's 1609 patron "W. H." when Herbert was 29, but I don't think Sonnets 1—17 were originally written for William Herbert's 17th birthday. He certainly doesn't fit with Kit and Aemilia. But with William Herbert's family connection to great poets like his uncle Phillip Sidney, he is a very likely patron in 1609 to pay perhaps five to ten pounds for the printing of a great, late sonnet sequence. He and his brother Phillip—thanks to their support for the printing of the First Folio in 1623—should be listed along with other major, post-Southampton patrons of Shakespeare such as King James I and George Carey (the next Lord Hunsdon).

In addition, another attractive but unlikely W. H. exists. He is William Harvey, who married Henry's mother Mary. He was her third husband. Mary died in 1607. Harvey married again in 1608 to a woman named Cordell, who was named after Cordilla in the old play about Lear that was Shakespeare's source (Duncan-Jones *Ungentle* ... 185). Was Harvey memorialized by the printer Thorpe because he gave his former wife's manuscript copy of the sonnets to the printer in 1609?

But what did she receive from Shakespeare beyond sonnets 1—17? I don't think Shakespeare would give Henry's mother all the 126 sonnets for her son. Will is both frank and brave, but he is not foolish.

So this W. H. doesn't seem to be the real W. H. Of course, if Don Foster's speculation is right, and W. H. is a typo for "W. SH.," then W. H. is a will-o'-the-wisp. But then, "W. H." could just as easily be seen as a typo for "H. W." if a typo is the explanation. But I think Thomas Thorpe (T. T., the publisher of the 1609 version of the *Sonnets)* would be really fussy about getting his dedication right for his own patron. Maybe it's all a mistake by T. T., who got wrong the youth Shakespeare first wrote Sonnets 1—126 for and confused him with the young man paying the printer's bills.

Since Katherine Duncan-Jones likes William Herbert for the youth, she brings up as part of her proof a fascinating detail from 1616—the year of Shakespeare's death in April—when Ben Jonson dedicated his *Epigrammes* to William Herbert. She and I both believe that Ben must have had the dedication to *Shakespeare's Sonnets* in mind when Jonson wrote his contrasting dedication. Ben gives Pembroke's full name and titles and goes on to state (below):

MY LORD. While you cannot change your merit, I dare not change your title: It was that made it, and not I. Under which **name**, I here offer to your Lo: the ripest of my studies, my Epigrammes; which though they carry **danger** in the sound, doe not therefore seeke your shelter: For, when I made them, I had **nothing in my conscience**, to expressing of which I did need a **cypher**.

(Duncan-Jones 61)

Duncan-Jones and I both think that **"cypher"** may refer to "W. H." And we both also think that Ben's words "danger" and "nothing in my conscience" refer to the daring honesty of Will's sonnets for the youth and the dark lady, which may have shocked people in 1609 and which may account for some of the silence surrounding their publication. I, of course, also wonder if Ben Jonson, perhaps the best of

Will's readers along with John Donne and Edward Alleyn, may have spotted some of the code, which I am doing my best to decipher.

I believe (with Harold Bloom) that Will may have started Sonnets 1—17 in 1589 (or Spring 1590—maybe even in April) to get them done in time for Henry's 17th birthday in October 1590. I also think that Shakespeare was still revising close to 1609. That may rule out William Harvey as W. H. because if he had a manuscript of the *Sonnets,* it would have been dated earlier and been incomplete. So maybe Will provided the manuscript, and William Herbert paid the printer. I think Will might have chuckled at all our fuss over "Mr. W. H." in Thorpe's dedication. He might point out that **HWWH** makes a nice chiasmus (ABBA) and ask, like Hamlet, why we would really like to solve "his mystery." Some say that "Mr. W. H." is simply "Mr. William Himself," a legalistic joke from an illiterate way of signing a will. But what about William Herbert? Before he received his title, he might have been called "Master" but not "Mister." What we do know is that later, upon Burbage's death in 1619, William Herbert says he was really close to this other of Shakespeare's dearest male friends and business partners, the great actor Richard Burbage (Wilson 400). Also, Herbert helped the actors with the printing costs of the First Folio of Will's plays in 1623 (Wilson 401). But William Herbert was not the only one in his family to be honored in the First Folio.

Other preliminary leaves dedicate the Folio to William Herbert, third Earl of Pembroke (the Lord Chamberlain), and his younger brother Philip, first Earl of Montgomery, and offer commendations of the playwright in verse and prose (Schoenbaum 258).

This rounds off Shakespeare's posthumous patrons nicely with Phillip, who is the nephew and the namesake of Sir Phillip Sidney. It also argues that this wonderful patronage may have been a family, literary affair, not the grieving tribute of the young man of the *Sonnets.*

Gary Schmidgall reviews some of the key patrons of Shakespeare's era and gives the numbers of works dedicated to them. William Herbert (Pembroke) received "nearly ninety" dedications (73). The King's oldest son, Prince Henry, received "almost a hundred" (74). Lucy, Countess of Bedford, received "about thirty" (76). Edward de Vere received "fewer than thirty" (76). And although Henry Wriothesley lived almost as long as Pembroke, his census is much more modest. He received twenty-two dedications... Aside from the Shakespearian dedications, the only other noteworthy volumes represented are Florio's *Wordes* (1598), Ferrabosco's *Lessons* (1609), and Nashe's 1594 *Traveller* (76). From 1591 to 1613, Southampton also received other literary dedications from Clapman, Barnes, Lok, Markham, Knight, Davies, Daniel, Wither, and, finally, Chapman—but after 1609 (77).

So, from 1591 on, we have a list of possible "rivals" to make up "nine Muses" competing for Henry's attention, but it does not include Will's chief rival, Marlowe, whose life was cut short in 1593. I'm not sure anyone knows how many of these were rewarded with a response from Henry.

Although "almost fifty" of the "nearly ninety" works dedicated to Pembroke "can be classified as religious" (73), most of them were unexpected and unrewarded. He may be a very logical choice for Thorpe's W. H., but is there any evidence for him in the *Sonnets?* I am willing to let the younger William Herbert in the "back door" of the *Sonnets* and consider him to be possibly **"another youth."** In Sonnet 110, line 7, Shakespeare in a pun confesses to Henry he got close to "another youth" (perhaps while Henry was in the Tower for three years after the failed Essex rebellion). In this Sonnet, Henry has been released by James I, and Will is reunited in line 11 with his **"older friend"** in 1603 when Henry Wriothesley was 30, William Herbert was 23, and Will was 39. Once again, this youth and patron confusion of ours might seem odd to Shakespeare. He might like the rhetorical puzzle enclosed in the chiasmus: **HWWH** and tell us not to get too worked up over it. If Henry can have "rival poets," I see no reason why Will can't have "rival patrons." But in Sonnet #110, Will is quite blunt and firm: "... **worse** essays proved thee my **best** of love" (line 8). If W. H. read this, and if he were "another youth," he must have been at ease with Shakespeare's earlier youth and

patron, "A god in love, to whom I am confined" (line 12).

But all this is part of Will's difficult dance for Henry. He may be trying to keep his lines open to any and all patronage if he needs it in the reign of the new king. The elite have "the power to harm." And no matter what true feelings Will has for Henry, he must follow Horace's advice to the poet as translated by William Webbe in 1586:

> Let a Poet first take uppon him, as though he were to play but an Actor's part ... so to hide one's cunning ... every part is polished ... is a speciall gift.
> (qtd. in Schmidgall 132)

Webbe's Horace goes on to name this "gift" with a word that Aristotle uses, which Schmidgall describes as "a word that provides the root for cryptic" (132). Shakespeare may have had to construct some of his **code** to protect himself against being fully understood by his patrons or their enemies. The courtly world was thus one of extreme circumspection in letters, elaborate ciphers, codes, spying, intrigue—all part of the background against which the speaker courts the Young Man.
> (180)

Both Wyatt and Donne report extensively about this background. Not only did it make Shakespeare and others better "actors," it also forced them to use tricky rhetorical devices that could voice their inner conflicts without revealing from which of Janus the Gatekeeper's faces they were speaking. Of course, in the plays, Shakespeare can give his characters dangerous words and not be blamed for them. In the *Sonnets,* he faces a trickier situation. Although many commentators want to say that the voice of the Poet in the *Sonnets* is a character in a fiction, Will names himself and is responsible himself for building in the autobiographical clues and dodges. So, in part, one of his Poet's faces may be a fiction, but the other face may be the real Will. How are we to sort this out? We are in the same position as those people Will wanted to entice and deceive.

He does protect himself perhaps with code and definitely with tricky rhetorical constructions. Schmidgall sums these up well:

The final psychological challenge ... to integrate deeply mixed feelings— derived inevitably from the suitor's subjection to the charisma of power and his consciousness of self-injury. ... the Renaissance experience of courtly life... often found expression in **equivocal figures such as the paradox and the oxymoron.** To this can be added the figure *amphibole,* which Abraham Francis says occurs "when the sentence may be **turned both ways,**

so a man shall be uncertain what to take." (188 f.)

To define the pressure that all poets found at court, Schmidgall quotes a telling, satiric sonnet, which he says is "attributed to Wyatt:"

Driving to desire, adread also to dare,
Between two stools my tail goeth to the ground.
(189)

I heard a version of this in the 1970s presented as a Russian proverb: "You can't put your ass on two barstools, comrade." John Donne sums up with an "oxymoronic synopsis" his experience of life at court: "Suspicious boldness to the place belongs" (189). This double consciousness, a mix of "boldness" and "suspicion" is what makes *Shakespeare's Sonnets* so exciting.

The psychological pressure is very high; the written response is full of rhetorical figures that contain explosive contraries and loaded ambiguities. One key word that could go two ways or more might be the best way to avoid detection while still speaking the plain truth. The court is an intense pressure cooker. But the court is just a small part of the English landscape of the *Sonnets.*

Chapter 17 Literary Time Frame: Summer Sun and Moon

Trying to put all these people's lives and sonnets in both a literary framework and a timeline of Shakespeare's life is really a challenge. Let's tackle the literary framework first. There are **two great parts**: Sonnets 1—126 for the youth and Sonnets 127—154 for the lady. I do agree that the seemingly incomplete, twelve-line, rhymed couplet Sonnet 126 is an *envoi* between the youth's and the dark lady's Sonnets. It may also have been written oddly because it ends the time period covered by the sonnets. I also think that the twin, "ending" Sonnets 153 and 154 are more mechanically written, a repeated, expanded translation of Marcianus Scholasticus's 5th century AD Greek epigram. "Giles Fletcher translated it as a sonnet in his *Licia* (1593), and that is possibly where Shakespeare got it..." (Levi 108).

This **double** translation or two versions with differences is a **double** *envoi* written to cap the dark lady sequence and the whole sequence as well. They are less passionate, more classical, and they are about Cupid's problems and Will's leftover illness, probably written after the end of the affair but in what year? They are more about a creation myth of how hot springs came to be and more about venereal disease than love. But including these two, there are 28 dark lady sonnets, and many scholars agree that this number reflects the cycle of the moon and women's menstrual cycle. For me, four of Will's code numbers interlock in the older calendar of the Moon: **14 ÷ 2 = 7 and 2 X 14 = 28.**

The Romans had a pretty piece, which Shakespeare knew, a rhetorical riddle, so they could remember lunar astronomy. They called the Moon the **"liar Moon"** (*Luna mendax*) because she made a **DCCD** **chiasmus** when she made a **D** in the sky looking ahead at the sun as she was in**C**reasing (waxing and Latin **C**receres) and a **C** in the sky looking back at the sun as she was **D**ecreasing (waning and Latin **D**ecreceres). So we can look up at the Moon and decide whether she is waxing or waning by telling us a lie with a **D** or a **C**. This plays right into Will's portrayal of the Dark Lady as the Moon and as a liar. Of course, in Sonnet 152, he says he lied to her ten times as much as she lied to him. Under the seductive power of the Moon, he lies to lie with her.

In Sonnet 152, Shakespeare shows this Roman Moon shape shift from **D** to **C** in lines 9-12:

For I have sworn **D**eep oaths of thy **D**eep kindness,	**waxing**
Oaths of thy love, thy truth, thy **C**onstan**C**y,	**waning**
And to enlighten thee gave eyes to blindness,	
Or made them swear against the things they **see:**	**(C)**

This is a fine embedded trick from Roman rhetoric. And, as for making oaths upon the liar Moon, we can't help but hear young Juliet's warning to Romeo: "O swear not by the moon, th'inconstant moon" (*R&J* II.2.109).

In contrast, in the group of sonnets to the youth, there are many references to him as Sun or son (by way of punning) or solar hero (two examples: Sonnets 18 and 33). As mentioned before, there's a fascinating temporal anomaly that may refer to Hamnet's death: Quatrain 3 of Sonnet 33, which is 3 X 11. The sonnet starts off lamenting that both the sun in the sky can be covered with clouds and so can the youth's face. Will suspects the youth of an "ugly" action that stains himself and the poet. The early lines sound as if they were written in 1592, and the stain comes from Henry not turning down Aemilia's advances for Will's sake. Suddenly, there's a reference to a deeper wound, the death of 11-year old Hamnet Shakespeare, and this third quatrain could have been added as a revision in or after 1596. Or could it have been added in one of the two intensive revision sessions, either in 1604 or 1608? Here are lines 9—12:

"Even so my **sun** one early morn did shine
With all triumphant splendor on my brow;
But out alack, **he was but one hour mine,**
The region cloud hath masked him from me now."

I see this "Even so..." acting like a Homeric simile, an aside from the future comparing two devastating disappointments, alike in causing tragic grief. I also wondered if Hamnet's age at death, eleven, was remembered in the numbers 11 X 14 = 154, the total number of sonnets (just as 17 is remembered as a number about Henry, and 17 X 9 = 153). This loss of a son, some, including James Joyce, have noted, carries over into the play *Hamlet*. It's interesting, too, that Aemilia lost a baby daughter in 1599, who she had named "Odillya" by combining "ode" with her own name (Woods *Lanyer* 28).

I find it touching to suggest that these two lost children gave

96

their names to the tragic love affair between Hamlet and Ophelia. A friend and colleague of mine, Paul Snyder, a computer and library media specialist, whose Dad was a cipher man on a U.S. submarine in World War II, read an earlier version of this paper. Paul is descended from Walsingham's messenger—Davisson—in the Mary Queen of Scot's case, and Paul wondered if Odillya were Shakespeare's biological daughter. So many Shakespeare detectives, so many possible answers! Who knows about paternity?

Shakespeare's love life was stained by tears, by loss of his son, and by accusations and disgrace. In his time, he was not the literary superhero he is for us. Some people simply call that hero and icon "The Bard;" I call that icon "Shakespeare, Inc." William Shakespeare may be the Wolfgang Amadeus Mozart of the theater, but there's a real man under there, and I'm interested to see if I can see him through his wonderful disguises after four hundred years of reruns, dumb-downs, hoopla, icon making, theatrics, theater history, and evolution. In the 1590s, this man was hurt by personal betrayal of the grossest kind. His best friend has slept with his lover; Will had hoped she would be faithful to him. But why shouldn't "Suns of the world" be expected to "stain, when heaven's sun staineth"[?] he asks to end Sonnet 33. I wonder if "heaven's sun" is a reference to Jesus. If it is, his stain could be his wounds and his death as clouds covered the sun. This is another hard, inexplicable loss, despite all the Christian dogma justifying it. And Jesus' cry "Why

hast thou forsaken me?" is as mysterious as ever and could apply to Will asking God about the death of Hamnet or asking the youth about sleeping with the dark lady.

Sonnet 34 continues the solar image of 33 with a question in line 1 that is set against the joy of Sonnet 18; the youth has broken his promises: "Why didst thou **promise** such **a beauteous day** [?]" Will feels the loss of love and trust yet must accept the youth's tears as pearls that "ransom all ill deeds" (line 14). Will sounds like a fatherly older brother in the first seventeen sonnets. But especially after the death of Will's son Hamnet in 1596, puns on son and sun become thicker, and Henry becomes, in the final solar sonnet, Sonnet 126, line 1, "my lovely boy."

I think the 126 sonnets represent the Sun's summer cycle and theater season, starting in late April or early May depending on which calendar we use to count. Key numbers also line up here: 14 X 9 = 126, and 18 X 7 = 126, also. In fact, if—just for the sake of speculation—we count Sonnet 1 as May first (May Pole Day) and count the sonnets as one day each, we reach September 3rd of our calendar at Sonnet 126. Those 126 days (or 18 weeks) could correspond to the (outdoor, summer) theater season. I could not find, in the many biographies I've read, the dates for the summer theater season. I suspect that line 4 of Sonnet 18 refers to the shortness of that season and the theater lease: "And summer's lease hath all too short a date."

In the summer of 2001, on the 26th of August, my wife and I loved every minute of seeing *King Lear* performed in Shakespeare's New Globe Theater in London in light, intermittent rain. I quickly went to their web site for ordering tickets. They are working under almost the same weather conditions as Shakespeare's company, and their summer season runs from early May to September. So as an experiment I want to start the 126 solar Sonnets on May 1st of our Gregorian calendar and end them on September 3rd. We will get to the calendar problem and the Old calendar of Julius Caesar that Shakespeare was using later.

The **method of the naming code** is also used in support of establishing a timeline. Time is the great enemy of all these people, but time is also a river of stars they live under. It is as if the people named are players, and time is the backdrop for their scenes. The named principal people of the sonnets are the fish, but the ocean is time. They are the dear, endangered ones, and time is their habitat. There is one sonnet in particular which uses the doubled letters and sounds of the naming code to establish the midpoint of summer. **Sonnet #52** forms a **bridge** between the **name code** and the **time code.** It is like London Bridge over the Thames linking London to Southwark.

When we turn to Sonnet 52 and count the days from April 24th O. C. (our May 1st), we will reach **June 14th O. C.** (our June 24st) for that sonnet. Actually, I found the Solstice code first and counted back to Sonnet 1. Both the code and the lines will show this to be a **Summer Solstice** sonnet. Sonnet #52 is about that important instant in solar time, Summer Solstice, and all other solar feasts. When we do the count in the old, Julian calendar, a timetable in use in Shakespeare's day, then Sonnet #52 is on June 14th, and when we count back to Sonnet #1, we get April 24th, a day very close to Shakespeare's birthday! Perhaps Will is telling us that guess work about his birthday taking place on St. George's Day is not correct. Or perhaps he is simply looking back one day at the youth, H. W., who was "the only herald" at the St. George's Day Garter ceremony on April 23rd 1590.

There are **52** weeks in the year, so we have a reference to a key time number, seven: 7 X 52 = 364. Time words used include: "hour," "year," "time," and "instant." I believe that lines 4—8 (the second quatrain) describe in code the full year with its four "instants" of two equinoxes and two solstices:

"ThereFORE are **feasts SO SOL**emn and **SO** rare,	FOUR/SO/SOL/SO
Since, SeLdOm coming, in the long **year** set,	S/SLOw/**year**
Like **stones** of **worth** they thinly placed are,	**Stones/worth**
Or captain jewels in the **carcanet**."	Anagram of **Cancer**

The most "thinly placed" feasts in the necklace of "the long year" are the **four** solar feasts of equinox (vernal and autumnal) and solstice (summer and winter). These **four feasts** (which are important to farmers, pagans, and Christians) are placed like gems in a necklace around the sun's neck. Shakespeare uses the word "**carcanet**" for necklace for the rhyme and perhaps for the image of an "arc" and "net" of stars, the arcing net of the Zodiac as well as the odder sound of the word "carcass," or body of the year and of the lover. At Summer Solstice, the Sun is in the sign of **Cancer** the Crab, and "carcanet" is also an **anagram** for cancer. In books showing decorative clothing of the Elizabethan era, the French style *carcanet* comes in many shapes and was quite popular. Here, the youth is decked out like a solar hero wearing a necklace and a robe on the Summer Solstice. He reminds me of a heroic tenor in Mozart's *Magic Flute*. This solar sonnet is centered on the longest day (and its Moon mate, Sonnet 145, is set on the shortest night) of the year.

This pair of sonnets (52 & 145) could be compared and contrasted with Spencer's *Epithalamion* and the comedy *A Midsummer Night's Dream*, which may have been written before or rewritten for and performed at Henry's mother Mary's second marriage on May 2 but in 1594 to Thomas Heneage. The lead couple of that play—**Theseus** and **Hippolyta**—may be flattering portraits of the older host/groom and hostess/bride. Perhaps Shakespeare even delighted in some scrambled letter code found in their names:

THoma**S HE**n**E**age as
THESEuS and

Mar**Y** sout**HA**m**PTO**n as
HiPPOlYTA.

Such are the trivial coincidences of **word games** that people (including me) make too much of, celebrating a frivolity of happy luck at a wedding like the flowers and ribbons and music and play acting on a summer's evening. Perhaps even Henry's troubles with two Elizabeths (de Vere versus Vernon) are made light of in Lysander's fairy-dusted shift from Hermia, his true love, to Helena and back again, thanks to Puck's mistake and correction on the shortest night of the year. Of course, if **Bottom** portrays Shakespeare, he is as potent as the Roman Ass at weddings, and he gets to make love to Titania (perilously close to Britania) the Queen of the Fairies, suggesting the most outrageous identity fantasy of all. The timed parts about the four days of the Summer Sun and nights of the Moon in this early comedy may have helped Shakespeare organize his *Sonnets* into solar and lunar songs. Or maybe the Sonnets' solar/lunar split came first.

Were the *Sonnets* published in 1609 in the order that Shakespeare designed? Yes, I think the movements of both the Sun and the Moon help organize *Shakespeare's Sonnets* into his planned, countable sequence. His sonnets are like a mechanical, astronomical clock that includes Sun and Moon. They are also like a partial arc of Stonehenge with the gap between 51, the second horse riding sonnet (with its lunar night twin Sonnet 144), and **52** revealing Summer Solstice dawn. As one of my students pointed out, the word **"key"** is used in Sonnet 52, line 1: "**So** am I as the rich, whose blessed **key"**—so the dawn of Sonnet 52 may contain the **KEY to TIME**. And 52 lines up with 145 to represent the full 24 hours of the Solstice day and night. The *Sonnets* contain a partial (male), four month and three day, **solar calendar** and a smaller, internal (female) monthly (June for Juno) **lunar calendar** placed inside the arc of Summer. Seen in this way, the *Sonnets* can take their form from a medieval *Book of Days* or a contemporary *Farmer's Almanac*. This design is also repeated up on the "Heavens," the underside of the ceiling over the stage of the New Globe theater. Perhaps Will could have stood on stage at his Globe and looked up and seen painted both the Sun and the Moon as well. These great counters of Time dominate the sky, and Time is both the great enemy that the sonnets seek to defeat and the organizing flow of all our lives.

Time is best organized by breaking it into equal pieces. The pieces of time are given to us and to Shakespeare in a series of time numbers. If 1 sonnet equals one day, then 7 sonnets equal one week, and 2 times 7 equal a fortnight or 14 (a time word with reference to fourteen line sonnets), and 4 times seven equals one lunar month (28 nights—the dark lady cycle), and 22 weeks times 7 equal 154 days, which are actually 126 days and 28 nights. The **number seven** helps generate a lot of structure in the *Sonnets*. I believe that every group of 7 sonnets (at least for the first 77) represents a week, and #1 begins on a Monday, so that #7 is Sunday. If you study every 7th sonnet, you will find **key time words**. The days of the week start with the Moon day, and on the seventh day, in *Genesis*, the Creator rested on Sunday. Every 7th sonnet can be seen as a resting point, a Sabbath, where the consequences of the passage of time are reflected upon. After these eleven weeks—11 is a number associated with Hamnet's death—the series is interrupted by the Rival Poet series of nine sonnets, and a new time scale seems to begin. Life's experiences do not always line up with regular weeks.

Table 6. Every 7th Sonnet is a Sunday up through #77

1. Sonnet #7: the Sun's arc & passage across the sky from "Lo" to "Noon" to "low"
2. Sonnet #14: "astronomy" … "stars" … "date."
3. Sonnet #21: "sun and moon" … "April's first-born" … "gold candles"
4. Sonnet #28: "day and night" … "stars"
5. Sonnet # 35: "eclipses stain both moon and sun"
6. Sonnet #42: "lose both" … double cross
7. Sonnet # 49: "Against that time…" this phrase times three
8. Sonnet # 56: "Tomorrow" (twice) … "winter" … "summer's welcome"

9. Sonnet # 63: "hours" … "time's injurious hand" … "morn" to "night" and the phrase, "For such a time"
10. Sonnet #70: "wooed of time" … "young days"
11. Sonnet # 77: "dial" … "minutes" … "Time's thievish progress"

So, for the first eleven Sundays, at least, halfway through the 154-part sonnet sequence, time is a theme that comes up in multiples of climacteric seven. Does 11 X 14 = 154 have anything to do with these 11 Sunday sonnets? Does 11 introduce another important number, Hamnet's age at death? And do the weeks stop at double 7's or 77 or 11 X 7 for that numbered reason, like Hamnet's life? Sonnet #77, lines 7 & 8, state: "Thou by thy dial's shady stealth mayst know/ Time's thievish progress to eternity;" Sonnet #77 is a dedicatory sonnet, perhaps written for the inside title page of a gift, blank notebook from Will for Henry. Then, as said before, Sonnet #78 begins the Rival Poet sequence of nine poems (9 is the other climacteric number), and time changes its framework and may become, as Hamlet says, "Out of joint."

The numbers 7 and 9 were full of meaning for the Elizabethans. Her subjects celebrated Queen Elizabeth's 63rd year as her fortunate, double climacteric. For them, the number seven referred to the seven planetary gods and goddesses, the seven known "planets" (including the Sun and Moon) of their era. This number seemed to have "astronomical" connections to the days of the week: Monday (Moon), Tuesday (Tiw or Mars), Wednesday (Odin or Mercury), Thursday (Thor or Jupiter), Friday (Freya or Venus), Saturday (Saturn), and Sunday.

The oldest human calendar known is an elk bone with cuts in groups of seven on it. This may be the first attempt to count the phases and quarters of the Moon: 7 X 4. But for Shakespeare's contemporaries, this double "meaning" of **seven**—the days of the week and number of (known) planets—seemed liked magic. Shakespeare seems to be interrupting his sequence of orderly sevens with a group of nine sonnets. **Nine**, of course, refers to a different "magic" double number inherited from the ancients: the nine Muses and the nine numbers of mathematics (without zero). This nine is an appropriate number to use when conjuring up the rival poets for Henry's patronage and love. So, at 77, halfway through the 154, 9 interrupts 7, exactly 14 sonnets after Sonnet **63**, the mid point of 126, and the second half of the 126 sonnets to the youth (Shakespeare's double/ double climacteric number) leads up to 99 (9 X 11), a sonnet that has 15 lines and may contain an elegy to Lord Essex. So, at Sonnet 78, nine interrupts seven, and the numbers dance on until the super double climacteric at 126 = 9X 7 + 9 X 7. After that, the Moon takes over again for a four-week series of 4 X 7 = 28. And then, those 28 have a double "ending" of 9 X 17 = 153 and 14 X 11 = 154. Shakespeare uses key numbers to record how intricately time dances, and his design works like a series of wheels with inter-locking teeth. There is clockwork inside these *Sonnets*; Shakespeare works like a clock maker.

In addition to Sonnet 77, there are other key time sonnets embedded in the first 77: in particular, there are three other very important ones: **#19, #52, and #60.** Sonnet #19 establishes the ravenous and dangerous nature of time (and perhaps scheming old men against Henry). Sonnet #19 also puns on **hours** as the "whores" of time. It is a companion piece to #18, the first sonnet not only to promise immortality to the youth in poetry, but also, it is the first one to deliver it. Sonnet #52 ties two parts of the code together. Its number reflects the total number of weeks (or 7's) in a year. It is also, by repeated code letters and the number of days from the 24th of April (of the Old Julian Calendar) or May 1st (of the New Gregorian Calendar) found to be the **Summer Solstice Sonnet.**

The third and most famous Time Sonnet (#60) stands before the center of the 126-poem, solar sequence for the youth. It may be placed on June 29th of our calendar or the 22nd June of the old calendar—along with Sonnet 153—and may mark the end of the affair with the dark lady with Shakespeare's attempt to cure his disease by traveling to Bath for the waters. There at the seashore in Sonnet 60, he faces the great sea of Time. Sonnet #60 also introduces that magic time number from Babylon, which is also very useful in breaking time up into 60 pieces. The sonnet compares the waves of the sea to "our minutes" in lines 1 and 2, and 60 minutes make an hour. In addition, for us, 60

seconds also make one minute, so Time can now be collapsed in two sequences of 60 down to an "instant" (Shakespeare's word). The meter of these sonnets can tick along like the regular iambic pentameter in line 4: "In **se**quent **toil** all **for**ward **do** con**tend**." While the number of lines per sonnet is tied to twice times the week, the meter of the lines is tied to the 60 seconds that make each minute tick away. But the pendulum clock had not yet been invented, so maybe seconds are ticking for us but not for Shakespeare. Perhaps his ticking of instants came from the beat in music (and a metronome) or the stresses in his lines.

But how are the two key time numbers—**7 and 60**—related? The number seven comes from the days of the week and the old lunar calendar where 4 weeks of seven days equal one moon month. It was the Babylonians who first divided the hour into sixty minutes for their purposes in astronomy and math and the circle into 360 degrees. Mario Livio cites Ifrah, who argues that the Babylonians may have chosen a base 60 counting system to compromise the mix of their two immigrant cultures: a 5 base math culture with a 12 base culture (21).

Well, if each of *Shakespeare's Sonnets* is one day, then that unit can be thought of as 1/7th of a lunar week, and 24 hours times 60 minutes adds up to the same time. So, I can make a little equation: 1/7 = 60 X 24. I think it's odd that Sonnet #24, with twenty-four hours in a day, an obvious opportunity to discuss time, is not a major time sonnet, nor does it fall on a Sunday. Instead, its themes are geometric painting and perspective, with the sun gazing into Shakespeare's "shop" through the windows of his eyes. Perhaps Sonnet 24 contrasts 12 hours of light for the eyes to 12 hours of darkness for the heart. But two key time sonnets—#52 and # 60—express and link up two kinds of chronological numeral systems. And all the sonnets use a range of differing scales of time. In sonnets 1 through 17, each sonnet stands for **one year** in the youth's short life. But each sonnet also becomes **one summer day** with the comparison stated in Sonnet #18. Finally, a sonnet can be read in about **one minute**, and five musical beats per line times 14 lines equal 70 ticks, instants for Shakespeare or seconds for us. The sonnet can be said to be about a minute-long, little song. *Shakespeare's Sonnets* may contain Shakespeare's very mathematical number theory of the relativity of time.

There is also a sequence of key numbers with extra meanings in the sonnets, and it goes like this: 1, 2, 3, 4, 4.5, 5, 6, 7, 8, **9**, 10, **11, 14,** 17, 18, 22, **28,** 33, 52, 60, 63, 77, 99, 126, 128, 153, and 154. This is Shakespeare's sequence. This is not the sequence of numbers called "Fibonacci sequence" after their 13th century discoverer (Livio 101). (I wish it were. But what an odd "proof" of Shakespeare's plan and math knowledge that would be!) Interestingly, in Sonnet # 5, there is a pun in line 10 on the Greek word **penta** for five:

"A liquid prisoner **pent** in walls of glass,"

and Shakespeare is talking about rose water perfume that survives after the rose dies just as the youth's "substance" could live on in his children. I am looking at a graphic illustration of the Tudor Rose, a five-petal rose with a five-sided red rose on the outside and a five-petal white rose at its center (Kerr 39). It looks a lot like the all-important Pythagorean **pentagon with a pentagram** inside it (and another set of pentagon and pentagram nested inside them), which the mystical Greek followers of Pythagoras and Italian Renaissance mathematicians used to generate the "Golden Ratio" and the irrational number *phi* (Livio 34).

But instead of the Fibonacci sequence, Shakespeare uses a **personal** set of code numbers, neither mystical nor mathematical. I think this series is as revealing as the Fibonacci series would be, but it takes playfulness and awareness of the usefulness of **numbers as ciphers**. Shakespeare does show awareness of Pythagorean number associations. Like the obviously chauvinist Pythagoreans, in the *Sonnets*, he mostly associates **odd** numbers with male, light, and good attributes and **even** numbers with female, dark, and evil attributes. In Act V, Scene 1 of the *Merry Wives of Windsor*, Falstaff says, "They say there is divinity in **odd numbers**, either in nativity, chance or death" (Livio 31). In the Sonnets, three odd numbers 9, 11, and 17 stand for three possible males (The Rival, his son Hamnet, and Henry), and the dark lady is the even number 28, but Shakespeare shifts gender attributes and gives himself a "feminine," **even** number designation: the poetically important 14. So he is not a strict, sexist Pythagorean.

Three of his personal code numbers seem to have at least three meanings with at least triple generative powers:

14: WILL
1) 14 lines per sonnet
2) 14 sonnets with the word "name" in 17 lines
3) 14 X 11 = 154

17: HENRY
1) 1—17 are the first group written for one occasion
2) 17 lines containing the word "name" in 14 sonnets
3) 17 X 9 = 153

& 11: HAMNET
1) According to Schiller, "Eleven is the sin. Eleven transgresses the Ten Commandments" (qtd. by Livio 104).This is "an opinion that dates back to medieval times" (104). But Shakespeare associates 11 with the age of his son at his death on August 11, 1596.
2) 11 generates a series of sonnets up to #77, eleven weeks, up to the Rival Poet series, a new series of 9 sonnets.
3) In at least two sonnets, eleven reveals an elegy for Hamnet in quatrain 3 of Sonnet 33 and for Lord Essex also in quatrain 3 of Sonnet 99.

So, 14, 17, and 11 can be said to hold triple meanings or be **triangular**. Is Shakespeare trying to work autobiographical content into a relationship with a shadowy double design of numerical or geometric content? Seventeen is a number associated with Henry; fourteen is a number closely associated with Will and the sonnet form. Is Shakespeare doing a kind of formal, poetic geometry as the inventor of the sestina, the French mathematician Arnaut Daniel (c. 1190), did by making the sestina's sequence of 6 repeated words form two triangles into a Star of David or Solomon's Seal? (It is said that Arnaut invented the sestina to impress a young lady, but we don't know if it worked.)

I even wondered if the magic numbers of the **sestina—6, 36, 3, and 39**—reveal a sestina embedded in these sonnets. Just the fact that both Petrarch and Sidney wrote sestinas started me wondering. In 1590 and again in 1593, a double sestina titled "Yee Gote-heard Gods" by Sidney was published in the *Old Arcadia* by Sidney's sister, the Countess of Pembrooke. Suddenly, I remembered that in the first part of the sonnets to the youth, **only sonnets #36 and #39** have **"name"** in them. They also share **six** rhyme words: "me," "thee," "one," "alone," "twain," and "remain." I also wondered if the run of six sonnets—34, 35, 36, 37, 38, and 39—all about the "first separation"—held an internal **sestina.**

I really thought I was on to something. I had two sestets with 6 rhyme words in different order, but the problem is that Arnaut Daniel's formula for the order of repeating words is very specific. If we give numbers to the 6 rhyme words as they appear in Sonnet #36, they would line up like this: 1. twain, 2. one, 3. remain, 4. alone, 5. thee, 6. me. If Sonnet 39 were to follow Daniel's strict order, they would next line up thus: **615243.** Instead, they line up this way: 6. me, 5. thee, 2. one, 4. alone, 1. twain, and 3. remain. So close, but no cigar!

> **652413 is not**
> **615243**—

the outside numbers match, but the one has jumped over the **524.** Then Sonnet 37 has **5 & 6**; Sonnet 38 has **6 & 5**; Sonnet 40 has **none**; Sonnet 41 has **5 & 6** again; and Sonnet 42 has **5612 & 4.** So I have something which is "nothing." In some codes, agents wrote in **"nulls,"** inserted to mean nothing, designed to mislead.

I felt as if a hint of a sestina design led me down a dark passage in this maze until it turned into a **dead end** and left me feeling a **wall.** Was that part of Will's plan? There is enough of a pattern there to make me ask, but I do not know. Perhaps some numbers I have not used yet will generate an internal **sestina**, but I cannot find the next clue now. If any form that can generate two triangles as the sestina can—in the form of **the six-pointed Solomon's Seal**—is embedded in the sonnets, it could be a diagram with real, autobiographical meaning. The triangle pointing up was seen as male, and the triangle pointing down was seen as female. There are two triangles embedded in the *Sonnets:* the Poet/youth/lady triangle and the poet/youth/rival poet triangle. So

you can see why I worked hard to find an **embedded sestina**, but I failed.

In addition, when Sidney wrote *Old Arcadia* in 1581 and dedicated it to his sister, he constructed a very hard-to-read, rather funky prose romance about the land of the pastoral tradition in ancient Greece. It is written in a form called a "macaronic narrative." That is, it is a prose narrative with poems embedded in it. In fact, Sidney embedded 78 experimental poems in *Old Arcadia.* "Ye Gote-heard Gods," a 75 line double sestina and a debate between two shepherds about the beautiful shepherdess Urania, is just one of those poems. (For one more family connection to Philip Sidney and English poetry, Lady Mary Wroth, née Sidney, called her 1621 sonnet sequence *Urania.*) Should those 78 poems by Sidney be seen as 78 etudes that Shakespeare used to construct many of his sonnets and parts of the design of the whole sequence?

Given twenty years or more to write and imitate and parody and revise and design and come up with new correspondences, what did Shakespeare put into these Sonnets? I have great faith in Will's ability to play with the design and make it more intricate perhaps than any one of his plays. As we know, from the literal tons of volumes written by all of us commentators, that's quite a claim. I guess it's a funny variation of the joke about 50 chimpanzees with typewriters given infinite time to write. Give Shakespeare twenty years to revise, and what did he produce?

Well, in the Sonnets, the numbers help us just as dimensions on a drawing help us understand a cathedral. We can start with the "lucky" number 7 that links the solar calendar (52 weeks) to the lunar month and calendar (4 weeks) to the form of the sonnets (2 X 7 = 14 lines). Twenty-eight Sonnets make 4 weeks, and 126 Sonnets make 18 weeks. The more the numbers fit a coherent design that adds meaning and beautiful geometry, the stronger is the evidence that **these sonnets are arrayed in Shakespeare's order and that all of them count.** Since no notes or drafts have survived, we have only the structure without the plans, and I think the structure is lovely and inviting and full of meaning and exciting to visit.

In the *Sonnets* we have the almanac of Will's greatest loves. Will's love for Henry lasts a longer time (perhaps four and a half times—half of nine—or 126 divided by 28) and has a sunny, golden influence on his great career as a dramatist. Will's love for Aemilia lasts much less time, waxes and wanes like the Moon, begins in the passionate darkness of self-deception and ends in burning love, with the fever of venereal disease his final memory and pain. The 26th dark lady Sonnet ends with the sad pun on "lie." The 28th lunar poem, like a sliver of Cupid's bow in the sky, ends the whole sequence with the more powerful healing word "love," but it does not heal Will. Line 14 of Sonnet 154 ends with an ABBA chiasmus but without an end of time or love:

"Love's fire heats **water, water** cools not **love."**

And when we realize that Sonnet 40 (June 9th) and Sonnet 133 might be seen as contemporaneous (and W. H. Auden agrees), both written when Will **first admits in writing,** in the separate but joined solar and lunar sequences, that Henry and Aemilia were having an affair, then the smaller lunar cycle could be placed inside the larger solar time line, like one Moon "month" starting perhaps on June 3rd with 40 and 133 side by side like day and night. (This is not the Synodic month of astronomy that lasts for an average of 29.530569 days and goes from New Moon to New Moon. This is Shakespeare's lunar month that starts in the dark of the Moon and ends with a sliver of Cupid's bow 28 sonnet days and nights later.)

The Summer months surround the lunar June. The twenty-eight days of the Moon are caught in the embrace of a Solar Summer. We can draw an arc with a compass and mark two segments on it. (See Figure 3, page 116.) Remember, Time is the great enemy entity to be defeated by the sonnets. If any of these people are to be remembered, says the poet, it will be because they are named in these Sonnets. But, 400 years later, few can agree on who is named! Is it the code that finally gives the names of the people Will wanted to save from Time? Would Shakespeare be amazed to find out how much we disagree? Did he think his code of names and time was almost as obvious as Sidney's open secrets?

Then there are the problems everyone has with trying to get the narrative design of *Shakespeare's Sonnets* exactly right. But it's not a totally logical, modern narrative; it's a sonnet sequence. It shares some of the difficulties and strengths with the modern mosaic novel or essay, where the author writes a passage almost as well-written as a prose poem and then puts three little stars and moves on to the next piece of the mosaic. This narrative form was used wonderfully by two 20th century poets: Rilke in his *Notebooks of Malte* and by Pasternak in his *Dr. Zhivago*. But a Renaissance sonnet sequence is a narrative genre in its own right.

There are many ways to try to organize our thoughts about the design of the Sonnets, but many have found that it's too difficult to be exact. Let's use fuzzy logic instead.

Fuzzy is good enough if it helps us see overall patterns. For example, what if we try to see it as if it were Will's favorite narrative form, a play?

Remember, most of us use fuzzy logic in the theater to grok what Shakespeare is up to. We never get "it all." We have to experience the flow and go from what we understand to what we add from each performance. So I want to consider the Sonnets as a play. Let's give it act and scene numbers. Let's remember that such numbers were added to Shakespeare's plays after he finished them. Let's call it:

"THE HISTORICAL COMEDY OF *SHAKESPEARE'S SONNETS.*"

Table 7. The Acts and Scenes of the *Sonnets*

Prologue:	**Sonnet 1**	**24 April**
Act 1:	**Youth's Birthday**	**25 April—9 May**
	Sonnets 2—17	
Act 2, Scene 1:	**Our Love Begins**	**10 May—1 June**
	Sonnets 18—39	
	Moon Subplot: I love the lady!	
	Sonnets 127—132	**27 May—1 June**
Act 2, Scene 2:	**Our Love Triangle**	**2 June—23 June**
	Sonnets 40—61	
	Moon Subplot: we both love the lady!	
	Sonnets 133—152 & 153 & 154—the end	
Act 3, Scene 1:	**Loneliness & Rivalries**	**24 June—9 July**
	Sonnets 62—77	
Act 3, Scene 2:	**Rivals become Rival**	**10 July—18 July**
	Sonnets 78—86: death of main rival	
Act 4, Scene 1:	**Our Separations**	**19 July—25 July**
	Sonnets 87—93	
Act 4, Scene 2:	**New Century**	**26 July—31 July**
	Your arrest & death of Essex	
	Sonnets 94—99	

Act 5, Scene 1:	Youth in Tower	1 Aug—7 August
	Sonnets 100—106	
Act 5, Scene 2:	New Regime/Reunion	8 Aug—14 August
	Sonnets 107—113	
Act 5, Scene 3:	Continued Friendship	15 Aug—26 August
	Sonnets 114—125	
Epilogue:	Sonnet 126	27 August

I hope that fuzzy logic version is helpful. Of course, it's just analogical thinking from one genre to another. But someone could write an adaptation, a play or a film script based on this scenic, narrative framework and call it: *SHAKESPEARE IN LOVE II: HIS OWN VERSION.* (When I teach early or middle Shakespeare in ten weeks, I assign the Sonnets in the following bunches: 1—17, 18—33, 34—61, 62—77, 78—86, 87—99, 100—116, 117—126, 127—141, and 142—154.) But we should not expect Shakespeare to write a play-like, autobiographical sonnet sequence with a totally logical or linear chronology.

Perhaps the nearest models for writing his personal history might be his history plays. In them, according to John Julius Norwich, Shakespeare used time compression and scenic conflation and had "a cavalier approach to chronology" (357). Shakespeare added and subtracted characters, made up speeches and scenes, and always tried to insert scenes that created contrasting values—all this was in the service of heightened drama and more powerful theater. Just look at how bent out of shape those people get who are trying to reconsider *Richard III*. That rascal Shakespeare—he adds old Queen Margaret to heighten the female versus male tensions in his play. Margaret was in exile in France when the play begins and dies while she is still haunting Richard in Shakespeare's play. So why wouldn't Shakespeare feel free to dramatize his own life? Part of the experience of reading this sonnet sequence in order is to understand the spaces between sonnets and how to follow the shifts. No one should be surprised that Shakespeare used a variety of dramatic values to increase suspense and heighten the tensions he had experienced.

Wherever one tries to step in the meadows and groves of Shakespeare studies, it is very rare to find new, unclaimed territory. After I came up with my "Sonnets as a play" idea, I found that Oscar Wilde had proposed this first in 1889. He saw the *Sonnets* as a four-act tragedy and divided them up this way:

Table 8: Oscar Wilde's view—the Sonnets as a Play

Act 1:	Sonnets 1—32
Act 2:	Sonnets 33—52 & 61 Sonnets 127—152
Act 3:	Sonnets 53—60 & 62—99
Act 4:	Sonnets 100—152

Source of Data: Wilde 1191

108

I like how some of this, including the "out of sequence" placement of the dark lady sonnets, lines up with my scheme. I hope both of these "play" outlines help others in trying to see a design.

So much time has passed, and only the sonnets and the author Will are "immortal." Has all that time blocked us from ever reading these sonnets as a knowledgeable 1609 reader who knew Shakespeare might? Maybe that "knowledgeable reader" is a myth. Well, Ben Jonson or Henry Wriothesley would do for me: I wonder what they thought. We have to do the best we can. No matter what the odds, any study of *Shakespeare's Sonnets* must try to guide readers into and out of his labyrinth of Time where the names may be hidden.

I think it's a mistake to treat this sonnet sequence like a modern novel with a logical chronology. It may be that *Shakespeare's Sonnets* can be best understood as a series of segments (or gallery walls with each sonnet a word painting in a set). Sonnets 40, 41, and 42—all about the sexual triangle— form a neat set of three. But I also place them in a set of eight sonnets, as if they were three panels in a complex triptych.

(See Appendix D on page 173.)

Chapter 18   The Maze of Time
& the Shape of the Globe Theater

> "In this strange **labyrinth** how shall I turn?"
>   * * *
> "Yet that which most my troubled sense doth move
> Is to leave all, and take the **thread of love**."
>   Sonnet 77, lines 1 & 13—14, from the Crown of Sonnets,
>   *Urania* by Mary Wroth (1621)

For a moment, let's take the image of time as a labyrinth seriously. Is it possible that Shakespeare designed the *Sonnets* like a maze? In his time, both village-green, turf "labyrinths" and private estate, hedge "labyrinths" were popular. But Robert Field differentiates labyrinths from mazes, a more recent distinction:

> ... the word **'labyrinth'** should only be applied to two designs ...the 'Classical Labyrinth' and the 'Medieval Christian Labyrinth'.... A labyrinth ... [has] only one pathway to the middle and ... no choices are offered. Such designs are called ... **'unicursive'**.... The word **'maze'** is used where at various points you are given a choice of pathways. In such designs, it is possible to get lost.... Such designs are called ... **'multicursive.'** (3)

So the Minotaur of Crete was kept in a **maze**, not a labyrinth. What does it feel like inside the *Sonnets?* Well, there is one path to follow. That path has straight parts as in the first seventeen sonnets, but at Sonnet 18, the reader takes a turn. Sonnets 18 and 19 are a pair. Then we take another turn: Sonnets 20 and 21 form a pair, and so on. Many have tried to read the *Sonnets* in a **linear** way, as a "unicursive labyrinth." The other way to read them is to notice all the choices Shakespeare builds for exploration of themes. When you read the Sonnets **thematically** or look at separated sonnets as **pairs**, the overall design feels more like a "multicursive maze" in a tall hedge, where you can make wrong turns and where you can't see the center.

Sir Thomas Wyatt, one of Shakespeare's favorite poets, used the maze as "an image of the lover's confusion" (Schmidgall 91). Wyatt writes of his "long error in a blind maze chained" (qtd. in Schmidgall 91). In a ballade, Wyatt exclaims, "Alas, I tread an endless maze" (91). Wyatt and other Renaissance writers also used the maze as an image for the court (175). In Sonnet #58, Shakespeare calls himself his patron's love "slave," and like an angry suitor, he shows, in lines 13 and 14, his frustration at being stuck waiting for the young lord to get around to seeing him:

"I am to wait, though waiting be so hell,
Not to blame your pleasure be it ill or well."

Gary Schmidgall quite rightly points out that in the poet/patron relationship, there can never be "equality." He points out that

> Time weighs heavily in the Young Man sonnets. It is no coincidence that **the word *time* occurs about seventy times** in them and **not once** in the Dark Lady sonnets.
> [My emphasis]

So, being stuck in the maze of the sonnets is supposed to feel frustrating. The music is complex, like sweet melody and dissonant counterpoint. But every musical composition or maze has a design. If only the reader could get a bird's eye view, the overall design might be seen. If only I were smarter or could fly higher like Shakespeare's lark! But I cannot see all of his design. I enter 126 solar sonnets first, and then I enter 28 lunar sonnets. I feel the earlier introduction of the dark lady's affair with the youth as an inserted triangle, Sonnets 34—61, an aside I can get lost in.

I had heard early rumors of the youth's lack of good faith. I feel Shakespeare's despair **twice (at the same time):** once in Sonnet #40 for betrayal by the youth and again in Sonnet #133 for betrayal by the lady.

In Sonnet #40, Will cries, "Take all my loves, my love, yea take them all" (line 1), and in Sonnet #133, he cries, "Of him, myself, and thee, I am forsaken,/ A torment thrice threefold thus to be crossed" (lines 7 & 8). So he doesn't feel twice the pain. He feels three times three or **nine** times the pain. And he doesn't feel double-crossed; he feels **triple-crossed**, forsaken even by himself. Each of the three relationships—to the youth, the lady, and himself—is multiplied by three. We experience a complex, kaleidoscopic vision when we take on his point of view. A triangle of internal mirrors bounces each image nine ways. This may make clear seeing in Time's maze impossible or very difficult.

In the youth's solar series, Shakespeare finally gets free of the youth's betrayal and into clear air; in the dark lady series, he does not. But the end of the sequence is not an exit from the maze. As we finish Sonnet # 154, we feel incomplete. Time bends back from the end of the lunar month to just before mid-point in the solar summer. Time really runs from Sonnet 154 back to #62 and then on until Sonnet 126. So the end of time happens before the end of the sequence. Time is a serpent with a loop and a double back and a tail.

I see the Rival Poet series as another inserted triangle. I get lost at first because there is more than one rival. But the series finally narrows to one main, more dangerous rival. And the series ends in the past tense as if the rival were dead and only his last written work was the ghost of a threat in a dark hallway. I am trying to "envision" Shakespeare's design.

Do the two triangles of the youth and the lady intersect in the maze like a **Solomon's Seal**? Or do the two triangles of lady and rival share one straight line from Will to Henry and form a **diamond**? The geometry of this maze includes straight lines, turns, pairs, opposites, parallel corridors, three interior triangles, an **end** that is not an **exit**, and an **exit** that is not an **end**. I am still trying to develop more ideas about the internal parts of this maze. But typical of any maze, the design does not reveal itself while you are lost inside it. Only a bird's eye view, a garden plan would reveal all, so I dreamed one up the best one I could envision. (See Figure 2, next page.)

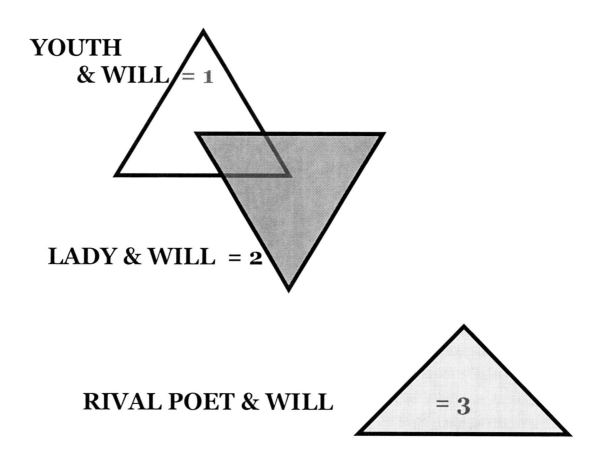

YOUTH & WILL = 1

LADY & WILL = 2

RIVAL POET & WILL = 3

Figure 2: Bird's Eye View of Maze
in Shakespeare's Sonnets

Note 3 triangles from prior page embedded in the Maze of Time

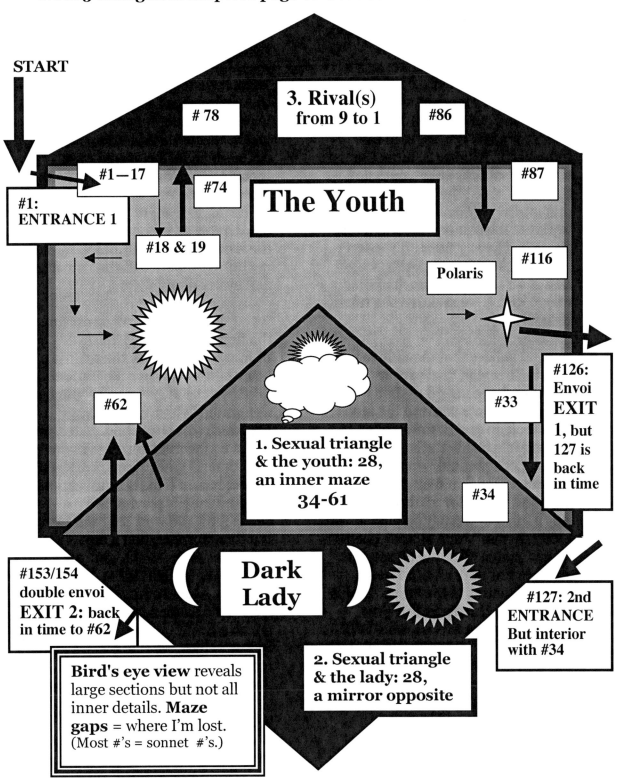

START

78

**3. Rival(s)
from 9 to 1**

#86

#1—17

#74

#87

#1:
ENTRANCE 1

The Youth

#18 & 19

Polaris

#116

#62

#33

#126:
Envoi
EXIT
1, but
127 is
back
in time

**1. Sexual triangle
& the youth: 28,
an inner maze
34-61**

#34

#153/154
double envoi
EXIT 2: back
in time to #62

Dark
Lady

#127: 2nd
ENTRANCE
But interior
with #34

Bird's eye view reveals
large sections but not all
inner details. **Maze
gaps** = where I'm lost.
(Most #'s = sonnet #'s.)

**2. Sexual triangle
& the lady: 28,
a mirror opposite**

This maze design seems like a draft to me. It helped me to understand more when I made it, but I also clearly see where I am lost. The problem of trying to represent the *Sonnets* with a garden maze is that this maze of time is also taking place in the sky. This sequence is a sophisticated maze of time. It is a 126-day summer with 28 nights represented in tandem with 28 days in May and June or just June in the New Calendar. We can read the sequence in a linear fashion; that lets us read about the solar youth and then read about the lunar lady, but that is also very confusing. And that is part of the confusion built in and generated by any maze. If we don't coordinate days with nights, we get lost. If we don't keep track of time, we get lost. If we make wrong turns, we get lost.

I believe that the only real Ariadne's thread Shakespeare provides is the thread of time we can follow under the sun and the moon. Let's look up and fit the smaller Lunar cycle inside the large Solar series. Let's pretend we can see the Moon and the Sun racing across the days and nights for 28 days. The lady's lunar cycle may be named with a silly rhyme: "June Moon." I believe we can match all of the 28 sonnets about her or under her influence with the phases of the Moon. In this astronomy, **Henry is the Sun, Aemilia is the Moon, and Will is the Earth** (or later, the Globe). If we do not look up at the sky to follow the Sun/days and Moon/nights, we will get seriously lost, and then "Devouring Time," like that fabled monster, the Minotaur, will eat us

alive, like the annual sacrifice of boy and girl virgins from Athens.

As in any encoded document, the names, the words, the letters, the dates, and the numbers all have to work together and be decoded together for us to get the full meaning of the message. Perhaps it is the code that provides the thread of Ariadne that keeps us oriented inside the maze. It is so easy to get lost in the *Sonnets!* Perhaps it is the code—in all its forms and even incomplete as my findings are—that gives us the string of clues to keep us on track. As readers we walk, picking up on puns as echoes, bits of logic, hints of embedded autobiographical meaning, snippets of word music, and cycles of numbers.

For example, we know that the first sonnet about music is numbered 8 because the scale is an octave. In it, we hear the tonic chord based on the 1st, 3rd, and 5th pitches as a sound "picture" of a happy husband, wife, and child. Later, we find a connection and clue in the only other sonnet about music #128. It, too, has an 8 in its number, and the dark lady is playing the clavichord. 128 = 12 & 8, and twelve is a time number, half a day. This may refer to the night, and 128 - 100 = 28. Twenty-eight is the Moon number. As one of my students, who is a music major reminded me, there are also twelve keys in every octave. By such clues, we find our way in this maze and wonder where we are. Sometimes I feel a bit like the clown or the butler following Ariel's music through a dark woods.

114

Overhead, there are the Sun and the Moon. It helps if we can look up and see them in the sky over the maze. The solar and lunar cycles seem to interlock something like Table 9 in our contemporary Gregorian calendar (below). Here is a list of **solar sonnets, June dates, other dates**, and **lunar sonnets** to fit with **days and nights and the phases of the Moon:**

Table 9: Solar & Lunar Sonnets: Our Gregorian Calendar (N.C.)

SOLAR MONTHS	Sonnet # Sun Cycle	LUNAR MONTH & DATES	Sonnet # Subject Moon Cycle		Phase of MOON
MAY	Son. 1	May 1	Sun Begins Summer		
JUNE	Son. 34	June 3	Son. 127	Dark Lady	Dark/New
JUNE	Son. 35	June 4	Son. 128	Virginal	Waxing Cres.
JUNE	Son. 40	June 9	Son. 133	Triangle	Half
JUNE	Son. 48	June 17	Son. 141	Heart as fool	FULL
SOLSTICE	Son. 52	June 21	Son. 145	And Hate-away	Waning Gib.
JUNE	Son. 58	June 27	Son. 151	Name spelled	Waning Cres.
JUNE	Son. 61	June 30	Son. 154	Cupid's Brand	Thin Bow/ Old Moon
JULY	Son. 63	July 2	Sun is 1/2 way to 126		
AUGUST	Son. 93	Aug. 1	Eve's apple grows		
AUGUST	Son. 116	Aug. 24	North Star		
SEPT.	Son. 126	Sept. 3	Sun Ends Summer		

Table 9 shows how to fit the 28 solar sonnets with all 28 dark lady lunar sonnets.

I also teach Technical Communications. My students and I know that there are times when simple sentences and paragraphs fail to communicate. That's when we have to reach for a chart or graphic to try to represent the true complexity of our discovered data. I have had to do that often in this study. Take a while to study Table 9. If the calendar of the *Sonnets* contains at least that much interlocked information, no wonder we can get lost! (Later, we will have to worry about conversion to Shakespeare's old, Julian calendar that adjusts Sonnet 1 to April 24th, Summer Solstice Sonnets 52 and 145 to June 14th, and Sonnet 126 to August 27th.) I have also designed a maze of the heavens, a diagram that fits Table 9 and calibrates the Sun with the Moon. (See Figure 3, next page.) This figure will help you set the twin sonnets 40 and 133 at the **half moon** & see all of **June.**

Figure 3: Calibrating the Sun & Moon
in *Shakespeare's Sonnets*
in our Gregorian calendar
Solstice: June 21
(June 14 in Old Calendar)
To convert: subtract 7

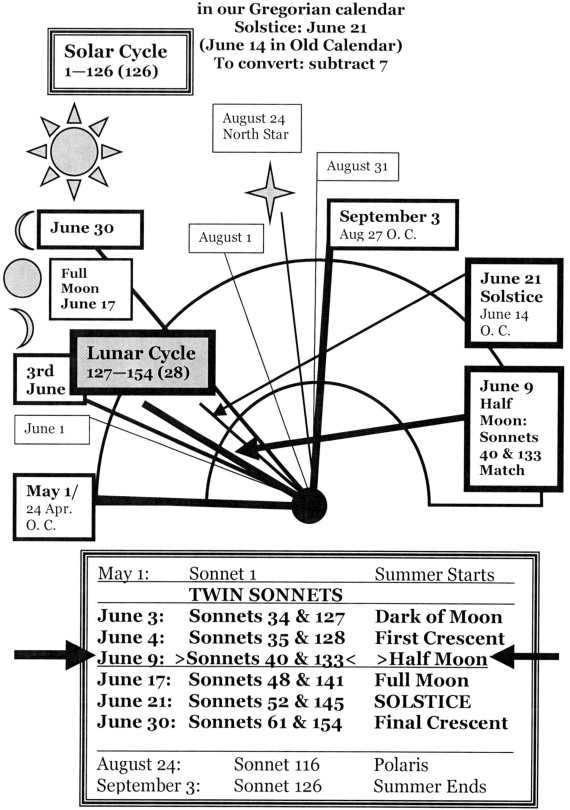

May 1:	Sonnet 1	Summer Starts
	TWIN SONNETS	
June 3:	Sonnets 34 & 127	Dark of Moon
June 4:	Sonnets 35 & 128	First Crescent
June 9:	>Sonnets 40 & 133<	>Half Moon
June 17:	Sonnets 48 & 141	Full Moon
June 21:	Sonnets 52 & 145	SOLSTICE
June 30:	Sonnets 61 & 154	Final Crescent
August 24:	Sonnet 116	Polaris
September 3:	Sonnet 126	Summer Ends

116

Shakespeare is not the only poet of his time to set up a calendar in his sonnets. Kenneth J. Larsen discovered a calendar in Spencer's *Amoretti.*

The eighty-nine sonnets of the *Amoretti,* as numbered in the 1595 octavo edition, were written to correspond with consecutive dates, beginning on Wednesday 23 January 1594 and running, with one interval, through to Friday 17 May 1594: they correspond with the daily and sequential order of scriptural readings that are prescribed for those dates by the liturgical calendar of the Church of England (qtd. in Weatherby 127).

Larsen's thesis was based on, "Dunlap's remarkable discovery (in 1969—70) ... Dunlap claimed liturgical status only for sonnets 22 through 68, which appear to correspond to the days of Lent in 1594" (127). A brief summation of Dunlap's claims would look like this:

Table 10. Calendar Days and Spencer's Sonnets		
Sonnet 22	"penitential"	Ash Wednesday
Sonnet 62	March 25, 1594	New Year's Day, Feast of the Annunciation
Sonnet 68	"celebratory"	Easter

(Data from Dunlap, qtd. in Weatherby)

So, in 1595, Shakespeare may have been inspired by the Christian poet Spencer to design his sonnet sequence with a different kind of built-in, secular calendar.

Later, I began to wonder if there is another, underlying image of Time in the *Sonnets,* not a maze at all but drawn from a famous piece of Elizabethan architecture. What if the sense of Time were both regular and irregular? What if Time runs regularly in weeks of seven sonnets up to a point and then becomes "out of joint" or irregular? It looks to me as if Sonnets **1—77 are regular solar time** and as if Sonnets **127—154 are regular lunar time.** If so, then we are looking at 11 weeks of solar time and 4 weeks of lunar time for a total of **15 regular time units of seven.** Then, if we try to break Sonnets **78—126** into regular units, we fail. Sonnets **78—86,** a group of **nine** and the rival poet sonnets, bring in a new sense of time. If Sonnet 86 announces the death of Marlowe in the past tense, and if it tries to encompass all that happened from 1593 (Marlowe's murder) to 1598 (the twin publication of the unfinished, original "Hero and Leander" and the marred, finished version by Chapman), then suddenly, "time is out of joint," as Hamlet discovers when he thinks about his father's murder and his promise to take revenge.

I have broken Sonnets 78—126 into five irregular units, and I have come up with **an interesting 5-part design:**

---

1. **Sonnets 78—86**   The Rival Poet(s) sequence, are **nine**.
2. **Sonnets 87—99**   Separation and Essex's death, are **thirteen**.
3. **Sonnets 100—106**   The Muse in Tower for three years are **seven**.
4. **Sonnets 107—116**   Regime change & reunion, are **nine** again.
5. & **Sonnets 117—126**   True minds and the rest of time are **eleven**.

Thus, we have the two climacteric numbers: **7 once** and **9 twice.** We have Hamnet's unlucky **number eleven once.** And we have the most unlucky number of all—**thirteen— once.** These five sections of irregular time add on to the fifteen regular sections and make **a total of 20 units of time.** Does the number twenty correspond to anything important? Until 1987, there was no consensus about how many sides the Globe Theater had. But in that year, thanks to archaeologists, 162 degrees (almost half) of the Globe's foundation were found under paving stones in a parking lot by an apartment complex only a short distance from the foundation of the Rose Theater. From extrapolation, it was discovered that the Globe was a **twenty-side structure** (Gurr 18). So I wondered, could it be that the structure of Time in the Sonnets was 20-sided like the Globe? Then the 15 regular segments would correspond to those architectural modules that made up the regular, three-tiered galleries around the stage. Could the five irregular units—**9. 13. 7, 9, &** **11**—correspond to major parts of the stage and the roofed house above it?

After I drew the following Figure 4, I convinced myself that the structure of Time in the *Sonnets* may be based on the architecture of the Globe. This may be my most far-fetched claim to date. But I imagine Will standing in the bare bones, oak-beamed structure of the Globe in the Winter or early Spring of 1599 and turning himself around to get a 360-degree view of the frame work of his company's new theater. Shakespeare might then have had a telescoped view of Time. In Sonnet 112.4, the youth and the Globe are both referred to as "my all-the-world." Of course, this world can also be blown up into the universe and/or all Time.

So I see an architectural plan for Time in the *Sonnets* shaping itself to the Theater. The 15 modular units that make up the three tiers for the higher paying audiences are the regular pieces of time as counted off by the Moon in 4 quarters of 7 nights each every 28 days. I see Will Shakespeare standing there, at the center drain on the groundling's floor, turning like a planet to view the proportions of the two 9 unit **columns** that hold up the roof over the stage. The three cross pieces of the **stage**, the **heavens**, and the **base** of the house roof triangle then seem to me to become **13 units, 11 units, and 7 units.** Perhaps Will had an architect's plan before him on a table set on the floor of crushed ashes and hazelnut shells. Perhaps, like the ultimate groundling, he saw that Time might be structured in the Sonnets like the wonderful, surrounding, open-topped cylinder of their new playhouse.

The youth and lady betraying him together (1592?), Marlowe's murder (1593), and Hamnet's death (1596) were the three rude shocks in his life before 1599. All three events could have knocked the regular passage of linked lunar and solar time out of order. As he stood watching the new stage front go up, Will was watching an irregular architectural order (not constructed in standard modules) take shape. This was the custom-designed, business center of a theater, not like the regular Renaissance inn with a courtyard. Of course, the workmen trying to get the joinery of the beams to fit, so they could drive home the oak pegs, would have taken a lot of time. If this gave Will an idea for the structure of the last 49 Sonnets and how time would change in the *Sonnets*, "time out of joint" could look like Figure 4 (next page):

Figure 4.
The Architecture of Time in the *Sonnets* & the Shape of the Globe Theater Stage Front

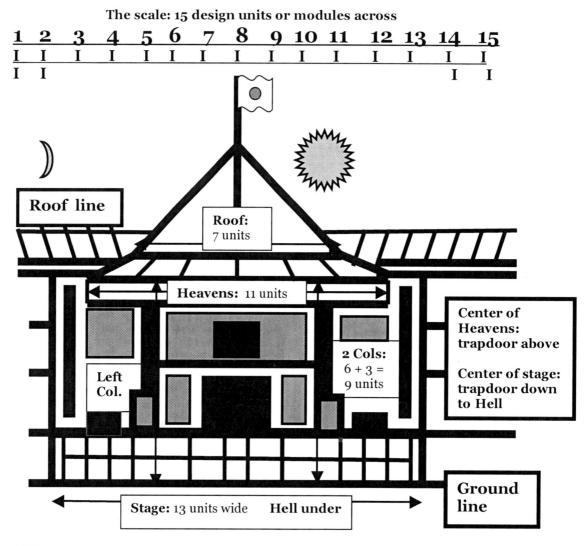

The scale: 15 design units or modules across

1 2   3   4   5   6   7   8   9 10 11   12 13 14   15
I I I   I   I   I   I   I   I   I   I   I   I   I   I
I I   I   I

Roof line

Roof: 7 units

Heavens: 11 units

Center of Heavens: trapdoor above

Center of stage: trapdoor down to Hell

Left Col.

2 Cols: 6 + 3 = 9 units

Stage: 13 units wide   Hell under

Ground line

TIME OUT OF JOINT: 5 irregular lengths of narrative time
<u>Sonnets 78—126 = 49 Sonnets break into 9, 13, 7, 9, 11 Sonnet units:</u>
1. Left column   Rival Poet(s)   Heavens to ground 9 Sonnets
2. Stage/Hell   Rejection & Essex Rebels   The Boards 13 Sonnets
3. Roof of house Tower & QEI—James I   Upper house 7 Sonnets
4. Right column   Reunion with youth   Ground to heavens 9 Sonnets
<u>5. Heavens   Life after reunion   Under roof   11 Sonnets</u>
These fit with 15 units of 7 day (week) long regular lengths of time:
15 X 7 = 105 Sonnets, made of 2 parts: 77 (1-77) + 28 (127—154) = 105
<u>11 sides (to youth) + 4 sides (to lady) = 15 regular X 7 unit sides</u>

15 Regular + 5 Irregular units = 20-sided Globe

What fun! If we see Time as the Globe and the Globe as the World and the World as the Universe and the Universe as Space-Time, we stand in the center of the spinning *Sonnets* with an altered sense of Time for the structure of the whole sequence. To tie this geometrical vision of time and the Globe to the Sun, Moon, and Stars would just take a few steps forward. All we need to do is to gaze up at the underside, painted surface of the Heavens, and then we will see, in reverse to what the actors on stage could see: the golden **Sun** to the audience's left, the golden **Moon** to the audience's right, the golden **cloud** covering the trap door at the center of the Heavens, and an arc of images of the star-etched **Zodiac.**

The painted Heavens' roof over the actors mimics the real heavens over the audience and London. In this kind of thinking, fuzzy logic, and speculation help get me started. Then I live with the implications of my guess work for a while and do the math or diagrams or rereading. The more I think about the rightness of this Globe Theater image, the more I think that in the structure of the *Sonnets* William Shakespeare tried—he had ten years from 1599 to 1609—to make a unified design of his theater, his world, the universe, the calendars, and his sense of Time, the maze in the *Sonnets*. At any rate, this metaphorical thinking helps us appreciate his multi-dimensional genius.

Astrology, Geometry, Astronomy, Architecture, Music, Poetry, and the opening of new ventures—all seem to run together in Elizabethan minds. In his *Biography* of Shakespeare, Peter Ackroyd points out that the Globe's opening night was carefully planned:

> A horoscope was consulted to determine the exact day for the opening of the Globe. The play chosen for that auspicious occasion was *Julius Caesar* and, from allusions in the text itself, it is clear that is was first performed on the afternoon of 12 June 1599. This was the day of the summer solstice and the appearance of a new moon. A new moon was deemed by astrologers to be the most opportune time "to open a new house." (374)

In the astronomy of the *Sonnets,* Shakespeare started a new affair on the new Moon. The opening of the Globe seven years later was to be much more fortunate. Also in the *Sonnets,* the Summer Solstice was recorded in Sonnet 52, 11 sonnets shy of the mid-point of Shakespeare's summer sequence, which is Sonnet 63. Shakespeare would have been delighted that his celebration of the young lord as a Whitsun Solar Hero in Sonnet 52 rang true again with an echo in 1599 when the Globe opened. Ackroyd goes on:

> That evening, Venus and Jupiter appeared in the sky. These may seem to be matters of arcane calculation but to the actors and playgoers of the late sixteenth century they were very significant indeed. **It has been demonstrated,**

for example, that the axis of the Globe is 48 degrees east of true north, and so was in direct alignment with the midsummer sunrise [my emphasis].

(374)

(See Appendix C on page 172 for a diagram of the Globe's alignment.)

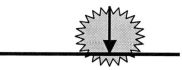

Given all this planning in 1599, it may not be very far-fetched to see the Globe's design in the *Sonnets*. Shakespeare had ten years to build these Sonnets to that structure after the Globe was opened with a performance of *Julius Caesar* on Summer Solstice, 12 June 1599 O. C.

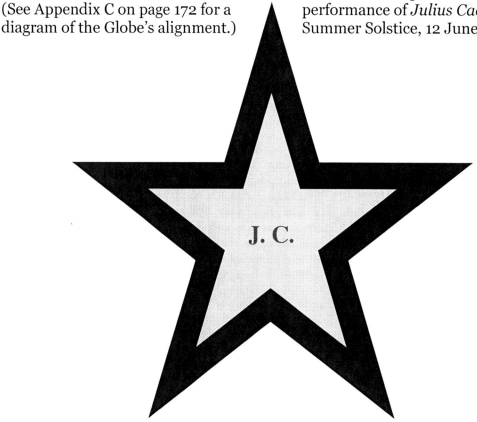

And the maze goes on. In addition to being one of Shakespeare's images for time, the **maze** was also the **name** of an Elizabethan dance, as named by Petruchio (to his friend Hortensio) as he begins his rough and sexy courting dance with Katherina:

"I have thrust myself into this **maze,** Happily to wive and thrive as best I may."

(*Shrew* 1.2.52-53)

Chapter 19   **Problems of the Calendars and Real Heavenly Bodies**

But there's another problem even with the simplest view of time only as a calendar: Table 9 (which is a pretty important start) is but one literary, textual solution for our time on our Gregorian calendar. I wondered what the Sun and Moon were really doing in the sky of June 1592. What year in the 1590s had the dark of the Moon been on or close to June 3rd? I called my colleague in the Science Department at Linn-Benton Community College, Greg Mulder. I asked him, "Greg, when was the full moon in June 1592?" He brought up the complex calendar problem and e-mailed me, "This problem makes your question much more difficult to answer as the switch between the Julian and Gregorian calendars happened between 1500 and 1850 depending on where you lived."

In turn, I called him up and reasoned, perhaps mistakenly, "Should we assume that Shakespeare was using the new Gregorian calendar because he lived and worked in London during the whole writing of the *Sonnets:* 1589—1609? Londoners in-the-know would have been influenced by that center of astronomical learning dominated by the needs of the Royal Navy, since the reign of Henry VIII, based in Greenwich, just down the Thames. [Later, Christopher Wren designed the octagonal observatory there on a high hill, and Greenwich became a world center for the study of the interrelated sciences of Time, Astronomy, and Navigation. It

became the place of the prime meridian as well.] So let's assume Shakespeare was operating from 1589 to 1609 on the more exact Gregorian calendar and Greenwich time."

"Okay, just a minute," said Greg, and I could hear his calculator clicking as I listened. He spoke as he calculated, "The phases of the Moon happen in a cycle 19 days earlier each next year. 1592 was 5,071 lunar phase cycles and 410 years ago. Hey, this is odd! It comes out that 1592 had the same phases of the Moon as we have this year, 2002. And the Full Moon is on June 24th this month." (See Table 13 on p. 135.) You can bet that on June 24, 2002 I was out in our garden at night with my wife Sandy and our two cats Emma and Sam looking up at the Full Moon. It's just wonderful—the strange and questionable places Shakespeare researching can lead us.

But the calendar problem is really much more difficult, and as an English "major," I'm not sure I'm trained to handle it. According to on-line pages by Mike Spathaky entitled, "Old Style and New Style Dates and the Change to the Gregorian Calendar: A Summary for Genealogists," Britain did not accept the Gregorian calendar until an Act passed Parliament in 1752. Spathaky writes:

> For 170 years, between the Papal Bull of Gregory XIII [October 1582] and the

Chesterfield Act of the British parliament, two calendars had been used side by side in Western Europe. England could not help being influenced by the Gregorian calendar. (n.p.)

I've seen sources that apply a subtraction of 8 to 10 days (11 after 1700) to correct our Gregorian calendar to the Old Style. This conversion of the calendar in *Shakespeare's Sonnets* plays some nasty tricks on my neatest solution. But in fact, it starts the *Sonnets* on or near Will's supposed birthday, April 23rd, and his christening was recorded in Stratford on April 26th in the Old Style.

Suddenly, the alignment of Moon and Sun in the *Sonnets* became much more difficult. Could Sonnet 141 be June 24th New Style? Then would it convert to June 14th Old Style? To convert or not? If we must subtract, some of the neat correspondences of the two sets of 28 sonnets, that I like best, seem odd. I would rather have the Full Moon on June 17tth (See Table 9) . But I can't seem to get it there! Well, but 17 is a magic code number. Does that make any difference? I think the wording of the genealogist Spathaky (above), "England could **not help being influenced by the Gregorian calendar**," gives us a lot of license!

Shakespeare's family has all the markings of being a mix of traditional rural people with progressive, middle class aspirations, with some hidden Catholic political leanings, but mostly with a "bend with the breeze" survivors' attitude as well. Shakespeare might wonder why Protestant England could not shift from the inaccurate pagan calendar of Julius Caesar to the more accurate Catholic calendar of Pope Gregory. Perhaps he built this bi-polar calendar problem into his *Sonnets* like the wobble of the Earth on its axis. Perhaps the conflicting pagan and the papal timelines are part of the maze in the *Sonnets* just as they were part of Shakespeare's age.

There is yet another way to make a calendar of the year with all the folk festivals and religious and royal holidays. For most people, who did not own almanacs or count each day, this is how the year was experienced. The scholar Francois Laroque researched a seasonal round for Renaissance England and applied that annual template to all of Shakespeare's work. In the back of Laroque's book, *Shakespeare's Festive World,* there is an Appendix 2, which divides the Elizabethan year up into the "sacred or ritualistic half" and the "profane or secular half" (308). These are also called the "Festive half—**Winter**" (November 1st— April 31st) and the "Working half—**Summer**" (May 1st— October 31st) in his Appendix 3 (309). The Summer Solstice is listed on June 24th (Saint John's Day) by the new calendar. To convert to the old calendar, subtract 10 days, so thc Solstice would occur on June 14th. This would realign the sun and moon sonnets from Table 9, so that Sonnet #52 would line up with a June 14th Solstice. Then Sonnet #1, the first of 17 birthday sonnets for Henry, would line up with April 24th (the day after birthday of William Shakespeare).

So does this prove that Shakespeare was born on April 24th or was the legend of April 23rd started to give his birth **festive** meaning? The fact that he died on this day in 1616 strengthens this possibility especially for those who like to find great meaning in numbers. Like both astrologers and astronomers, it's clear that Elizabethans loved number play and were into numerology. In this festive alignment with the old calendar, the dark lady sonnets begin on May 27th and end 28 nights later on June 23rd. The whole Summer sequence for the youth then ends on August 27th.

Once I started seeing the youth and the dark lady as the Sun and the Moon with painted on human faces, I realized that some of the fictional feel of the sequence for modern readers comes from the

St. George's Day and the legendary mythological content of the festive year as shown in Table 11. Some of this festive zodiac was painted on the underside of the Globe's "Heavens" that any actor standing on stage could look up and see. At least that is what the painters of Shakespeare's New Globe in London thought (Gurr 41).

But let's correct the *Sonnets'* calendar to the old Julian calendar and add in the festivals that would mark the days for most people instead of a paper calendar hanging on a wall. (See Table 11 next page.) This table hints at some of the complexity of thinking about time in Shakespeare's day. It may invite us to develop a very rich texture for time in the *Sonnets*.

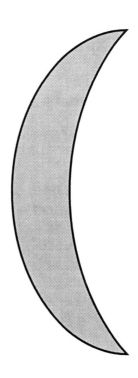

Table 11: Solar & Lunar Sonnets Corrected to the Old, Julian
Calendar (Ritualistic & Secular Festive dates
& *Agricultural Non-calendar Feasts* included)

SOLAR MONTHS	Sonnet # Sun Cycle	LUNAR MONTH & DATES	Sonnet # Subject Moon Cycle	Phase of MOON
LAST PART OF SACRED OR RITUALISTIC HALF OF YEAR				
APRIL	Son. 1	April 24	Sun Begins Sonnet calendar Will's Birthday (or not) & day after <u>St. George's Day</u> & <u>Order of the Garter</u>	
MAY	Son. 9	May 1	<u>May Day, Beltane</u>: Maypole, Morris Dances, Robin Hood	
MAY	Son. 18	May 10	<u>Whitsun</u>: "Fair" Youth as Whitsun Lord, King of Summer New series: "shake ...buds"	
MAY	Son. 34	May 27	Son. 127 Dark Lady "Black" Beauty as Queen of Summer	Dark/New
MAY	Son. 35	May 28	Son. 128 Virginal	Waxing Crescent
JUNE	Son. 40	June 2	Son. 133 Triangle	Half
JUNE	Son. 48	June 10	Son. 141 Heart as fool	FULL
JUNE			*Sheep-shearing*	
PROFANE OR SECULAR HALF OF YEAR STARTS WITH SOLSTICE				
<u>SOLSTICE</u>	Son. 52	June 14	Son. 145 And Hate-away	Waning Gibbous
JUNE	Son. 58	June 20	Son. 151 Name Double spelled: AEAYMMEELLYAEA!	Wane Cres.
JUNE	Son. 61	June 23	Son. 154 Cupid's Brand	Thin Bow Old Moon
JUNE	Son. 63	June 25	Sun is 1/2 way to 126	
JULY			*Rush-bearing*	
JULY	Son. 93	July 25	Eve's apple grows	
AUGUST	Son. 100	Aug. 1	<u>Lammas</u> (day after Juliet's b-day)	
AUGUST	Son. 114	Aug. 15	<u>Assumption</u>	
AUGUST	Son. 116	Aug. 17	North Star	
AUGUST	Son. 126	Aug. 27	Sun Ends Sonnet Summer in Old Calendar	
SEPTEMBER			*Harvest-home*	

Source of data on feasts: Laroque 306-9

126

If we like this old calendar set-up better than Table 9 (that was constructed with our newer, Gregorian dates) then the full moon appears on the night of **June 10ᵗʰ**. But according to astronomical data, the **actual full moons** shone on the following dates corrected to the old, Julian calendar:

> **1592—June 14ᵗʰ;**
> **1593—June 23ʳᵈ; and**
> **1594—June 4ᵗʰ.**

Darn! There's not one perfect alignment! (The new moon shining on the wedding night—June 15ᵗʰ old calendar—one night after the Solstice night in *A Midsummer Night's Dream* doesn't help us either.) So in the most likely years (1592—1594), we do not get a true alignment between the old calendar literary moon and the real moon. Perhaps this is all calendar lunacy based on the stubborn anti-Catholic refusal of England to join the continent in the more accurate calendar designed by Pope Gregory.

Doctor Dee advised Queen Elizabeth I that the Pope's new calendar (based on committee work which got its math from Galileo) was better science than the old. But Archbishop Grindall of Canterbury told Elizabeth he wouldn't support the change because the new calendar was "Papist" (Woolley 172 f.). Perhaps the stubborn and Protestant English liked their original, pagan Roman roots and decided to stick with the old calendar of Julius Caesar, the pagan J. C., to deny the Pope's claim to be the only representative of the Christian J. C. Perhaps Will preferred the old calendar of his boyhood. I'm sure he had heard of the more accurate Catholic calendar.

He has me more confused than Peter Quince and Bottom looking up in the almanac to see if there is a moon shining on the night they perform. There is. In scene one of *A Dream*, Hippolyta had reminded the impatient Theseus to wait four days for the new moon and their wedding night. I love this time maze stuff! I think Shakespeare was playing with both calendars and everyone's minds. I also wonder if the ritualistic and secular festive year—written about by Francois Laroque, from St. George's Day on April 23ʳᵈ through May Day, Whitsun, Midsummer's Day, Lammas, and on to the day of the Assumption on August 15ᵗʰ—is also built into this Summer Sonnet calendar (308). (See Table 11 above for such alignments.) Perhaps all this confusion about time is ours, not Shakespeare's.

In 1657, the invention of the pendulum clock "... made it possible to replace the old seasonal routines definitively with a stricter and more rational chronological system" (Laroque 30). So Shakespeare's concept of time fits with fuzzy logic and his hour-glass, not our atomic clock at modern Greenwich. I wonder even further if this new sense of "exact time" had anything to do with the switch in the use of punctuation from rhetorical to grammatical and logical. It seems to me that the mechanistic "Enlightenment" had a "scientific" influence on many areas of thinking between our time and Shakespeare's time. These great shifts—from word music to reason—may act to cloud our vision of Shakespeare.

Shakespeare often used "time's fickle glass" to tell time, as in line 2 of Sonnet #126. He goes on to warn the youth, in lines 7 and 8, that Nature can only protect him from Time for a short while:

"She keeps thee to this purpose: that her skill
May time disgrace, and wretched **minute** kill."

Of course, 126 is twice 63, and 63 is a key odd number for the Elizabethans. They called it the double climacteric because it is 7 times 9. Remember, there are 9 Muses, 9 Worthies, and 9 numbers (without counting zero), and there are 7 planetary gods and goddesses and 7 nights to each quarter of the Moon. Shakespeare **doubles** (again that key number 2) the double climacteric of 63 into 126 sonnets for the youth. The more I look, the more I am convinced that the design of this sonnet sequence clicks into place and reveals Shakespeare's thinking.

Most editors print the word in line 8 of Sonnet 126 as "minutes," but Duncan-Jones points that the word is printed **"mynuit"** in the 1609 Quarto. She thinks that may have been "a visual pun on the [French] minuit, midnight... so often associated with death, despair and the expiry of legal contracts, as in Marlowe's Doctor *Faustus*..." (366). Another editor reminds us that minutes were "the smallest units of time (seconds were not used till the mid-seventeenth century" (Orgel

129). No wonder so many of us get dizzy trying to figure out the Elizabethans. They had no standardized spelling or grammatical punctuation or precise sense of time. This seems like a variation on Einstein's joke that if you have more than one clock, you don't know what time it is.

To the imprecise, old calendar, first designed by Julius Caesar, the Elizabethans added their calendar of solar and lunar, pagan and Christian, secular and sacred feasts and rites. This annual round of festivals and feasts adds a whole new layer to the sonnet calendar. It invites me to speculate about the youth as Shakespeare's **Whitsun Lord**, the ceremonial King of Summer. He is certainly described as such in the Solstice Sonnet #52. He has a golden, sunny, god-like influence. In Sonnet # 97, line 11 says, "For summer and his pleasures wait on thee [.]" I like to think of Shakespeare thinking of the youth the way Michelangelo thought about his statue of David. People who model for statues or sonnets can become icons. (Of course, for the city of Florence, the statue of David became their heroic "Statue of Liberty," a fighter for the independence of their city-state.)

Perhaps Shakespeare wants to give his young "King of Summer" some of that kind of folk hero status. The youth is also a wealthy man and a patron and a military officer and one member of the Essex faction at court; Shakespeare is his older friend but also serves at his pleasure. But serving the "King of Summer" is not always a pleasure.

We can also speculate about the dark lady as his **Queen of Summer**—a "black beauty" he fell in love with and elected in Sonnet #127— a figure of the night like the Moon. But she is not at all like the myth of the "virgin" Queen Elizabeth, Diana, or the Fairie Queen. The dark lady is a secular, sexy, manipulative, frustrating Queen of Misrule over Shakespeare's heart. From the 27th of May to the 23rd of June (Old Calendar), she rules his almanac of nights and the dark side of his heart and gives him love sweats, love fits, and a fever. Unlike a typical beauty queen in the English countryside, she's dark, mature, manipulative, not faithful to Will, and ambitious. She's more like the goddess Fortune than Diana. Unlike the youth, she is Shakespeare's social equal. She has her own will and interests. She goes through her phases with him and forces him through all kinds of emotions. He is attracted to her "heaven" and has to go through "hell" to get there. Any hope he had that she would be a true love to him dies with four intervening realities: 1. his lust (Sonnet #129), 2. her tyrannous nature (Sonnet #131), 3. her starting an affair with the youth (Sonnet #133), and 4. his fever from disease (Sonnet #147). On the night of the full moon (June 10th and Sonnet #141), Will Shakespeare is howling like a lone wolf:

"But my five wits, nor my five senses, can
Dissuade one foolish heart from serving thee [.]"
(Lines 9 & 10)

So his Queen of Summer rules his heart, and his heart makes him lie about what he thinks and sees. The dark lady is not only a real woman to him as in Sonnet #130. She is also an allegorical, female folk festival ruler from the old English and Roman calendar. She is the Moon who rules the peak of the season in her 28-day period around midsummer, a more realistic rival to the Tudor myth of the Virgin Queen.

Gary Schmidgall wants to go quite a few steps further. He writes that if the youth represents the "10th Muse," the muse of the court, with Shakespeare sometimes feeling stuck as a poet who writes elegant poems for the lords, then the dark lady represents the Muse of the theater. It's clear that Shakespeare had two Muses. On his bad days, his Muse of lyric poetry seemed to be a snotty, spoiled brat with crazy political ideas, and his Muse of the theater was an illiterate whore, a material girl who laughed only at his dirty jokes.

In his book, *Shakespeare and the Poet's Life*, Schmidgall develops a complex allegorical list of qualities and keywords to contrast these two social forces to show that Shakespeare saw himself as the roped "love slave" being drawn and quartered by golden horses of the Sun and silver horses of the Moon. William Shakespeare led a passionate, disciplined life. His two Muses fought over him for his time and loyalty.

TABLE 12. **Theater Muse versus Poetry Muse**

Youth as 10th Muse of Poetry	Lady as Muse of the Theater
Court aristocracy	Theater's democracy
Poetry	Drama
A young lord	A company of men and boys
Private	Public
Petrarchian/Pastoral	Comic/Satiric/Tragic
Unequal	Equal
Dissembling	Truth telling
Treasure	Pleasure
London	Southwark
Rome	Alexandria
Octavius/Lavinia	Cleopatra
Uneven patronage	Steady income

Source of data: Schmidgall 191

Of course, Shakespeare's choice between these Muses was no contest. Despite the dominance of the youth in the *Sonnets*, there was not a one-time decision that Shakespeare made to favor poetry. Every time that freedom from the plague allowed, Shakespeare chose the Theater over the Court and writing plays over writing poems and sonnets. Even the two times of sonnet revision suggested by Wells and Dobson—around 1604 and 1608—are like black holes in time when plague closed the theaters, as soon as 13 or more people a day died in London. The Male muse of poetry may seem to win in the sonnets, but the Female muse of the theater wins in Shakespeare's life. Henry is important to Will as a person, but the theater was Will's first love. He was right to hedge his bets with patronage and writing poetry for the elite, but it only seems as if Shakespeare is stuck with patronage when you are a reader stuck in the self-important little world of his sonnets. When you see his plays, you know he was not stuck. The twenty years of his career includes some great poetry, but his thirty-seven plus plays overshadow the poems. It's just that the enduring power of the plays in our culture makes us more curious to see if Shakespeare left us any autobiographical clues in these sonnets.

The fun of all this thinking about the layers of meaning in the *Sonnets* belongs to the well-revised complexity of the work. So the old Roman calendar, the "festival year" of church, court, and town, the youth as Solar hero, and the lady as Lunar heroine add archaeological layers to time as designed in the *Sonnets*. I am sure that Shakespeare had heard of the new, more accurate, Papal calendar as well. I wonder about this modern calendar and what Will was thinking in 1609. I guess I need to know if the calendars of the Royal Navy and the British merchant fleet and their navigators shifted earlier than the rest of England.

Old impressions and fantasies die hard. From when I first started to study Shakespeare in high school in Brooklyn, I carry an imagined scene: Will is eagerly buying drinks for sea captains and sailors and returned explorers and is questioning them about where they've sailed as they are surrounded by theater people and other rogues in the Mermaid Tavern. He's as eager as a science fiction writer talking with astronauts and NASA scientists. In fact, I like to picture a painting of a larger than life-sized mermaid with huge breasts leaning out of a wave like a Muse and a bar maid floating over their heads as they talk about the far reaches of the Mediterranean and the Caribbean and as Will begs for details about India (for *A Midsummer Night's Dream*) and the Americas (for *The Tempest)*. In my view, he's also very interested in navigation. He reveals some new knowledge on emergency sailing techniques for avoiding wrecks in the opening scene of *The Tempest.*

My father Bill taught me both coastal and celestial navigation, and I worked on yachts and on coastal oil tankers with intelligent captains who told me stories as I stood at the wheel and as they navigated on the six-hour watches at night. I know how exciting the details of navigation can be. It is a practical science, always eager to progress all the way

from the astrolabe to the Global Positioning System (GPS).

It is interesting to remember that Shakespeare does tell us that he is thinking about exact science, not astrology. Way back in that sonnet with a very important number, number 14 (his number), in lines 1 and 2, he starts, "Not from the stars do I my judgement pluck;/ And yet, methinks, I have **astronomy**," so maybe he's up on the latest thinking about the more accurate, new calendar. The argument of Sonnet 14 states that Will cannot predict the fate of kings or wars from the stars as astrologers like Dr. Dee and Simon Forman pretend; rather he can predict the fate of love and friendship from the stars in the youth's eyes. Sonnet 14 also contains doublets on the youth's "truth" and "beauty" that sound like the source for the ABBA chiasmus on truth and beauty that Keats can hear much later like a slogan coming from figures on an ancient Grecian Urn.

As truth and beauty shall
together thrive ...
Thy end is truth's and beauty's
doom and date.
(Sonnet 14.11 & 14)

Sonnet 116 reminds us that precise astronomical science is most important for Shakespeare's time as a key to navigation. Lines 5—8 point like a sextant at the North Star and echo Wyatt's translation of Petrarch's sonnet about a galley in a storm with an important difference: Shakespeare compares the focus on Polaris and the ability to navigate not to reason but to true love.

"O no, it is an ever-fixed mark,
That looks on tempests and is never
    shaken;
It is the star to every wand'ring bark,
Whose **worth's** unknown, although
    his **height** be taken."

Hear are name pun words **"shaken"** and **"worth"** again, with a nice companion h-word in **"height."** Henry's true worth as a lover, friend, and patron can never be known even though his height in the world as one of England's eighteen Earls up on the very steep sides of the Elizabethan social pyramid can be brought down to the horizon, measured, and "taken." He can also be brought low by the Queen's old men and locked in the Tower. But seeing him after his release by the new king and feeling a true mind, says his dear friend Will, is like spotting the **North Star** (Polaris) from the deck of a **"bark."**

Shakespeare had portrayed himself as "a saucy bark" when compared to the large warship or pirate ship who was his main rival, Marlowe. "Bark"—a type of small, three-masted sailing ship in Sonnets 80 and 116—also gives us an odd pun for the sharp voice of a dog. Perhaps Shakespeare was portraying himself as a salty sea dog. It's also interesting that Henry captained a warship—*The Garland*—in a fleet that raided Spain under the command of Essex (Rowse 115). Henry's ship was the only ship to sink a Spanish ship on that raid. Shakespeare portrayed Henry as if he were a Spanish treasure galleon. But we must upgrade and toughen our views of Henry as a sea captain and as a cavalry general in Ireland, too.

In Shakespeare's time, **latitude**—the angular distance north or south from the Earth's equator measured through ninety degrees—could be measured from the fixed stars including Polaris; but **longitude** was still a huge problem waiting on the construction of accurate clocks that could be used at sea. Greenwich would be placed on a great circle numbered zero or named the prime meridian, but no one on a ship in Shakespeare's time could measure accurately the degrees or length of time away from England.

Shakespeare had compared himself to a "saucy bark" in Sonnet 80. But here, in Sonnet 116, after all the betrayals, trials, deaths, separations, and changes in regime, he has discovered in himself and the youth true love and lasting friendship, "the marriage of true minds [.]" This discovery takes place late in the solar summer on August 24th (August 17th of the old calendar). Does the change in regime and shift in the month to August make the new King James I "august" or even Augustus? As a premature pro-James rebel, Henry is released from the Tower. Shakespeare has already done much of his great play writing. The end of Summer is just ten days away on September 3rd of the new calendar, August 27 of the old. Shakespeare's sonnet Time is coming to an end with triumphant love.

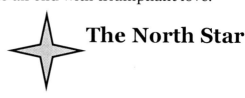 **The North Star**

Chapter 20   "The Man in the Moon is a Lady"

Looking back at June and in interpreting *Shakespeare's Sonnets,* should we choose the literary Moon or the real Moon? How long did Will's celestial, triangular affair with the lady and youth last anyway? In navigation, we find our position by triangulation. When describing his shock at betrayal by the youth, it is significant that Shakespeare takes 3 Sonnets—40, 41, and 42—to get it right. When he tries to triangulate to find his way, he feels lost between the sun and the moon. But does he give us any time clues about the length of this triangular affair? Well, it could have lasted at the very least for 28 days in June of 1592. No, it had to last at least until Aemilia was married in October 1592. Or it might have stretched over a few years. Shakespeare may even have kept in contact with the Lanyer musical family long after their affair ended. How can we know?

Suppose we take one other known celestial event and find its date. In Sonnet 107, line 5, Shakespeare referred to a total eclipse of the Moon in 1595: "The **mortal** moon hath her **eclipse** endured," and most scholars agree that this is a reference to Queen Elizabeth I. Rex Gibson, in his excellent teaching edition of the *Sonnets,* gives **seven possible events** that might be referred to in the Queen's reign as her "eclipse" (123). Shakespeare, of course, may be referring to all seven in this one line, but the one I think is the most likely is the death of Elizabeth in 1603. The next lines say that the

predictions of civil strife after her death without an heir did not come true.

Shakespeare's contemporaries had invested a lot of worry about the civil war that might follow Elizabeth's death. Shakespeare had written eight English history plays propping up the Tudor myth that their dynasty had stopped the chaos of the War of the Roses and brought prosperity. In 1604, Shakespeare seems to be propping up the dynasty of another peace-making king, the descendant of the man who killed the Scottish dictator Macbeth. Line 7 of Sonnet 107 proclaims, "Incertainties now **crown** themselves assured," and the succession of James I brought peace with Spain and a kind of Augustan *Pax Romana.*

King James' first official act was to name Shakespeare's company "The King's Men" and give them license to play any where in England. James knew the power of the London theaters as national propaganda, and Shakespeare was next to the top of the list of James's newest servants— under the newcomer, Lawrence Fletcher, who was personally known to James because he had played twice at James's court in Scotland (Schoenbaum 196). And what did Will give back to the new king, who was obsessed with witchcraft? "Double trouble,/Boil and bubble"— as predicted by three witches or Norns, the good Scottish ancestor of James appears and slays the evil Macbeth. Shakespeare had earlier done this for Elizabeth's grandfather

133

Henry VII showing him as a hero whose rebel army slays the hunchback king in *Richard III*. Shakespeare is very political; he is also willing to take lots of chances. It is this high tension between royalist flattery and anarchic revelry that still makes Shakespeare's politics useful to us today. He is also fascinated by the heady and confusing, celestial connections of politics and astrology and astronomy that most people of his time made, even if he is skeptical.

Up to 1603, almost any reference to the Moon or Diana can be seen as a reference to Elizabeth and her cult of herself as "The Virgin Queen." But, I wondered, is the dark lady also the Moon? And does the eclipse of 1595 have anything to do with her life or even mark the end of Will's affair with her? When was she eclipsed? I called Greg Mulder again for more lunar science. "Greg, how can I find the date of the total lunar eclipse over England in 1595?" He referred me to a web page that listed all solar and lunar eclipses. The lunar eclipse observed in the Northern Hemisphere in 1595 occurred on April 24th our calendar, and it belongs to the Saros series #115 of eclipses that returns every 18 years, 10 and 1/3 days (Espenak n.p.).

Should I take William Shakespeare literally, or is that just the thinking of a "rude mechanical?" Did his affair with Aemilia start on our calendar's June 3, 1592 (was this just after she was cast off by Hunsdon?) and end near his 31st birthday on April 24, 1595, a period of almost four years? What other evidence is there? I was interested in the ratio set up by the number of

solar sonnets (126) to the number of lunar sonnets (28). That reduces to a ratio of 4.5 to 1. If Will and Aemilia were involved for almost four years, then 4.5 times 4 equals 18, and 18 years are close to the actual number of years elapsed in the longer relationship between Henry and Will: 1590 to 1608. I always tell my students to, "Do the math," when they make number claims. So I always try to "do the math" as well.

Is this Shakespeare's "sum of sums," or is it astronomical lunacy? I'm so far into speculation (with some evidence) and moonlight, and I still don't know. (I feel my literary guide here is Borges; he delights in mixing scholarship—real and imaginary—into his fictions. Thinking of Borges frees me up to imagine. But the reader and I are still left with puzzling questions of: what is real and what is imaginary?) I am not trying to write fiction here, but let's not stop speculating now.

If this almost 4 year period is the timeframe of the lunar sonnets, then there would be **three Full Moons** in three Junes: June 24, 1592; June 5, 1593; and June 14, 1594. Then, on April 24, 1595, Will (the Earth) comes between Aemilia (the Moon) and Henry (the Sun), and Will's shadow eclipses her. I do want to point out that the literary line-up back in Table 9 has on June 29th the solar Sonnet 60, which is one of the great Time sonnets, and this sonnet starts with ocean waves coming ashore (perhaps at Bath, where Will may have tried the hot water cure as in lunar Sonnet #153, the companion sonnet to Sonnet #60). #60 contains in lines 7 and 8 a worried idea about the eclipse of the solar hero,

"Crooked **eclipses** 'gainst his glory
    fight,
And **Time** that gave doth now **his
    gift confound.**"

But this is more dangerous than the eclipse of the Moon. Darkness in daytime is much more dangerous than darkness at night. Who is plotting "crooked" plots against Henry now? Does this reference to struggle between the Sun and Time point to when Henry and Elizabeth Vernon secretly started their own affair in 1594 or 1595? Does it refer to pregnant Elizabeth (disguised as Henry's male page) running off with him to exile in France in 1598? [I see material here for *As You Like It*.] Does it refer to pregnant Elizabeth and Henry ordered back to Britain by the Queen and put into jail for secretly getting married without her permission in

1598? I admit it; I'm lost in questionable time over 400 years back then. But I'm still looking for clues.

Let's get back to the **Full Moon** (sonnet 141) and the Lady, who is driving Shakespeare wild as a wolf-man. If we want to look at how the real Moon and Sun make the sonnets line up over a 3 year, 10 month affair, from 1592 to 1595— perhaps conducted mostly in the summer theater months from May to September while Will was in London— here is another table (13) with new calendar dates. Finally, we get at least three options this way. These options may have something, much, or nothing to do with Shakespeare's sonnet pairs. Since the **dark of the moon** happens in sonnet 127, we have three real, astronomical dates to **start** with leading up to a real, lunar eclipse, perhaps the **end** of the affair.

Year	Dark of Moon	Solar Sonnets	June Full Moon	End of 28 day cycle	
Lunar Sonnets:	**#127**	**#127**	**#141**	**#154**	
1592	June 10	#41—68	June 24	July 8	See
1593	May 22	#22—49	June 5	June 19	p. 123
1594	May 31	#31—58	June 14	June 28	for 6/24

Table 13: 3 Years & 10 Months

1595 — **Total Lunar Eclipse: April 24**
Of course, this date rhymes with Old Calendar Sonnet 1 & is close to Will's Birthday.

See p. 123 for 6/24 Full Moon

Chapter 21   **Reading Sonnets in Pairs**

One of the most exciting games to play while reading the *Sonnets* is to read them in pairs. Table 13 (page 135) will force some interesting and some weird pairs. I really like the pairs that are forced by Table 9 much better. But isn't that how any book of changes goes? Some alignments are full of meaning; some seem meaningless. Choose the literary Moon or the literal Moon. Choose astronomy or astrology. See what meanings you can find by linking sonnets up to each other.

Some sonnets (like 50 and 51, the two horse-riding sonnets) are paired as if they were one long, 28-line, double sonnet. They may record, back to back, Will's ride on a slow horse to Stratford on the Oxford Road and back again to London. Reading them with their "moon pairs," Sonnets 143 and 144, reinforces the realities of this important and frequent round trip. Sonnet 143 seems to be set in a comical back yard full of chickens and babies in Stratford or even at the Davenant family inn in Oxford. Sonnet 144 seems to return to the serious Faustian, angel versus devil, either/or tug of war in London. Other sonnets dialogue with each other over the heads of sonnets in between them by imagery or theme. Each sonnet becomes like a walking player at a fair willing to talk with any other sonnet it meets.

For example, even in the "regular times" of the first 77 sonnets, there are parts that do not reinforce the sense of regular, seven-day, weekly cycles. If we start after the three, youth betrayal sonnets—40, 41, and 42—then we next face a unit of ten sonnets, which can be broken down as one **solo** sonnet 43, then four pairs of **twin** sonnets or eight—44/45, 46/47, 48/49, and 50/51—and then, that series of ten ends with the **solo**, solstice sonnet #52. So, even when we see the calendar rolling along in regular weeks with the moon, there is also a rhythm counter-pointing below time based on ideas, emotions, and content: 10/7, a new ratio.

If the affairs of the Summer Sun, Moon, and Earth line up in three different ways over the course of three years and ten months, there are many conversations among these poems that can be calculated and overheard by reading in pairs. But even my favorite alignment, considering Sonnets 40 and 133—the solar and lunar twins when Will first admits the lady and youth are having an affair, thus **calibrating** the two scales of Sun and Moon—to be **contemporaneous** (as W. H. Auden does), creates a major problem. How could the youth's "stain," first mentioned in Sonnet 33, start before Will's affair with the lady —unless that stain is some other act than Henry's making love to her, too? Or maybe Shakespeare the reviser is messing with his own timeline and breaking the prime directive of nonintervention so valued in *Star Trek!*

All I am saying is this: if this text were written and revised by

William Shakespeare over a twenty-year period, which spanned the great arc of his play-writing career, then shouldn't we consider all its possible complexities? As I see it, *Shakespeare's Sonnets* are beginning to look more like Julio Cortazar's novel *Hopscotch,* and some kind of radical Renaissance creative mix of autobiography and metafiction. I think Borges would agree. Recently, I saw a Robert Redford video that analyzed the Anasazi solar and lunar architecture of Chaco Canyon. I found that the complex theories and geometry of time in Chaco Canyon were not that different from Shakespeare's **Sun/Moon structures** in the *Sonnets.*

I cut my sharpest text-chewing teeth in Donald Hall's class on Yeats and Joyce at the University of Michigan in 1963. In *Ulysses,* we found that Stephen Dedalus thought Shakespeare was very autobiographical and "Joycean." In fact, Joyce was the first writer to give me more room to speculate about Shakespeare and play what-if games. It seems odd to me now that the main characters of *Ulysses* are a lovable and funny, older man (Bloom), a bright youth (Stephen), and an unfaithful, sexy woman (Molly). Did Joyce borrow his main characters from *Shakespeare's Sonnets* as well as from Homer's *Odyssey?*

I'm not sure it's really justified, but Joyce scholars have a license to have more autobiographical and punning fun than Shakespeare scholars. I found an essay by Michelle Burnham that likens the love triangles in the *Sonnets* and *Ulysses* much more precisely than my first take. Burton proves to me that Joyce was thinking of Blazes Boylan (not Stephen) as the youth (43). After all, it is Blazes who makes Bloom a cuckold, not Stephen. Joyce was faced with a problem in his Homeric model. Odysseus is blessed with the faithful Penelope to come home to.

Joyce had a lot of weird ideas about creative tensions caused by love triangles and his jealous rages. But how weird are Joyce's ideas if they also form one creative incentive for Will in his *Sonnets*? Joyce may have leaned on Shakespeare to help him solve his Homeric problem. For Molly Bloom to be an updated, 20th century Penelope on June 16, 1904, she must also be the dark lady. Yes, I said yes. It's "Bloomsday" all over again. Balding Will Shakespeare was Leopold Bloom before Bloom ever existed. Does that make sense? Bloo who? I think Joyce found Shakespeare (as most of us do) very stimulating like Mozart's music. This idea of dialectical pairing is very rich. Shakespeare's two-way rocking and triangular intellect seems to move like Hegel's thesis, antithesis, synthesis—triads way before Hegel and Marx.

Chapter 22   Guessing at Shakespeare's Timeline

Do the *Sonnets* contain a very heady mix of fact and fiction? How literally and deeply does the autobiographical material flow in this great work? I think that the hardest task for anyone trying to help others think about these sonnets is to try to put dates on sonnets and give something of a timeline to the whole sequence. But I do want to try! My opponents in this game always say, "We can never know." I call that the position of "Saint Agnostic" (he who must piously doubt everything), and since I want to apply science to these time puzzlers, I consider it a fun challenge to speculate. Literary critics must remember that no matter what their thesis committees say, most mathematicians and scientists make room for speculation and find the proofs later. I will take the risk of entering my best guesses in the following Table 14 in hopes that others will find these interesting and debatable.

Of course, if Shakespeare revised these *Sonnets* up to 1609, when he left London and did not supervise the printing (because 1609 was a bad plague year), whole sonnets or new lines or quatrains or couplets or code words from later years up to 1609 could appear anywhere in the sequence. Did Will go back and mess with his own timeline? I think so. Perhaps like the elder, revising Yeats, Shakespeare at age 45 revised Will at 25 and made our attempts at dating the sonnets much more puzzling. But, once we

get into upper division classes, aren't we supposed to be attracted by puzzles? Shouldn't we try speculation and experimentation? Shouldn't we—as physicists did when I was an undergraduate at the University of Michigan—find the design of the bubble chamber in a glass of foaming beer?

What else can we say about that year 1609 in Shakespeare's life? There are major personal events before and after his 1609 publication of the *Sonnets*. In 1607, Shakespeare's granddaughter Elizabeth Hall was born. This may have increased the attraction of life in Stratford for him. In 1608, Shakespeare's mother Mary died. This may have given his sadness new depth and liberated Shakespeare from worrying about what his aging mother might think of his affairs. I think that Anne already knew and does not "hate" him. In 1609, he published the *Sonnets* and got out of London. In 1610, the attraction of family life in Stratford wins. He semi-retires or is forced to retire by a shift to the right in royal politics against the values of tolerance. In 1610, perhaps from Henry Wriothesley (but it could have been from William Herbert as well), he gets ahold of one of three copies of William Strachey's letter about a shipwreck in the Bermudas. Will begins to write a farewell to the theater, a proper exit from the Globe, full of homey details about being a father and worrying about an unmarried daughter and her upcoming marriage as well as bright spirits and dull oafs who serve him because he practices good magic as well as a three goddess masque to bless a wished for wedding.

In May 1609, he was probably no longer worried about the "secret" affairs hidden in the *Sonnets*. Then, a year later, he semi-retired to Stratford, perhaps working on four more plays: possibly *Cymbeline* and most certainly *The Tempest*, and he enjoyed a brief collaboration with his young replacement, John Fletcher, a more acceptable Anglican writer, on

King Henry VIII and *The Two Noble Kinsmen*. But think of him in 1609 looking over the last 20 years, publishing too late for the sonnet craze but not wishing to leave his sonnets behind in manuscript form only. He had worked very hard in those twenty years. His main accomplishments were his plays. The sonnets may shut the door on his life in London. I have constructed a tentative timeline to hang the sonnets along like wet laundry on a sunny day. My hope is that many others will help make this difficult job more precise.

Table 14: The Sonnets and the Life

A SPECULATIVE TIMELINE

Numbers	dates	themes and groupings
1—126		**SOLAR SUMMER CYCLE: 126 days for Henry**
1—17	1589	Henry's 17th birthday message in 1590: "Reproduce!" a new kind of *carpe diem*
18—19	1591	Henry's beauty at 18: "You are my sunshine" like Sidney's Stella. #19: de Vere's attempt to arrange marriage?
20—32		#20 heterosexual/ #27 **Separation #1**/ #31 bisexual?
33	1592	Sun that stains: quatrain 3 about Hamnet's death: 1596
34	**June 3, 1592?**	Broken promise: Is #34 a reference to Aemilia & **#127?**
35—39		Sweet thief, thorns, clouds, eclipses; #38 10th Muse, rival
40—42	**1592**	**SEXUAL TRIANGLE: Aemilia/40 same time as 133**
		AGES: Will is 28, Aemilia is 23, Henry is 19
43—53		**Separation #2,** #48 Rival poet, Kit Marlowe mentioned?
54—63		Struggle over Henry's defects and his own
60	1594?	**Great Time** Sonnet. Will is worried about "crooked eclipses" of the Sun. Sonnet #153, first of the Cupid envois, is its companion sonnet.
64—73		Loss and fear of death, my **NAME**: vile vilest
74/75		Better part of Will is Henry's
76—78	1592?	MUSE: #78 visits Greene's insult: Henry's eyes taught ignorant Will to fly and added feathers to the wings of those rivals who are more learned than Will.

78—86		**RIVAL POET: Marlowe: from polygon to triangle**
79—81	1592	From many rivals to one? From Florio, Nashe, Chapman, & finally just Marlowe
82		Rival(s)
83		Your **NAME:** Hence, Worth (2X)
84		Focus on one main Rival: Marlowe, Kit Morley
		#84 Kit's **NAME:** K + … it 2X, **present tense**
86	1593	86, Line 1 about Kit in **past tense:** after his murder age 29
	1598?	Revision adds references to Kit's *H&L* & Chapman's rewrite published in 1598
87—126		**Back to Henry and Will**
87—96	1594-8	Farewell and loss: Henry and Elizabeth Vernon's affair. They were secretly married in 1598.
	1596	Hamnet's death (See quatrain 3, Sonnet 33)
	1599	The GLOBE Theater opens on Bankside.
97—99	1601	**Separation #3:** Essex rebellion Feb. 1601
		Essex executed, Henry in Tower for 3 years
100—103		Henry as Will's MUSE during absence?
104	1593	A flashback & 1603?
105—106	1603	His love: 3 years apart: 1601/02/03 Henry out of Tower
107—109	1603/4	Queen Elizabeth's death and James I crowned
110	1603	H.W. versus W.H. [?]: who was "another youth?"
112		Crows twice over Greene: all-the-world 2X: The Globe
111—115		Separation #3 and time
116		True love/true minds: love is like the **Pole Star**
117—125	1605	"I bore the canopy"—for James I.
		Henry hosts a performance of *LLL* for Queen Anne in his London home. Gunpowder Plot 1605-06
126	1609	**ENVOI.** Henry , a life long friend 1589—1609
		Post-Sonnets: 1610—16. 1617—23 Commemorative bust.
127—154		**LUNAR/MENSTRUAL CYCLE: 28 days for Aemilia**
127—130	1591/2	**DARK LADY:** Excitement and humor about Aemilia
131/132	1592	Sudden sexual tyranny: Will confronted her about Henry?
133/134	1592	**SEXUAL TRIANGLE** (back to time of 40—42)
135/136		His **NAME:** WILL: 14 and 7 uses of word "will"
137—140		Blinded eyes, lies
141		**Full Moon:** all 5 senses wide open to foolishness of love
142		Love/hate: pity me, so you deserve pity, too
143		Housewife leaves baby and chases hen: **HEN.** = **NAME**
144		Two loves: Will torn as Faustus in morality play
145	1582 &	His wife's **NAME:** And/Anne and hate away/Hathaway
	1592?	**Solstice:** shortest night = shortest, tetrameter lines
146—147		Repents but still has fever

148—150		Half Moon: eyes deceive, blind, "abhor" (twice) her power
151		Aemilia's **NAME** pointed out: **AEAYMMEELLYAEA** perhaps even with joke about variant spelling of her name Double spelled
152	Date?	Disease, eye. End of affair? Last word: pun on "lie"
	1595?	Length of affair: 28 days to 3 years and 10 months?
153/154	1595?	**DOUBLE ENVOI**: Two versions & "translations" of
	1609?	Cupid's tale are doubled: eros and illness: "mistress' eyes" "new fire"/"... water cools not love."
	1609	**ABBA:** last word: "love"

In addition:

1603—4 **A LOVER'S COMPLAINT**:

Published in 1609 with the *Sonnets:* in rime-royal

A young, female-voiced companion piece, a wronged woman. Added to Sonnet sequence as was Daniel's "Complaint of Rosamond" to his sonnets, "Delia," in 1592. Woods says Aemilia read "Rosamond" and retold her story in her own poem (*Lanyer* 40).

Cast of characters: Maid, Poet (who overhears), Reverend Man (once a courtier who now herds cattle), Youthful Seducer, and a Nun (who tried to seduce youth).

Note: For a detailed discussion of the connections between "A Lover's Complaint" and the *Sonnets*, see my essay in Appendix E, pages 174—182.

I don't know if I can line up any of the year dates in Table 14 with the solar and lunar annual dates in other Tables. If I had to pick any year as a key year, I would choose **1592.** Like the year of the Essex rebellion (1601), that may have been a very stressful and dangerous year in Shakespeare's life. 1592 was the year before Marlowe's murder and the year that pregnant Aemilia was married off to a court musician.

But **Time** is a very slippery slope. Galileo came up with a theory about the **relativity** of motion in **space**. A follower of Galileo's, Giordano Bruno, lived in the French embassy in London from 1583 to 1584. Bruno regularly met at dinner parties with Sir Phillip Sidney and an Italian scholar born in England, John Florio (Bossy 106). Florio became Henry's Italian tutor. Thus, a chain of idea men could link Galileo to Shakespeare. Perhaps the reason why so many of us find such trouble in pinning down a timeline in the *Sonnets* to Shakespeare's life is that Will is trying here to introduce his theory about **relativity in Time.**

Chapter 23   Reading Protocols, More Work to be Done

That's as far as I can go now. I did find many more possible **name code clues** outside of the **fourteen name code sonnets** and all the sonnets I have quoted so far. The sheer numbers of them do add weight to my case. (I list all key name code and possible autobiographical clue words I found in a five page **Appendix A,** pages 164—169.) There may be many more code and timeline clues hidden in both the words and numbers of the Sonnets. For those who enjoy or doubt or want to continue this work, I quote Sherlock Holmes: "You know my methods, Watson. Apply them!"

I will freely admit that when I read a particular sonnet, I am still and often baffled by the four-hundred-year-old, compacted English written for the *Sonnets* by Shakespeare. And even when I am able to do a clear, logical prose paraphrase, I know it is a reduction and not equivalent to the poetry's ability to enclose complexity. I think that the code adds an **extra formal challenge** for the writer and the reader, which may or may not detract from each sonnet's clarity and may make some of his wordings seem odd at first. It's not an accident that the top favorite twenty sonnets are the ones that read most clearly. They are truly great poems, but isolating them from the sequence works best at the Introduction to Poetry level. Once we try to read the whole sequence as a work, we have to struggle with all the sonnets in the current order.

Some of these sonnets are harder to read than John Donne's brainy, metaphysical sonnets. But I hope that the code I've found and the system I've described will help others find more understanding. The code may explain many of Shakespeare's word choices, and, I hope, it adds new meanings to lines that have been interpreted so many times that our collective notes threaten to force the sonnets off their pages. I try to both see and listen for *double entendres* and other rhetorical tricks of Shakespeare's trade. I know he is a master of word play. I try to make my mind match his moves.

Just remember, the *Sonnets* were published in 1609, only a year before he went into semi-retirement in Stratford. We know that 1609 was a plague year in London; he may have fled to the relative safety of Stratford without checking and correcting the proofs or the differences introduced by the two type compositors at the printer's shop. What role these introduced compositor mistakes have on the code, I do not know. I tried to correlate the facsimile 1609 copy published by Helen Vendler to the Arden edition I am quoting, and I believe that none of my key pieces of code were introduced by the two typesetters. On the other hand, we may never know what pieces of code were in Shakespeare's handwritten manuscript or a professionally copied fair copy used for the text that the typesetters may have revised out of existence.

I do think that the shift from the rhetorical syntax, grammar, and punctuation of the Renaissance to the so-called logical grammar and punctuation we use now can keep us from understanding Shakespeare. Stephen Booth's edition of the *Sonnets* is the most useful with this problem. I also think it is odd for me to be teaching 400 year old printers' and grammarians' rules of grammar and punctuation to my students rather than Shakespeare's more creative usage. It's very clear that we are captives of those inherited "rules." Booth is also very good at showing us what meanings of words we can have as we interpret the *Sonnets*. His careful use of *Oxford English Dictionary* (OED) entries can help us separate current word meanings from acceptable meanings in the late 16ᵗʰ and early 17ᵗʰ centuries.

There is only an occasional problem with using the OED. Since so many thousands of its entries are from Shakespeare's using, for the first time in print, a word with a new meaning, how are we to rule in or out our sense of when he is coining a more modern meaning for a word? Shakespeare did more than any other author to modernize English usage. When can one say this is a **new use by Shakespeare** or that new use came after him? He is a powerful wordsmith. He is clearly inventing better and newer ways to use English words than can be found in Florio's dictionary and perhaps even the OED.

I don't think it odd for Shakespeare—in the middle of a major publishing project—to flee London in 1609. Even King James I put off his triumphal entry as King into London until 1605 because 1604 was also a plague year. Although Shakespeare may have sent the *Sonnets* to the printers as he left town in a hurry, in them he combined all his figurative, story-telling powers with his desire to leave behind a great and baffling and perhaps unfinished, autobiographical memoir on the theme of love.

I know that "my discoveries" are based on the speculations of many other writers. Sometimes what I considered wrong answers were the most useful to me. Bad science can generate good science. When I scribbled in the margin in response, I was forced to offer alternate conclusions. I offer all this in the same spirit. Throw away what can be proven wrong or silly. Take what is useful and proven and go with it where you will. Most of all, delight in these *Sonnets*. They form one of humanity's most passionate texts. As my grandmother Sadie told me in the 1950s, they are one of the greatest, most honest explorations of earthly love written in a great age of exploration in the Renaissance world and in the history of our language. Cracking their code has just let us in on a deeper layer to explore.

I think this guessing at identities from clues was always part of the sonnet sequence writing and reading game. I consulted the on-line source, *Voice of the Shuttle,* and had fun finding and studying their link to a list of twenty-two "Elizabethan Sonneteers." Even though he publishes late, Will Shakespeare is really the pick of the Elizabethan litter. Placed in his Renaissance literary setting, his sequence imitates, follows the rules, outwits, and outshines them all. Who were Laura, Beatrice, An Hind, Stella, Delia, Phyllis, Licia, Elizabeth, Idea, the youth, the rival poet, and the dark lady? In any allegorical literary work, the reading protocols include setting up equations and analogies. I think that part of the original reading protocols for sonnet sequences is looking for magic numbers and hidden names. I think Shakespeare's code is both conventional and far more extensive than the use of code by many others.

Another link I found was to a page called "Sonnets on Sonnets." I read them all avidly and found 2 lines from two of them by famous poets, Burns and Poe, that fit my purposes here. Lines 1 & 2 of the sonnet by **Burns** read:

"**Fourteen**, a sonneteer thy praises sings;
What magic myst'ries in that **number** lie!"

Of course, fourteen is Will's base number. By the use of his other favorite number 2, he generates two other magic numbers: seven and twenty-eight. And then he numbers a whole sequence and uses their numbers as an organizing principle.

Poe also wrote a sonnet about sonnets. His last two lines, 13 and 14, pointed to the possible code of concealed words for names:

"Stable, opaque, immortal—all by dint

Of the **dear names** that lie **concealed** within't."

If, with this kind of deciphering curiosity, we start with Will's most obvious uses of his name Will, we can generate two magic numbers, 14 and 7, which lead us to the all-important 2. Those numbers help us to possible other hidden names. But if we remain stuck within the text of each sonnet, we can generate lots of strong, new critical structure and meaning and aesthetic appreciation, but we won't be playing **the full sonnet game.**

Remember, it is not just peasants and amateurs and 19th century Romantics and loonies who want to know identities. Biographers and historians and all lovers of Shakespeare are also fascinated by who was who. I remember here and honor three of my best professors who were very good at linking the lives and the works: Leon Edel on Henry James at New York University; Richard Ellmann on Yeats, Joyce, and Wilde at Northwestern University; and Samuel Schoenbaum on Marlowe and Shakespeare, also at Northwestern University. They taught me to think without a bias against autobiographical clues.

I think that at the core of playing the sonnet sequence game is the guessing game. The sonneteer is obliged to drop clues or hit you over the head with them. Once you get it, each clue opens an inner room into other sonnets or not. When you're in that room, you say to yourself, "Ah, I understand now what this means." And if Shakespeare has constructed a complex, encoded text—where puns, names, letters, numbers, and time are all interwoven—then this is a maze that is quite a wonderful puzzle to explore. This is part of the fun and illumination or delusion of sonnet sequence reading. You want to say, "The others are deluded, but not me." Sidney hits us over the head. So does Shakespeare, or he taps us on the left shoulder from where he's standing, behind us on the right. We look around to the left, but then he runs away and comes into and out of focus like a laughing lover at a masquerade garden party. That old joke! What fun! Can you guess who the guests are under their clever masks?

The *Sonnets* have been linked most closely with three of the plays: *A Midsummer Night's Dream, Romeo and Juliet, and Love's Labour's Lost.* But if the range of writing and rewriting in the sonnets spans from 1589 to 1609, then we should be able to hear and see feedback between the sonnets and many more plays. And the sonnets should contain pieces of all of Shakespeare's styles from this twenty-year span. If all this is so, then those of us working in isolation have been working like the blind men all around that elephant. We each describe a part, and we feel disappointed about those who come up with such different descriptions. Perhaps we should work more like the sixty top physicists in the world on their own list-serve, at least until we get a better, richer consensus about the main parts of *Shakespeare's Sonnets.* It seems to me these *Sonnets* are a very large work, like a series of 154 detailed

scenes—Renaissance paintings—on the horizon of time past. What a great opportunity for collaborative work this wonderful text presents. I offer my views on Shakespeare's autobiographical code as one view into that larger project.

After reading eight annotated editions of the sonnets, I feel that the qualities of Shakespeare's sense of humor are largely missing from the critical record. Somehow, this comic genius—who can be cheerful, wacky, silly, dirty, nasty, and dark and fill whole theaters with all kinds of laughter—does not show up much in the notes on his sonnets. I know that not all puns were considered funny by the Elizabethans, but they also considered the pun as a better form of joke than we do when it is well done. Could it be that we are still under the influence of religious and academic Puritans? Yes, we are, but I believe that the **code of puns** will give us back some of Shakespeare's amusing views of his own life. The only commentators with good senses of humor that I found and enjoyed were Roy Neil Graves and Oscar Wilde, and Oscar can't help himself: he must report that his fictitious discoverer of the identity of W. H. was "**wild** with delight" (1153).

My friends Lance Sparks and George Venn and my wife Sandy Jensen read early versions of this study. Because of their encouragement and their questions, I have taken the time to do more research and expand this work. Lance suggested that I try to write a much more marketable, biographical novel on Shakespeare and his code. I did start such a fictional narrative. I have also read the novels, *The Da Vinci Code* by Brown and *The Rule of Four* by Caldwell and Thomason. I did enjoy these popular novels, but I often wished they had all included an essay of their historic findings at the back of their books for those of us interested in keeping separated, as clearly as possible, historic fact, educated speculation, and fiction. Since my finding of code encourages me to favor autobiography over fiction, I did not want to cloud over any newfound, substantive content with my own fictions.

I'm not sure the youth or the dark lady had good senses of humor, but I am certain that Will Shakespeare did. Think of Falstaff in the tavern and on the battlefield. Think of Hamlet teasing Polonius and Claudius. Think of Hamlet seeing Yorick's skull flying up out of its grave to make room for Ophelia. One more pun may be hidden in that jester's name. I wonder if Yorick's name is a pun for "your rick;" "rick" is the Danish word for "man" as in the name of many Danish kings—Frederick—which translates to "man of peace" (*fred*). In addition, "Your Rick" is a name pun reference to the

dead and famous, theatrical clown, **Ric**hard Tarleton. So let's not leave Yorick's or William Shakespeare's skull in the cold ground. Once we've dug them up, let's remember how these men "of infinite jest" made us laugh. Shakespeare's sense of humor is tied to his intellect and, I believe, to his playing with numbers and code and name puns and calendars.

Stanley Wells believes that Shakespeare may have composed the sonnets over "a long period of time—perhaps as much as twenty-five years [1609 − 25 = 1684?]—and rearranges them in a sequence that only fitfully reflects their order of composition" (*Looking* 52). If you agree or not, let's try to read **all** of his sonnets. This is not often done. Even a fine Shakespearean like Sir John Gielgud left Sonnet #136 off his recorded reading of selected sonnets. But listen to its lines 13 and 14. This is Shakespeare's voice, too, at its most plain and clear:

"Make but my **name** thy love, and
    love that still;
And then thou lov'st me, for my
    name is **Will**."

Chapter 24　Names and Code in the Plays and Other Poems: a Start

There is a deep set of connections between the *Sonnets* and Shakespeare's other poems and almost all his plays. There are all kinds of datable, topical references that will please both biographers and historians. Some of these will enrich interpretations and how we read the plays and poems. If it's possible, we will find new depths in Shakespeare. We will also come to love his Chaucerian, jolly side even more. Above all, we will better understand him as a great Renaissance artist who used all the tricks of his trade. In the following chapter, I want to draw some of the dotted lines between the name code of the *Sonnets* and the most obvious uses in the plays and poems. Although the *Sonnets* are self-contained and well designed, their exuberant ideas overflow like tide pools into the plays, and the ocean of the plays rushes ashore in waves of clear, rough water back into the *Sonnets*.

1. Two Gentlemen of Verona

Shaking Launce: Launce is one of the first of many clowns whose name is a pun on all or half of Shakespeare's name. For Will, it must have started in grammar school, "Here comes Willie Shake a Lance! Shake Spear! Shake Spear!" The Shakespeare family even explained the origin of their "Norman" name with a pun and a story about 1066 when they said their ancient relation "shook a spear" for King William the Conqueror. But in the heart of middle England, the Shakespeare name has over forty spellings and forms; some of them don't even shake a spear. In 1592, Robert Greene joined a long line of schoolboys and insulted Will by naming him "shake-scene." In the *Sonnets*, Will spreads his last name out into 6 separate sonnets, and the words change into an expanded chiasmus—A-ABBA-A—**shake shake spur spur shake shaken.** He is riding high on his horse and laughing.

All those who wish to prove that someone besides William Shakespeare of Stratford—whom playwright and dear friend Ben Jonson called the "Sweet Swan of Avon"—wrote the plays and the poems have got to explain why there are so many name puns and auto-biographical details all over these great works scattered, from beginning to end, as if tagged by a graffiti artist named Will Shake-speare. Ben Jonson, one of Will's closest friends, could not resist name punning twice in his 1623 intro-ductory poem to the First Folio. He calls him "shake a lance" and "shake stage." Face it—most Elizabethans and Jacobeans loved name puns. They also used ciphers, numerology, mottos, crests, rebuses, and word games. All of these verbal and visual elements are good pieces of evidence.

2. Titus Andronicus

In a book that is mostly about the Bessano musical family, Lasoki and Prior remind us that there is a character named Bassanius (the Latin form of Bassano) in *Titus Andronicus* (136). They also translate and unpack the name of the barbarian Queen Tamora. In it, they find the Italian: *"T'amo, Mora,"* or in English: **"I love you, Moor!"** They believe this is a hidden exclamation by Will toward his dark lady, Aemelia Bassano. They also remind us that Tamora is in love with a Moor who has a Jewish name: Aaron (136). Like me, they had picked up on Shakespeare's pun on "more" in Sonnet 40, which calls the dark lady a "Moor," and much more. They go on to remind us that after 1592, Shakespeare entered an "Italian phase." In his two plays about Venice, he presented in *Merchant of Venice* a Italian lover named **Bessanio,** and in *Othello* he presented a servant and wife to Iago, **Emelia.** Both of these Venetian plays also explore two key parts of Aemelia's family background by exploring the fates of a Venetian **Jew** named Shylock and a **Moor** named Othello. Both are non-Italian **outsiders** with crucial roles to play in the Republic of Venice: the first, a interest-charging moneylender Shylock with a rebellious daughter Jessica; the second, a Mars of a man, a mercenary general who is defeated in love (137). It looks as if Shakespeare was close to Aemelia's family during most of his London theatrical career.

3. *Love's Labour's Lost*
Seven and a half embedded sonnets: several weaker sonnets are offered to beautiful women in this somewhat academic comedy. Although the world's most famous sonnet writer,

Shakespeare also thinks that the sonnet writing craze of the 1590s and the lousy sonnets written by love-sick, French noblemen are great subjects for parody. Specifically, he has his wittiest nobleman Berowne write sonnets for Rosaline, a witty, dark heroine who shares many qualities with dark Aemelia. This couple foreshadows the much more famous Beatrice and Benedick and may embody the fun times Will and Aemelia had together: two very verbal people both in love and out of love determined to give life their all and learn from each other despite their big differences.

4. *A Midsummer Night's Dream*
Theseus and Hypolita:
These may be fuzzy logic code names—

THESEAS and
HYPPO-YTA—

for **TH**om**AS** H**E**n**E**age and Mar**Y** **SO**ut**HA**m**PT**on, as the lead couple in this layer cake comedy, which played at their wedding in May 1594.

Lysander and Hermia: I think these are joking names for Henry Wriothesley (perhaps after Leander) and his lover and later wife Elizabeth Vernon (the female form of Hermes). The other couple, Demetrius and Helena, may be a glancing reference to Lord Strange and Elizabeth de Vere. They marry in January 1595, and there is no reason why Shakespeare's company couldn't have been hired to play the *Dream* at their wedding, too. Three ladies' names that start with H in this play may lead us to speculate about three Elizabeths: Tudor, Vernon, and de Vere. But, of course, if Hippolyta is

148

Mary Southampton, then Titania is dangerously close to Britania, and we know with whom this mother of Titans is made to fall in love! Nick Bottom the Ass—his name has the same sound syllables as Will Shakespeare, the dream weaver and joyous comedian. As for the outrageous fantasy of this Ass making love with Titania—blame it on Puck and Oberon, fairy trickster and king of the fair folk.

5. *Romeo and Juliet*

Montague House: Both the name of Romeo's family and the name of Henry Wriothesley's mother's mansion in Southwark across the Thames from London was Montague. Romeo's family belongs to the Ghibeline, republican faction of Italy. The Capulets are royalist Guelphs. Of course, there is a dangerous gulf (named Tybalt and the blood feud) between them. I think there is some reason to wonder if the liberal Henry Wriothesley and his middleclass friend Shakespeare had some of the same little r republican, pro-Parliament, factional sympathies as Nicolo Machiavelli and his good friend Leonardo da Vinci. Shakespeare shows us plenty of bad monarchs and their abuse of royal power.

He and Henry may not be anti-monarchy activists like the Puritans. But Henry does risk his life and join the Essex rebellion against the old men around Queen Elizabeth, and Shakespeare goes about as far as he can in *Hamlet* to plead for Henry's life and good character. Shakespeare's company did get paid to play *Richard II* before the Essex rebellion. Shakespeare may not be a republican, but he did take many political risks and try to use his theater as a center of guarded free speech. In King James' later campaign against nonconforming believers, Shakespeare sounds like a voice for religious tolerance. I think there is a strong line of good, democratic values starting from William Shakespeare to John Milton and leading to Thomas Jefferson. At the very least, Montague House in London was where Shakespeare and his company performed plays for Henry and his mother Mary. Another generation's iteration of this famous mansion in Southwark later became the first British Museum. After he was freed from the Tower in 1603, Henry Wriothesley used his legal training as a senior statesman to negotiate between opposing factions, and he was often on the Parliament's side in their growing feud with King James over his supposed "Divine Right." This division eventually led to the English Civil War.

Three and a half embedded sonnets: The prologue, the dialogue sonnet, and the transition to Act II of *Romeo and Juliet* are all full sonnets. The last 6 lines of the play—spoken by the Prince—are a sestet from the tail end of a rhymed, English sonnet. This 6-line, rhymed sestet was also used as a stanza form in "Venus and Adonis."

"What's in a name?" In wondering about names, Juliet uses one of the *Sonnets'* key name code pun words for Henry Wriothesley's last name, a "rose." She is trying to separate her true love at first sight from his dangerous name, Montague. The rose is a very rich symbol. Most of the nobles of Britain, including the Tudors, took some form or color of rose as an emblem. The War of the Roses was only its most public blood feud. The five-petal, red and white, Tudor rose enclosed both sides of the war, two sets of embedded five-pointed, pentagram stars and pentagons, which also enclosed the geometric key to the Pythagorean, golden ratio number *phi* or Φ. Tudor legend named the Tudor Kings and Queens as peace-makers after the death of Richard III, and Shakespeare supported that view.

6. Venus and Adonis

Dedication: There are seven uses of forms of the word "honour" in the dedication letter to Henry Wriothesley. As in the *Sonnets*, there is also a pun on another of Henry's honourable titles, Baron: in the word "barren." Two times **Baron** multiplied by seven times **Honour** equal fourteen. Shakespeare is playing some of his favorite name and number games even in this 1593 public dedication to Henry Wriothesley.

Internal Tagging: In addition to the public naming of Will and Henry in the dedication, Shakespeare makes puns on his own last name when describing Venus as a she eagle in line 57: "**Shaking** her **wings** [Will's family crest & his name in heraldry he designed] devouring all in haste" (Roe 82). The other half of his name is delayed until line 103, when Venus is describing her conquest of Mars to Adonis: "Over my altars hath he hung his **lance**" (Roe 84). In 1563, this "**shaking ... lance**" prefigures

Shakespeare's design of family punning heraldry by three years.

Sacred Geometry: The downward pointing female triangle of the **V** in Venus contrasts with the upward pointing triangle of the **A** in Adonis. But in this encounter, these two triangles **(V + A)** will not mate and make Solomon's Seal, the six-pointed star.

Adonis: This beautiful young man is used literally and figuratively as an identity for the youth in the Sonnet 53, lines 5 and 6:

Describe **Adonis**, and the
     counterfeit
Is poorly imitated after you;
   (Duncan-Jones 217).

Henry is like a real Adonis. Just as Will fell for an older woman, Anne Hathaway 26, when he was 18, so Henry fell for an older woman, Aemelia Bessano 23, when he was 19. Of course, Will wished Henry had not fallen for Aemelia, so the cold young Adonis in this poem may be a private joke of forgiveness from Will to Henry, about a year after the affair between Henry and Aemelia ended. Remember, the *Sonnets* were not published until 1609. Whatever the length of Will's affair with Aemelia, I believe she was one of three main, life-long influences on his imagination and writing—Henry, Aemelia, and Kit—all immortalized and identified in code in the *Sonnets* (1589—1609).

7. The Rape of Lucrece

Dedication: Here is the clearest evidence for Henry

Wriothesley being the youth of the *Sonnets* and the clearest evidence that the code of the *Sonnets* spills over into the other poems and plays. The word **"honourable"** is used twice in the dedication letter, and so is the word **"worth."** These are both also code name words used in the *Sonnets*—also as doublets—so both the method and the actual words of the substitution code carry over in this very public document that so clearly identifies Henry Wriothesley (H. W.) in its 1594 publication.

"All for one, one for all:" This is the Wriothesley family's French, chiastic motto: *Tout pour un, un pour tout*. It is translated in line 144 (Roe 151). This motto is also played on in the *Sonnets,* whenever Will plays with the number words "one" and "all."

Internal Tagging: Just as Shakespeare punned on his last name in "Venus and Adonis," he does so again in "The Rape of Lucrece." Just as the rapist Tarquin is threatening Lucrece with his sword, we find line 505: "This said, he **shakes** aloft his Roman **blade**" (Roe 168). And in the stanza that follows, we find three references to a falcon (bird) or a falchion (blade), which echo the three silver falcons on the Wriothesley family crest (168). This stanza ends by describing Liucrece's "**trembling fear**, as fowl hear falcons' bells" (168). Trembling is a kind of shaking, and fear rhymes with spear. Perhaps these tagging puns mean that both Will and Henry (as men) are associated with the more powerful rapist by gender and by the lady's blame.

But the real rapist, I think, was Lord Henry Carey, Hunsdon, who forced himself on Aemelia after her forced marriage in Fall 1592 and the birth of their bastard son Henry in 1593. Perhaps Shakespeare even dares to name Hunsdon in a stanza, where Lucrece is pleading with Tarquin not to rape her. She says a rape would not be worthy of his own royal name: "Thou wrong'st his **honour, wound'st** his princely **name**" (Roe 172). In the words "honour" and wound'st, we can find the letters of Hunsdon's name: **HONoUr wouND'St**. We have found this kind of embedded name code in the *Sonnets*. Why wouldn't Shakespeare use the same identification tags in other works? But why does he need code in publicly dedicated works? He needs it to name a powerful man like Hunsdon and his crimes, and Will needs it to reinforce the less obvious code of the *Sonnets*. These uses also show that Will believes in embedded code as a neat way of giving clues and proof. The code is part of the complex patterns of his mind.

I think the *Sonnets* and the two poems dedicated to Henry Wriothesley are very intimately connected. What was Shakespeare thinking about Aemelia in these 3 great poems of the 1590s, all written, in part, for Henry: *The Sonnets, Venus and Adonis*, and *The Rape of Lucrece*? In them, we seem to see three different forms of a woman's tragic or at least painful love life:

1. As an unwillingly shared and independent mistress in *The Sonnets*
2. As a spurned, older lover and

goddess Venus (from Venice) in *Venus and Adonis*

3. And as a grief-filled, raped wife in *The Rape of Lucrece*.

I was most familiar with seeing Aemelia in her rebellious complexity as a woman Shakespeare wanted as his sole mistress. She is sexually attainable, but also, in an opposite way from Petrarch's ideal, she is not always attainable. That is, she must be shared with other men. Young Henry was seduced by her. She has a husband, Alphonse, forced on her. Lasoki and Prior think that after he "discharged" Aemelia, Lord Hunsdon still felt entitled to sex from her (118). No wonder Shakespeare is uptight about "having" her as "his" mistress. Perhaps her 1611 book conveys her mature, feminist feelings best about how she felt.

Venus and Adonis may be a lightly pornographic joke between Will and Henry, commemorating when Henry stops his affair with Aemelia. Venus goes off mourning her loss of Adonis. Shakespeare compares the youth of the *Sonnets* to Adonis in Sonnet 53. Not even the goddess of love can keep Henry. Shakespeare politely portrays Adonis as never giving in and being more interested in hunting than in love. There may even be a good joke in the hunting scene where Adonis is killed by a boar—what a bore!

But I could not relate Aemelia's fate to Lucrece's until I read Lasoki and Prior's book on the Bessano family. In a packed Chapter 8 on Aemelia as the dark lady, Roger Prior writes that Aemelia may remind Shakespeare of Lucrece

because not even her forced marriage to Alphonse Lanier protects her from unwanted, continued sexual attention from Lord Hunsdon (118). Not only does Alphonse have to put up with the rape of Aemelia, but so do Aemelia and Shakespeare. Lord Hunsdon is a royal Tarquin; perhaps this made Aemelia feel suicidal. She certainly complained to Shakespeare. This adds a lot of confusion and danger to his love for her. This adds a lot of loathing and stress to Aemelia's life at age twenty-three. This helps explain some of the pain and confusion of the dark lady sonnets. When Will sends Henry *The Rape of Lucrece*, it is a serious communication between two friends about the fate of a woman they shared. Perhaps Hunsdon read it and stopped and became patron of the Lord Chamberlain's Men in 1594—the power of Will's pen. I think all three portraits in poetry—the dark lady, Venus, and Lucrece—show a very complex mix of sympathy and revulsion, Shakespeare at his best. Suddenly, we have a three-way portrait of this very important woman in Shakespeare's life.

8. Merchant of Venice

Bessanio and Antonio: Is Bassanio's name also derived from the name of the Italian town outside Venice, which the musical family, the Bessanos, took for their new Italian name? Yes, and in this name, Shakespeare combined two English spelling of their name: Bessan**o** + Bessan**i** = Bessan**io**. Here is another curious doublet, name game, key to the code and to Shakespeare's invention of characters. Their Bessano forebears had come to Italy from Sicily. Before that, they were descended from Sephardic Jews, who were exiled from Spain with the Moors—perhaps to Morocco—by the new nationalistic, Spanish regime of Ferdinand and Isabella in 1492, which also attacked gypsies and drove them to live in caves in the mountains and help create flamenco culture with other internal exiles. Antonio is a loaded choice for the Merchant's name because Antonio Bessano was the oldest brother of the generation that went to England as musicians in the court of Henry VIII. And it's odd that Antonio should be an anti Semite because, although they were converts first to Catholicism and then English Protestantism (as a matter of advancement and survival), the Bessanos don't strike me as haters of who they used to be.

Aemelia's conversion and her long poem on the passion of Christ strick me at first as sincere and unambiguous. But when she became the first English woman to publish her own book of poetry in 1611, the poet titled her work, ambiguously, "Hail to the God who is King of the Jews." That's the Hebrew title for Jesus that drove Herod insane. Aemelia gives voice in her poem to Pilate's wife warning him not to execute Jesus, just as Aemelia's Eve reminds Adam that he is a greater sinner than she is after the Fall. So Aemelia does express irony in an early modern feminist form.

Jews of Venice: The Bessano's family crest contained three silkworm moths and a mulberry tree, which show their strong roots in the domestic Italian silk industry, a common occupation for Sephardic Jews. Venice built one of the first ghettos in Europe, a gated area that was locked up at sundown. The Venetian Republic said it was for "the protection of the Jews," and I suppose every time a state raises up a wall and a curfew, we could ask that old question best raised by Robert Frost: what is being walled in and what is being walled out?

Isaac Asimov thinks he has tracked down the root for Shylock's made-up name. In an Old Testament grab bag of odd taboos, Leviticus says, "Don't eat cormorants!" Actually, in the *King James Bible*, 1611, it says,

"And these are they which ye shall have in abomination among the fowls; they shall not be eaten ..."
(*Leviticus* 11.13)

And in a long list of forbidden birds, here are three not to be eaten:

"And the little owl, and the **cormorant**, and the great Owl..."
(*Leviticus* 11.17)

These are all considered unclean birds. But the Hebrew word usually translated as **cormorant** is *"shalakh,"* and Asimov thinks that is where Shakespeare got the name for his Jewish money lender, who is forced by Venetian law and the cross dressed lawyer Portia to give up his claim to a pound of Antonio's flesh and to convert to the supposedly more "merciful," Catholic religion. Could some of this incident come from Bessano family history in Venice after they converted to the Catholic faith but got in debt to a very difficult money lender?

9. *Henry IV.1*

A knight named Jack: In *Henry IV, Part 1,* Will wanted to poke fun at an old Protestant family name, so he named his fat knight Sir John Oldcastle. But the knight's powerful family objected, so Shakespeare—who may have based his knight on his own father—changed the name to Sir Jack Falstaff, very close to its real original, John Shakespeare. I think the old man had a drinking problem, which led to his real decline and which led his son to reject him as Hal does Jack. But when it came time to pick up John's quest for a family crest, Shakespeare himself designed a piece of punning heraldry, which shows a falcon with its wings in the shaking position and a diagonal spear that looks (when I squint) like a pen. So the family crest repeats the old story of shaking spear, and the motto says, "Not Without Right," a reference to a legendary someone who fought for William the Bastard way back when he came from Normandy and became the Conqueror.

10. *Merry Wives of Windsor*

A boy named Will:
Shakespeare goes back to grammar school and his Welch teacher to recreate a schoolboy's nightmare: a meeting between his mother and his teacher. The mother, Mistress Page, asks, so how's he doing? And the teacher makes up an impromptu Latin test in the street, complete with double translation, vocabulary, and verb and pronoun forms that have plagued all of us in English or in Latin. Little Will Page is a wit, and he makes up what he doesn't remember using everything from puns to pig

Latin. His mother is impressed. His teacher lets him pass. The great author, who has Ovid memorized, remembers all the school boy tricks. But it is not the best students who need these tricks. I remember French classes in high school when my best friend knew all the words (his father was a French teacher) while, if there had been prizes for coined "anglicisms," I would have won first place. At least, I made my French teacher Monsieur Desmé shake his head and laugh and give me a nick-name, *mon petit ver*, my little worm.

I also like actor and author John Southworth's speculations about the Page family being drawn after Shakespeare's family, with Mistress Page as his own mother Mary, Mr. Page as the sensible side of his father John, and I'd like to add daughter Anne Page as a portrait of Anne Hathaway as a girl eight years older than William (who may have been a childhood visitor to the Shakespeare house), and Will as a little school boy (183).

Perhaps Shakespeare is humorously showing himself and his future wife as youngsters (more like sister and brother), when the eight years between them was really a unbridgeable gap. The other Windsor middle class family is named Ford, the second syllable of Will's hometown of Stratford. The parson, Sir Hugh Evans, may have been a Welsh teacher of Will's, whose name can become an exclamation: H. Evans! (Heavens!)

Falstaff in "love:"
Shakespeare brings back his fat

knight as a con artist who is out-conned by two middle class housewives. To escape angry husbands, Jack has to be carried out in a laundry basket and is dumped in a watery ditch. Perhaps Falstaff is no longer based on John Shakespeare, and the unflappable Mr. Page, who trusts his wife, is. Falstaff also has to dress up as an old woman and is beaten with sticks. His ultimate humiliation comes when he is pinched by children dressed up as fairies. All of this middle class fun and the opening jokes about the crest of the Lucy family with luces (fish) as louses on an "old coat" comes from family life in Stratford like the comic Sonnet 143, which compares the dark lady to a housewife chasing a chicken (the youth) while Will portrays himself as a big baby crying for a kiss.

11. *Much Ado About Nothing*

Hero: I think her name is a reference back to Marlowe's "Hero and Leander," written by Marlowe before his murder in 1593 but not published until 1598. Instead of dwelling on the Hellespont, this Hero is a governor's daughter, who lives in Messina, Sicily, near the infamous whirlpool and rocks called Scylla and Charybdis in *The Odyssey*. This Hero is chaste but wrongfully accused. Marlowe's Hero is successfully seduced in a scene that tries to please the soft porn tastes of law students and one law student in particular, Henry Wriothesley, more than Shakespeare's 1593 "Venus and Adonis." But, as recorded in the rival poet sonnets, it was Marlowe's portrayal of Leander as a feminine looking young Henry Wriothesley,

made love to in the sea by Neptune that really twisted Shakespeare's shorts and made his codpiece limp. But then, Marlowe was murdered by "a coward's knife," and Will could compete only with the ghost of his rival from then on.

Beatrice: I think this wonderfully witty, woman character is based on the love of Shakespeare's London life, Aemelia Bessano Lanyer. He gives her the name of Dante's muse but the character of the dark lady. So, unlike Dante's chaste, ideal lover, Shakespeare picks as his female muse a real and unpleasantly difficult, educated woman, a poet and a musician and a cast-off mistress of Queen Elizabeth's cousin.

Jokes about sonnets: Benedick (or good dick) is a bit like witty Shakespeare himself. But, when he wants to woo Beatrice with sonnets, he brings up that old problem of rhyming in English. Rhymes have stumped many a would-be sonneteer, and Will jokes that even this witty couple writes less-than-wonderful sonnets. But when they both try to wiggle out of marriage, their friends prove they love each other by finding a sonnet by Benedick in Beatrice's pocket and a sonnet by Beatrice in Benedick's pocket. Gotcha! Mutual sonnet writing is a sure sign of true love or at least the crazy games of courting. Those old, cobbled together, Italian love songs of eight and six lines to make 14 have come a long way from that creative Sicilian lawyer Lentini at the dawn of the Italian Renaissance.

Dogsberry is "an Ass:" In 1584, three Bessano brothers had a run-in with a Sheriff, whose men were confronting a mob opposed to the walling up of a popular gate used by poor people and immigrants in London. It's interesting to note that the cops identified the Bessanos as "black" men because of their black hair and dark skin. When the Sheriff threatened to arrest the three brothers, who were the Queen's servants and immune from arrest, one of the brothers said (according to the Sheriff's report), "...send us to the ward? Thou wert as good ... (be the words with reverence named) kiss our etc" (qtd. in Lasoki & Prior 244). Another officer reported the missing word as "arse" (244). This may be proof that Shakespeare heard all sorts of Bessano family stories from Aemelia and/or her many London relatives and remade them into scenes in his plays.

12. Henry V

Sonnet as epilogue: As in *Romeo and Juliet*, Shakespeare uses the flexible sonnet form to sum up what will happen after his hero king dies young. And since Shakespeare played the Chorus, he got to say this final sonnet himself. What's in a name? All those King Henry plays—IV, V, VI, VII (at the end of *Richard III*), and VIII—must count for something in Shakespeare's quest to make his favorite lord, Henry Wriothesley, immortal.

13. As You Like It

Rosalind: Here's another witty heroine, cross-dressing as Ganymede. She may refer to Elizabeth Vernon, who dressed in disguise as a page of Henry Wriothesley's, when they eloped to exile in France in 1598 after a secret wedding not approved by Queen Elizabeth I.

Poor sonnet writing: Rosalind's literary criticism of the poor sonnets and songs that Orlando hangs on trees for her shows her educated tastes and her valuing Orlando more as a wrestler and good man than as a poet. She is both intelligent and realistic. If Shakespeare showed any of his sonnets to the dark lady (and I think he did), what did she say to him?

14. Hamlet

Polonius: A double-written name that combines the character of Lord Burleigh with the name of one of his spies, Robert Poley. Poley was present (with two other operatives and crooks) when Marlowe was murdered at a safe house for spies (run by a distant, female relative of Burleigh) near the Deptford navy base down the Thames from London. Perhaps, if we see Hamlet as Marlowe, then Polonius, Rosencrantz, and Guildenstern can be seen as those three spies. When Shakespeare uses name code and political allegory, there are no rules that say he cannot mean multiple identities and meanings.

Hamlet/Hamnet: A great name elegy for his son, who died at age 11 on August 11, 1596. Shakespeare played the ghost and left us the spooky scene of a living father coming back to haunt his dead son.

Essex and Henry: After the failed Essex rebellion, Essex was executed and Henry Wriothesley was in the Tower. I believe that the friendship between Hamlet and Horatio was double written from the relationship between Essex (Hamlet) and Henry (Horatio) as well as Henry (Hamlet) and Horatio (Will).

Marlowe: I also believe that third ghost embedded in Hamlet's multiple personalities was Will's greatest rival, Kit Marlowe. At court and in the public theater, Shakespeare's audiences might have heard the echoes of two famous thirty year old men, who were both dead: Essex and Marlowe. Marlowe's street name Kit is encoded in the *Sonnets* (See page 74); he's called a dead "shepherd" in *As You Like It* by Touchstone; and Kit's play *Dr. Faustus* is one of the sources for contrast in Shakespeare's 1611 play *The Tempest*. All of Shakespeare's parodies and tributes to Marlowe may drive some authorship loonies nuts, but in London before May 1593, no one would have mistaken the dramatic rivalry of these "two mighty opposites" and all the distinct differences that show up in their best early, competing plays. The playbills and the London crowds could tell Kit from Will, and Will probably acted in Marlowe's plays as well.

15. Twelfth Night
Name subtraction code: In *Twelfth Night*, as instructed by the cipher writing character Maria, I uncovered a pretty piece of Shakespeare's name code. Unlike Malvolio (bad or sick or evil will in Italian), I looked under the MOAI initials that Maria used as a "fustian" cipher to lure him into self-deception. I have realized that Shakespeare sometimes plays a name subtraction game with his characters. He did so in one sonnet: "Take honour from thy name." (See page 36.)

So, **Olivia — Viola = I.**

Viola loves the Duke without ego or "I." Olivia is all wrapped up in the self-love of her grief until she falls for the disguised Cesario.

Then I wondered what Malvolio minus MOAI equaled, and it was **LLOV.** So Maria got Malvolio to believe that those four letters— MOAI—in his name were equivalent to his name. But all they are equivalent to is his name minus LLOV, and he winds up **loveless.** Now I was on a roll. I had "I LLOV..." but I also had a blank. I messed around with other names, but then I asked myself, who else winds up loveless? Of course, it's Antonio. So I subtracted Sebastian from Antonio, and the remainder is **BASSANOO.** Thus, by subtraction and some kind of fuzzy logic I arrived at an embedded code in *Twelfth Night:*

I   L-LOV   BESSANO   O!

This exclamation is a later form of the code found in the name Tamora in *Titus Andronicus,* as in the Italian *"T'amo, Mora,"* made in English into "I love you, Moor" (Lasoki and Prior 136).

Antonio and Sebastian: I wonder why these two paired and named characters are good guys in *Twelfth Night* and bad guys in *The Tempest.* What happened between Shakespeare and Antonio Junior, the head of the Bessano family between

1601 and 1611? I also wondered about the name Sebastian. Could it be unpacked this way: Sebastian = Sea Bastion = Sea Fort = Venice? Is that why Antonio's name is linked with Sebastian? I did find one curious accident of passport misspelling from one of many trips between England and Italy taken by Bassano brothers. I wonder if "Baptist Bassani" was misspelled by an official as "Bastian Bassaine" (Lasoki & Prior 27). Name spellings are often unpredictable and quite wild in Shakespeare's day. But were the name forms Baptist and Sebastian linked? Alvise Bessano's first name could take the form of Alinso or Alonso or Alvixus (23). Alonso is the King of Naples in *The Tempest*. Do many of Shakespeare's character's Italian names come from the rich storehouse of Bessano family names? At any rate, Shakespeare needs Sebastian to subtract the right letters from Antonio and result in Bessanoo.

Viola and twins: Viola joins a lot of other later, female characters—most of them good daughters, whose names have three syllables and end in a: Ophelia, Viola, Emilia, Cordelia, Perdita, Marina, and Miranda. Of course, written just after the heavy father/son, William/Hamnet tragedy *Hamlet, Twelfth Night* supports the nice fantasy that the dead twin brother Sebastian/Hamnet will return, and, in the meantime, the plucky twin daughter Viola/Judith will survive in life dressed up as him. Viola is also the name of a musical instrument, as Toby Belch names it, the *viola de gamba*, not a bad pun for Aemelia, the daughter of the

musical Bessano family, who actually made and repaired violas.

16. Othello
Emilia: Poor Emilia is married to the ambitious, racist, manipulative, Spanish Ensign in the Venetian army, Iago. She is used by Iago to steal the silk, strawberry handkerchief, which Iago plants as false physical evidence to make a case where there is no evidence, only misguiding misinterpretation. The other Aemelia (Bessano) was forced to marry her second cousin, Alphonse Lanyer, who had inherited her father's musical position at Queen Elizabeth's court and who went to war under Essex and along with Henry Wriothesley to a raid on Spain and to Ireland to try and improve his social standing. Aemelia was hoping he could, but they were both disappointed. Was Alphonse at all like Iago?

Venice: Named for the Goddess of Love, Venus, a rich maritime sea power and top-down republic was the first city where the large Bessano family became successful as musicians, players of wind instruments, and makers of musical instruments. Aemelia Bessano may have been Shakespeare's most intimate informant on life in Venice and Italy.

17. Anthony and Cleopatra
Anthony: Is the English form of the Roman, Latin name Antonius. There is also a Bessano relative by the name of "Mark Anthony."

Rome versus Egypt: Late in life, Shakespeare may see himself as an aging theatrical campaigner and

158

compare himself to Anthony, lover of the "dark lady" Cleopatra, that sexy Macedonian Queen of Egypt. He may see himself as a Anglicized Roman playwright of the north. To him, Aemelia Bessano brought the whole, Mediterranean south: her Italian, Jewish, musical, "gypsy," mistress, sexy background.

18. The Tempest
Antonio and Sebastian: Here are these two names again. Sebastian is not a Bessano family name, but his name coupled through letter subtraction with the name Antonio (See page 157.) helps generate again the **Bessano+ o** family name. But here, Antonio is the evil usurping, younger brother of Prospero, the Duke of Milan. And Sebastian is the younger brother of Alonso, the King of Naples. Antonio almost succeeds in teaching Sebastian how to usurp the place of his brother, too.

Marlowe's Doctor Faustus versus Prospero: The contrast between Faustus' "black" magic and Prospero's "white" magic continues Shakespeare's career-long dialogue with his one-time, chief rival and long dead doppleganger, Christopher Marlowe. The name of Will's spirit Ariel echoes the name of Dr. John Dee's good angel, Uriel. (A third great play about magicians is *The Alchemist* by Ben Jonson, but there, the magician is only a con artist.)

"Shake + spurs" & "break + staff:" Twice, Shakespeare has Prospero pun on the above phrases that echo Shakespeare's own last name. This pattern is consistent from beginning to end in Shakespeare's plays and poems. It is one of his favorite rhetorical tricks, and those who deny it are not looking for the real Shakespeare. (Such critics are stuck in the famous but anti-funny worlds of Dr. Johnson and gloomy Coleridge.) But in order to follow the real Will, we must follow his trail of name puns along with all the rest of the crumbs dropped from his very full bag of rhetorical tricks.

Farewell: These name puns and other markers, like the word "globe," tag William Shakespeare's four speeches of farewell (3 of ten lines each and one of 20) said by Prospero to the court and his London audiences in the last scenes of *The Tempest*. When Will says good-bye, he says so with a smile and his truthful honesty. The last words of the last play written completely by William Shakespeare ask both his King and his audiences to "set me free." But did Will play Prospero or did Burbage? John Southworth, an English actor, thinks that Will played Alonso instead (272). So maybe Burbage delivered Will's famous lines, and, once again, we have only a second hand actor's recitation we can count on. Southworth also thinks that Shakespeare did not retire to Stratford but continued to act almost to the end of the 1615-1616 theater season when he went home ill and missed the final presentation at court on April 1, 1616. He died three weeks later close to or on his birthday (275 f.). I like Southworth's rethinking of the last five years of Shakespeare's life. Southworth doesn't believe in that old saw that Shakespeare retired (for health or religious or political or any other reason). He has Will still acting on tour in the Fall of 1615 with his company.

But in Southworth's final portrait of the man Shakespeare, he says we have "no evidence" about the man from his texts we can rely on. Then he cleans up Will's life far too clean for me. Once again, it's best when all kinds of people work together to see Shakespeare. Southworth convinces me that people who do not act do not know enough to write about Will as an actor or as he was seen by some as a mere "player." But will Southworth and others ever see the many pieces of encoded, autobiographical details that I believe Shakespeare left for us in his systematic texts?

But wait, there's more Will to consider from 1613 to 1615 in *The Two Noble Kinsmen (TTNK)*. I hesitate to go there because no one knows what parts Shakespeare wrote and what parts Fletcher. But are we really that stuck? Don't we know the meaning of the word "collaborate?" Can we believe that both authors—Shakespeare and Fletcher—didn't read the whole finished text and both approve of every word? So we can look at all elements of this last play and look for a piece of **Shakespeare's mind** and focus on the **patterns** of his code.

I think the play is better and wackier than critics say. There are Shakespeare **name tags:** "shake .. stir," "shake ... bones," and "shake ... javelins" (*TTNK* Prologue 5 f & 17 & 2.2.48 f). And the three key characters of the sexual triangle are defined as if **Arcite** were Henry Wriothesley, **Palamon** were

Shakespeare, and **Emilia** were Aemelia Bessano Lanyer. I think the following **character points** were written in (beyond the Chaucer source) to pin down these identities:

1. Arcite as Henry: skilled "horseman" (*TTNK* 2.5.12 ff, 3.1.106, 3.6.74 ff, 5.3.115 f, 5.4.48 ff; "pretty" (2.3.79); **name code**—"worthy" (2.2.69), "worthily" (2.5.1), "hence" (4.2.22); "honor" & "worthiest" (5.1.17); "If I were a woman" (2.5.64 ff); "thief in love" (3.1.41); "soldier" & "fair foe" (3.6.4 ff); apology (3.6.39 ff); worships Mars (5.1.49 ff); & see details of his picture (5.3.41 ff).

2. Palamon as Shakespeare: "saw her first" (*TTNK* 2.2.161); **name code**—"will" (2.2.67); "he has a tongue will tame tempests" (2.3.16 ff); "brown manly face" (4.2.42); great "singer" (4.3.86 ff); worships Venus & her music (5.1.69 ff); & his picture (5.3.44 ff).

3. Emilia as Aemelia: lesbian "faith" (1.3.48 ff, 2.2.76 ff); "lords got maids with child" (4.3.41 f); converts to hetero faith (5.3.84 ff); worships chaste Diana (4.2.57 ff, 5.1,137 ff); "recorder" music (5.1.137); "moon" (5.1.137); no **name code** needed.

In fact, *TTNK* has so much author winking, self-parody, and self-referencing—mainly *Two Gentlemen of Verona, A Midsummer Night's Dream, Hamlet, Much Ado About Nothing, Macbeth*, and *Othello*—that it's a great play to end on and rest my case. But wait, then there is *Cardenio*.

Cardenio: Or the Second Maiden's Tragedy is a difficult nut to crack. In all the good books I've read about Shakespeare written in the decade from 1995 to 2006, the same cliché about *Cardenio* rules: it is a "lost play." These authors say its plot was derived from Cervantes' *Don Quixote,* and it was co-authored by Shakespeare and John Fletcher: a very intriguing consensus.

But oddly enough, an L. A. theater troupe can be found on the internet (on a poster) performing "Shakespeare's *Cardenio."* One of my best students ever—Erica Jones, a young, Corvallis costumer and total Shakespeare nerd like me—sent for and showed me a book by Charles Hamilton (1994), which contains the full text of *Cardenio* and attempts to prove it is Shakespeare's and Fletcher's. But this book seems to have suffered the same fate as Nicholl's great book about Marlowe's murder, now in a new edition (2002) but originally published about the same time in the mid-1990s. Both books were mostly ignored by the Shakespeare Ph. D. club. Even though Hamilton discusses at length all kinds of proofs happily within the mainstream of literary Shakespeare studies, perhaps it is his expertise and claims from the field of handwriting analysis that caused the biased "club" to deny him membership.

But if Shakespeare had a hand in this **Cardenio**, what would we expect to find in its text? Hamilton labors mightily and comes up with great circumstantial evidence. Here is a list of most of the notes Hamilton hits:

• **Two Noble Kinsman** is the

nearest model:
• The plot and subplot fit as tightly as the 2 plots of *Lear* and are on the Shakespearean theme of sexual jealousy. Both come from Cervantes, and both contain sexual triangles: 2 men compete for 1 woman in both—a total of 6 characters. 2 of the men are brothers; the two women are sisters.
• The Lady Luscinda is like Emilia in *TNK.*
• There are many echoes of the *Sonnets, The Comedy of Errors, Othello, The Winter's Tale,* and *Hamlet.*
• In addition, Hamilton wants to prove that the ms. is written in the handwriting of William Shakespeare, and it is this claim that may lead to his banishment from the "club."

Of course, I read the text looking for code and name puns. Here is what I found:

• One nasty theme of the play is the Tyrant's love for the dead body of the Lady. Is this a pun by Will on necr**ophilia**?
• I came up with a long list of what I like to call "Leonardo's thumb prints" or Shakespeare name tags. They are concentrated in two key speeches by Cardenio, the deposed king and hero, a. k. a. Govianus.
• These two "code" sections come in two key speeches: one at the end of Act I (lines 240—247), the other at the end of the play (V.2.2212—2130). In both of them, I find the familiar code **name pun "honour"**

doubled. In the first, there may be a **name-tag** on Will's last name: "prick + spur" as well as "content" doubled and the word "key." There are other name-tags of "shake" and "stiff" (IV.4.1756) and "quaking ... judge" and "shake ... fit" (I.2.373—375). And in the second speech, there are key words: "lady," "admired mistress," "will and we'll," "Queen of Silence," and the music of **"recorders"**—the instrument of the Bessano family to end the play.

In addition, there are all kinds of Shakespeare's favorites tricks like mini-masques, a play within the play, 2 suicides of wronged women like Lucrece, an exiled leader like Prospero, a foolish father like Polonius but with 2 daughters, a reference to the *Tempest*, Ariel singing, and a ship wreck.

Before Hamilton's book, the coverless playbook of this play spent 400 years "lost" in plain view with the censor's title of *The Second Maiden's Tragedy* mistakenly attributed to either Tourneur or Thomas Middleton for the last 200 years (Hamilton 12). Whatever you think of my findings, I hope more people will read the text of this play and Hamilton's fine book. I think it would make fantastic theater and a good addition to Will's last years.

So Shakespeare may have ended as he started. Back in 1590 or so he may have recorded his ties to the Bessanos in *The Taming of the Shrew:* he shows us an analogous father named Baptista with a dark, shrewish daughter and a "white," milder daughter. The inverse ratio goes: dark **Aemelia** is to Katherina as older, "sweeter" Angela is to younger Bianca.

William Shakespeare's plays belong to all of us to dig through, but they belong most in live theater productions and in the movies. I don't pretend that much of this word gaming and code breaking will be relevant to performance. I leave any decisions about how the code may change performance up to actors and directors. I can't see a contemporary actor speaking a Henry Wriothesley code word and winking at someone in the audience. The code is a creature more appropriate to the poetry texts and silent reading. I believe the code may have been born in the *Sonnets* and then carried over into the plays especially when a friend in the know, like Henry Wriothesley, was going to be a reader or in the audience. Beyond Henry, I just have to wonder how many people got it. Was there a circle of dinner friends and co-workers to whom Shakespeare read the *Sonnets* and other pieces? Perhaps we can now see the *Sonnets* as the code key and the plays as public encoded speeches with hidden jokes and identities only for those in the know. Once again, it would be lovely to know what Henry Wriothesley, Edward Alleyn, Ben Jonson, the Bessano musicians, Richard Burbage, or major Court figures got as they sat in the theater.

My purpose is not to reduce Shakespeare to rags and tatters of words and fragments of words. My purpose is to encourage all kinds of

Stratfordians to play and to see that we have a valid code from Shakespeare to work on. My ultimate purpose is to put to rest that silly, old saw that Shakespeare left us "no clues" about his personal life in his poems and plays, especially in the *Sonnets*. So many false leads have been offered with so many crazy code ideas before people considered the most obvious—that the author Shakespeare is William Shakespeare, and he left us many clues to prove it, and, as all the documents Sam Schoenbaum found and published prove, he really did grow up in Stratford as Da Vinci grew up in Vinci. We owe Shakespeare the further investigation of this code and much deeper word play work.

Then, of course, after we have snuffled around in all the texts—the poems and the plays—like a herd of moles, let the actors, actresses, and directors give us what we should all really love: performance! I offer all this speculation and evidence to you in a spirit of inquiry and friendship. I simply want to know all of Shakespeare better. In the spirit of scientific speculation I have tried to see if Shakespeare himself left us any friendly data. This is the whole question about my method: are these details biography or autobiography? What if the man left us clues? Don't we all hope to know this man better than before? I go to the theater and deeply enjoy his works. I will look for you there. If we cannot be friends in the theater, what have we done to the spirit of Will? We are all, after all, shameless friends and lovers of William Shakespeare, aren't we?

"We are star dust."

—Joni Mitchell

Appendix A:

A list of possible NAME code words and autobiographical word clues in
Shakespeare's Sonnets
(including and in addition to those cited in the body of text)

Use this list to go there and look around for even more clues.

Sonnet #	Possible CODE WORDS for names and other CODE

In the Sonnets for the Youth:

1	**rose, herald**, tender 2X, heir/memory, code: o-n-a-n 2X, theme: procreate, don't masturbate: 1—17, **17th Birthday**
2	forty (fort) winters (carpe diem), **will, worth**, made/maid
3	thy glass, face 2X, some mother, mother's glass, **April,** windows
4	lend, lends, usurer, sum of sums, traffic with thyself alone, unused beauty, th'executor [of **will** implied]
5	hours, will, hideous, **rose** [implied] water
6	vial, willing, willed, happies [sic], self-willed, heir
7	son [sun implied]
8	wilt
9	will 2X, wail, well, waste, himself
10	deny ... love, possessed with ... hate, love 4X, hate 2X, for love of me, beauty
11	wilt, kind-hearted
12	**hence, wastes**
13	love as personal address 2X, yourself 2X, beauty, Who? husbandry, honour, uphold, father/son
14	truth 2X, beauty 2x, (Keats' ABBA), stars 2X, eyes, art, date
15	rich, youth, wasteful, he + engraft? = he + n = Hen. N + you = new.
16	**happy, worth**, pencil, pen, drawn
17	will, high, heaven, hides, half, numbers number, faces, metre, twice
18	summer's day (each of the Sonnets is one), **shake, rose** [implied] buds of May, summer's leasc (theater season), lines to time
19	Devouring, **devour, wilt, heinous**, hours, **worst, wrong**
20	A woman's face, master mistress, heart, hue, hues, **wrought**, pricked
21	muse, heaven, rehearse, couplement, sun and moon, heaven's, huge, hems, hearsay
22	thou (in youth), heart 3X, wary, will
23	unperfect actor, heart, rite, dumb, recompense, writ, wit

164

24	eye, played the painter, heart 2X, sun, eyes 5X, perspective
25	**honour** 3X, titles, marigold, sun's eye, happy
26	Lord of my love, witness, wit 2X, worthy
27	weary, travel, pilgrimage, imaginary, jewel, black, night 3X
28	happy, **shake**, day 5X, night 5X, nightly
29	disgrace, heav'n, rich, featured, art, scope, **Haply**, lark, arising, heaven's, wealth, state 2X
30	sessions, waste, woe 3X, bemoaned moan, pay, paid, all, restored
31	**all 7X,** thou ... hast all the all of me
32	hearts, all 7X, hidden
33	**sun**, heavenly, rack, suns, heaven's sun, 3 X 11 (Hamnet's #)
	Quatrain #3: about Hamnet's death
	Line 11: "But out alack, he was but one hour mine,"
	a revision after 1596 referring to Hamnet's death
34	sun [implied], [broken] promise implies Henry and Aemelia get together?—brought out in the open in Sonnet 40, pearl
35	**roses**, moon and sun, bud, sweet thief
36	Unless thou take that **honour** from thy **NAME**
	honour 2X, in two there is one, mine 2X
37	all 2X, **worth, entitled**, engrafted, happy
38	rehearse, worth, **10th Muse**, 10X
39	And our dear love lose **NAME** of single one
	worth, all, NAME, him, here, **hence**
40	all 5X, **more 2X** (Moor? [dark] *mors*, L. [mulberry tree, symbol of the Besanno family]), wilful, love 10X, love (10) ÷ all (5) = more (2)
41	heart, beauty 4X, beauteous, woman 2X, **woo-man, woe-man**, twofold
42	all, wailing, lose/loss 6X, both ... cross = doublecross
43	**darkly** bright/bright in **dark**: ABBA, shadow 3X, shade 2X, dreams 2X, **happy, heavy**
44	**wrought**, heavy, naughts
45	air, fire, health
46	divide, heart 8X, eyes 6X, heart wins war 8 to 6
	8 + 6 = 14, octet and sestet of sonnet
47	heart 6X
48	trifle 2X, truest, thrust, trust, **worthy, whence, thence, wilt**
49	Against that time 3X, sun
50	heavy, weary, wretch, heavily, horse, **spur**
51	thence, wilful, horse, **spur**
52	**Solstice**: key, so 4X [sol], seldom 2X, Therefore (there 4)
	carcanet (necklace) contains both "arc" and "net"
53	Begins second half of Summer
	every one 2X, one 5X, none 2X, shadow 3X, **Adonis, Helen**, beauty, bounty, heart
54	beauty, beauteous 2X, **rose, roses** 2X, bud, sweet 3X, sweetest
55	record, memory, wear, **arise**

56	hungry, two contracted new
57	slave, happy, fool, **will**
58	slave, vassal, charter, privilege, **will,** wait, waiting, ill, well
59	nothing new, five hundred, sun, wonder, wits, **worse**
60	waves, minutes, eclipses, **worth**
61	**will**, weary, watchman, watch, wilst, wake, far off, others, near
62	all 3X, heart, **worth, worths**, beauty, code: o-n-a-n
63	memory, beauty, vanishing, vanished
64	will, store loss loss store: ABBA
65	beauty 2X, **honey**, hold, **wrackful**
66	all 2X, unhappily, honour, wrongfully, ill
67	beauty, **roses, rose, wealth**
68	beauty 3X, beauty's, **fleece**, holy, all, yore = your
69	all, hearts, outward, beauty, weeds, soil, common
70	slander's mark, crow, buds, ambush, ill, hearts
71	Do not so much as my poor **NAME** rehearse bell, vile, vilest, implies youth's name is not the same as the poet's Will
72	My **NAME** be buried where my body is worthy, **willingly**, well, **worth**
73	time of year, **shake**, well, translation of Ovid's line & Marlowe's motto: "Consumed with that which it was nourished by."
74	Note: I think this sonnet contains some interesting use of code, but, as of now, I'm less sure. Line 11 seems to refer to Marlowe's murder, "coward conquest of a wretch's knife," and there are **4 key K-sound words**, and **"it"** is prominent in line 13. contented, fell, all, bill, shall, coward conquest (is conquest a glance at "inquest?") wretch, **worth**, it contains worth = that = that = it = that = this = with thee
75	food, show'rs, wealth, anon, counting, alone, all 3X,
76	That every word almost doth tell my **NAME** [like a bell implied] Why write, still 3X, all 2X, sun, telling, told
77	glass, will 3X, beauties, how 3X, waste 2X, memory 2X, wilt, profit, enrich, book
78	**10th Muse**, grace 2X, graced, art 2X, "added feathers to the learned's wing," "As high as learning my rude ignorance."
79	call, all, another, a **worthier** pen, he 6X, thee 7X, thy 5X, thyself
80	Knowing a better spirit doth use you **NAME** **worth, wilfully, will, wracked, worthless, worst**
81	Your **NAME** from **hence** immortal life shall have **from hence 2X**, memory, rehearse
82	writers, hue, **worth**, true 2X
83	**worth 2X**, beauty, both, eye, 2 poets, 2 eyes
84	Who is it...? **c**opy/wr**it**, **worse**, **c**ounterpart/w**it**, **worse**
85	"that able **spirit**," all whilst, others

166

86	Was **it** the proud full sail of his **great verse**
	"Was this the face that launched a thousand ships?"
	in-hearse, it 2X, spirit/spirits, compeers,
	"that affable familiar ghost," thence, **countenance, his line**
87	Farewell, dear, estimate, charter, **worth 2X**, had, dream, waking
88	vantage 2X, **right** (Risley/sound gag),
	wrong (Wroithesley/sight gag)
89	Thy sweet beloved **NAME** no more shall dwell
	will 4X, ill, I'll 2X, **haply**, tell
90	wilt 2X, while, heart, rearward, woe 3X, windy, rainy, worst, will
91	**wretched** 2X
92	worst 2X, happy 3X
93	deceived husband, shall, still, heart, hatred, heart's 2X, history,
	thence, Eve's apple, beauty
94	**will**, heaven's, husband, **worse**
95	**NAME 2X, naming, rose, budding name,** heart, privilege,
	knife
96	youth 2X, grace 3X, **will,** well, translate 2 X, lamb 2X, all, mine 2X
97	summer 2X, summer in winter, widowed wombs, w-words
98	absent in the spring, hue, any summer's story, rose, all, shadow
99	15 lines: violet, whence, sweet 3X, breath, roses: elegy for Essex?
100	Muse, **worthless, rise, resty**, satire, wastes
101	beauty, truth 4X, **wilt**
102	merchandized, publish, Philomel, her mournful hymns, hush, night
103	muse, worth, glass 2X, disgrace, well, graces, verse 2X, more 2X
104	"eye I eyed," beauty, **3 winters and 3 summers, 3 Aprils,**
	3 Junes, hue, beauty's summer
105	fair, kind, and true (3X)
106	chronicle, wasted, all 2X, skill, **worth**
107	moon (for QEI), her eclipse, and crown (for James I)
108	Even as when first I hallowed thy fair **NAME**
	implies **herald/rose** from Sonnet 1
109	**heart, rose**
110	**another youth, worse essays**, newer proof, **older friend,**
	heaven, most 2X
111	**Thence** comes it that my **NAME** receives a brand, #11
112	**o'er green**, brow, care, calls, well or ill, allow, **all the world 2X**
113	I/eye, heart, **crow**, dove
114	**whether** 2X, kingly, cup, poisoned
115	**reckoning**, beauty, love is a babe, growth, grow
116	true minds, **worth's height**, star, If logic: "Inever writ"
117	**hoisted, winds, wakened hate (HWWH)**
118	healthful, **rank, ill, thence**
119	hopes 2X, **wretched**, heart, fever, ill, ills
120	hell of time, woe, hard, true, hits, you 2X, humble, ransoms, ransom
121	**vile 2X, wills, I am that I am, reckon**

122	memory, **heart, razed**, record
123	**heard, registers, records, haste**
124	weeds 2X, heretic, witness
125	honouring, ruining, heart, **Hence**
126	lovely Boy, **hour, hast, withering, wrack, wretched**

In the Sonnets for the Lady:

127	**not** beauty's **NAME, no NAME**, black 3X, eyes are raven black
128	music 2X, wood 3X, would, happy, fingers 2X, lips 3X
129	waste, lust 2X, mad, well heaven
130	sun, **wires 2X, roses 2X**, breath, reeks, music, mistress, heaven
131	art 2X, beauties, heart, jewel, **face**, groan, **1,000 groans**, black 2X, thence
132	eyes/ayes, thy heart 3X, ruth, sun heaven, [Evening] star [Venus], morning, mourning 2X, mourn, beauty, black
133	Beshrew, heart 5X, my friend and me, engrossed, **wilt**
134	he is thine, he 4X, **will** 2X, wilt 3X, bond/bind, him 3X, **whole,** confessed, covetous, statute of thy beauty, anagram: usurer—use, sue
135	Whoever hath her wish, thou hast thy **Will**
136	Make but my **NAME** thy love ... for my **NAME** is Will.
137	blind (Cupid), eyes 4X, **worst, heart** 4X
138	lies 2X, youth/young, lie, false 2X, faults
139	**wrong, heart**, eye 2X, pretty looks, looks 2X, enemies/foes
140	wit, tell, health, physicians, ill 2X, mad 2X, heart
141	eyes, 1,000 errors, heart 3X, five 2X, wretch
142	sin 2X, sinful, pity, pitied, **and echo with last 2 lines of Wyatt's "They flee from me:"** If thou dost seek to have what thou dost hide, By self-example mayst thou be denied.
143	**Hen.** [implied], **Will**, chase 2X/catch 2X, **housewife (hw?)**, babe 2X, flies 2X, hope, behind/be kind.
144	two loves, **worser**, ill, angel 5X, spirits, spirit, saint/devil, fiend, both 2X, another's hell
145	**And** (Anne**) 'hate' away** (Hathaway), heart, fiend, heaven
146	Poor soul, soul 2X, **fading mansion**, death 2X, dead, dying And death once dead, there's no more dying then. An inspiring line for John Donne writing his "Holy Sonnets"
147	Fever, **fair** : bright = **black** : hell = **dark** : night, physician/ prescriptions, past cure/past care, speaking ill of her
148	**String of exclamations:** O! No! Aye! Not so! Yes so! No! O! eyes 2X, eye 2X, sun, Cupid [implied], blind
149	cruel, thine eyes, "love, hate on ..."
150	power/powerful, lie, worst, **abhor 2X** (not a nice name for her), **unworthiness, raised, worthy**

151	But rising at thy **NAME** doth **point** out thee
	conscience 2X, Double embedded anagram: betr**AAY**ing 2X, m**E**,
	MMy 2X, tr**EE**ason, te**LL**, m**Y** bod**Y** th**A**t, h**EE** m**A**y
152	forsworn 2X (four sworn), sworn 2X, swear 2X, bed-vow, vowing,
	vows, 2 oaths versus 20, oaths 4X, deep 2X, perjured 2X, I,
	eye, lie: I'm 10 X worse than you
153	Cupid: holy fire, **bath** 3X, mistress' eye 2X: **17 X 9 = 153**
154	Little love god: maiden hand/virgin hand, brand 2X, quenched,
	bath, men diseased, mistress' thrall, came, cure,
	14 X 11 = 154
	153 & 154 are two versions of a "translation"
	final line **ABBA** construction:
	Love's fire heats **water, water** cools not **love.**

Appendix B:

A web site by Nigel Davies tries as hard as I do to prove that **the sequence in Shakespeare's 154 Sonnets is by the poet's design.** I don't always agree with Davies, but I decided to make a list out of his best insights to show how he lines up some of the numbers of sonnets with their content and with the meanings of numbers to prove that **their positions in the sequence are no accident.**

# Sonnet	Reasons from content or the relationship of numbers
Sonnet 5	The word "pent" means "confined" but *"pente"* is 5 in Greek
Sonnet 8	Music has 8 notes in the octave; in line 12, there is the word "note." There are 12 notes (black and white keys) in the standard octave.
Sonnet 10	The first double digit sonnet introduces the speaker as the specific 2nd character (like the second actor in an Aeschylus play).
Sonnet 12	12 hours of day, 12 of night, with 12 numerals on the clock's face.
18—126	After 1—17, there are 109 sonnets, one more than Sidney's 108.
10 Sonnets:	21, 32, 38, 78, 79, 82, 85, 100, 101, & 103 refer to the muses. There were 9 classical muses. The youth was the 10th muse.
26 & 126	Two formal break points in sonnets to the youth 100 apart.
44 & 45	2 sonnets centered on the 4 elements: 4 & 4 start at 44.
Sonnet 49	7 & 9 are "climacteric" numbers. 7 X 7 = 49. "Against that time..." begins all 3 quatrains. Another climacteric sonnet (7 X 9 = 63), begins with the word "Against..."
Sonnet 52	52 weeks of the year
Sonnet 55	There may be a "visual pun" here between the digits 55 and the book's initials: SS. (But, there's a problem since Shakespeare used Roman numbers.) There is mention of "Mars"—it was the 5th planet in the "Ptolemaic system of astronomy."
Sonnet 60	A pun on "our" and hour.
Sonnet 63	7 X 9: the Grand Climacteric. Drayton had 63 sonnets in *Idea*. 63 X 2 = 126. QE I's 63rd year was celebrated.
Sonnet 71	Our years are "Three score and ten" or 70. Sonnet 71 is a like a "funeral dirge" after the allotted 70 years.
Sonnet 75	It centers on the Seven Deadly Sins but only mentions five of them: 7 [− 2 =] 5.
Sonnet 81	It "reaffirms the poet's belief in the power of his verse." The climacteric number 9 is squared to make 81.
Sonnet 99	It has 15 lines. 15 + 99 make 1599, the year Jaggard published two of the sonnets just before the 16th century turned.
Sonnet 105	Plotinus's doctrine of the One is referred to 5 times. 1-0-5—One, Zero, Five. When a person has reached a state of oneness (five times over), he has need of "nothing."
Sonnet 114	Its opening line, containing the word "crowned" may glance at the concept of a perfect crown of sonnets at 100 plus 14.

# Sonnet	Reasons from content or the relationship of numbers
Sonnets123, 124, & 125	a triad that forms the climax of the first 126. They all contain "pyramids" and "great bases" and refer to time. The word "No" shows up in all three. It begins the 1st quatrain in 123 , the 2nd quatrain in 124, and the 3rd quatrain in 125.
Sonnet 126	It is comprised of 12 lines or 6 couplets: 12 and 6 put together make 126. 126 is twice 63 and can be called the "Super Grand Climacteric." And 126 divided by 14 equals 9. Shakespeare could have written 126-14 line sonnets for a total of 1,764 lines. But since one sonnet has 15 and one has 12 , the total lines = 1,763. Does this point up the importance of 17 to him with the grand climacteric 63 as in 17 and 63 make 1,763? And is it important that the digits of 1,763 add up to 17? The 17th birthday of the youth generated the whole sequence.
Sonnet 127	Sonnet 1 desires the youth to have an "heir." Sonnet 127—the first for the dark lady—names "black" as "beauty's successive heir."
Sonnet 128	The keyboard of the virginal: there are 12 keys and 8 notes in the octave for 12 & 8.
Sonnet 133	Line 8 is: "A torment thrice threefold thus to be crossed." 133 represents 1 (one torment), 3 (thrice), and 3 (threefold).
135 and 145	Both are playful punning sonnets on Will (135) and Anne Hathaway (145) positioned 10 sonnets apart.
Sonnet 144	This is about the battle of two spirits. In alchemy the number 4 is closely associated with spirits. Here, there is 1 speaker, one angel spirit (4), and one devil spirit (4).
Sonnet 154	154 divided by 14 equals 11, the age of Hamnet when he died and was buried on August 11, 1596. In Sonnet #11, there are the words "threescore year" or 60. If we insert 60 in the tens column of 154, we get 1564 or the year of Shakespeare's birth. Thus, Shakespeare "has left his own fingerprint, a water mark, his unique signature, a personal irrefutable date-stamp of the year of his birth in these contents."

Source of data: Davies.

Appendix C:

The Alignment of the Globe Theater
Opened 12 June 1599 O. C. (Summer Solstice)
with a performance of *Julius Caesar*
on the night of the New Moon with Venus & Jupiter
appearing in the evening sky

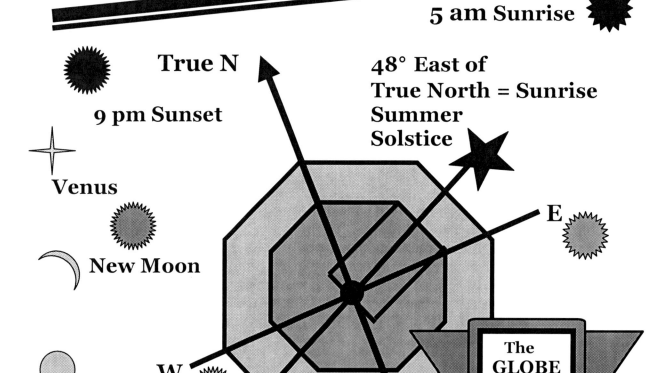

The 20-sided Globe is represented by an octagon (not drawn to scale).
Note how the Elizabethan imagination links up Roman & English history, fate,
time, both solar & lunar calendars, & opening a new, commercial enterprise.

Source of data: Ackroyd 374.

Appendix D:
Two 4-sonnet segments
seen as a traditional altar triptych design

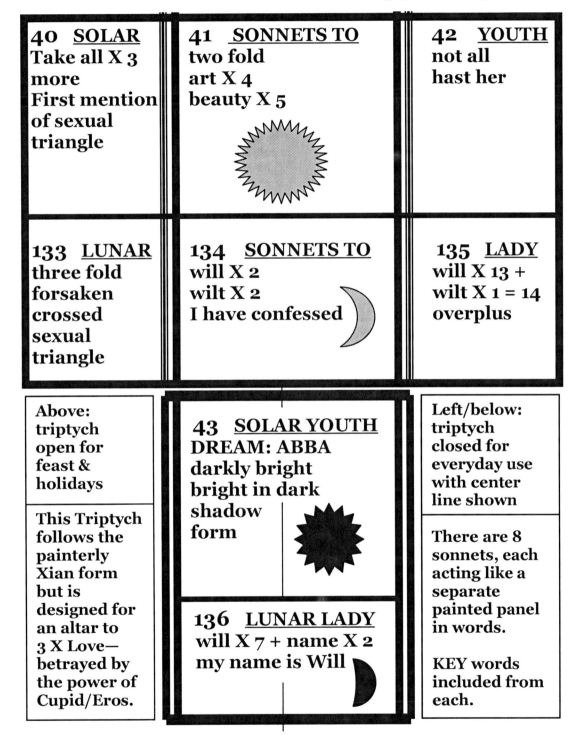

40 SOLAR Take all X 3 more First mention of sexual triangle	41 SONNETS TO two fold art X 4 beauty X 5	42 YOUTH not all hast her
133 LUNAR three fold forsaken crossed sexual triangle	134 SONNETS TO will X 2 wilt X 2 I have confessed	135 LADY will X 13 + wilt X 1 = 14 overplus

Above:
triptych
open for
feast &
holidays

This Triptych
follows the
painterly
Xian form
but is
designed for
an altar to
3 X Love—
betrayed by
the power of
Cupid/Eros.

43 SOLAR YOUTH
DREAM: ABBA
darkly bright
bright in dark
shadow
form

136 LUNAR LADY
will X 7 + name X 2
my name is Will

Left/below:
triptych
closed for
everyday use
with center
line shown

There are 8
sonnets, each
acting like a
separate
painted panel
in words.

KEY words
included from
each.

The power of a popular image—an opening altar triptych—can help us rethink the relationships of 2 sets of 4 matching sonnets: 40—43 (solar) & 133—136 (lunar).

Appendix E.
A Lover's Complaint by William Shakespeare:
Questions & Speculations

In 1603—4, during the first of two periods when he did major revisions on his *Sonnets,* William Shakespeare wrote "A Lover's Complaint." This is an odd work that too few have commented on, and it has been treated oddly as well because he had it published in 1609 as a contrasting, companion poem to his very famous Sonnet sequence. Perhaps John Benson started the odd treatment; he pirated the *Sonnets* in 1640 and rewrote them to please readers and make money. His weird rewrite became the misleading, off-standard version for almost 200 years. The "Complaint," a 329 line narrative poem, "was long thought to be the work of another poet and was not solidly attributed to Shakespeare until the 1960s" (Dunton-Downer and Riding 455). Although Shakespeare's name was on the title page, this was not proof enough for many. In fact, many scholars still believe that Thomas Thorpe pirated the *Sonnets* and the "Complaint" in 1609. Based on detailed evidence in the texts, I believe Shakespeare authorized the 1609 Quarto printing, got out of town in a plague year, perhaps to tour with his company, and certainly never complained about theft.

Most major modern editors of the *Sonnets*—consider Booth and Vendler—do not even include "A Lover's Complaint." In the Cambridge edition of *The Poems* edited by John Ross, it is given good notes, but it is separated from their edition of the *Sonnets*. It is correctly present in the Arden edition of the *Sonnets* also with good notes edited by Katherine Duncan-Jones. But mostly, "A Lover's Complaint" has been treated like a poor stepchild.

Yet it is Shakespeare's fourth, long narrative poem after "Venus and Adonis" in 1593, "The Rape of Lucrecre" in 1594, and "The Phoenix and the Turtle" in 1601. It is more than one third the size of "Venus and Adonis" (329 lines versus 1,194 lines), and it is just less than one fifth the size of "The Rape" (329 lines versus 1,855 lines). "The Complaint" is written in the same rhyme royal, seven-line stanza as "The Rape of Lucrece, " a form like half a sonnet with pentameter lines and an ababbcc rhyme scheme, "first used in English two centuries earlier by Chaucer" (Dunton-Downer & Riding 452). The number 7 —one of the fateful, climacteric numbers of the Elizabethan age, tied to the 7 Planetary gods and goddesses and the days of the week—is an organizing number here. This poem is 47 stanzas of seven lines each. In both "The Rape" and the "Complaint," the climacteric number seven may indicate sexual disaster.

But the main speaker is not like the poet of the *Sonnets,* who may be recast as one of the two older men of the initial frame before we get to the leading voice, which is a young, female voice, a wronged woman. The "Complaint" is a recognizable genre piece; it offers a contrasting female voice to the male voice of the poet and lover in the *Sonnets*. In 1609, it was attached to Shakespeare's Sonnet sequence just as Daniel's "Complaint of Rosamond" was attached to his sonnet sequence, "Delia," in 1592. Aemilia Lanyer, the first English woman to publish her own book of poetry, herself a wronged mistress of Lord Hunsdon in 1592 and perhaps the dark lady of the *Sonnets*, also read Daniel's "Rosamond." Lanyer retold part of the story of King Henry II's poisoned mistress (Rosamond) in one of her major poems published in 1611.

"Faire Rosamond, the wonder of her time,
Had bin much fairer, had she bin not faire..."
(Lanyer 61)

Elizabeth Woods, a leading expert on Lanyer, doesn't know if she read Shakespeare's "Complaint" or his *Sonnets* in 1609, but she does think Lanyer read "Venus and Adonis" and "The Rape of Lucrece." I think Aemilia Lanyer is the best and leading candidate for the dark lady of *Shakespeare's Sonnets,* and this opinion colors some of my views of the "Complaint."

According to Duncan-Jones, there was a group of Sonnet and Complaint sets published in the 1590s along with Daniel's: Thomas Lodge's "Complaint of Elstred" followed his Sonnets *Phillis* (1593); Michael Drayton's "Matilda the Faire" followed *Ideas Mirror* (1594); and Richard Barnfield's "Cassandra" followed *The Affectionate Shepherd* (1595). Duncan-Jones writes that Shakespeare's maid is "unique" because she is "unnamed" (431). But the point is that Shakespeare, in sonnet revision time in 1604, decided to create a "Complaint" to make a recognizable "box set." But perhaps it was not finished until a second revising period in 1608 and then, I believe, Shakespeare authorized their publication in 1609.

Read after *Shakespeare's Sonnets*, the "Complaint" is a let down, but it brings an interesting change of diction and style. According to John Roe's notes, there are at least five key words in "Complaint" that Shakespeare used only once:

Table 1.	
1. "fluxive"	line 20
2. "appertainings"	line 115
3. "acture"	line 185
4. "extincture"	line 294
5. "unexperient"	line 318

None of these words went anywhere but into the OED as odd, nonce words, used only once by Shakespeare. Duncan-Jones points out others in her notes. Shakespeare coined words in all his works, but here in the "Complaint" they seem to be used more often, they stand out more, and there seem to be more that did not get "picked up" and used by others. These words seem like odd, metal words coined once but never sent to the mint. I wonder what Shakespeare's playful mind was doing, placing them where he did. Of course, he did not know they would not catch on. It's just indicative of his kind of writing and diction in 1604—perhaps as he was writing *Othello* and thinking about *King Lear*—that he would use so many odd, shiny coins.

And, unlike the powerful four characters of the *Sonnets*, the lead character of this poem is somewhat odd, too. She is the pathetic yet very moving voice of a maid who has been seduced and left by a young lord, who sometimes sounds a lot like the young man of the *Sonnets*. Hers is a feminine voice, more like that of the Roman wife Lucrecre, a lamenting voice. I wonder whose voice this is.

Like the *Sonnets*, this poem has a cast of characters: the **Maid,** a **Poet** (who overhears her), a **Reverend (Old) Man** (once a womanizing courtier, who now herds cattle, who sits down to listen to her), the **Youthful Seducer**, and a **Nun** the young man boasts about (who was seduced from her sacred vows by the youth's beauty). The poet speaks first and sets the rural scene—in a female-shaped, womb-like landscape—and describes the lamenting maid (lines 1—56). The reverend man sits down next to her to listen (lines 57—70). The maid retells the story of her seduction (lines 71—329). In her retelling, she repeats the winning lies the young seducer used to conquer her doubting heart.

"Gentle maid,
Have of my suffering youth some
        feeling pity,
And be not of my holy vows afraid."
            (Roe lines 177—9 274)

In fact, she gives him a long speech, the second longest single section of the poem, in the middle of her lament (lines 177—280). Then she recounts her ruin and ends with a sad pledge that she would be taken in all over again (lines 281—329).

"Ay me, I fell, and yet do question
        make
What should I do again for such a
        sake."
            (lines 321-2 282)

After she cries "O!" five times in the final stanza, she ends with:

"Would yet again betray the fore-
        betrayed,
And new pervert a reconciled maid.'"
            (lines 328-9 282)

So even our sympathy or our advice would be useless to change her second lament, which is to say that she would fall all over again. Then, a little oddly, there is no second half to the frame. It would be useless. Neither the Poet nor the Old Man get to comment on her sad tale.

176

The maid's second lament ends the narrative. She has her own last word. This gives the "Complaint" a five-part structure, with a two-part introduction and a long speech, with a speech inside of that. These five parts and the five O's at the end remind me that the five-pointed star, the pentacle or pentagram, is an ancient female symbol. For the Greeks, it is the symbol of the Goddess Kore in the apple core, and for the Celts, it is the sign of Morgan (Walker 782—3). The Pearl poet of "Gawain and the Green Knight" makes it the sign of the Virgin Mary on the inside of Gawain's shield. Set up in a table, the five parts of "A Lover's Complaint" would look like this:

Table 2.	
1. The **Poet's** discovery of the Maid, frame	56 lines
2. The **Old Man's** approach, frame	14 lines
3. The **Maid's** story, first two-thirds	107 lines
4. The **Youth's** deceptive speech	103 lines
5. The **Maid's** story, last third	49 lines

Thus, we have an odd testimonial to the power of insincere speech to seduce, a complaint that undermines itself, which may even be said to be an instructional piece for young men to learn how to lie to get love. These young men—who enjoyed "Venus and Adonis" as a piece of light pornography and made it Shakespeare's most popular published work in his lifetime—may be Shakespeare's only real, reading audience, but he also shows them what lies do to young women who are taken in. (See Sonnet 152 for Will's echo, the last personal sonnet addressed to the dark lady, in which he says that all his vows to her were lies to get her love.) As usual, William Shakespeare builds in lots of lines of conflicting moral tension and difficult intellect.

Based on prior evidence I've considered in the *Sonnets*, I can speculate that the autobiographical material in "A Lover's Complaint" runs deep. What if the poet is a pastoral version of younger Will in 1592 (age 28) listening to the dark lady (perhaps Aemelia Lanyer at age 23) justifying her giving in to the youth? Will must have asked the dark lady, "Why did you do it?" What did she answer? Does this poem give us some evidence? Then suppose that the Reverend Man or "Father" is Will in the countryside at 40, already thinking about retiring from London, perhaps rethinking his sympathies for the dark lady (and perhaps, from the perspective of a father of 19 and 21 year old daughters, worried about young men leading them astray).

Duncan-Jones associates this Old Man with Lord Hunsdon, the cousin of Queen Elizabeth, instead (435). Her insight makes me wonder if Shakespeare used him as a model for the Old Man, who took Aemilia Bessano as an 18 year-old, orphaned mistress in 1587 and discarded her when he got her pregnant at age 23 in 1592. Once a major scholar like Duncan-Jones brings up such a clue and says, "sounds like Lord Hunsdon," then I'm inclined to spin out a whole story that lights up the Aemilia Bessano Lanyer connection and describe her as both the dark lady and the wronged maid. Of course, in 1603, when Shakespeare started to write the "Complaint," his own daughter Judith was also 18 years old, and his sympathies for the "bastard shame" of the dark lady, expressed in Sonnet 127, may have deepened.

Suppose the silver-tongued seducer is the youth of the *Sonnets,* perhaps Henry Wroithesley at age 19 in 1592. Then we must assume that Will at 40 has a very complex view of the double-crossing sexual triangle that he admits to being part of twelve years before. After all, the youth used the love-making and speaking skills taught to him, in part, by Will's early sonnets. But even though the youthful seducer of "Complaint" reminds many of the youth in the *Sonnets,* this man has brown hair and perhaps a youthful, reddish beard (Duncan-Jones 437; Roe 269). He is not as fair as Henry. Perhaps in 1604, Shakespeare is drawing a composite seduction of Aemilia by Henry Wroithesley in 1592, of Mary Fitton by William Herbert in 1601, and even of Judith Shakespeare by

an unknown youth in 1603 or before. I am open to all of Will's possible echoes and suggestions. I cannot shut down any of them with a pretense at one literal-minded reading.

It seems to me that it is sometimes very misleading to propose that only one limited, literal, reduced reading is possible when we are up against Shakespeare's richly suggestive and multi-leveled poetry. When doing literary detective work, it's best to stick to the facts, but if the "facts" are William Shakespeare's rich texts, then we have to open ourselves up to the nature of our evidence. We have to speculate and call it that. In the investigative stage of any exploration, "what ifs" can get us much further than "we can never know," but they can also get us in trouble. But it is Shakespeare who suggests what-ifs. He combines levels of reality and periods of time. He constructs analogies and formulas. He makes use of word and number codes. He cuts what he doesn't like. He dramatizes. He jokes. He plays all kinds of rhetorical games. He never stands still like a target on the village green.

Let's start with the most obvious wronged maid. This maid reminds many of Ophelia, sitting by a stream and weeping, rereading Hamlet's love letters and tearing them up and throwing them in the river as well as breaking ivory and crushing gold rings and stamping them in the mud. But Ophelia is not the only wronged daughter of middle and late Shakespeare—the plays are full of them. After the father and son obsessed *Hamlet* in 1600-1601, which many think records his double loss of son Hamnet at age eleven in 1596 and his father John in 1601, Shakespeare's landscapes are peopled by daughters: Viola and Olivia in *Twelfth Night* (1601), Desdemona in *Othello* (1604), Goneril, Regan, and Cordelia in *King Lear* (1605), Marina in *Pericles* (1607-08), Imogen in *Cymbeline* (1609-10), Perdita in *Winter's Tale* (1610-11), and Miranda in *The Tempest* (1611). The maid of "A Lover's Complaint" is just one of many young woman and daughters who speak through him and to whom he listens with a fatherly ear. Of course, during the first decade of the 17th century, there are always at home in Stratford Shakespeare's real daughters with their life and love problems for him to think and worry and write about.

But Shakespeare's "Complaint" is not just a simple maid's lament complaining of false love. In the middle of her lament, as proof of her innocence, she gives the youth's silver-tongued, clever, devilish speech. Her lament is divided by the young seducer's long speech. Like the plays within plays, we have here a genre enclosed in a genre. That is, we have the battle-tested model of a successful man's seduction speech that other men may use to seduce. Such how-to models were common fare in Shakespeare's time. But this cynical speech is enclosed in a female lament, so we can see the sad result of its (his) success even while men may admire and even plan to abuse these skillful lies and strategies that include reversing the blame and shedding false tears. It is the male lover's tears that convince the maid of his love. She knows his deceitful reputation from other women, but she cannot imagine that tears can lie as well as words.

And then comes the maid's pitiful confession. Even though she knows he was lying, she would fall for his sweet lies all over again! This is the stance that Shakespeare himself admits to in the *Sonnets*. He believes the lady's lies. He lied to her to make love to her; he says so in the last personal sonnet to her #152, line 7: "For all my vows are oaths but to misuse thee..." (Duncan-Jones 421). But Will has also been betrayed by the youth. Will must also accept the young lord's explanation of his betrayal and value his tears as if they were "pearls." He ends Sonnet 34, lines 13-14,

"Ah, but those tears are pearls which thy love sheds,
And they are rich, and ransom all ill deeds."
(Duncan-Jones 179)

He is forgiving the youth and patron with acceptance even before he names the betrayal in Sonnet 40. So the maid is like Will; her complaint includes the admission that she would fall all over again.

In Shakespeare, the image always makes a reflection. He is neither a simple cynic nor a simple moralist. Whenever a person or character makes a strong figure, that figure generates its opposite or at least a contrasting shape off on an angle like a shadow. And that is true of the wronged Maid, who, at first, seems like such an obvious figure for our sympathy. Soon, we may feel uncomfortable like the Old Man, who is a reformed courtier and rake, listening to her confession. In fact, I could construct a complex chain of positions that start out from her lament. Most of us who care about young women—daughters, daughters-in-law, nieces, granddaughters, and students—start with compassion.

Table 3.

1. Pity the poor Maid. She has been deceived.
2. But her seducer may have learned his skill from the "deep-brained sonnets" ("Complaint" line 209) of his women lovers or even a poet like Shakespeare.
3. Will does blame himself (in the *Sonnets*) for the youth's subtle, erotic words and misadventures in love.
4. Here in the "Complaint," Will writes a successful, seduction speech for this young lord, who boasts that even a nun was willing to betray her vows for his beauty.
5. The Maid says she would fall for his fine words and especially his tears all over again.
6. In the *Sonnets*, Will falls for the tears of the youth, and he cannot cure the love sickness he feels for or the VD he caught from the dark lady with reason or hot water.

"A Lover's Complaint" (1604) forms a small and often ignored bookend piece with the *Sonnets* (1589—1609) as "The Rape of Lucrece" (1594) was a promised bookend to "Venus and Adonis" (1593). Both "The Rape" and "The Complaint" are laments by wronged women: Lucrece's rape is large, violent, political, and tragic; the Maid's seduction is personal and deceptively attractive. These laments seem to warn us about women's wages from men's lust. On the other hand, both "Venus and Adonis" and the *Sonnets* are explicit celebrations of the power of love, lust, and worldly affairs to move us in almost every direction and teach us truths about ourselves. Some of the lessons may be very surprising. Not even the goddess of Love, Venus, can seduce the righteous young Adonis, who is killed while hunting a boar. And the youth and the poet and the dark lady are locked into a sexual triangle of their own making, having all seduced each other.

"A Lover's Complaint" seems a pale reflection in the mirror to show up the *Sonnets*. These are not equal tragedy/comedy twins like *Romeo and Juliet* and *A Midsummer Night's Dream* or especially the larger twin works *Hamlet* and *Twelfth Night*. Taken together, with the overpowering *Sonnets* and the short "Complaint," these can be thought of as the 1609 version of those twinned poems of the mid-1590s both dedicated to the Third Earl of Southampton, "Venus and Adonis" and "The Rape of Lucrece." But the "Complaint" is a worthy work for much more study. Although it does not justify or counter-balance the perceived and sometimes exaggerated sexism in the *Sonnets*, it does give a flawed, young woman her voice in an age when men played the love game with all the advantages of unequal power. The much-neglected "Complaint" should come into its own as a minor work and companion to the *Sonnets*. In the Quarto of 1609, "A Lover's Complaint" does physically follow the last dark lady sonnet. It may be a flashback to the time of Sonnet 133, perhaps in 1592, where Will confronts the dark lady's betrayal of him with the youth with this question:

"Is't not enough to torture me alone,
But slave to slavery my sweet'st
        friend must be?"
            (Duncan-Jones 381)

And it may be a whole lot more as a genre piece and a fatherly poet's attempt to give us the voices of his daughters and even his ex-mistress.

This lament does really follow the *Sonnets* and must modify the views we formed reading that very complicated text like another echo. It does restart the arguments of the *Sonnets* with a whole new female, "**concave**" landscape and a whole new set of narrative notes. Just as we end the *Sonnets* with the doubled envoi story of the origin of hot springs from "Cupid's brand," a phallic torch, we turn the page and start to hear (with a poet recording them) the cries of a young woman wronged by a more powerful lover. The "Complaint" does come next reverberating from a womb-like cave. The *Sonnets* are incomplete without their counterpart, "A Lover's Complaint." After all, William Shakespeare put it there.

"From off a hill whose concave
        womb reworded
A plaintful story from a sist'ring
        vale..."
        (Duncan-Jones lines 1—2 431)

Sisterhood is powerful. Shakespeare can listen to two sisters in Stratford. He can also continue his love for the dark lady by giving her a voice in this poem.

Works Cited
(for "A Lover's Complaint")

Duncan-Jones, Katherine (ed.). *Shakespeare's Sonnets*. London: Arden Shakespeare, Thomson Learning, 1997.

Dunton-Downer, Leslie, and Alan Riding. *Essential Shakespeare Handbook*. London: Dorling Kindersley, 2004.

Lanyer, Aemilia. *Salve Deus Rex Judaeorum*. Edited by Susanne Woods. New York: Oxford UP, 1993.

Roe, John (ed.). *The Poems*. New York: Cambridge UP, 1992.

Walker, Barbara G. *The Woman's Encyclopedia of Myths and Secrets*. San Francisco: Harper & Row, 1983.

Works Consulted
(for "A Lover's Complaint")

Bell, Ilona. *Elizabethan Woman and the Poetry of Courtship*. New York: Cambridge UP, 1998.

Oxquarry Books, Ltd. "A Lover's Complaint." "The Amazing Web Site of Shakespeare's Sonnets." 2002. December 13, 2004 <http://www.shakespeares-sonnets.com/lcall,htm>.

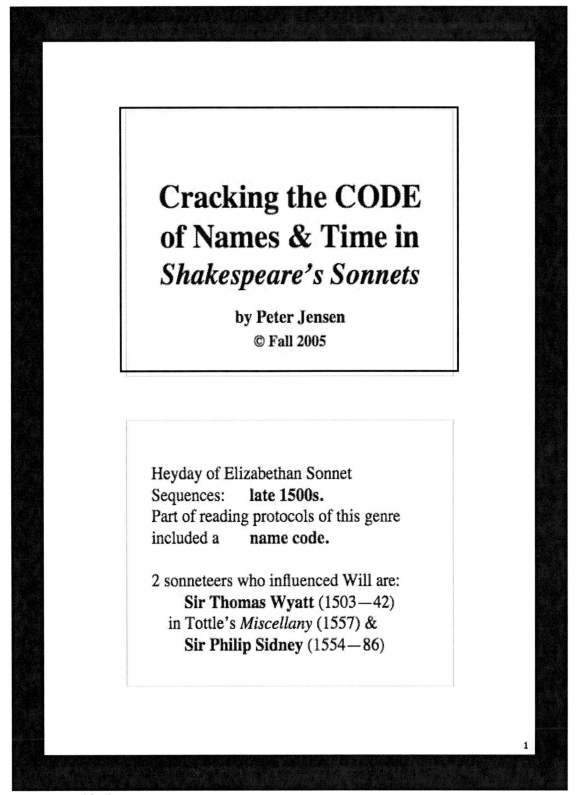

**Cracking the CODE
of Names & Time in
*Shakespeare's Sonnets***

by Peter Jensen
© Fall 2005

Heyday of Elizabethan Sonnet
Sequences:　**late 1500s.**
Part of reading protocols of this genre
included a　**name code.**

2 sonneteers who influenced Will are:
Sir Thomas Wyatt (1503—42)
in Tottle's *Miscellany* (1557) &
Sir Philip Sidney (1554—86)

Two slides per page

Sir Thomas Wyatt

(1503—42)
Diplomat,
translator of
Petrarch, &
sonneteer

Sir Thomas Wyatt's pun on name of
Anne Boleyn (QEI's mother):

"Whoso list to hunt, I know
where is **AN HIND**."
ANNE DEAR
Or even: **Anne B. Hind (deer)**
Does Will pun on Wyatt's name when
he uses **"Yet"** or **"Why … it?"**

2

184

Queen Anne Boleyn "B"
d. 1536

Sir Philip Sidney
(1554—86)
Protestant war hero and sonneteer

3

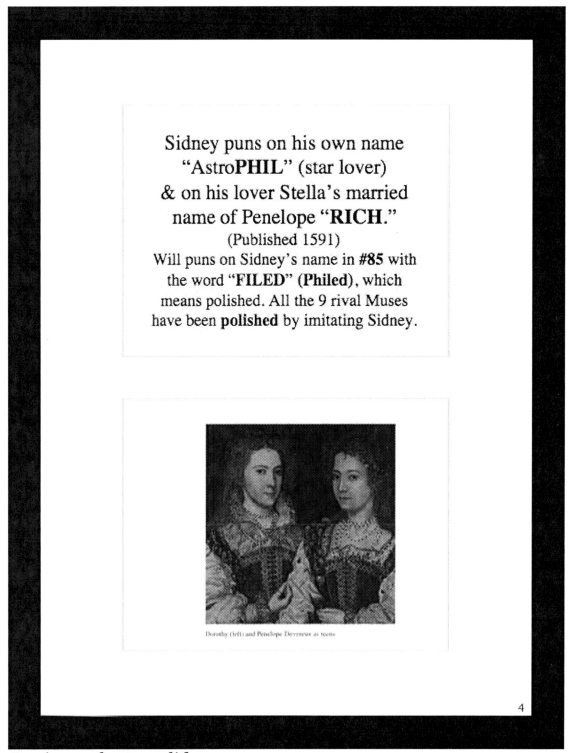

Sidney puns on his own name
"AstroPHIL" (star lover)
& on his lover Stella's married
name of Penelope "RICH."
(Published 1591)
Will puns on Sidney's name in #85 with
the word "FILED" (Philed), which
means polished. All the 9 rival Muses
have been polished by imitating Sidney.

Dorothy (left) and Penelope Devereux as teens

4

Caption on bottom slide:
Dorothy (left) and Penelope Devereaux as teens.

186

Sidney's sonnets published: **1591**
5 years after his death.

Shakespeare began
1st 17 sonnets **1589/1590**
for youth's 17th birthday
celebrated in Oct 1590.

Will's 4 people or characters

- The Poet: 154 sonnets
- The Young Lord: 126 sonnets
- The Dark Lady: 28 sonnets
- The Rival Poet(s):   9 sonnets

Total sequence: 154 sonnets

5

The **KEY** to the **CODE** is
"NAME"
"Name" is used 17 times in 14
sonnets (+ one use of "naming")
Look for **DOUBLETS** that
sound or spell like a key name.
In Sonnet 52, the code sets **TIME.**

Elizabethans enjoyed **numerology.**
Will's code **substitutes numbers** for people:

14 = Will

17 = the youth

11 = Will's son Hamnet

28 = The dark lady

9 = the rival poet(s)

7 = key to time (1 week)

2 = doublet word code

6

Looking for the word **"name"**
in the couplet of **Sonnet 136:**

"Make but my **name** thy love,
and love that still;
And then thou lov'st me, for
my **name** is **Will**."

The Poet
**William
(Will)
Shakespeare**
?
The Chandros
portrait
c. **1590s?**

7

EXAMPLES of puns: Sonnet 121
The Poet's NAME:
Line 1: **Two** uses of word "**vile.**"

"Tis better to be **vile** than **vile** esteemed"

Line 8: the **plural** word, "**wills**"

"Which in theirs **wills** count bad what I think good?

Plus Line 9: "**I am** that **I am**,"

No, **I am** that **I am**, and they that level"

(NOTE: "**I am that I am**" is what God told Moses
when Moses asked for God's **Name**)

Equals: 2 **Will+I-am-s**

Recently rediscovered painting: Henry as teen?
Sonnet 20: "the master-mistress of my passion"

8

Names of youth in Sonnet 1?
"Herald" + "Rose"
(His family = Heralds to the Order of the Garter,
which celebrates its rites on St. George's Day)
Harold Writh (old form)
Harry Rizley
Henry Wriothesley

The Young
Lord at 21,
**Henry
Wriothesley,**
3rd Earl of
Southampton,
1594
Miniature by
Hilyard

9

Sonnet 36, line 12:
"Unless thou **take** that **honour** from thy **name:**"
Honourable Henry
The word **"honour"** is used a second time.
Take (subtract) **"honour"** from Henry. What
do you get? Is the answer in the leftover vowels?
HEnrY
— HOnOUr
(ey[e]) **I O O U** (you)!

Is that **I. O. U**, with **double O** for **owe?**
For **owe** a lot!?

**Henry
Wriothesley**
in the Tower for
3 years
(1601-03)
1603
with cat Trixie

10

192

Sonnet 39, line 6:

"And our dear love lose **name** of single one,"
KEY CODE WORD points to:
a single use each of **worth (Writh**/Wriothesley**)**
& **hence (Henry)**

Line 1: "O, how thy **worth** with manners may I sing"

Line 14: "By praising him here who doth **hence**
[Henry] remain."

Hence + Worth

Henry Wroithesley ★ 1623

Died 1624 in Flanders with son Thomas

11

★ Wriothesley

Sonnet 81, line 5:

"Your **name** from **hence** immortal life shall have,"
"Hence" (for Henry?)

Doubled in line 3:
"From **hence** your memory death cannot take"

MODEL use of CODE:
"Name" turns on code,
and **doublet** reveals **name.**

The Dark
Lady, poet
**Aemelia
Besano
Lanyer?**
(1569—1645)
"Unknown Lady in
Black" by
Marcus Gheeraerts
1592

12

194

Sonnet 151, code **key** line 9:
"But **rising** at thy **name** doth **point** out **thee**[.]"

Lines 5—12:   **2X CODE**

"For, thou betrAying mE, I do betrAY   **AE/AY**
My nobler part to My gross body's trEAson;   **MM/EE**
My soul doth teLL my bodY thAt hE mAy   **LL/YAEA**
Triumph in love; flesh stays no further reason,

AEAYMMEELLYAEA!?

But rising at thy name doth point out thee   **KEY**
As his triumphant prize, proud of this pride:
He is content thy poor drudge to be,
To stand in thy affairs, fall by thy side."

**Christopher
(Kit)
Marlowe?**
(1564—1593)
at 21
Cambridge
University
1585
Rival Poet

13

195

Sonnet 84, lines 9—14:

"Let him but [K sound] **Copy** what in you is wrIT,   **KIT**
Not making **worse** what nature made so clear,   **WORSE**
And such a [K sound] **Counterpart** shall frame his wIT,
                                          KIT
Making his style **admired** everywhere.
        (Lord **ADMIRAL**'s Men)

You to your beauteous blessings add a curse,
Being fond on **praise**, which makes your **praises worse**."
                                        WORSE

Doubled words & letters & sounds + clue word

More Marlowe evidence:

Marlowe's motto at Cambridge:

"QVOD ME NVTRIT ME DESTRVIT"

from Ovid & on 1585 portrait
Sonnet 73, line 12 translates it:
"Consumed with that which it was nourished by."

Sonnet 86, lines 1 & 2, on rival poet:
"Was it the proud full sail of his great verse,
Bound for the prize of all-too-precious you"
      Line 1 sounds like Marlowe's line:
"Was this the face that launched a thousand ships?"
                          from *Dr. Faustus*

14

196

**Code list
drawn by
Robert
Poley**
1 of 3 spies
present when
Marlowe was
murdered
May 1593

Does Will pun on **Poley's** name in
Hamlet,
with the name for spymaster
"Polonius," who is also a parody of
Lord Burghley & sounds like
"felonious?"

15

197

In 12th Night, Malvolio is fooled
by a false NAME code in a letter:
He turns "**MOIA**" into his **name.**
Will plays with name
subtractions in *12th Night:*
Olivia — Viola = **I** (ego)
Malvolio — MOIA = **Llov**

Drawing of
**Anne
Hathaway
Shakespeare?**
(?1556—1623)

16

Sonnet 145, lines 13 & 14:

"'I hate' from HATE AWAY she threw,
HATHAWAY

AND saved my life, saying "not you.'"
ANNE

Tetrameter sonnet = TIME CODE: shortest night of
the year & moon mate to Summer Solstice Sonnet 52.

TIME CODE: 52 X 7 = 364

Sonnet **#52 sets** the **sun dial**, lines 4—8:

"ThereFORE are **feasts SO SOL**emn and **SO** rare,
    FOUR   **SO/SOL**   **SO**
Since, SeLdOm coming, in the long **year** set,
   S   **SLO**   **year**
Like StOnes of **worth** they thinly placed are,
       LSO   **worth**
Or captain jewels in the carcanet."

52 is the **SUMMER SOLSTICE** Sonnet: June 14th OC

17

If Sonnet #**52** = **14 June** O. C.,
then #1 = **24 April,** &
126 sonnets to youth are
126 days (18 weeks) of
summer theater season &
#126 = 27 August,
end of Summer & TIME.

Sonnets **40 & 133**:

Time twins happen at the same time,
when Will admits in writing youth &
lady are having an affair: double/double
cross. That day is **9 June,** and this pair
calibrates **the Sun** with the **Moon.**

1st sonnet to lady **127 =**

3 June (Twin with Sonnet 34)

18

200

The **youth** is the **SUN.**

The **lady** is the **MOON.**

The **28** sonnets to the lady are night **twins** to **28** day sonnets to the youth:

MOON: 127—154

SUN: 34 — 61

3 June—30 June O.C.

TIME & Numbers

1 = "a summer's day" = 1 sonnet

2 = KEY CODE multiplier/doubles

7 = a week X 2 = 14 & 7 X 4 = 28

14 = a fortnight & # lines/sonnet

28 = 7 X 4 = a lunar month

52 = weeks/year X 7 =364 days

60 = minutes/hour (not seconds)

126 = 7 X 18 = 18 week summer
         theater season = end of Time

19

201

1623

(7 years after Will's death in 1616) was a
memorial year. His family (& Henry?)
placed a **bust** above his grave, & 2 actors
(Hemings & Condell)
edited & published the
1st FOLIO edition of his **plays**.

Memorial
bust of
**William
Shakespeare**
in Stratford
church
1623

20

Sonnet 72, line 11:
"My **name** be **buried** where
my body is,"
"Buried" doubled words in **2** pairs:

1. **"willingly/well**:" **Will** buried in
"willingly" & **2.** **"worthy/worth**:"
"worthy" buried in **WRiOTHesleY**

Sonnet 126:
12 rhymed couplet lines + 2X
(   )
(   )
End sonnets to youth & present
image of an empty hour glass =
End of **TIME**
1609

Engraving of
**William
Shakespeare
1st Folio
1623**

Shakespeare's Sonnets
**1609 Quarto rediscovered in
1800s**
versus John Benson's pirated &
changed, misleading edition of
1640 ★

22

★ **Note:** Actually, by 1711, Lintot had republished the 1609 version
(Burrow 99).

204

The End
but not Will's
END

23

Appendix G.

How Many People are Hiding in Sonnet # 127?

The answer to my title questions is obviously two: the poet and the dark lady. But is that the only answer? Suppose this sonnet is like one of those Renaissance paintings; the more you stare at it, the more you see. Since this sonnet presents a long gaze of the poet's eyes into the dark lady's eyes, like a painter at his model, we must feel its hypnotizing effect of eye contact and falling in love. Yes, let's have fun and stare with the poet and trade eyes. But let's also see what else is going on. Since this is the first sonnet about the dark lady in Shakespeare's sonnet sequence, it makes sense to analyze it as if it were a prologue, too, like its counterpart for the youth, Sonnet 1.

Let's do two things at once. Let's go line-by-line, and let's also point out possible hidden persons as we go. Let's pretend this poem is a Renaissance portrait of a lady with a landscape behind her and with people hidden in the bushes and maybe even up in the trees. Line one starts us with a looking back in time, an invitation to compare black with fair:

**"In the old age black was
not counted fair,"**

and we wonder how far back is this "old age?" Perhaps Will is thinking back to Chaucer in the late 1300s, or perhaps Will is thinking back further, to the famous mistress of King Henry II (1154—1189), who always had the word "fair" attached to her name, the "fair" Rosamond. So, maybe we've flipped all the way back to the late 1100s; maybe Henry II and his mistress and his jealous Queen Eleanor of Aquitaine and their sexual triangle are suddenly referred to here. Yes, I think so. He starts with an historic shift in the ideal of female beauty, back to when "black" was not seen fairly. He makes this historical contrast, and we'll hear more of the fair Rosamond later in line 7 when Will says the dark lady has "no holy bower" to use as a refuge or hiding place in the middle of a large maze constructed by the king.

The second line states a negative contrast:

**"Or if it were it bore not
beauty's name;"**

and here he says no one called a dark woman beautiful then. In the first two lines, we've already encountered two "nots," and if these are pun words for "knots," then we might have something tangled to untangle:

knot fair and knot beauty. And we may wonder if the word "knot" is also a reference to a knot garden, a common companion planting to a garden maze in Shakespeare's time. Of course, we'd also love to know the dark lady's name, so the very word "name" gets us very curious wondering about her identity. But we may not get it here. The whole sonnet seems to say "no" (know) and "not" (knot). We also must remember that "men of name" were royals only. At the end of *Richard III,* when Richmond (incoming King Henry VII) asks who was killed, he's only interested in the knights with titles from Baron on up who can be named.

Line three brings us back to "now" and our interest in the lady of this sonnet series:

"But now is black beauty's successive heir,"

and this reflects a fashion shift in taste in the 1590s in England to a new ideal, a new taste for "dark women." There was a very famous African-English Madame of a London whorehouse in the 1590s, whose name was Lucy Morgan, and some have been fooled by the word "black" to claim that she is the dark lady. But I don't think the twenty-eight dark lady sonnets describe this lady as African. Shakespeare says that darker women (in the time when he's writing this sonnet) are now the new ideal. "Black is beautiful." Notice that he uses the same word "heir" that he used in Sonnet 1 for the youth, the only other sonnet in the position of an opening prologue in this two-part sonnet sequence.

Back then in Sonnet 1, it was a new form of carpe diem: seize the day, get married, and beget heirs. Here it means that darker women have inherited beauty's crown from the blondes. Of course, in both poems, the word heir sounds like a pun on hair, and the youth is fair or blond while the dark lady has "black wires grow [-ing] on her head." But in this sonnet of love at first sight—mutual or not—only her eyes are described as "black." Perhaps his sympathetic gaze can see her grieving eyes, but he cannot see into them to her heart. Perhaps he is falling in love, but she is thinking darker thoughts.

Line 4 introduces a new idea:

"And beauty slandered with a bastard shame:"

which may mean that beauty itself is insulted and called illegitimate because of this new, darker ideal. But the word "bastard" is so harsh, I wonder how personal this reference is. In 1592, Lord Hunsdon disowned and married off his pregnant, 23 year old mistress, Aemelia Bessano, who had been kept by him since she was 18 and an orphan, and then he arranged to have her married off to her second cousin, Alfonso Lanyer, a court musician. If Aemelia is the dark lady (and I think she's the best candidate), then this line may refer to the shame she feels for getting pregnant as an unmarried mistress and being cast off from her privileged position as mistress to Queen Elizabeth's first cousin. Thus, the first quatrain may take us from a flashback of a famous, medieval mistress forced to commit suicide by drinking poison in her "holy bower" by a jealous queen in the 1100s to a mistress cast off by a royal, male relative in 1592. Who says Shakespeare can't time travel in the Sonnets? He does so all the time in his plays.

The beginning of quatrain 2, line 5 starts up a new connection:

> **"For since each hand hath put on Nature's power,"**

and we know this is a very conventional theme and complaint about Elizabethan women taking on Nature's power to give us hair color, skin color, and the color of lips with make-up and wigs and false arts. Queen Elizabeth herself wore red-headed wigs made from the hair of younger women. She also colored her skin with China white, so she would look more like alabaster, more virginal, and more like the marble sculpture of a Greek or Roman goddess. Of course, she is often called Diana, huntress and goddess of the Moon. Could it be that here we have a criticism of the aging queen, who set the standards for make-up use and wig wearing in her court? After all, she also had been called a "bastard" by her Catholic half-sister Mary and all her Catholic enemies. (Of course, in an orgy of competing, Christian insults, Bloody Mary also was called a "bastard" by the backers of the Protestant Princess Elizabeth.)

So if Elizabeth is peeked at here, do we also have to let into the background her father, another randy King Henry VIII and his first queen (the Spanish Catherine of Aragon) and Elizabeth's mother Anne Boleyn? Does Shakespeare imply that royal history repeats itself in sexual triangles that might even happen to poets and youths and dark ladies?

Using the key word "fair" again in line 6, Shakespeare (like Ben Jonson) seems to make fun of or be disgusted by the use of make-up to disguise age or lack of beauty:

"Fairing the foul with art's false borrowed face,"

and the pun here of "foul" and fowl is both traditional and quite a sting. He seems to be saying that "the old hen" can use art to borrow a younger person's face. How neat—he made a verb out of the noun and adjective "fair." Can Shakespeare even be referring to art as painting in a grander sense? Elizabeth Woods, the Aemelia Lanyer scholar of our times, found two paintings in the collection of the heirs of Lord Hunsdon. They were both done by the same painter, Marcus Gheeraerts the younger, who painted Lord Hunsdon in 1591 and then painted a lady called "Unknown Lady in Black" in 1592. Quite rightly, Woods wonders if this is a painting of Hunsdon's shamed mistress and mother of their illegitimate son Henry, the wronged Aemelia Lanyer. Woods thinks it so likely that she uses it on the cover of her Lanyer biography. Did Shakespeare get to see both of those portraits? In 1594, Hunsdon became the patron of Shakespeare's company, and they were renamed the "Lord Chamberlain's Men." So perhaps Will saw this painting (and he would know if it were Aemelia), and maybe he thought the painter idealized the lady, perhaps even lightening her skin color and giving her a red-haired wig. Or, perhaps as my wife Sandy reminds me, Aemelia simply powdered her skin and hennaed her hair in fashionable imitation of her Queen and to look sexy at court.

In the 7th line, we get the tantalizing word "name" again:

**"Sweet beauty hath no name,
no holy bower,"**

and this repeats what line two said with a big difference. Instead of just referring back in time to Rosamond the fair, this beauty, although heir to former beautiful ladies, doesn't have a name or even a holy bower to hide in. She lacks both title and shelter. King Henry II, the popular story goes, had built a garden maze near or in a forest and kept Rosamond there at its center in a "bower" or a locked house. He was the only one, he thought, with knowledge of the route in and a key, but his French Queen was suspicious and found out. She asked the mirror on the wall, "Who's the fairest of them all," and the mirror told her the truth: fair Rosamond. So the Queen got some soldiers and went to the bower with a bottle of poison. She gave Rosamond

a choice: "Drink this or I'll have you drawn and quartered, and then I'll have you killed." Rosamond became famous for taking Socrates' way out. She was so famous in the 1590s that Thomas Lodge wrote a companion piece to his sonnet sequence, *Sonnets to Phyllis* (1593), to give Rosamond's voice a female lament to contrast with the male lover's voice in his sonnets. In 1604, to imitate Lodge as other sonneteers had done, Shakespeare wrote "A Lover's Complaint," in the voice of a wronged maid that he published later with his sonnets in 1609. In 1611, Aemelia Lanyer was the first English woman to publish her own book of poetry. In it, one of her main poems, "In Defense of Eve," uses Rosamond's example as just one of many wronged women (like Eve), who were blamed for the actions of men. So perhaps there is a direct thread of Ariadne from Rosamond to the dark lady to the poet Aemelia Lanyer.

Line 8 laments that beauty is no longer worshipped like a statue or Venus or a goddess or a mistress kept in the center of a maze in a "holy bower:"

**"But is profaned, if not lives
in disgrace."**

Beauty is either not worshipped as she once was, or she is cast off by His Grace to live in disgrace. We find another knot to untangle, the knot of disgrace. Perhaps Shakespeare has heard the lament of Aemelia Bessano, after five years at court as the mistress to a very powerful man, disgraced because he got her pregnant. Even though Lord Hunsdon is 45 years older than Aemelia, perhaps with an older wife and family, and even though he is within his rights to force Aemelia to leave her position as his mistress, this may remind Will of when he was only 18, and Anne Hathaway was pregnant, when he did the right thing and married her, even though or maybe because she was eight years older than he. Will may be setting up another contrast here between himself and Hunsdon. Of course, since he will call the lady "my mistress" in the very next line, he may also be hoping to inherit her as a hand-me-down lover.

As usual, line 9 turns the argument:

**"Therefore my mistress'
eyes are raven black,"**

Suddenly, the lady is "my mistress," either a title of respect or a title of real or wished for sexual alliance. She may already be the mistress of his heart. Later, she will have black hair and "dun" breasts and do black deeds, but right now, the only part of her he's looking at is her very dark eyes. The use of "raven black" brings in all that is associated with that large bird. Another, even older sexual triangle from legendary English history may be peeking out of the trees like a raven. The raven is the bird of Morgan, Arthur's half-sister, his immortal lover, and mother of the son who will kill him in battle, Mordred. In the Pearl

Poet's "Gawain and the Green Knight," written at the time of Chaucer, Arthur's court will be tested by Morgan. Of course, Arthur is then on the throne and rules with fair Guinevere. Only his young nephew Gawain can pass the old beheading test and go on to almost pass the test of the perilous bed. Gawain's shame mythically leads (in a French motto added to that poem) to the founding of The Order of the Green Garter by Arthur. (It was actually founded by Edward III in c. 1350.) Is there another connection here? Back in Sonnet 1, I think the youth was celebrated as the "only herald" at the April 23, 1590 celebration of the Order of the Garter, when he was still 16. Both his uncle and granduncle had been Heralds to that Order. So how many of these people are hiding behind that one rich word, "raven?" We know that Renaissance imagery was heraldic, symbolic, full of suggestive history, and loaded with associations. We also know that Shakespeare's use of such associations was rich and very complex. Is this one word that powerful? Of course, Will had been insulted by Robert Greene as an "upstart crow" in 1592; but no insult is meant by reference to the more powerful raven.

In line 10, Will goes on looking deeply into her eyes:

**"Her eyes so suited, and
they mourners seem"**

and makes her out to be like the "sad-eyed lady of the lowlands." Her eyes are "dressed in black" as if they were mourners at a funeral. When Shakespeare met the dark lady, she

210

may have been in tears like the wronged young maid of "A Lover's Complaint." He may feel that he can rescue her from her sadness; he may be falling for her. We know that certain animals—dogs especially—get to us with their sad eyes. This may be twenty-three year old, pregnant Aemelia Bessano, crying out because she has been dumped in the Spring of 1592. She will marry the court musician Alphonso Lanyer, an admirer and inheritor of her father's position as a court musician, in October and give birth to Hunsdon's "illegitimate" son Henry early in 1593). Here, in Sonnet 127, before she is married off, Will may be a twenty-eight year old poet falling in love with her.

Line 11 feels harder than the rest to explain:

**"At such who not born fair
no beauty lack,"**

so she seems to be mourning because she was not born fair, yet she does not lack dark beauty. She was not high born with all the "fair" protection of social rank. Is this simply a restatement of the modern cliché, "gentlemen prefer blondes?" Aemelia's mother Margaret Johnson was a fair English woman, but Aemelia's father was dark. He had come from Venice to England with his family to be hired as musicians to Queen Elizabeth's court. There is a well-known miniature of Queen Elizabeth playing a lute by the painter Nicholas Hilliard; this may be the same lute that Aemelia's father was known to have given the Queen. Baptista Bessano was Italian, and perhaps he was Jewish. He died when Aemelia was very young, but Will's knowledge of any possibly Jewish family, who came from Venice, may form a little of the background for his powerful and bitter "Merchant of Venice." In Venice, the Bessano family had had the emblem of the Mulberry tree, *morus* in Latin, which may refer to some link to the Italian, home grown silk trade centered around Milan or the import silk trade of Venice. When in Sonnet 40, Will refers to this same lady as "more," he may be referring to her family emblem, not that she is a Moor. After all, the same word "Moor" was used to describe Leonardo da Vinci's Italian patron, Ludovico the Moor, Duke of Milan, who was also "dark" and involved with the silk trade.

Line 12 of this sonnet repeats the charge of lies being told:

**"Sland'ring creation with a
false esteem:"**

and we seem to have returned to the tone of line 4 with the verb "slander," but it is "creation" that is slandered, perhaps because the baby to be born will be dark or perhaps because the young, dark mother has been slandered while pregnant. This is a kind of racism or bigotry against all "dark" people. Fashionable fops and ladies may say that "black is now beautiful," but they are false. Once the dark lady is in trouble, neither her darkness nor her beauty can protect her. So quatrain 3 ends with an accusation that the new fashion of admiring blackness is only skin deep. Once that superficial attraction is tested, it fails.

Line 13 and the couplet starts with another turn:

"Yet so they mourn, becoming of their woe,"

and once again we are focusing on her dark eyes. They are becoming. That is, they are beautiful. The dark lady's woe makes her an attractive woe-man. Her grief is deep and gives her character. Perhaps Shakespeare is also referring to her darkness being lost in England in exile from Italy and the Middle East. Will probably met Florio, the Italian tutor of Henry Wroithesley, in 1589 or 1590. He may have written a sonnet to Florio (in 1589 or 1590) that Florio published as a forward to one of his books in 1591. But the dark lady may be the first partly Italian and/or Jewish, educated woman Will has met. Perhaps he refers to this when he calls her a "jewel." To Will, she is definitely "exotic." Her darkness turns him on. And if she is Aemelia Bessano Lanyer, then she is also a musician and a poet. He will publish his sonnets in 1609; she will publish her Protestant and feminist book of poems dedicated to "the King of the Jews" in 1611. Perhaps here, Shakespeare is hoping to have met his dark, romantic soul mate. This first dark lady sonnet is full of mystery and longing. But, of course, in 1592 and 1593 the bitter joke may be on Will. She is also in need of a patron and interested in the youth as a lover, or he is interested in her. Later in the dark lady series, Will becomes the mournful one when he is betrayed by both the lady and the youth. He admits it in writing in Sonnets 40 and 133.

He ends Sonnet 127 with a return in line 14 to what people should say:

"That every tongue says beauty should look so."

Praise of her raven black eyes should be on every tongue. He sees her eyes that look beautiful and look at him. He is captivated. Here is a woman who may counter balance the fair youth (as the moon counter balances the sun). In the very next poem, Sonnet 128, he is watching her play a keyboard virginal at a crowded party, and he will call her "my music." This is very close to "my Muse," but it is not the same. Even as he revises Sonnet 127, he is aware that his excitement over meeting her gaze will be short-lived.

Now we must revisit the title of this study. How many people are hiding in Sonnet 127? I don't really know. But I could make a list and ask you if you can see these people, too, or if you see even more people than I do. The dark lady is as mysterious a figure in the literary world as Mona Lisa is in the art world. I may be wrong, but I think both of these famous women are known middle class Italian women in their twenties, one a young wife, the other a spurned mistress. But Shakespeare is a very social, dramatic poet. He's a history buff, and he is fascinated by correspondences, allegories, and repeating patterns. If Sonnet 127 is a portrait of Shakespeare's Mona Lisa, who is in the background that he wants us to see? Here's a list of the 18 people I can see:

1. William Shakespeare, the poet and lover
2. The dark lady
3. The fair Rosamond
4. King Henry II
5. Queen Eleanor of Aquitaine
6.   Aemelia Bessano (Lanyer)
7. Lord Hunsdon
8. Queen Elizabeth I
9. Henry VIII
10. Anne Boleyn
11. Catherine of Aragon, Henry VIII's first Queen
12. Bloody Mary, Queen of England
13. Anne Hathaway
14. Morgan, the immortal dark sister of Arthur
15. King Arthur
16. Queen Guinevere, Arthur's fair Queen
17. The youth and young lord
18. Henry Wroithesley, the Third Earl of Southampton

Perhaps there are under this first contact poem between two lovers, the affairs of at least three famous English kings, their wives and mistresses, Will's wife, and a real Lord who has discarded a young mistress. Perhaps all these sexual triangles undermine Will's hopes at this very moment of eye contact.

To me, Sonnet 127 has the dark atmosphere of a large garden maze in the moonlight. Or perhaps this is the dark of the Moon when ghosts of famous people can be dimly perceived wandering on the pathways of our imaginations.

Appendix H.

Pyramus & Thisbe & Good Bad Writing in *Shakespeare's Sonnets*

When my community college students and I "do" the *Pyramus and Thisbe* skit from Act V of *A Midsummer Night's Dream* in class, I often wonder how indestructible it is. No matter how badly they act, they cannot mess it up. The more they do mess it up, the ruder they are, sometimes the funnier it gets. We are just doing readers' theater with no rehearsals and with everyone wearing funny hats. They love it, and so do I. I have a soft spot in my heart for this silly stuff. When my son Daniel was nine at a Magnet Arts grammar school, he played Thisbe in a long skirt with a mop on his head, and a very aggressive girl, who Daniel thought was " really cool," played Pyramus. I know—gender reversal in grammar school—all very naughty, but the kids and parents loved it. When my students finished acting up this fall, while the joking magic was still in the air, I said, "Well, that will look good on your resumé."

I know I do encourage them. And I love all the professionally crafted jokes that Kevin Klein (as Bottom) and his friends put into the Michael Hoffman movie version. They act badly better than any other production I have seen. I wish I could have seen the Lord Chamberlain's Men act it out perhaps on the 4th of May 1594 at Mary Browne Southampton's wedding to Sir Thomas Heneage. I'm sure those rude professionals had a few tricks for accentuating the awfully funny lines. It would have been a gas to see Will Kemp play Bottom, a part Shakespeare may have written to make fun of Kemp. So Kemp plays Kemp acting like an ass, and the crowds loved it. And Shakespeare smiled a complicated smile, which says, "It works, and I've pegged him perfectly as an ass." But did Shakespeare play Peter Quince? The broken sonnets of his Prologue—in ten and fourteen and ten line segments—and Quince's role as a amateur director say that this may have been Shakespeare's part. William Shakespeare was a genius at creating very good bad writing.

And I wish I could have seen this first written, detached skit's first performance at the Inns of Court for a law school graduation party in the late 1580s. Shakespeare knew how to write for rowdy crowds, and this skit is a real crowd pleaser—the climax of *A Midsummer Night's Dream,* the play within the play we've all been waiting for. Who can keep from laughing at Thisbe's pathetic lament for dead Pyramus?

214

"His eyes were green as leeks!"

Shakespeare was such a mix of pathos, bathos, and goofy clowning. But it is the mix that saves it from being a clunker. It is the intelligence in that pun "leeks," a very funny word that shows Will's skill. Her eyes are leaking from tears of grief; our eyes are leaking from tears of laughter. The leek is also the green Welsh national vegetable that will show up again in *Henry V* at war when Pistol is force to eat a leek for making insults against the Welsh.

When we shift to the *Sonnets*, most people also catch on and hear silly wit in two of the clunkiest lines perhaps ever included on purpose in a sonnet. The first is:

"That in the breath that from my mistress reeks"
(130.8)

which rhymes with Thisbe's line and may share another tie to *MSND* in lines for Bottom, where he warns the actors:

"And, most dear actors, eat no onions or garlic; for we are to utter/sweet breath, and I do not doubt to hear them say it is a sweet comedy."
(*MSND* IV.2.32—34)

But the line from Sonnet 130 that tops that smelly bad breath is perhaps the ugliest good line of all:

"If hairs be wires, black wires grow on her head."
(130.4)

Notice he wrote "if." Sonnet 130 is a very intense literary parody making fun of Petrarchian sonnets and clichés and all the sonneteers who followed Petrarch down the garden path lined with lily white hands, snow white breasts, red coral lips, and, worst of all, rosy cheeks. I can't help it. I see a less than rosy bottom when Shakespeare writes,

"But no such roses see I in her cheeks"
(130.6).

After all, "her breasts are dun," a gray brown, so her bottom must be, too, and that's not a rosy set of cheeks. O Will, did you expose the dark lady's cute ass in your sonnet? Sometimes, because I know he likes to write good bad jokes, I don't know when to stop, so I don't.

Everyone agrees that Sonnet 130 is a masterpiece of literary satire. But some portray it as "the only funny sonnet" out of 154. This is very misleading. There are other very funny, satirical dark lady sonnets. Here's a short list: 128, 135, 136, 143, 151, and perhaps even the twin envois, 153 and 154. Let's take a closer look at all these sonnets and not dismiss them as "not as good" or "unworthy of Shakespeare" or "juvenilia." Most commentators still have deep puritan prejudices against finding comedy in the sonnets. I, on the other hand, have a built-in, comedy seeking muscle.

I think these seven sonnets and some additional lines from other sonnets are meant to be funny. I think they have been wrongly dismissed and misunderstood as if Shakespeare (one of the greatest comic writers ever) were not allowed to make fun of his predicament of being stuck in a love triangle, not allowed to make fun of himself (a silly Will), and, most of all, not allowed to make fun of the dark lady and maybe even the young lord just a little. I think we have here some more wonderful examples of Shakespeare's great "bad" writing, and we must wear our fools' caps with bells on to figure out his jokes. In the spirit of Sonnet 130 (which everyone can laugh at) and the Pyramus and Thisbe skit, let's look at the others.

Sonnet 128 is the second of two musical sonnets. Its number suggests, like Sonnet 8, the octave of the scale as well as the 12 notes on the keyboard inside each octave. 128 is a funny version of the dialogue first kiss, pleading sonnet of *Romeo and Juliet*. Like that pilgrim/saint dialogue, this sonnet takes place at a public, musical celebration or party where the dark lady is playing the keyboard virginal (or Bessano built clavichord), and Shakespeare is looking at her swaying back as she plays. Like Romeo, he is hoping for a kiss, but in this sonnet he envies the jacks (the wooden keys) that are being tickled by the lady's playing fingers. Perhaps he also envies the other men (Jacks) standing around the lady. Surely this is a comic scene, and Will is laughing before his affair with the dark lady. He decides not to envy those keys—although he'd like to be tickled, too—but hopes instead to receive a kiss on his lips. I think this sonnet was first written in 1592, when Shakespeare was first attracted

to my best candidate for the dark lady, the musical, cast-off, and pregnant ex-mistress, Aemelia Bessano (later Lanyer). Then, I think Shakespeare wrote the lovely, teasing dialogue sonnet for his teen-aged lovers in about 1595. Then, he may have revised sonnet 128 in 1604 and/or 1608. So this comic sonnet's creation—with its good bad puns on "jacks" and finger tickling and lips itching for a kiss—may come both before and after *Romeo and Juliet*. And although she's playing a virginal or some other keyboard instrument, Shakespeare may know she has been an experienced mistress, since she was 18, of the Queen's cousin, Lord Hunsdun, two years before he became the patron of Shakespeare's company. At the time of Sonnet 128, it is 1592, and she is now 23, pregnant, and looking for male protection.

Sonnet 135 is the first of twins with Sonnet 136. These two sonnets make the most of the puns possible on his name Will. If you don't like puns (and Dr. Sam Johnson hates them) you won't giggle with Will here. You will conclude that this is bad writing, but I will argue that these are good bad writing. If you like his groaners as well as his serious art, then these two poems are for you. This means that you, like me, accept Shakespeare's values and wit when you are trying to understand Shakespeare. If you will read Sonnet 135 out loud, you will experience "Will" in "overplus." If you count the times, you will find 13 uses of "will" and 1 use of "wilt" for a total of 14. And if you go on to its twin Sonnet 136, you will count 7 uses of "will" as well as 2 uses of "name" and the most direct naming of himself the poet in 136.14:

"my name is Will."

I think all these wacky words and exact numbers have a point to make. I believe he has inserted in almost all his sonnets a standard Elizabethan nomenclature code, complete with embedded numbers, symbolic key words, doublets, rebus symbols, and nulls. It is not my purpose to prove here—a Stratfordian name and time code in the *Sonnets*—what I've tried to prove elsewhere. But in these, twin, silly sonnets, 135 & 136, he allows himself to overdo it and also to show us his encoding methods. If you don't like puns on his name and the sexual organs of both genders and about six other meanings of "will" as well, then you won't get his jokes here, and you won't understand the comic spirit of this "bad" writing. But if you roar with laughter like the fake lion in the Pyramus and Thisbe skit, then you will allow Will to be silly and count these sonnets as valuable with all the rest. When he first imagined these twin sonnets, he was the proud father of 5-year old twins, his little Gemini children, Judith and Hamnet. Later, after tragic losses, he did not censor his own naughty, child-like word games. He may have even added more wit and more precise numerological jokes.

Sonnet 143 is another neglected funny poem. It is mock heroic like Pope's "Rape of the Lock." It warns you from word one, this is not high art; it is "Lo." This sonnet is a domestic comedy like his "Merry Wives of Windsor." It's about a housewife running after a runaway fowl and leaving her baby crying. I think this is a joking poem about the sexual triangle he's stuck in with the youth and the lady. He calls himself the housewife's "babe," so the runaway fowl may be a comic reference to the youth, perhaps even a foul name pun on Henry, that is, a clucking hen.

He proposes that if she catches what she wants, she should come back, "play the mother's part," and give him a kiss. Here is Will portraying himself as a big baby, once again begging a kiss. Given the double betrayal of these two important people with each other, he is as helpless as a baby, and he might as well laugh at himself. If this housewife is Aemelia, then this scene could date from the time when her (bastard) son was a baby (also named Henry). That would have it written late 1593, when Aemelia was married to her second cousin (to save face) but still carrying on her affair with Will. Or it could be that this sonnet was first written about Anne when Susanna was a baby in 1584, or in 1608, when Susanna herself might have been running after her baby daughter Elizabeth. Whenever it was written or rewritten, it's placed in the 28 dark lady sonnets as comic relief between two very serious sonnets, 142 and 144. We are familiar with Shakespeare going from high to low to high in his plays. I think he does the same in his *Sonnets*. Once again, he saves himself from total tragic thinking with good bad writing. "Love" may be his "sin" in 142.1, and he may be trapped between "Two loves ... of comfort and despair," in 144.1. but between those two serious busted love poems, he's laughing at his predicament like a little kid in Sonnet 143.

Sonnet 151 may be the bawdiest sonnet of all. If you don't like dirty jokes, how could you enjoy this climactic sonnet placed near the end of Shakespeare's dark lady sequence? He is still celebrating their sexual affair. This poem has Shakespeare's erection rising, a lot of up and down motion, a climax of p-words, and it may even have him crying out the dark lady's name as he comes. I think he finally gives us the dark lady's name in quatrain 2, where he embeds doubled letters or sounds in the following way:

AA—in the doubled "betrAy" of
    line 5
MM—in the doubled "My" of
    line 6
EE—in the sound of the rhyme
    word "trEAson" of line 6
LL—in the word "teLL" in
    line 7
YA and EA in line 8's words
    "flesh staYs no fArther
    rEAson."

The key I think to this naming may be found in the turn line, line 9, where he jokes, "But rising at thy **name** doth **point** out thee." That is, full of sexual laughter, he points out her name in the quatrain above with his erection, a neat use of the rhetorical trick called *deixis* in Greek, where the word "point" acts as a pointer. This is a carefully planned, sophisticated joke where the word and his penis are the same figure. If I'm right, he rises, enters her, names her, comes, and falls—all inside this 14-line bedroom poem.

The wording may be a little stiff, but remember the principles of good bad writing: even if Shakespeare has to force the language a bit, he thinks it may be worth the constructed joke.

Sonnets 153 and 154 also have their detractors. But they have a sonnet sequence job to do. They must sum up the sequence and end it as a doubled envoi. The story embedded twice in these two twin sonnets can be seen as a light-hearted Roman, neoclassical folk tale. They answer the scientific question—How did hot springs come to be? with an Ovid-style minor myth: virginal nymphs of Diana come upon the sleeping Cupid and try to do a good deed for all of us by putting out the fire of his phallic torch in a cool pool of water. Aristophanes used the reverse of this joke to put out the fire of the old men with the old women's pots of water and pee in *Lysistrata*. In these sonnets, based on a Latin original or an English translation from the 1590s, Cupid's brand is so hot that it does not go out in water. It makes the cool pool seethe with heat, and healing hot springs are born. These poems may be minor neoclassical, Renaissance pieces like Cellini's salt bowls, but they also end Shakespeare's 28 dark lady sonnets and the whole sequence like the double bars at the end of a symphony.

The funny idea is that the little love god triumphs over inexperienced girls, who worship the chaste Moon. Neither male nor female puritans can defeat Eros. Nor can Shakespeare's venereal disease, which he caught from the dark lady, be cured by the hot waters of the Roman baths at Bath. And his love and lust for his "mistress" go on after the end of his 28 sonnets for her. Line 14 ends with his fitting chiasmus:

**"Love's fire heats water,
    water cools not love."**

This enables the last word of the sequence to be "love." The love joke is on all of us including poor Will. These two sonnets are like miniature, marble erotic statuettes. They are in the tradition of Shakespeare's "Venus and Adonis" and should be read with a worldly smile. After you have finished reading these twin poems, you can go either of two places in the 1609 version of the *Sonnets*. You can go ahead in **time** to Sonnet 62 for the youth, or you can go ahead in **space** to the female, womb-like hills that echo a wronged, young woman's lament in "A Lover's Complaint."

    This is all a very pretty formal trick set up by Shakespeare, ending Sonnet 154 with a sad smile, still a form of comedy in keeping with this great series about the powers of love. And if you don't allow for Shakespeare's funny tricks, if you don't understand his good bad writing in the *Sonnets* and laugh with him, then it's as if you are accepting his tragedies and his histories but not his comedies, and what's the fun of that? Three of his best comedies—*Love's Labour's Lost, Much Ado About Nothing,* and *As you Like It*—make fun of lovers so tongue twisted by trying to write sonnets, they wind up looking silly. Cupid has forced them to pad their fourteeners with filler feet and clunk their rhymes like loose junk. Perhaps Shakespeare was too wise and economical to throw away his rejected sonnets. He used them to mock the "art" of love with scribbled refuse.

    Almost no one else but Will—of about twenty Elizabethan sonneteers—writes even one funny sonnet. But Shakespeare writes at least eight in his sequence, and he adds many more good bad sonnets to his plays about lovers as sonnet-making fools. All these poems are an essential part of the rich diversity that defines his genius and his smile.

Works Cited

Abrams, M. H. (Ed.) *The Norton Anthology of English Literature*. 7th ed. Vol. 1. New York: W. W. Norton, 2000.

Ackroyd, Peter. *Shakespeare: The Biography*. New York: Doubleday/Talese, 2005.

Asquith, Clare. *Shadowplay [:] The Hidden Beliefs and Coded Politics of William Shakespeare*. New York: Public Affairs, 2005.

Augarde, Tony. *The Oxford Guide to Word Games*. 2nd ed. Oxford: Oxford U P: 2003.

Bevington, David, *Shakespeare's Romances and Poems*. New York: Pearson/Longman, 2007.

Booth, Stephen. (Ed.) *Shakespeare's Sonnets*. New Haven: Yale Nota Bene, 2000.

Bossy, John. *Giordano Bruno & the Embassy Affair*. New Haven: Yale UP, 1991.

Burnham, Michelle. "'Dark Lady and Fair Man': The Love Triangle in *Shakespeare's Sonnets* and *Ulysses*. *Studies in the Novel,* Spring 1990, 22.1: 43 ff.

Burrow, Collin. (Ed.) *William Shakespeare [:] The Complete Sonnets and Poems*. Oxford, UK: Oxford U P, 2002.

Carroll, D. Allen. " The 'Charge-House on the Top of the Mountain' (*Love's Labour's Lost* V.1.72)." *English Language Notes*, March 1996, 33.3: 8 ff.

"Chlamydia." *Wikepedia*. January 3, 2007. Jan. 3, 2007. <http://en.wikipedia.org/wiki/Clamidia>.

Davies, Nigel. "The Place 2 Be." March 3, 2003. April 29, 2003. <http://www.geocities.com/Athens/Troy/4081/Sonnets.html>.

Duncan-Jones, Katherine. (Ed.) *Shakespeare's Sonnets*. London: Arden Shakespeare, Thomson Learning, 1997.

———. Ungentle Shakespeare [:] Scenes from his Life. London: Arden, 2001.

Espenak, Fred. "Lunar Eclipses: 1501 to 1600." *Eclipse Home Page*. July 31, 1998. June 9, 2002 <http://sunearth.gsfc.nasa.gov/eclpse/eclipse.html>.

Field, Robert. *Mazes [:] Ancient & Modern*. Norfolk, UK: Tarquin, 2001.

Foster, Donald W. *Elegy by W. S.[:] A Study in Attribution*. Newark: U of Delaware P, 1989.

Gibson, Rex. *Shakespeare: The Sonnets*. Cambridge, UK: Cambridge U P, 1997.

———. *Teaching Shakespeare*. Cambridge, UK: Cambridge U P, 1998.

Graves, Roy Neil. "Shakespeare's Sonnet 126." *Explicator*. Summer 1996, 54.4: 203 ff.

Gurr, Elizabeth. Shakespeare's Globe. London: Spinny, 1998.

Hamilton, Charles. *William Shakespeare with John Fletcher [:] Cardenio: Or the Second Maiden's Tragedy*. New York: Marlowe, 1993.

Hammerschmidt-Hummel, Hildegard. *The True Face of William Shakespeare*. London: Chaucer P, 2006.

Haynes, Alan. *The Elizabethan Secret Services*. Phoenix Mill, UK: Sutton, 2000.

Hedley, Jane. "Since First Your Eye I Eyed: *Shakespeare's Sonnets* and the Poetics of Narcissism." *Style,* Spring 1994, 28.1: 1 ff.

Joseph, Harriet. *Shakespeare's Son-in-law John Hall [:] Man and Physician*. Westchester, NY: Author, 1993.

Jungman, Robert E. "'Untainted' Crime in Shakespeare's Sonnet 19." *ANQ*, Winter 2003, 16.2: 18 f.

Kerr, Jessica. *Shakespeare's Flowers*. Boulder: Johnson, 1997.

Kerrigan, John, Ed. *William Shakespeare [:] The Sonnets and A Lover's Complaint*. London: Penguin, 1995.

Langmuir, Erika. *Masterpieces from the National Gallery*. London: National Gallery, 2000.

Larkin, Chris. Personal Interview. January 2, 2007.

Laroque, Francois. *Shakespeare's Festive World [:] Elizabethan Seasonal Entertainment and the Professional Stage*. Janet Lloyd, Trans. New York: Cambridge UP, 1991.

Lasoki, David, and Roger Prior. *The Besannos: Venetian Musicians and Instrument Makers in England, 1531—1665*. Aldershot, UK: Ashgate, 1995.

Levi, Peter. *The Life and Times of William Shakespeare*. New York: Holt, 1989.

Lewalski, Barbara K. "Lanyer (Book Review)." *Shakespeare Studies*. 2002, 30: 337 ff.

Livadas, Nikolas G. *Odysseus' Ithaca [:] The Riddle Solved*. Ed. & trans. Constantine Bisticas. Athens: Author, 2000.

Livio, Mario. *The Golden Ratio*. New York: Broadway 2002.

Logan, William. "The Sins of the Sonnets (Book Review)." *Parnassus: Poetry in Review,* 1999, 24.1: 250 ff.

Luke, Mary M. *Gloriana [:] The Years of Elizabeth I*. New York: Coward, McCann & Geohagen, 1973.

Magill, Frank N. (Ed.) *Magill Surveys [:] English Literature Middle Ages to 1800*. Pasadena, CA: Salem P, 1980.

Marani, Pietro C. *Leonardo Da Vinci [:] The Complete Paintings*. New York: Abrams, 2000.

McBride, Kari Boyd. "Biography of Aemelia Lanyer." *Lanyer Home Page*. n. d. May 5, 2002 <http://www.u.arizona.edu/lc/mcbride/lanyer/lanbio.htm>.

Mulder, Greg. Instructor of Science, Linn-Benton Community College, Albany, OR. Personal Interview and e-mail exchange. June 2002.

Nicholl, Charles. *The Reckoning: The Murder of Christopher Marlowe*. New York: Harcourt Brace, 1994.

Norwich, John Julius. *Shakespeare's Kings*. New York: Simon & Schuster, 1999.

Orgel, Stephen. (Ed.) *The Sonnets*. With an Introduction by John Hollander. New York: Penguin, 2001.

Oxquarry Books, Ltd. "The Amazing Web Site of Shakespeare's Sonnets." 2002. January 18, 2003 <http://www.shakespeares-sonnets.com>.

Roe, John. (Ed.) *The Poems*. New York: Cambridge UP, 1992.

Rowse, A. L. *Shakespeare's Southampton [:] Patron of Virginia*. New York: Harper & Row, 1965.

Schmidgall, Gary. *Shakespeare and the Poet's Life*. Lexington: UP of Kentucky, 1990.

Schoenbaum, S. *William Shakespeare [:] A Documentary Life*. New York: Oxford U P, 1975.

Schwartzberg, Mark. "Shakespeare's Sonnet 33." *Explicator,* Fall 2002, 61.1: 13 f.

Sidney, Sir Phillip. *A Selection of His Finest Poetry.* Ed. Katherine Duncan-Jones. Oxford and New York: Oxford UP, 1994.

Singh, Simon. *The Code Book [:] The Science of Secrecy from Ancient Egypt to Quantum Cryptography.* New York: Anchor, 1999.

Spathaky, Mike. "Old Style and New Style Dates and the Change to the Gregorian Calendar: A Summary for Genealogists." 2000. November 26, 2002 <http://www.genfair.com/dates.htm>.

"Sonnets on Sonnets." n. d. November 26, 2002 <http://www.sonnets.org/about. htm>.

Southworth, John. *Shakespeare The Player [:] A Life in the Theater.* Phoenix Mill, UK: Sutton, 2000.

Trevelyan, Raleigh. *Sir Walter Raleigh.* New York: Henry Holt, 2002.

Truss, Lynne. *Eats, Shoots & Leaves.* New York: Gotham, 2004.

Weatherby, H. L. "Edmund Spencer's Amoretti & Epithalamion (Book), Shakespeare's Sonnets (Book), Art of Shakespeare's Sonnets (Book)," (A review). *Sewanee Review,* Winter 2002, 108,1: 124 ff.

Wells, Stanley. *Shakespeare [:] A Life in Drama.* New York: Norton, 1995.

———. *Shakespeare [:] For All Time.* London: Macmillan, 2002.

———. *Looking for Sex in Shakespeare.* Cambridge: Cambridge P., 2004.

———, and Michael Dobson. (Eds.) *The Oxford Companion to Shakespeare.* Oxford, UK: Oxford UP, 2001.

———, and Lena Cowen Orlin. *Shakespeare [:] An Oxford Guide.* Oxford, UK: Oxford UP: 2003.

Wilde, Oscar. "The Portrait of Mr. W. H." *The Complete Works of Oscar Wilde.* New York: Barnes and Noble, 1994: 1150—1201.

Wilson, Ian. *Shakespeare: The Evidence.* New York: St. Martin's Griffin, 1993.

Woods, Susanne. *Lanyer [:] A Renaissance Woman Poet.* New York: Oxford UP, 1999.

———. (Ed.) *The Poems of Aemilia Lanyer [:] Salve Dues Rex Judæorum.* New York: Oxford U P, 1993.

Woolley, Benjamin. *The Queen's Conjurer [:] The Science and Magic of Dr. John Dee, Advisor to Queen Elizabeth I.* New York: Henry Holt, 2001.

Works Consulted

Armour, Richard. *Twisted Tales from Shakespeare*. New York: McGraw-Hill, 1957

Berry, Ralph. *Shakespeare and Sex* (Book Review). *Contemporary Review*, July 2001, 279.1626: 55 ff.

Biemiller, Lawrence. "A Sonneteer Thy Praises Sings." *Chronicle of Higher Education*. 4/19/2002, 48.32: A48.

Blakemore-Evans, G. (Ed.) *The Sonnets*. Introduction by Anthony Hecht. Cambridge, UK: Cambridge UP, 1996.

Bednarz, James P. *Shakespeare & the Poets' War*. New York: Columbia U P, 2001.

Bevington, David. (Ed.) *The Necessary Shakespeare*. New York: Addison-Wesley, 2002.

———. *Shakespeare's Comedies*. Pearson/Longman, 2007.

———. *Shakespeare's Histories*. Pearson/Longman, 2007.

———. *Shakespeare's Tragedies*. Pearson/Longman, 2007.

Bloom, Harold. *Shakespeare: The Invention of the Human*. New York: Riverhead, 1998.

Bowmer, Angus L. *As I Remember, Adam [:] An Autobiography of a Festival*. Ashland, OR: The Oregon Shakespearean Festival Association, 1975.

Borges, Jorge Luis. "Shakespeare's Memory (1983)." *Collected Fictions*. Andrew Hurley (Trans.). New York: Penguin, 1998: 508—515.

———. "Everything and Nothing (1960)." *Collected Fictions*. Andrew Hurley (Trans.). New York: Penguin, 1998: 319—320.

Brown, Dan. *The Da Vinci Code*. New York: Doubleday, 2003.

Brubaker, E. S. *Shakespeare Aloud [:] A Guide to his Verse on Stage*. Lancaster, PA: Author, 1976.

Budiansky, Stephen. *Her Majesty's Spymaster [:] Elizabeth I, Sir Francis Walsingham, and the Birth of Modern Espionage*. New York: Viking Penguin, 2005.

Burgess, Anthony. *Shakespeare*. Chicago: Ivan R. Dee, 1970.

———. *Shakespeare*. New York: Knopf, 1970.

Burto, William. (Ed.) *The Sonnets and Narrative Poems*. Introduction by W. H. Auden. New York: Knopf, 1992.

Caldwell, Ian, & Dustin Thomason. *The Rule of Four*. New York: Dial P., 2004.

Campbell, Lily B. *Shakespeare's "Histories" [:] Mirrors of Elizabethan Policy*. San Marino, CA: Huntington Library, 1963.

Casey, Charles. "Was Shakespeare Gay? Sonnet 20 and the Politics of Pedagogy." *College Literature*, Fall 1998, 25.3: 35 ff.

Charney, Maurice. *Shakespeare on Love and Lust*. New York: Columbia U P, 2000.

Cheaney, J. B. *The Playmaker*. New York: Knopf, 2000.

Cheney, Patrick, Ed. *The Cambridge Companion to Christopher Marlowe*. Cambridge, UK: Cambridge UP: 2004.

Chrisp, Peter. *Eyewitness Shakespeare*. New York: DK Publishing, 2002.

Crewe, Jonathan. "Punctuating Shakespeare." *Shakespeare Studies*. 2000, 28: 23 ff.

Crystal, David, & Ben Crystal. *Shakespeare's Words [:] A Glossary and Language Companion*. London: Penguin, 2002.

Dickson, Andrew. *The Rough Guide to Shakespeare*. New York: Rough Guides, 2005.

Doebler, John. *Shakespeare's Speaking Pictures [:] Studies in Iconic Imagery*. Albuquerque: U of New Mexico P, 1974.

Duncan, David Ewing. *Calendar [:] Humanity's Epic Struggle to Determine a True and Accurate Year*. New York: Avon, 1998.

Dunton-Downer, Leslie, and Alan Riding. *Essential Shakespeare Handbook*. New York: Dorling Kinderlsey, 2004.

Duffin, Ross W. *Shakespeare's Songbook*. New York: Norton, 2004.

"Elizabethan Sonnets." n. d. November 26, 2002 <http:member.aol.com/erichl omqu/eliz.htm>.

Ferber, Michael. *A Dictionary of Literary Symbols*. Cambridge: Cambridge U P, 1999.

Ferington, Esther, Ed. *Infinite Variety [:] Exploring the Folger Shakespeare Library*. Washington: Folger Library, 2002.

Fisher, Adrian, and Georg Gerster. *The Art of the Maze*. London: Seven Dials, 2000.

Foster, Don. *Author Unknown [:] On the Trail of Anonymous*. New York: Holt, 2000.

Go, Kenji. "Unemending of 'Still' in Shakespeare's Sonnet 106." *Studies in Philology,* Winter 2001, 98.1: 114 ff.

Greenblatt, Stephen. *Will in the World [:] How Shakespeare Became Shakespeare*. New York, Norton, 2004.

Guedj, Denis. *Numbers [:] The Universal Language*. New York: Harry N. Abrams, 1997.

Gurney, Alan. *Compass [:] A Story of Exploration and Innovation*. New York: W. W. Norton, 2004.

Haffenden, John. (Ed.) *Berryman's Shakespeare*. New York: Farrar, Straus and Giroux, 1999.

Hagen, Rose-Marie & Rainer. *Bruegel [:] The Complete Paintings*. Koln: Taschen, 2005.

Hamill, John, and Robert Gilbert, Eds. *Freemasonry [:] A Celebration of the Craft*. London: Angus, 2004.

Harting, James E. *The Birds of Shakespeare [:] or the Ornithology of Shakespeare Critically Examined, Explained and Illustrated*. Chicago: Argonaut, 1965.

Hilton, Della. *Who Was Kit Marlowe?* New York: Taplinger, 1977.

Holden, Anthony. *The Drama of Love, Life & Death in Shakespeare*. London: Octopus, 2000.

———. *William Shakespeare.* Boston: Little, Brown, 2001.

Honan, Park. *Shakespeare [:] A Life*. Oxford, UK: Oxford U P, 1999.

Hughes, Geoffrey. *Swearing [:] A Social History of Foul Language, Oaths and Profanity in English*. Oxford, UK: Blackwell, 1991.

Hughes, Ted. *Tales from Ovid*. New York: Farrar, Straus, and Giroux, 1997.

Hutson, Lorna. *Elizabethan Women and the Poetry of Courtship* (Book Review). *Journal of Gender Studies,* March 2001, 10.1: 94 ff.

Instituto Geografico De Agostini. *Leonardo DaVinci*. Novarra, Italy: Artabras/ Reynal, reprinted and translated from 1938 edition.

Jensen, Peter. "William Shakespeare: A Literary Friend." *Oregon English Journal* 31.1 (Spring 1999): 93-94, 97.

Joyce, James. *Ulysses*. New York: The Modern Library, 1961.

Kermode, Frank. *The Age of Shakespeare*. New York: Modern Library, 2004.

———. *Shakespeare's Language*. New York: Farrar, Straus, Giroux, 2000.

Lawlor, Robert. *Sacred Geometry*. London: Thames & Hudson, 1982.

Legin, Philippe. *The astronomical clock in pictures*. Stan and Rita Morton, Trans. Colmar, Fr.: Cathedral of Strasbourg, 1978.

Magnusson, Lynne. *Shakespeare's Sonnets* (Book Review). *Shakespeare Studies.* 2002, 30: 318 ff.

Marcus, Leah S. *Puzzling Shakespeare [:] Local Reading and Its Discontents*. Berkeley: U of California P, 1988.

Marowitz, Charles. *Murdering Marlowe*. New York: Dramatists Play Service, 2005.

Martin, Reed, & Adam Tichenor. *Reduced Shakespeare*. NYC: Hyperion, 2006.

Martineau, John. *A Little Book of Coincidence [:] Pattern in the Solar System*. New York: Walker, 2001.

Meagher, John C. *Shakespeare's Shakespeare [:] How the Plays Were Made*. New York: Continuum, 1998.

Mowat, Barbara A., and Paul Werstine, eds. *Shakespeare's Sonnets*. New York : Washington Square P, Folger Shakespeare Library, 2004.

Nelson, Jeffrey N., and Andrew D. Ching. "Love's Logic Lost: The Couplet of Shakespeare's Sonnet 116." *ANQ,* Summer 2000, 13.3: p. 14 ff.

Nicholl, Charles. *Leonardo da Vinci [:] Flights of the Mind*. NYC: Viking, 2004.

———. *Elizabethan Writers*. London: National Portrait Gallery, 1997.

———. *The Reckoning: The Murder of Christopher Marlowe*. London: Vintage UK, 2002.

Nolen, Stephanie. *Shakespeare's Face*. New York: Free Press, 2002.

Norman, Marc, and Tom Stoppard. *Shakespeare in Love [:] A Screen Play*. New York: Hyperion, Miramax, 1998.

Norris, Herbert. *Tudor Costume and Fashion*. Mineola, NY: Dover, 1997.

Nye, Robert. *The Late Mr. Shakespeare*. New York: Penguin, 1998.

Padfield, Peter. *Armada*. Annapolis, MD: Naval Institute P, 1988.

Palmer, Alan, and Veronica Palmer. *Who's Who in Shakespeare's England*. New York: St. Martin's, 1999.

Partridge, Eric. *Shakespeare's Bawdy*. London: Routledge, 1955.

Pierce, Patricia. *Old London Bridge [:] The Story of the Longest Inhabited Bridge in Europe*. London: Headline, 2001.

Prescott, Anne Lake. Book Review. *ANQ,* Winter 2001, 14.1: 49 ff.

The Reduced Shakespeare Company. *The Complete Works of William Shakespeare (abridged)*. Silver Spring, MD: Acorn: 2001.

———. *The Complete Works of William Shakespeare (abridged)*. [DVD]. Silver Spring, MD: Acorn Media, 2003.

Riggs, David. *The World of Christopher Marlowe*. New York: Henry Holt, 2004.

Rosenbaum, Ron. *The Shakespeare Wars [:] Clashing Scholars, Public Fiascoes, Palace Coups*. New York : Random House, 2006.

Rowse, A. L. *William Shakespeare [:] A Biography*. NYC: Harper Row, 1963.

———. *The Elizabethan Renaissance: The Cultural Achievement*. Chicago: Ivan R. Dee, 1972.

———. *The Poems of Shakespeare's Dark Lady [:] Salve Deus Rex Judoerum by Emilia Lanier*. New York: Clarkson Potter, 1979.

Sams, Eric. *The Real Shakespeare: Retrieving the Early Years, 1564—1594*. New Haven: Yale U P, 1995.

Schoenbaum, S. *Shakespeare's Lives*. New York: Oxford UP, 1991.

Scott, Gray. "Signifying Nothing? A Secondary Analysis of the Claremont Authorship Debates." *Early Modern Literary Studies* 123 (Sept. 2006). <http://purl.oclc.org/emls/12-2/scotsig2.htm>.

Shapiro, James. *A Year in the Life of William Shakespeare [:] 1599*. New York: Harper Collins, 2005.

Shellard, Dominic. *William Shakespeare. The British Library, Writers' Lives*. New York: Oxford U P, 2000.

Sobel, Dava. *The Planets*. New York: Viking, 2005.

Somerset, Anne. *Unnatural Murder [:] Poison at the Court of James I*. London: Phoenix, 1997.

Sonnets [:] Shakespeare. Selected and read by Sir John Gielgud. CD. New York: Caedmon Audio, Harper Collins, 1963, 1996.

Spain, Delbert, *Shakespeare Sounded Soundly [:] The Verse Structure and the Language*. Santa Barbara: Capra P, 1988.

Snodgrass, W. D. "The Use of Meter." *Southern Review*. Fall 1999, 35.4: 806 ff.

Starkey, David, and Paul J. Willis, Eds. *In a Fine Frenzy [:] Poets Respond to Shakespeare*. Iowa City: U of Iowa P, 2005.

Stoppard, Tom. *Rosencrantz and Guidenstern Are Dead*. New York: Grove, 1967.

———, and Marc Norman. *Shakespeare In Love*. Miramax: 1998.

Tey, Josephine. *The Daughter of Time*. New York: Berkeley, 1975.

Thomson, Peter. *Shakespeare's Professional Career*. Cambridge, UK: Cambridge U P, 1992.

Tiffany, Grace. *Will [:] A Novel*. New York: Berkley, 2004.

Vendler, Helen. *The Art of Shakespeare's Sonnets*. Cambridge, MA: Harvard U P, 1997.

Washington, Peter. *Bach*. New York: Borzoi/Knopf, 1997.

Wells, Stanley, and Paul Edmondson. *Shakespeare's Sonnets*. Oxford, UK: Oxford U P, 2004.

Willen, Gerald & Victor B. Reed, Eds. *A Casebook on Shakespeare's Sonnets*. New York: Thomas Crowell, 1964.

Wolf, Norbert. *Holbein*. Köln: Taschen, 2004.

Wood, Michael. *Shakespeare*. New York: Perseus Books, 2003.

Wrixon, Fred B. *Codes, Ciphers & Other Cryptic & Clandestine Communication*. New York: Black Dog & Leventhal, 1998.

Index

Sonnet #/pages

*ff*inis

Printed in the United States
103435LV00003B/110/A